W9-CRF-020

SHE CAME IN DRAG

"Mary Wings is a national treasure—funny, zany, outrageously original and a terrific crime writer, too. Wings's latest, *She Came in Drag* is sure to expand her audience. This is not just a book for the lesbian reader. The mainstream reader will enjoy it greatly, for beneath the glitter, the fun, and the beautifully drawn San Francisco milieu, Wings has, without the slightest pretension, woven in universal truths."
—David Hunt, author of *Magician's Tale*

SHE CAME TO THE CASTRO

"God bless her, the girl knows how to have fun. . . . San Franciscans will enjoy recognizing the thinly disguised local politicians and institutions that Wings weaves into the narrative . . . the beloved Castro Theatre plays a starring role under its own name . . . nothing's too weird to be true anymore. Wings does take on some serious subjects, but *Castro* is primarily fast-paced and fun, and hey, it's well written."
—San Francisco Bay Guardian

"What's really noteworthy about Emma's fourth case . . . is her tough professionalism on the job, and Wings's success in tying high-level social debates about gay rights into the mystery, right down to the blissful final surprise."
—Kirkus Reviews

SHE CAME BY THE BOOK
A *People* Page Turner of the Week

"What can you say about a mystery that begins by quoting Gertrude Stein, ends by quoting Eleanor Roosevelt, and wickedly satirizes couples counselors, body piercing, and black-tie gay fundraisers . . . except buy it!"
—Feminist Bookstore News

continued on next page

"Irreverent, fast-paced and fun . . . a mystery you'll puzzle over, stay up with, and really enjoy."

—Rita Mae Brown and Sneaky Pie Brown

More praise for Mary Wings and the Emma Victor mysteries . . .

"Bravo!"

—Nancy Pickard

"Wonderful writing."

—Sandra Scoppettone

"Wings has a saucy, witty way with dialogue and description."

—*Elle*

"An unorthodox, likable protagonist."

—*Library Journal*

"Intricate descriptions and grin-getting dialogue . . . strong and appealing lesbian characters."

—Sally Gearheart

"Hip, witty, and fast-paced . . . the cast of characters is outrageous!"

—*Boston Phoenix*

"Riveting . . . written with great skill."

—Michael Nava, author of *The Hidden Law*

"Immensely readable, tightly plotted."

—*Bay Area Reporter*

"Well-paced . . . vibrant . . . enjoyable . . . Wings writes straightforward, intelligent prose."

—*Publishers Weekly*

SHE CAME IN DRAG

MARY WINGS

BERKLEY PRIME CRIME, NEW YORK

SHE CAME IN DRAG

Lyric excerpt from "Trouble in Paradise." Written by James Wirrick, Jeffrey Mehl, and Sylvester James. Copyright © 1984, Silly Music/Sequins at Noon Music/Wirrick Music/Jaymel Music. Used by permission. All Rights Reserved.

A Berkley Prime Crime Book / published by arrangement with the author

PRINTING HISTORY
Berkley Prime Crime edition / June 1999

The Penguin Putnam Inc. World Wide Web site address is http://www.penguinputnam.com

ISBN: 0-425-16935-9

Berkley Prime Crime Books are published by The Berkley Publishing Group, a division of Penguin Putnam Inc., 375 Hudson Street, New York, New York 10014. The name BERKLEY PRIME CRIME and the BERKLEY PRIME CRIME design are trademarks belonging to Penguin Putnam Inc.

PRINTED IN THE UNITED STATES OF AMERICA

10 9 8 7 6 5 4 3 2 1

This book is dedicated to Lorrie Sheets, who came to stay.

Due to remodeling, conversations were by candlelight: Thanks to Nancy Boutelier, Jane Cottis, and Kathleen Mullen for joining in on this latest tale.

Rachael Royer came in colors and Sue Bachman took me to a bank robbery.

And to my colleagues at Pasqua's who kept me caffeined up: Bob, Carlos, Clee, Corey, Lance, Junior and Sandra. Thanks for your good humor every single day.

"Fly them, screw them, just get the guest."
   —a former booker from *A Current Affair*

host 3. a living animal or plant from which
   a parasite obtains nutrition.

Trouble in Paradise

So much, so much trouble, trouble in Paradise!
Where do we go from here?
Now that we've come so far, baby?

I—I just think there's trouble,
Trouble, trouble in Paradise,
Need a solution!

Trouble, trouble in Paradise
So much confusion!
What am I gonna do?

So much, so much trouble, trouble in Paradise
Where do we go? Where do we go from here?
Now that we've come so far, baby?

—Sylvester James (1948–1988)

CONTENTS

SHE CAME TO TALK

Thirty-three thousand letters have been written to find you. Newspapers, tabloids, television news shows are hot on your tail; private detectives have been hired and have found your friends and neighbors. Once cornered, the bloodhounds descend upon you, invoking familiar titles: Jenny, Oprah, Jerry, Geraldo, Sally, and Johnny. Their first names are unwanted kisses in your ears. They call *you* Rita. They said it was about *truth*.

You have no idea how they found you. Later, you remember the high school yearbook; the tennis team, the final photos of your high school career, the young muscled arms slung around shoulders. The hazing, the crushes, the social life that could be more lethal than an Elizabethan court. The axes that ground, the kisses that were given, the wedding to the code of silence.

Sex, violence, and oddity are not your thing. You are a mycologist with a garden full of cats. The truth of your science is elusive, something you have spent a lifetime researching. The truth was never absolute, always fallible to the next result, the next experiment, the next cat that died on your hands.

Nevertheless bookers, talent coordinators, segment producers, and field agents think they know your truth. They

1

write you letters, they knock on your door. They reach way, way inside you. They use your bones for telephones and they tell you a big opportunity is waiting in the wings. You are going to be on national television; *you* have the topic that is hot. They make you many offers.

All you can think about is the forty-million-year-old mushroom. Encapsulated in a piece of amber, with only a mite for a roommate, a colleague of yours discovered it in the mountains of the Dominican Republic. *Coprinites dominicana* would arrive any day at your doorstep, and then you would be immersed in work, immune from pain, freed from the memory of the flesh. Meanwhile, the cats need to be watched, monitored. Millions of spores had to be cultivated, brought to maturity, and distributed. Your work was a matter of life and death. Or life and life. *Toklastaki*.

The last thing you care about is a first-class seat on a flight to L.A., a limousine to tour you around town, and the five-star cuisine of a Beverly Hills hotel. But they extend their offers, anyway. This is their promise: your bed will be soft, made of feathers, and your mind will be clear, having told the truth. Their voices flatter and cajole. You—you!—have the truth the whole country is waiting for.

But you don't want to go on the airplane, direct flight or otherwise.

You are only interested in the significant, neglected organisms of forest ecosystems.

You don't want a limousine tour or the five-star cuisine.

You have Mariposa to take care of the cats, to take care of you.

You laugh at the ten thousand dollars they end up offering you.

You don't want anything to do with national television.

You're tired of people dying.

You just want to continue your work.

Indinavir adefovir had nothing on nature.

You're almost there; remissions have been duly noted.
Toklastaki. Or what they liked to call TKTK1477.
How clever Mariposa is: the world of fauna
Has yielded an antidote for every poison.
There's not a lot of time to lose.
Except when Audra Léon is in your arms again.

*"So, let me get this straight—so to speak. You and Audra
were both on the tennis team in high school, right? Would it
be fair to say that you were lesbian lovers? For two years?
And you met in high school?"*

Gasp from the audience.

They start talking faster, offering more money, a trip to
Paris on the Concorde and blue point oysters flown in from
Nova Scotia. Twenty grand, enough to cover the mortgage
for years. An advanced hydration system. Why, you could
excavate another cellar, import the proper oak logs, and generate a hundred pound *Grifola frondosa* from Japan! The
capital would give you the time to quit your job. You could
devote your time to the cultivation of the fussy *Polyporus
umbullatus,* a mushroom said to reduce tumors. Maybe then
you will be able to forget her once and for all, stop hopping
on planes three times a year. Djerba, Tunisia, wasn't that the
last location? On Valentine's Day? All went well until the
fateful trysting in Phoenix—*found out!*

You had loved her long, loved her well.

The absolute truth is that Audra Léon is the love of your life.

You haven't heard from her in six long months.

Fame made Audra a household name. And freaked out.
Gale was a problem, as usual. The singer needed someone
from her past, she had ventured shyly on the telephone. Not
just anyone. You. And that old-time religion.

That fact doesn't exactly make you want to appear on national television.

The bloodhounds bark louder up your tree in San Francisco. You can almost hear the licking of their lips over the phone line.

They are taping two shows a day, three days a week, but they still find time to talk to you. They have only twenty-four to forty-eight hours to make all the arrangements and conduct the final interviews. The invitations to San Francisco's finest restaurants and funkiest coffee houses come faster. If only you will say it: Audra Léon is a lesbian. Your voice will not utter those words, not even in Audra's ears. You are becoming deaf to it all, hiding in your house. Friends, ex-girlfriends, and fuck buddies are concerned.

But the voice of another high school friend gets through. Her name is Bevin. Bevin Crosswell.

All you can think about is the past traumas of adolescence, the bad-girl bathrooms, the secrets kept at slumber parties, the unzipping of sleeping bags and late-night ceremonies. Bevin, who would pronounce judgment and carry out sentence. Flames, wreckage, trauma, and toxic shame. You didn't think therapy would ever fix *your* past. Except for those moments with Audra. You still wear the golden tennis racket necklace as a reminder of just how good and how shitty life could be.

But Bevin is remembering the you from high school as if nothing bad had happened. Do you remember her? How could you forget. "It's the revenge of the nerds, Rita." She counts you in the same club from high school. "We rule now." You wonder what Bevin rules, a lightning rod for the cruelty of teenagers, the torments of adolescence. In high school she was nearly an untouchable. And of course she would be the one who loved to mete out the punishments of the powerful.

"How could I forget you, Bevin? You got me kicked off the tennis team, not to mention a lot of things I never wanted to remember."

"Rita, I would like to make amends. I like to think that as

adults we've become something different than we were in high school. Not only that, I also wanted to thank you. I had so much trouble in biology—you saved my ass, girlfriend. And I never got to repay you the favor!"

High school, a time that you'd walled off. Here was living memory, and you have no taste for exhuming the past. But you're curious. Where could adult life have landed *her?*

Bevin is in San Francisco for a week. She invites you for coffee, drinks, and dessert at Top of the Mark, for old times' sake, for helping her in biology. Her voice is confident now. *"It's the revenge of the nerds, Rita."* You and Bevin both understood instinctively, like a pack of animals, how low you were on the rung of social acceptability. You were a science nerd. You still are. But a very important—and potentially rich—science nerd. The old feelings come flooding back; there must be a way to exorcise the past. Perhaps Bevin is offering it to you. The invitation comes floating over the line and, standing in your stunning bedroom suite, something makes you say yes.

You are successful. You are silk and vanilla. Years after high school you've made it. You're a babe. So what is Bevin these days? Revenge of the nerds.

A nerd in a mansion. A mansion with two fireplaces in Forest Hills. One of the fireplaces is in the huge bedroom that overlooks the ocean. There's a thick rug, and Mariposa would set a roaring blaze in the hearth for your evening trysts, on the few occasions that you left the house. No, you live very much in the happy present. Only the altar—the *offerta*—on the mantle keeps you tethered to the past.

Sugar skeletons laugh, perching in rows as they always have; you have saved them from childhood, safely tucked away in the fancy shoeboxes of Italian and French designers. You light the candles on the *offerta;* fires sprout from glittering craniums. The hand-tinted eyes on the portrait of your father are soft and forgiving. Chocolates, shells, a bottle of

mescal, and glittering marigolds in crystal vases made their
way through all the flames.

Inside your closet, a wardrobe of the finest materials, the
hottest designers, awaits you. You have power suits for the
board meetings and play clothes from Saks Fifth Avenue and
evening wear custom tailored by Ina Cho. Ina Cho, a marvelous designer, a woman who had just discovered a malig-
nant lump in her breast. She joked about making the Amazon
suit. "Who needs reconstructive surgery? Just wait, Rita, the
asymmetrical silhouette will become a *trend.*"

She gave you a drawing of a Spartan virgin, one breast revealed. The pain of disease was everywhere. One in nine.
They invited you to benefits. Your name got around. You
were doing incredibly good work, at last. And the closet full
of gorgeous clothes was just a symptom of success.

It was all a far cry from the hand-me-downs of high
school. Everything was neatly sorted. Lab coats and field
pants, roomy things for your luscious *zaftig* body. And the
suit you bought especially for the Cancer Society Award for
Outstanding Achievement. A cherry red cashmere suit with
tiny silver buttons cast in devil's heads. Ina has fitted it perfectly to your figure. Soft and tailored, it fits you like a glove,
hugs you like a long-lost lover, like a long-legged model.
You've only worn it once.

A long, vanilla bath suits you. After a moment, sinking
into the hot water, you decide to make the effort. You will
wash your hair.

Your long, black hair was the envy of all in high school. It
was the only thing the giggling popularity crowd admired
about you. Except, maybe, just maybe, your grades. Isn't it
funny, how the science nerds, the creeps, the intellectuals in
high school were the ones that ruled, once adult life made its
destiny clear? The cheerleaders were whining, married and
saddled with kids. The football boys were resenting the children, the mortgage, the wife.

You smile. Three years ago, you took a trip to the Amazon. The results have kept you busy ever since. The fruits of your journey, the help of Mariposa, are better than you could have ever expected. Slowly, you lower your torso into the water. Then your shoulders. Your hair, now streaked with silver, floats on the surface of the water. Long, wavy strands make a star around your head. Two washings and a five-minute condition with one of Mariposa's unique elixirs. You return to the bedroom. Why are you going to meet this woman? She wasn't a chum; she had just been a fellow outcast—and an executioner. You sigh. You will go anyway, and you do not know why. Maybe it's because Audra hasn't called you since she finished shooting *Wet Kisses Only*. Six months.

Taking the suit out of the dry cleaner bag, you pick a strand of cat fur off the velvet collar. You light a fire in the fireplace and unwrap your hair. Wet strands stripe your shoulders. You take a boar-bristle brush and stroke until the long mane is dry and shiny as an ebony sheet. And then, almost with regret, you twist it into a long braid at the base of your neck. It will trail down the back of Ina Cho's suit, the beautiful black plait that Bevin will remember. You blow out the candles on the *offerta* and leave the house. The air is warm and kind.

People turn their heads as you walk down Portola to the BART station. Jack-o'-lanterns grin, and cardboard skeletons want to sign your dance card. Halloween, Guy Fawkes, *Día de los Muertos*, it was all the same. The entrance into the dark season: fires and spirits, masks, merriment, and atonement. The drunken men raise their paper bags in salute as you descend on the escalator to board the BART. Your father could have been on that sidewalk with them. Whizzing through the tunnel, you think about Bevin, about your senior year of high school, the year that had started with a dream and ended in a nightmare on Halloween. *How different life is now,* you think.

You are one of the most respected researchers at University of California. You are on a sabbatical that could last a lifetime. You are glad you don't have to trek across the bridge to Berkeley. Your colleagues are green with envy; they whisper that you have made a deal with Corporate America, and they are not entirely wrong.

Your suits are made of cashmere, and awards line your office. Bevin might not even recognize you when you walk into the bar! You wear contact lenses and your five-foot-eight height is dramatic and fashionable, not like the giraffe days of high school. You take the elevator up to the top floor where the maître d' greets you with the prim smile reserved for the privileged.

Through the lights of skyscraper windows, you see her. It's Bevin, the same cat green eyes, her drab and mousey hair has been hennaed a deep but gaudy red. She's all in black, the fashionable existential statement in a silk Edwardian-cut suit, emphasizing an almost wasp waist. The snazzy little number sports diagonal zippers and a short box-pleated skirt, which reminds you of a tennis court. *Revenge of the nerds, indeed.* She stands up; she's shorter than you remember.

You look into her eyes, and suddenly you're both hugging, as if no time has passed. It is, indeed, a reunion. A reunion of the nerds. It is also an evening you will come to regret for the rest of your life.

"Rita, you look wonderful!" Bevin crows. "And you still have that gorgeous hair." She had trouble keeping her hands off the shining plait that falls down your back. All the girls wanted to touch your hair in high school, like you were their pet.

The coffee is sweetened with sugar, and you never guessed at the bitter taste it would leave in your mouth as you sat across from Bevin and looked into those green eyes, like the cat's-eye marbles Juan used to play with. You remember the long nights on the bus, traveling to tennis tournaments at high schools all over the Bay Area.

Audra would take your hand in the darkness of the big school bus. And Gale was always sitting behind the two of you. She was quietly making plans, you realize now. Gale Petros was a parasite. Not a friendly one, not like the mushrooms popping up in the green darkness below.

Bevin still has those shapely calves, is in condition. She had kept the weight off, you think. Her suit is stone-washed silk, her short nails manicured, her fake red hair all spiky and hip, an expensive salon job. Bevin must be doing well in the world. There was no reason to think about the days of old.

"Nice suit!" Bevin remarks, her hand gliding over the soft, brushed cashmere. "Those buttons with the tiny devil's heads— Is it—?"

"Ina Cho," you confirm.

You'd bought it right off a model at one of your few social activities. Runway women and white wine at the annual Bay Area Career Women Fashion Benefit. You'd been a little drunk, but you weren't the only woman who had undressed a model that evening.

Once you had gotten up your nerve, it was easy to pounce. The next morning she'd called it The Lesbian Lion's Club. You'd taken her home, taken off her clothes, and taken her. She'd found it more than pleasant, her screams still rang in your ear. Too bad you only roared in season; waiting, always waiting for Audra to return your calls. The model would return next year, with a new suit, she promised. What was her name again?

"I hear Ina is designing for Audra now?" Bevin suggested.

Audra. Audra. Audra. You would think Bevin would want to forget about the tennis team. She was never very good, and worse, never noticed the snickers and comments that came her way from the other girls on the team. Audra used to make fun of Bevin's valley girl accent and ski-jump nose.

"What kind of work are you doing at the moment? I hear you're Dr. Huelga now. Congratulations. Does that mean you're a Ph.D. or what?" Bevin's eagerness hadn't dimmed in the ensuing years. Every remark hit the same enthusiastic cheerleading tone of optimism. You remember wondering, even back then, if Bevin was all surface, if she had an internal life. She always burned a little bit too bright, too anxious for approval. The popular girls could smell her neediness a mile off. You just shut down and crawled into your world. You were good at building walls, but Bevin had never learned.

"I did my post-doc at Sloan-Kettering. I got my medical degree at Harvard. I'm working with the . . . the Women's Cancer Research Institute."

"A medical doctor and a researcher! Talk about revenge of the nerds! You're a real heroine, Rita. I've read about your achievements."

"You have?" Strange, Bevin didn't seem the type to read scientific journals.

"Sure, in *The Lancet*."

Before you can develop a feeling of sudden suspicion, Bevin is ordering one cognac for you and Thai tea for herself.

"*The Lancet?* Didn't think that would be the usual fare to make its way into your mailbox in Las Vegas."

"I do a lot of research. Your name came up in the data bank. Mushrooms, right? Some kind of—anyway I didn't get too far with it."

The drinks arrive. Bevin watches you take a tentative sip and a pink glow descends. The past is but a bumpy highway of old memories and a girlhood that never died. *Time heals all wounds,* you think.

"I was afraid you wouldn't remember me." Bevin's voice is a hopeful whisper.

"Really?" You stop for a moment, wanting to forget a certain night and not being able to. Shame. You are feeling shame. "How could I forget you?" There are many things you don't care to remember, like the night you were kicked. And kicked off the tennis team. How mean girls could be. How Audra intervened on your behalf.

"Have you seen any of the old crowd?" she asks.

"I didn't run with the crowd," you remind her. "Neither did you."

"The old *tennis* crowd?" she pressed. The tennis crowd was different. The jocks and smell of the locker room. The black girls and the brown girls, the white girl who came from the wrong side of everybody's tracks, Bevin, the white girl who didn't fit in. Rita, whose backhand left far too much to be desired. You played doubles with Bevin and lost a lot.

Tennis, bleachers, and late nights coming home on the bus. The smell of the green cracked seats, the feeling of the big vehicle lurching around corners, Audra spilling into your lap. Audra saying they were a special sorority, the tennis girls. Rita was close, she could almost be one of the popular girls. But Audra said that Bevin wouldn't fit in. She was just too white. Audra wanted Bevin *out*. Audra fed you these kinds of hopes. Until it became clear: Audra wanted Gale, not you.

Bevin has a husband now and a rock-solid marriage. A suburb of Las Vegas, it's not so bad, actually. A gated community, of course. You're wondering how the short, red, spiky hairdo goes over in the desert. Well, it was a place full of showgirls, wasn't it? Entertainment people.

Dessert arrives. Napoleons appear on plates, you smash the crusts with your fork and laugh as you lick the pudding off your lips. You wonder if she's flirting with you.

You and Bevin remember home economics, the strict disciplinarian, Carmine Wright. Mrs. Wright, who had accused you of being more than a bad cook. How you said nothing, preferring, as usual, to build walls. As if you were born with an extra gene for shame, whether you deserved it or not. But Bevin is laughing about how she almost sewed her fingers together once. And Audra, why, Audra was actually good at sewing and embroidery. She started making her own clothes. But in the second semester, she cooked everything on high and smoked cigarettes on the edge of the asphalt playground. Once Gale had lost her shot at being a professional tennis player, Gale started smoking with Audra.

"Remember the Halloween slumber party we had at your house?"

Yes, you remembered. The beginning of your senior year of high school and you knew you would reach every goal: honor society, class valedictorian, an acceptance to Harvard. But Halloween and hard times had hit the family. No money for clothes, much less costumes. Miranda, your older sister, had no money for books, for heat. She was cold in Canada,

In September, the arrival of Juan, a dark, squalling thing, didn't feel like a joyous occasion. You were ready to launch your ship, but Juan stretched the family budget to bankruptcy. And worse, seemed to ruin Mama's health. Varicose veins started popping out in her legs.

Then, in the beginning of October, Father was laid off from his job as an X-ray technician. He drank, they said, and they were right. The photos came out all wrong, and after awhile, Father didn't care about it, didn't put the lead shield around the chest, the throat, the thorax. The job at the hospital was history. Any job was history. Father was drinking again. The stinking *borrachero* had been on a binge for days this time. Usually, the police scraped him off the sidewalk and phoned the family when he was sober. He would come home, make trouble, feel guilty, and leave again.

Mama doted on little Juan, forgetting just about everything else. Miranda quit school, took a job as a waitress in Montreal, and started sending money home.

Then Miranda had called one night, right before Halloween. The mortgage was way overdue. Miranda had been keeping track of the family finances from afar. Payments hadn't been made in months. Scanning some of the unpaid bills, arriving with red stripes, you started opening them. *Foreclosure*. The word itself had a terrible sound to it, like an accident that was surely going to happen. You knew what foreclosure meant. You were too young to hear these words. You wanted to be a child.

In a way, you hoped for any kind of change. A cloud of depression had fallen with finality on the Huelga household, a cloud you thought would never lift. You counted the months to graduation.

Then Mama got the bright idea of having a slumber party on Halloween. There would be jack-o'-lanterns and a bobbing for apples contest. She would make little sugar skeleton heads for favors. You wonder if Mama had gotten you mixed up with Juan. You had gone over your record collection with great precision that evening; your little pink LP player was poised and ready by the time the other girls had gotten there. Your copy of "Sweet Sweetback's Baadasssssss Song" had no skips. Audra loved that song.

Mama was so excited that you would have your friends over. As if she knew: You don't have any real friends; you were just a satellite of the popular girls. If it weren't for Audra, you wouldn't have any friends at all. She picked you out. She had protected you.

And then, when one of their own fell, even Audra couldn't help: You were blamed. Gale had been selected as athlete of the year. The fall exhibition tournament would bring a scout. Gale would get signed up, and a tennis career would spring her out of Visalia, out of California, out of the United States even. Then the horrible happened. Gale was sick on the court. People mentioned poison. And the Ex-Lax had been found in your purse. When fingers were pointed, they were pointed at *you*. The walls went up, and your face turned to stone.

But the slumber party the next night was not canceled. The

girls had insisted that the party must go on, despite your alleged deceit. You said nothing, just crawled behind a mask and hoped for the best.

Mama served American cheese sandwiches on day-old bread. She put apples in water and made everyone bob. Pumpkins had to be carved and candles lit. You died of shame a hundred times that night. And more since. You had never had a party at home. Long strings fraying from the carpet actually tripped people as they walked through the living room.

Mama had put up a giant piñata of Minnie Mouse. You had taken it down; Minnie's crepe paper ear tore in half. But the Betamax was ready for *Scream Blacula, Scream!, Coffy,* and Audra's favorite, *Foxy Brown.* Mama carried the piñata away, sulking.

"All right, I'll just leave you alone!" She'd been hurt by your refusal of offerings. "It's been so long since you've had anyone over—"

"Is Daddy going to be home tonight?"

"I don't think so."

"Thank God."

"Don't talk about your father like that."

"He hasn't been home in three days. Maybe we'll be lucky, and he'll stay out for the rest of his life."

"He's a good man—he's just—" Mama started crying.

"It's just that he's a hopeless drunk."

The crack of Mama's hand came hard across your cheek. "Never speak of your father that way!" Her black eyes danced with anger.

"Sure, Mama, sure," you say, cheeks burning.

"I'm sorry, baby." Mama reached out, but you pushed her hand away.

"It's all right, Mama. You go take care of Juan. I think I hear him waking up."

"Oh, Rita! I just want you kids to be happy." She was crying. You grab her, hug her hard, holding the strong, stocky motherness of her close to you. "I'll go get Juan," she said, drying her tears. She looked so old, it was impossible to imagine that she had ever been a girl. She had been a mother forever. Juan, in his crib, was probably starting to cry.

"I know, I know." You hugged her harder, and she cried. "I'm in high school, Mama, I'm not a baby," you said. "We just want to stay up and dance."

Bevin prompted you back into the present. "Remember the night Audra dressed up like Pam Grier and sang 'Pretty Woman'?" she prompted.

You remember the costume, the makeup. *"Pretty woman, walking down the street."*

"Hey, Rita, you're just as quiet as you ever were!"

Later that night, Mama parked in front of the television set with Juan, the baby squalling. You heard the snickers of girls coming from inside the sleeping bags: *"Cheese sand-wiches!"*

"That was a pretty heavy night for your family." Bevin was persistent but cautious. What was she driving at?

"Yes?" Don't go there. The past will only burn a hole in your head. And you're so close. You must be chatty and bright, the Rita Huelga of *today*. The Rita Huelga that will go down in history for her research, not the tragedy of long ago.

You search your brain for suitable material. You reminisce about the old days, keep the conversation going about high school teachers, the sleazy janitor who tried to cop a feel from Bevin in the locker room. The home economics class where all the drama started.

Bevin remembers something else: how you passed her the answers to the biology final. She's still really grateful, she wants you to know. It's the only way she could stay on the tennis team. Do you remember the songs we used to sing on the bus? *"Found a peanut, found a peanut, ate it anyway, ate it anyway."* Bevin remembers the way Audra wanted to sit next to you on the bus. Bevin winks and waits, but you say nothing.

You remember smoke and fire. Audra, who needed help with her botany exam; crawling into your sleeping bag for excitement, later joining Gale for satisfaction. And then the fire, and Audra had gone to join a rock and roll band, to meet her destiny. Gale Petros had a blown tennis career; she joined Audra, and your heart crumbled slowly. The tennis team suffered one humiliating defeat after another. Dad was dead, and a big piece of insurance money kept the family afloat. As the last months of your senior year dragged by, the only thing that propped you up were long hours in the lab. A science project: rats running through an endless maze, like a heart that will never find its home again.

"Just recently—I—I bumped into Audra." The words are out of your mouth before you can stop them. The liquor burns a path down your throat.

"Really?" Bevin is remotely interested. Her fingers find a spiky henna strand. She curls it around and around her fingers. Then she settles her hands, like errant children, in her lap.

You don't tell Bevin that it was no bump at all.

The first bump was by accident: You were returning from Brazil with Mariposa. There she was, Audra Léon! High school crush who not only remembered you but kissed you on the lips, right there in the airport! You dropped your luggage on your foot. Audra laughed. Mariposa mentioned that she needed to visit some friends in L.A., and Audra took you back to her place for the afternoon. It was Audra's dream come true, and yours, too.

A sumptuous palace, fifteen thousand square feet, Audra had said. Not including the garages and the guest house. The bedroom had a huge round bed and a view of Los Angeles's air. Gale was in Visalia, and soon, Audra was in you.

The return to San Francisco from Brazil was difficult, even with Mariposa around to help out. Audra was always on your mind. Your high school flame started keeping in touch after that.

Wet Kisses Only was a wonderful script. Shooting would start soon. Maybe you could meet up on location. A discreet hotel rendezvous. Audra celebrated your research victories, although she didn't really understand the scientific terminology. You were comforting when Audra didn't get the Grammy. "That Grammy was *mine!*" she had insisted. Audra hadn't changed at all. The world still revolved around her. But she had created her own fiefdom: castles, security guards, caterers, moats full of spin doctors and publicists. She was a self-created goddess. Her grandiosity only amuses you now, as it did in high school. Especially now that she has made the improbable dream come true, with only a voice and incredible willpower.

There was also the kind of sexual thrill fed by its forbiddance: Audra didn't have to ask you twice before you got on a plane, checked into the Phoenix Royal Hotel or any other hotel on earth. Audra, in her usual supersexy disguise, entered the room where you waited patiently on the bedspread, looking out at the desert. Your magic was still there for her. She still screamed when your tongue dove inside her, and soon, flames rose out of the ashes of your past. Gale never suspected a thing.

"Yeah, I saw Audra in Phoenix," you say to Bevin.

"In Phoenix, you say?" Bevin's voice is cautious as she herds the end of her dessert around the plate. "No mushrooms in that climate!" she quips.

Old times' sake, you explain, shortly. Your lips still hold the memory of Audra's kiss good-bye. It was just too difficult: the closet, the press, Gale. There was a deadly silence in your life that you filled with nightly tears and the memories of the flesh and the skinny runway model.

You shiver, take a deep draught of cognac. Gale was used to the heat, used to the closet. And Audra had said that she was going to figure it out: the closet, the press, Gale, and *you.* She had a plan. A grand plan that made you laugh. You watched the progress of her life-scam on *Entertainment Tonight.* But then the silence had lasted six months. Why didn't she call? Maybe she was waiting for things to settle down.

You look across the table. Does Bevin seem flirtatious? Maybe Bevin was looking for a little roll in the hay, you think. An old high school chum from out of town. Maybe Bevin's husband would understand. Maybe he wouldn't know. Her hennaed hair looks a bit greasy. Suddenly, you're choking, fumes collecting in your mouth.

"How was it? Seeing Audra?" Bevin asks, her tongue cleaning custard from the side of her mouth. "I'll bet she's still the same: mischievous, funny? Full of herself?"

"Audra has a lot of compassion." Your words come out soft, a secret whisper that you could almost share with Bevin. "Why, when Pam Grier came down with that terrible fever on the Roger Corman film, Audra sent her own specialist down to help." You are speaking in between quick sips of cognac. Bevin looks sympathetic and signals the waiter for more liquor. "Audra always thought Grier was the best black actor—the best actor—of her generation. But the scripts were silly in that earlier decade. Grier had a 105-degree temperature and had lost her hair and her eyesight. When Audra heard, she flew down personally."

"Gee, I never thought of Audra as the *compassionate* type." Bevin's hand crawls over the table. Her fingers are cool from the ice tea she's been drinking. Bevin, you recall, had quite a backhand. "Do you think she's still with Gale—*that way?*"

Gale, your nemesis. You would have shared the closet with Audra, stayed well out of the limelight, but you'd never had the chance. Gale understood what it was like to be black, like Audra. Not like you or Bevin. But you don't tell her this. You shrug. You don't say anything.

"It was too bad you got blamed for the demise of Gale's tennis career," Bevin whispers into the silence.

"Time heals all wounds," you lie.

"How is Audra, anyway?"

Audra had changed much, you say, but yes, she was in many ways just the same.

Bevin is squeezing your hand harder. "But Audra didn't do so well with the new hubby, the white guy from Vegas. Did you see the debut video of no-talent Tyrone Warren?" She chuckles.

"Yeah, they just released it last month."

"Well, you won't see it anymore. His career is washed up, just like his vocal cords. The guy couldn't even carry a tune. Pathetic. Embarrassing! That song sank on the charts faster than the *Titanic*. They say he's in seclusion, that he's just a househusband for Audra. They are never even seen together in public."

You say nothing.

"I guess he just hangs out with his Vegas pals," Bevin prods.

"Audra has her own life," you lie. Audra, after she told you of her impending marriage to Tyrone, said everything was *very much* the same. You smile as you remember her lunging across the big pink bedspread after you. And afterward, she explained the trials of stardom. "It's like you gotta survive all these people trying to use your life. People making decisions for you. Trying to build you up. To keep the product coming out of you. Ripping you off in the process." And then Audra pulled out a video of *Coffy*. You watch the old blaxploitation, just like before. Hugging each other in the afterglow. The lurid costumes, the urban action scenes populated by prostitutes and pimps, the ridiculous, self-conscious

dialogue are familiar. High school was, indeed, a long time
ago. But Audra's still there, still entranced by blaxploitation's
most memorable actress.

"It's like Coffee's making a decision on her own; people
are out to destroy her. Every day, a goddamn building falls on
the chick, and she just crawls out from underneath and walks
away. And that's what I gotta do. Even though it sure looks
like I'm standing on top of the building now, baby. And Coffee didn't even have my mama on her side!"

Audra's mother had undoubtedly helped create her ego, if
not her success. But back in high school, Charlene Léon had
decided Audra was too good for Rita. You blamed your father. He had brought shame upon the family. But Audra was
Charlene's only daughter, only *child*. And Audra's family
was solid backbone black community; Charlene was one of
the altar ladies and active in all the local charities. Audra's father, a thin, quiet shadow of a man, raked the front yard down
to the bare dirt. They were oil and water, the Huelgas, the
Léons. Mr. Léon had died a few years ago, liver cancer. But
the family never faltered with Charlene at the helm. Audra
was never interested in boys. Did Charlene know then? Did
she know now? The cognac goes down your throat like
honey.

You think about the gentle orbs of Audra's breasts and you
gasp, remembering the moment of your surprise and a memory of intense pain and the ecstacy that followed. Audra always said you are the best lover she ever had. So why is she
still with Gale? Why doesn't she call? It wasn't like Tyrone
Warren was keeping her heart locked up.

You find yourself wanting to defend Audra. "Audra has
her own life," you say. "Her career has never been stronger.
Wet Kisses Only is a great script, tailor-made for Audra. And
she has never looked better," you find yourself saying. "She
is in great shape."

"Oooooo! Rita, go girl, Audra in the buff. Does she still

have the tennis arm?" The penciled eyebrows shoot up and down.

"No . . ." You find yourself excited, wariness slipping off your shoulders like a coat that was far too warm for the weather. The cognac is warm; it has erased all your defenses. *Careful, Rita.*

Bevin keeps on talking. She works in Las Vegas. Something about that city always makes you freeze. You tell Bevin about the people from national television and their competing offers, their hunger, their greed, the many offers from Jenny and Johnny and Sally. Bevin orders more cognac. Slowly, she swirls the beige tea, ice clinking in the glass. She pokes at the cubes with her straw.

Bevin starts carefully, very carefully. You don't know what she is going to say, but you have a horrible idea. A bad fantasy that comes true. Your head is spinning, but its not just the cognac.

Bevin, it seems, works in television. "I work for the *Johnny Lever Show*," she says.

The restaurant seems to stop. The harpsichord waterfall of melody stops. No food is served, and diners stop chatting. "I work for the *Johnny Lever Show*." You might as well be falling into the floor, a huge hole opening up in the red carpet, taking you down through the floorboards, the hotel rooms, into the damp and cold basement.

She's still talking; she doesn't seem to stop. She works for the *Johnny Lever Show*. What is she saying? Soon they will start taping in San Francisco. She's scouting locations, that's all.

You're thinking: She doesn't want to commiserate on the revenge of the nerds. She doesn't want to sleep with you at all. Bevin is just another bloodhound barking up your tree. She just wants you on her television program. How ever did she find you? But Bevin's green eyes are sparkling with gold;

they bring you back to the present. Maybe she wasn't looking for you, after all.

Three easy words come to mind: "Go to hell," you say.

"Hey, no pressure, Rita. Don't worry. I'm just here scouting locations," she repeats. "That's all! San Francisco is such
a beautiful city." Bevin squeezes your hand again. You pull
your arm away as if you'd been touched by poison.

"Chill, girlfriend. There's nothing to worry about."
Bevin's noticing some look on your face, some expression
you cannot control. What is she saying? "Seeing you is great.
You look so good, Rita." Not like before, not like when you
were a science nerd in high school, she means.

"Of course, if you wanted to go on the air to talk about
Audra, I would be glad to help you get on the show."

You are paralyzed in your seat. The restaurant around
Bevin's head is still blurry, like an Impressionist painting.
Only Bevin's face is in focus, in dreadful focus. "I work for
the *Johnny Lever Show*." What is she saying now? That the
dessert and the cognac and the shared memories are something they should do more often. Bevin loves San Francisco
so very much.

"Look, I know you and Audra have been close for years."
Something in her tone reminds you of your therapist. "Even
though she's been with Gale all this time."

Gale. Why did she keep bringing up Gale?

"Go to hell," you say again. It's the only thing you can
think of: a paltry shield against the bright lights of media par-
asites. *Damn you, Rita! She's played you well.*

"You know, Audra isn't fooling anyone," Bevin is saying.
"The reporters always pick up on Gale. Gale sits at the table
behind Audra and rides in the backseat. Gale, in the shadows.
A real second-class citizen. Of course, now that Audra and
Tyrone are in happily married seclusion . . ." Bevin is taking
your pulse with the comment. "I hear Audra's hired an army
of bodyguards to protect their privacy."

Your face is a mask. She prattles on: "I used to watch you and Audra in the hall together, in front of your lockers. You didn't seem to care who knew. Making out in the back of the bus, late at night. Why, you and Audra were my first lesbian role models."

"But you're married."

"I'm *bi*," Bevin confirms. "You and Audra were quite a turn-on in the back of that bus."

"It was just a natural kind of thing. We didn't even know the word *lesbian*." You start to relax. Lesbians, you are all lesbians. Bevin, Gale, Audra, and you. Television producing lesbians, secretary lesbians, mycologist lesbians, and the biggest pop star to top the charts in a half century. Lesbians.

"But you *were* lovers, Rita. And that's the point. Why don't you consider, just *consider*, coming on the show?"

"No."

You remember Audra stretched out on the hotel room bed, crawling toward you over the sheets, whimpering with desire.

"That truth should not be denied," Bevin says.

Bevin's words ring in your ears: *"That truth should not be denied."* Audra, begging for your hands.

Talking faster, Bevin cannot believe that Audra remains in the closet, issuing denials and homophobic comments. "Rita, Audra is denying your relationship. As if it never happened."

"As if it never happened."

"Rita, won't you consider coming on the show?"

"No."

"Rita, you are not an island." Her fingers find yours again, a warm, trusting squeeze that doesn't let go. "Telling the truth can only be good," Bevin says, and you find yourself nodding. The truth, the truth about Audra on that hotel room bed was more absolute than any science you've ever practiced. "And Johnny Lever *is* different. Think about his charity, Tree of Life. It's a fund that has given away millions of dollars. I know you're on the board of the Women's Cancer Information Center. Johnny would be happy to give the organization two hundred and fifty thousand dollars.

Two hundred and fifty thousand dollars. The Information Center could buy its own building.

Two hundred and fifty thousand dollars. The Information Center could hire an assistant for the overworked executive director.

"Just *think* about it." Bevin withdraws her hand and sighs, a professional sound, exasperated but not without hope.

"I'm sorry, my private life is not for sale, Bevin."

But the woman's little pink hand crawls toward her velvet handbag. Fingers reach under the flap, there's the sound of a snap being undone. Tiny fingers in a tiny handbag. The object that emerges is also small. It's silver and square. It's a pack of matches, a very old pack of matches, a souvenir from a sleazy bar called El Trebol. A map of Mexico is etched on its back. You remember the stars, twinkling with the beautiful names of Mexican cities: Monterrey, Durango, Torreón, Veracruz, Guadalajara. You haven't seen the matches since high school. And it sends a cold dagger of fear through your heart. Bevin unfolds the cover. She tears off a match and strikes it. It bursts into a tiny, deadly flame. "Your private life is not for sale?"

"This isn't evidence of anything, Bevin."

"Are you absolutely sure, Rita?"

Bevin puts the tarnished book of matches on the table between you.

Monterrey, Durango, Torreón, Veracruz, Guadalajara. Such matches had been struck in the secret spaces of the bad-girl bathrooms in high school. And more. You could remember the rough feel of the smoke in your lungs. "I work for the *Johnny Lever Show*."

"This book of matches would certainly support my testimony, Rita." The flame flickers, and you see the rats in their endless maze. How did Bevin get the matches? You smell the fungus, the mushrooms, the damp sanctuary tucked inside your home. You want to run out of the restaurant, out of the world, and hole up in your own secret cave. But you cannot move. "I work for the *Johnny Lever Show.*"

Quick as a snake, you reach for the matches. Even quicker, Bevin has the matchbook hidden in her palm.

"Not so fast, girlfriend." The matches have been ferreted away in her handbag. "There's no statute of limitations on murder, Rita."

"What do you want?"

"I just want a short appearance. You can have your matches back. After the show."

"Why are you doing this to me?"

Bevin laughs, the penciled eyebrows moving up and down. "It's my *job,* Rita. The revenge of the nerds, remember?"

The words come out of your mouth like dry sand. "You want me to go on the television show."

"Hey, how long has it been since Audra has called you, Rita?"

You don't tell Bevin. It has been six months. Ever since her marriage to Tyrone. The plan that was supposed to make their affair safe. But now there was no affair.

"I'll bet she hasn't called you in a long time. Am I right?"

How come Bevin seemed to know everything?

"Come on, Rita. Just a brief appearance. That would get Audra's attention!"

"What do I have to do?"

"I just want a detail, Rita. Something you—or only someone *intimate* with Audra would know."

"How do you people sleep at night?"

"Easy. We don't sleep with Audra Léon." Bevin pats her purse.

"You're a disease, Bevin."

"No one's immune from television, Rita. Or from agents and book contracts and movie rights."

"I am."

"Fine. All I want is a brief appearance. And a juicy tidbit. Come on, everybody's got a scar . . . a mole . . . give me something good, Rita."

You remember what was good. The pain and pleasure of Audra's breasts. Even putting alcohol on the sterilized bandage was exciting. And then the phone calls had stopped.

"We actually do know about a certain . . ." Bevin whispered the delicious secret. You nod your head. The information is correct. How did they get it?

"Audra Léon isn't just selling *you* out," Bevin explains. "She is keeping all lesbians in the closet as well."

You don't know what to say. You don't say anything. You are frozen with alcohol, memory, and the knowledge of who you are. Bevin is right. You are angry; crushed at Audra's silence. There's nothing to think about anymore. Your mind runs like a rat down all the mazes. There is no escape, not for you.

"I work for the *Johnny Lever Show*." Bevin *owns* you.

A disturbance just on the edge of your peripheral vision attracts your attention. A worried maître d' is approaching your table with several guests in tow. Two members of Generation X had penetrated the tower. In their early twenties, they bear the requisite angry expressions common to their kind. They seem to size you up: corporate lesbian, you see them think. The maître d' is having second thoughts, as he seats the two Xers at your table. He seems to size you and Bevin up; you are not the ladies he thought you were. He's more right than he could ever imagine. *I work for the* Johnny Lever Show.

"Hi," the first ruffian growls.

"Hi! How ya doin'?" Bevin has a false pleasantry.

You recognize them from a television appearance, from the Dyke March last year. They are the generals of the Lesbian Revengers. They tongue each other in suburban shopping malls and pass out questionnaires asking heterosexuals how they got that way. They wear T-shirts that say My Body Is a Bomb. Their blue jeans have very few threads left. One of them is bald. They are not exactly *your* kind of lesbian. Their conversation seems far away. You watch them, listen to them as if they are trapped behind a veil of stupidity.

Bobbing their heads excitedly, they crow over this unique opportunity. They have heard about Audra Léon for years. The one named Gertrude says Audra cruises L.A. bars wearing wigs, looking for girls, when she and Gale have fights. It's not exactly information you want to hear. That deep-throated scream, you know, could only be meant for you. The memory of that sound fades, fuses with the memory of a whining police siren outside. *Fire!*

The generals are planning their attack. They have talked to Bevin on the phone for hours. Audra's sham marriage to wanna-be singer Tyrone Warren is a travesty. The wedding video that was leaked to the press looked dispassionate, to say the least. Why wouldn't anyone tell the truth? Immediately after the marriage, Audra had hired a virtual army of bodyguards to protect their privacy.

"I heard he hits her," Bevin said sadly, red spikes bisecting her penciled eyebrows. The glinting of her green eyes warn you to be careful.

"No," you hear yourself saying, remembering your own unique wedding gift. A little garden of rare, carnivorous plants. Audra liked to watch the flies get trapped on the sticky leaves. And then she never called you again. "He's never hit her," you say.

"What *we* hear," the one named Gertrude announced, "is that they're not even living together!"

"You may be right about that." You shrug. Bevin is baring her teeth.

"There. You see?" the Revengers swear, gritting their

teeth. Audra herself made homophobic remarks to the media, they remind you. "Whadda y'all think, that I'm some kinda queer!" Audra had supposedly lashed out at the paparazzi. It was a remark she later denied making. But you could imagine her, in a moment of ill-advised passion, lashing out. Still, the word hurt you, too. *Queer.* A name the Revengers had taken for themselves.

The Revengers are especially excited by the opportunity to out Audra Léon on national television. Chattering, giggling, they nearly leap off the upholstery.

You feel sick, but by that time, more cognac arrives. You start to drift on a sea of alcohol. Bevin's voice and the voices of the Lesbian Revengers all seem to merge into the background, and all you can feel is the softness of Audra's mahogany thighs, the lavender scent of her breath.

It was *not* a one night stand, a mercy fuck, a souvenir for old times' sake.

It was Audra loving you once again, once again, once again.

Wasn't it? But now you have no choice. As Audra would say, if a building falls on you, you have to pick yourself up and crawl out from under it. And walk away. And now you will have to walk away from Audra. Forever.

"Johnny would be happy to give the Women's Cancer Information Center *two hundred and fifty thousand dollars.*" Bevin announces with righteousness. The words fall on the table, like big bundles of cash. The generals applaud.

General Gertrude presses their case. "Dr. Huelga, you have to do it! *Two hundred and fifty thousand dollars.*" The Revengers have big eyeballs as they scream, "This goes *beyond truth;* its big money for the women's community, for breast cancer—all the money that goes to AIDS—"

"The body is an interrelated organism," you intone. "It's pointless to pit one disease against another."

"Except the boys have gotten all the bread. *Two hundred and fifty thousand dollars.* You have to do it."

"I don't have to do anything," you say, pepper in your eyes, but you are wrong. You will do it.

That's when Bevin's pager bleeps. She leaves the table and heads for a phone, the pleats of her skirt flaring as she flies across the deep red carpet. You look at the Lesbian Revengers, suddenly lonely. General Gertrude fought the war on the streets and in the city's best eating establishments. Kissing and handing out forms. They were the grass roots; you were the boardroom. It was all the same cause, wasn't it? But there was no reason why you have to ruin your personal life.

The Revengers are taking this opportunity to liberate the Top of the Mark. The bald one has her pierced tongue out, circling the ear of the other general, but none of the stockbrokers or waiters seem to notice them. The room is spinning around you, circling just like the tongues of the Lesbian Revengers. You drink more cognac, hoping this moment will fade into memory. You will take a taxi home, crawl into bed, and try to sleep without dreaming.

Bevin has returned, just as you are slipping into your coat, ready to flee into the night. Her hand slides across your cashmere jacket, stopping you from putting your arm into the sleeve.

Bevin has got some very exciting news! Johnny Lever has just called her. The message is *too* exciting! Bevin moves closer; you all lean together and join in a conspiracy that will change history. If you could reach over and strangle General Gertrude, you gladly would. Although she wouldn't be the first on your list.

It doesn't matter about the twenty grand, the limousine, or the big hotel. What matters is Bevin's handbag. She holds it close as she tells you the exciting news. Johnny Lever has pulled on the moral heartstrings of the famous singer and made her see the light. And the light is lavender. Audra herself will appear on the show!

Yeah, yeah. The two positives that make a negative. How

gullible does Bevin think you are, anyway? Audra will never show.

The show will be taped right here in San Francisco and aired on National Coming Out Day, Bevin tells the Revengers, who are beside themselves with righteous glee.

On October 11, you will be picked up by a limousine. You will tell your story on national television. And then the curtains will part. And three to thirty million people will hold their breaths, and you will out Audra Léon as a gay woman, a lesbian, as your lover.

Bevin calls a cab and escorts you home. Her purse sits beside her, wedged in between the door and her hip. You pull up to your house, and Bevin is impressed. "This is a fucking mansion! Look at that gate! And such a lovely garden!"

A row of white mums circles the drive; they wave in the wind, their long stalks bending, beckoning.

"You have a lot to lose, Rita," Bevin says quietly. The sentence is like a shadow that is creeping across your life.

"You give me back the matches," you say, "as I walk onstage. Or the deal's off."

"After the show, Rita." Bevin loses no time pulling a piece of paper out of her little black purse. It says Release across the top, but the rest of the letters are too small. They are swimming across the page like microscopic spores. You are signing the death warrant of a love affair. A love affair that could have lasted a lifetime. Except Audra hasn't returned your calls for half a year. A pen is in your hand, and Bevin is telling you that the taping has already been set up. You won't have a lot of time to think, you realize. You don't want to think. "Wear the Ina Cho suit, honey. It looks beautiful on you; you look beautiful in it."

The limousine will pick you up at 5 A.M.

"You know, Rita, I think you *do* want to out Audra. Revenge can be sweet," she says softly, leaving a wet kiss on your lips. It tastes exactly like phosphorus.

CHAPTER ONE

nO OBITS!

"No Obits!" cried the headline of the *Bay Area Reporter* in sixty-point type. "No Obits!" 1998 gave us the first week that the gay and lesbian paper hadn't received any obituaries. For a decade the obituaries list only grew longer. Dead friends filled those pages. Now activism, money, research, and drug companies had changed the course of the AIDS epidemic.

Halloween seemed, once again, something to celebrate. And Halloween belonged in the Castro, where the happy havoc tangled up traffic and Muni lines in a show of anarchy that had seemed impossible to suppress. Castro clones who had never worn a dress giggled and teased each other with the newfound freedom to wear frocks. The words of the late, great Sylvester rang from the café: "You're a star, you only happen once," reminding us all of the differences in camp: the low camp that was sexist and high camp that was proud.

Unfortunately, it was to be the last Halloween in the Castro: Next year, the overwhelming street party would be moved to the Civic Center. The large, flat area with a square

pond and a bureaucratic ambience was just going to be no
fun at all.

Cruising through the Castro, I could feel the high holy
day was nearly upon us. If October 11 gave gay people permission to come out, October 31 gave gay San Franciscans
a chance to wear those size-fourteen heels, ruby slippers, or
knee-high pirate boots they'd always dreamed of. Hundreds
of tasteless take-offs on dead movie stars were in the making. The bars were doing a brisk business, and in between
burritos and smoothies, gay men held hands and kissed,
sometimes blocking the sidewalk so badly a lesbian could
hardly make her way to a frozen yogurt. And Halloween
would be a lot worse.

I had avoided the Halloween festivities in recent years.
The traffic jams were one thing, the tourist crowds who
came to gawk were something else. Already there were rum-
blings of discontent; ACT UP was planning a massive photo
shoot, taking aim at rubbernecking heterosexuals. The bully
boys just might show up later with a less benign protest of
their own. A lot of the spontaneity had gone out of the annual celebration. And my life.

As a freelance people-finder, serving summonses and taking out other people's trash, I'd done pretty well. My last gig
had helped me buy out my house partner. Police Officer
Laura Deleuse didn't like living over a private investigator.
I didn't like living under a cop, either. Our real estate relationship ended amicably, and the financial rewards from my
last venture helped put the title of the old Victorian in my
name. And my name only.

With less than a 1 percent vacancy rate in the city, I found
just the tenants I wanted. Creole and Jessie were masseuses.
While the police officer was tired, grumpy, and suspicious,
my new tenants were positive, soothing, and healthful. Their
tenancy would probably help my blood pressure, circula-

tion, and flexibility. I hoped it was a relationship that would last a long time.

I moved upstairs, to the roomier apartment with the bay view. I let Jessie and Creole carry on their sensuous business in the building. It didn't create any parking problems, and all I ever heard from downstairs was the occasional blissful groan. Their business was doing great.

But detective gigs hadn't been coming my way. Suddenly, there weren't any people to find or summonses to serve. I'd been out of the loop for too long. But today was different. At nine o'clock, the phone rang with a nice, boring gig. I lifted the receiver, fingering my earlobe: a sign of trouble.

"Emma Victor, private investigator." A representative from Guaranteed All Risk wanted me to watch some guy walk away from his crutches and record it on film. It would save the company hundreds of thousands, and I expected my fair share for sitting in a car and waiting for that particular moment of truth. I would meet the client later at noon. Guaranteed All Risk hired a lot of freelance detectives—contract workers, these days. They were trying to keep as many people off the payroll as they could, just like everyone else. Cost-cutting and don't forget to catch them at the disco. Chump change, but a chance to look out my windshield for a few days.

Meanwhile, Rose called with something far more interesting and lucrative. It was time to take out the trash.

"Did you see the television program that outed Audra Léon, Emma? It was a history-making event."

"I'm getting back into the reading habit," I grumbled, reminding Rose of the past. "Twenty years ago, women crowded into women's bookstores to discuss the latest manifesto. Remember the Myth of the Vaginal Orgasm?"

"Yeah, I remember vaginal orgasms, too."

"Ah, what has happened to us, Rose? Lesbian sex used to be a revolutionary act. Now the sisterhood returns to the bookstore to watch television: famous people coming out on *television*. And afterward we go to the Safeway and pick up an *Enquirer* with a lead article about Martina and Rita. Then we return to our highly mortgaged home to search for our G spots."

"What's wrong with that?"

Apparently, the outing of a famous comedian, a famous actress, a famous pop singer, a famous anyone, mattered to everyone in my circle, everyone but me. What was fame to the pioneers against patriarchy?

"So our friends have stopped reading and writing manifestos. Now they return from work and reach for the remote. What's wrong with that?" she repeated.

"Oh, nothing," I sighed. "It's just that I had a million calls and E-mails before the show, reminding me of the rebroadcast of the *Johnny Lever Show*. My tenants downstairs rang me up to come down and watch the spectacle. Afterward, they offered me a tape. I never watched it."

"You'll see it here, girlfriend."

Great. How could I miss the outing of Audra Léon? The tabloids screamed about her supposed homosexuality while I waited in line at the Safeway, Audra's copper pageboy and signature cat suit were displayed in Cliff's notion store; the window dresser did better than Madame Tussaud in recreating the diva of pop.

The *Bay Area Reporter* strung "Audra Léon **OUT!**" in sixty-point type on the front page. Audra Léon was one of us, they said. I found myself getting almost angry. "Maybe she's one of *them,* but as far as I'm concerned, Audra Léon does not belong to our tribe."

"Not to mention all her lyrics, a woman who desperately needed a *man*. Her wedding with Tyrone Warren, that white, wanna-be-black rap artist, doesn't make me feel particularly sisterly toward Audra Léon, either," Rose agreed. "Remember the interview with Barbara Walters? 'A lesbian? Don't be silly! I am a devoted mother.' If you listened to her words, Emma, she never said that she *wasn't* a lesbian. Oh, hell, what do we care, eh?"

"Not a lot. What's up, Rose?"

"The producers say the woman who outed Léon is in danger. Needs security."

"Why did she go on that show in the first place?"

I guess it was the money they promised to the Women's Cancer—"

"Sounds nice, but I'm not sure that would be reason enough."

"Whatever, Emma. Are you interested? They're coming over in twenty minutes."

"It doesn't cost anything to listen to someone's problem."

"And the media is a monied medium. By the way, what are you doing for Halloween? Planned your costume yet?"

"I don't know, Rose. There's too many tourists that come to gawk."

"Come on, Emma. It's the last Halloween in the Castro. You always look good in whatever drag you cook up. Next year, they're moving to the Civic Center."

"That's progress for you."

"Page Hodel is going to DJ from the sound stage. And there's a drag king contest at the club Lex! It's always nice to dress up as a guy. All the young women are doing it at the Club Lex. You get all those boy privileges and people move out of your way on the street. Hey, why don't you do that costume you did a few years ago? The butch/femme thing."

The costume Rose meant had been ingenious but nearly impossible to wear. I had cut a dress in half and sewn it over a three-piece business suit. Half my face was done up in false eyelashes and blusher, the other half featured a mustache and five-o'clock shadow. One foot wore a high heel, the other, a lawyerly wing tip. Depending on what angle you approached me, I was a boy or a girl. From the front, I was a gender schizophrenic, unable to make up my mind. A startling effect, it was, nevertheless an awkward concept; the difference in the shoes gave me a backache, and my arms were tired, the femme side crooked at the elbow, the butch side with hand in pocket. I had even mastered giggling out of one side of my mouth, grunting out the other.

"We'll talk about Halloween later. Get in your car and get over here, Emma."

"Yes, ma'am."

"TV people, Emma. Look sharp."

What kind of drag would that be? I splashed water on my face and pinched my cheeks for color, the Victorian equivalent of blusher. I tried to thread the scroll-engraved golden hoop earring through my right earlobe. An allergy to nickel was ruining my accessory plan. First rubbing my earlobe with alcohol, I managed to thread the wire that was supposed to be gold through the inflamed skin. The earring continued to be a problem. I took a starched white shirt out of its plastic bag and threaded a silk scarf around my neck. My leather coat fit me like a second skin. I checked the mirror. White shirt, shoes shined to a mirror finish, a kid leather coat, and earrings twinkling at my ears. I looked sharp enough for the media sharks.

Soon I was driving up and down the hills, my car precariously perched at stop signs and then dipping down into Eureka Valley. I passed the rows of Italianate Victorians that lesbians and gay men had painted in happy colors. They marched down the hill, glorious Gold Rush palaces, all done up in a merry-go-round of rainbow colors. The window of Cliff's Variety was showing an Audra Léon look-alike mannequin. The black cat suit and copper pageboy were unmistakable. Across her cauldron was written Last Halloween in the Castro.

Rainbow flags gave way to piñatas as I cruised down the hill toward the Mission. I rolled over the freeway to the

steep-hilled district called Potrero Hill. Gilded Italianates
perched on sixty-degree slopes, overlooking skyscrapers,
bridges, and water. The hills gave way to the long industrial
landfill of Third Street. San Francisco's shipping industry
had, for the most part, moved over to Oakland. Santa Fe rail-
way rented out the waterfront property as storage. A few
boats wandered in and out of the harbor. Sometimes the
Russian Navy would drop anchor. But live-work lofts, the
planned Mission Bay project and the mayor's cronies would
soon change all that.

Still, the real estate was relatively cheap, compared to the
rest of San Francisco. Rose had rented a warehouse where
you could smell the french fries and the diesel fuel. The
warehouse, with the wooden storefront, could have been the
meeting place for Alcoholics Anonymous. Instead, the initi-
ated had to salute a video camera hidden behind a twist of
blackberry bushes to gain entrance.

I walked through Rose's idea of a security gauntlet. Three
more cameras and I had to press the code before I was
admitted into the office park. A hive of activity, Rose's bur-
geoning workforce tended the phones and banks of computers. Indoor palm trees stretched toward the big industrial
skylights. Secondhand oak furniture, wooden desks, and
fireproof file cabinets, heavy as anchors, were massive bul-
warks in the interior. No wooing the clientele with a suite of
downtown offices, brocade wallpaper, leather-topped desks,
and overpriced downtown lunches. Rose took her clients to
little-known bistros and saved money on location and furniture. The big bucks she spent on computers and an extensive
private security system guarding some of the biggest art
collections in San Francisco.

I went directly into Rose's office. The place was architec-
turally designed to make it amenable to a wheelchair: lowered tables, nothing important over four feet from the
ground. Only a half cup of coffee was present, a paper-

weight on today's *San Francisco Chronicle*. Rose must be somewhere on the floor; the cup was still warm. The paper was turned to page four: "Shop Today, Super Halloween White Sale at Macy's!" It seemed Macy's would use any excuse for a white sale: Easter, Veterans Day, Valentine's Day, the Linen Department worked them all. Underneath the pictures of fluffy towels, a headline blared, "New Hunter Virus May Help Kill HIV . . . It might take a virus to kill a virus, say researchers who think they have discovered a biological weapon that can seek out HIV-infected cells. . . ."

"Want some coffee?" Rose wheeled into her office, glancing over at a coffeemaker. Its pot held a half-inch of black, oily substance.

"No thanks; I've had enough caffeine to power Rome this morning."

"I like the earrings, Emma." Rose wheeled up to me. I bent down as she examined the jewelry, the unique little etched pattern. Something Indonesian? Your right earlobe is a little red."

"Hard to get solid gold these days. What's up, Rose?" My sometimes employer was being evasive. "Make with the fast forward; I've got a meeting with a new client at noon."

"What's the gig? A new client?"

"Insurance gig. Guaranteed All Risk."

"I think I recommended you for that," Rose murmured.

"Trash television? What's the story?" A white label with a red border emerged. I could read the careful black printing as she came closer: the *Johnny Lever Show*. A date had been written underneath it in hand: October 11. National Coming Out Day.

"I've recommended you to a few insurance firms. Who did you say called?"

"Guaranteed All Risk. A Mr. Fremont. Thanks for the plug." The VCR grabbed the tape out of Rose's hand and gulped it down. We watched the plastic box disappear inside the black, rectangular mouth.

"Hmm," Rose grumbled. "As I said, Lever wants me to hire a bodyguard. The woman who had the affair—Dr., Dr.—what's her name. The one with the black hair—"

"I heard she had a great left hook. So why are you working for them?"

"The situation intrigues me. The ins and outs of being out and in kind of interest me. I like this Dr. Huelga character, Emma. And I could use some entertainment business money, diversify my clientele."

"You're going behind the Orange Curtain, Rose?"

"There's a lot of money in Southern California. Right now I'm just guarding a whole lot of old-master paintings in Pacific Heights bedrooms. *Bo-ring!* I'll just show you the *salient* bits of this," Rose promised.

The tape began to whir. Soon we'd see a prime-time pimp outing a big pop star. I didn't care very much. Once again, I felt irritated. It didn't matter to me if Audra Léon was a lesbian or not. There were fifty thousand lesbians in the Bay Area, having children, paying off mortgages, walking their dogs, and teaching in the school system. They were in the front lines, fighting to keep the kids and keep the home fires burning. Lesbians who worked hard, had their portraits taken at Kmart, lesbians who didn't lie. Who cared about a pop singer who'd been forced out of a closet filled with satin and bodyguards? What difference could it possibly make?

"So, how exactly did you get *this* gig?" I asked the director of Baynetta Security Services.

"Bevin Crosswell, an old college buddy. She works for Johnny Lever. So you heard about the show—"

"Yeah, the lady with the left hook. Her high school love was—is—a closet case with golden vocal cords and more money than God. How'd Lever find Audra Léon's old girlfriend, anyway?"

"How do these people find anybody? It's their job."

"It's their job to ruin people's lives."

"Don't get moralistic, Emma. Besides, Johnny Lever made good on his promise. He donated two hundred and fifty thousand dollars to the Women's Cancer Information Center, where Huelga is on the board."

"Lever got his money's worth. The Lesbian Revengers who initially supported the deal withdrew their support from Lever because of the way he treated Rita Huelga."

"Bevin will be here any minute with Dr. Rita Huelga."

"Does she really think this woman is in danger?"

"Just take their money, Emma. What's the problem?"

I let a silence crash in the room.

"Here, let me cue the tape up." Rose pushed the fast forward button and the image was divided by eight lines. Soap commercials raced by frantically. Actresses jerked their heads, playing housewives that barely existed: women who didn't need to generate a second income to keep the family afloat. The American dream: stay at home and crow about the wash. Their red mouths were frantic, chattering mutely across the screen. "Whiter than white!" Then the logo popped up: *"The Johnny Lever Show!"* and Rose released the fast forward button.

A big, pale blue stage showed a rear projection of the San Francisco skyline. The Transamerica pyramid looked jaunty, piercing a lone cirrus cloud that hung over downtown. The Bay Bridge twinkled with fake lights. In front of the screen, two deeply upholstered chairs waited, empty, expectant. A dapper blond man holding a microphone like the sword of Damocles stood in front of the backdrop. A shiny grin competed with the sheen of his silver suit. Applause was heard as the tape slowed to normal speed, and the camera panned across a studio audience. "Hoo! Hoo! Hoo!"

"Here it comes!" Rose turned up the volume.

"Welcome to the *Johnny Lever Show.* It's October

eleventh, and we're taping here in San Francisco. But it isn't only Indian Summer that's heating up the city by the bay." Johnny's eyes twinkled and he tilted his head in mock reverence. "Today, we've got something very exciting for you! For all you fans—or soon to be former fans—of Audra Léon!" Johnny Lever loped back and forth across the stage like a tiger, wagging the microphone at the audience. A circus atmosphere was engendered, underscored by Johnny's bright green bolo tie, which matched the lizard skin boots on his feet.

"Hoo! Hoo! Hoo!"

The camera came closer. Johnny Lever affected an expression of carefully cultivated compassion. His words dripped like honey into the microphone, belying the hostile excitement of the crowd as he greeted them and cut suddenly to a commercial.

Rose fast forwarded past a NyQuil commercial. An actress in a negligee fell asleep across the screen, full makeup upon the pillow. I wondered how Audra Léon was sleeping these days.

Rose paused the tape. Behind Johnny Lever, four portraits came into focus from the rear projector. Audra Léon, white teeth flashing, framed by the highly burnished copper pageboy, two wings curling around her face in parentheses. A black cat suit looked like it had been painted on her long limbs. Another square showed a different Audra emerging out of the Pacific. She was a black-headed crane, impossibly long legs, a tiny string bikini; she'd been careful to keep her pageboy dry. A third image showed Audra in a scene from her upcoming film, *Wet Kisses Only.* On her back, a cat suit of sequins had been pulled down off her shoulders, the sequins pooling around her waist. The camera had teased the audience with a shot that ended just above her nipples.

The fourth shot showed an Audra we never could have guessed at. Out of focus, out of the past, she must have been

fourteen or fifteen. A fuzzy Afro and a tennis racket clutched
under her arm, a tight T-shirt over small, adolescent breasts,
this Audra was pure tomboy. The copper pageboy and cling-
ing cat suits were something no one could have predicted.

"And now, please welcome a very special guest—"
Johnny's hand extended out toward the blue curtain. He
waited, and nothing happened. "Once again, please welcome—" The curtain wasn't moving, and Johnny's smile
became a little fixed, when a woman was suddenly pushed
from behind the curtain into the national spotlight. Perfectly
polished loafers tripped onto the stage on thick soles. A
large-boned but not quite heavyset woman stood still, like a
deer caught in the headlights. A dark red suit with black velvet collar had been carefully tailored to her body. Her hair
was smoothed back over her head, ending in a long, impres-
sive, thick plait down her back. A white streak began at a
widow's peak and made a straight line across the top of her
head, a Bride of Frankenstein effect, but offset by the shy
warmth of the jet eyes, which blinked in the lights. The velvet collar echoed the black hair, the black eyes. Underneath
the jacket, the tiny butterfly collar was open just enough to
reveal a medal that nested at the base of her brown throat. A
close-up showed the dramatic heart-shaped face that was
nervous to the point of desperation. The medal was revealed
to be sectarian; a tiny tennis racket.

Above the medal, wide-set, coal dark eyes showed terror
under a high forehead. A nearly unbroken line of black eyebrow made a thick black line over her eyes. The shiny ebony
cap of hair, untouched by the people in Makeup, was
brushed into a sleek helmet. On camera, the bright red lips
and porcelain white teeth that bit them leapt out at the
viewer. It was a beautiful face: naive, dramatic, frightened.
Smiling shyly at the audience's applause, she squinted into
the spotlight, her dark eyes glittering. The long-legged im-

ages of Audra Léon, hovering in the background, disappeared as she came onstage.

Johnny Lever slung a casual arm over Dr. Rita Huelga's shoulder and turned her toward the stage. The one corner of her mouth twitched, gathering her lips to the left, lopsided.

"I know its a little nerve-racking, all the wires and cords—" he whispered, sotto voce, and escorting her. "Watch the stair," he crooned. But Dr. Rita Huelga's step was careful; the loafers scuffled up the stairs to the appointed chair. He set her down gently, like a pie cooling on a windowsill. He turned and faced the audience.

"Ladies and gentlemen, I'm proud to present to you a woman who is not afraid to speak the truth and address some of the most important issues of our day. Thank you so much for coming here to share your story, Dr. Huelga."

Dr. Huelga nodded, gulped. She was sitting up so straight in her chair, she might have been waiting for electrocution. Johnny kept on with the honied exposition.

"Ladies and gentlemen, the lesbian and gay movement has made great strides in our society. Let's face it—a hundred years ago, people were burned at the stake for the love that dare not speak its name. We know now that homosexuality is *completely* genetically determined. Homosexuals, in fact, are *born that way*. There's nothing we—or they—can do about it. Isn't it time for society to change? Isn't it time to come out of hiding, for love to speak its name? Right now, our brightest stars are wrestling in their celebrity heavens with their own consciences, their own careers, their own passions—their own genetically determined impulses! And we ask ourselves the question: Why don't they come out? And what better role models can there be than those men and women in the entertainment business?"

"I can think of a few million at least," I groused.

"Shut up, Emma, just watch."

"Now, Dr. Huelga—" Johnny slowed his pace. He got out

of his chair and leaned toward her, bending down on one knee, a gesture of marriage proposal. "I can't tell you how important it is that you've come here," he said softly for all to hear.

Behind Rita Huelga, the four images of Audra Léon suddenly flashed back upon the screen.

"Dr. Huelga, you live here in San Francisco, right?"

"Yes." Her voice was a rich, controlled contralto.

"And what do you do here, in this beautiful city by the bay?"

"I'm a mycologist."

"What's that, exactly?"

"I study mushrooms."

"And why do you study mushrooms?"

"There are a lot of health benefits."

"Such as?"

The audience shifted in the background, but Johnny knew what he was doing; establishing the credibility of his witness.

"Some mushrooms, particularly the *Polyporus umbullatus,* actually have been shown to shrink tumors." Rita Huelga's face began to relax. "Who would have thought that fungus could be so important!" she quipped, and the audience laughed. Smiling, her eyes tilted over her high cheekbones.

"Dr. Huelga here has won an award for outstanding achievement from the Cancer Society, haven't you, Rita?"

"Yes." Rita was uncomfortable. She didn't want to mix her career into this interview. She didn't want to be there at all.

"And Rita, I know you went to high school with one of today's most important stars, didn't you?"

"Yes."

"And, if I understand this correctly, you had a passionate—a sexual relationship with someone who is well known to us all."

"Yes."

"And Dr. Huelga, that person, that star, was Audra Léon, wasn't it?"

Gasp from the audience.

"Yes." Rita Huelga's knees clamped together.

"So, let me get this straight—ha-ha-ha. You and Audra were lovers in high school, right?"

"Yes."

"And you met on the tennis team?"

"I want our audience—and Rita—to know that she is not here to talk about a brief love affair in high school. This isn't about an adolescent crush. You and Audra were together for two years. Am I correct?"

"Yes." Her sensuous mouth loosened unconsciously with the memory, the full lower lip was licked by a cautious, nervous tongue. The concreteness of their relationship. The weekend sleepovers? The discovery, the play? Dr. Huelga's moving mouth told a story without words.

"Now, Dr. Huelga, you are a very brave woman for coming here. And, ladies and gentlemen, let me remind you, this is National Coming Out Day, isn't it Rita?"

"Yes. Yes it is."

"The fact is," Johnny addressed the audience, "Audra Léon is a lesbian. Her carefully orchestrated marriage is a sham. That's true, isn't it?"

"Yes." Dr. Huelga seemed to gather some strength, her full mouth relaxed with the words of truth that passed through them. "Yes, it's true."

"Hoo! Hoo! Hoo!"

"And—you know that because—" The silver ball of the mike came closer to her lips, as if it were a wand that would raise the ratings.

"Because . . ." Johnny's voice was so intimate, their heads might have been lying on the same pillow together.

"Because three months ago, I spent a week in a hotel with Audra. In Phoenix."

Johnny nodded, feeling the ratings rise. "She was on location, wasn't she?"

"Yes."

"For her upcoming feature, *Wet Kisses Only*. Am I correct?"

"Yes."

"And what happened in that hotel?"

"We, uh, just spent time together, like we always did."

"Like you always did?"

"Sure. We talked about the old days. What she's doing now. The pressures of her career. Just—uh—normal—kind of stuff."

"And you made love?"

Dr. Huelga's face froze for a moment. Behind her, Audra's image seemed to loom, malevolent.

"Uh—" Rita's heart-shaped face froze, the lips clamped shut.

Johnny's body snapped upright at rigid attention. With a concerned glance at the audience, he loomed over Dr. Huelga, who sank deeper in her upholstered chair. "I mean, you are here because you had—have—a lover relationship with Audra Léon? Am I not correct?" Johnny's demeanor had changed from compassion to cross-examination.

"You made love in that hotel in Phoenix, didn't you?"

"Yes."

Johnny smiled, breathed a sigh of relief. Addressing the audience, he said, "Now, we all know that there are a lot of people who would like to—who would even pretend to have had sex with major stars. This show gets calls all the time. When Greta Garbo died, we had people lining up around the block to talk about the woman who just wanted to be alone.

But ladies and gentlemen, this is different. Now, Rita."
Johnny was on bended knee. "Tell our studio audience what
you told our assistant producer."

"Huh?"

"About Audra—you know—"

Dr. Huelga was a statue on the chair.

"Come on, Rita. Look at those pictures of Audra behind
you."

Dr. Huelga, turning around, saw for the first time the
looming images of Audra Léon. Her face went gray.

"Rita, it's all going to come out now. Remember, it's National Coming Out Day. Remembering Audra as your high
school lover, and your surprise at the Phoenix Royal Hotel
when you discovered—"

"Huh?" A stage manager offstage waved at her. The heart-
shaped face drifted away from the lens. Johnny's strong
but gentle hand landed on her shoulder and brought her back
to the moment at hand. "But, Rita. If I may get a little
graphic—"

Rita bit her lip. She seemed to look into the lights and go
far away.

"Rita-a-a-a-a-a-a-a-a-a-a-a—what was different about
Audra?" Johnny's voice was singsong now. "It's just a few
words, Rita. We need to know that you're not afraid. That
you're not just making this up. You can tell us. Tell us about
Audra. And how she's different . . ."

"Her nipples," Rita whispered.

"What—what about her nipples, Rita?"

"Her nipples." Dr. Huelga's hand came up to her throat,
as if she would strangle herself. White fingers curled around
the edge of her velvet collar.

"Yes?"

Silence.

"Audra's nipples are—" Johnny Lever leaned toward her,

willing the word to come out. The lights dimmed, went pinker, as if to soothe the woman on the spot.

The broad lips parted, the slightly asymmetrical mouth twisted. I could almost see her thought processes. She'd walked the plank, blindfolded by her own foolishness, vanity, and desire. Why not jump? The word was like a hard, cold stone out of her.

"Pierced."

Gasp! Applause!

"You heard it, ladies and gentlemen. Finally, someone has come up with the incontrovertible truth. Audra Léon is of the Lesbian persuasion. And always has been and always will be!"

"Hoo! Hoo! Hoo!"

"Hoo! Hoo! Hoo!"

The camera panned over the photos of Audra Léon. Despite the cleavage revelation, all her clothing was carefully constructed to obscure any hint or shape of a nipple accessory beneath.

"Hoo! Hoo! Hoo!"

"Hoo! Hoo! Hoo!"

"Hoo! Hoo! Hoo!"

Rita's face was frozen.

"Rita," Johnny's smile was slick, triumphant. "Maybe you can tell us what's the difference between a vibrator and a dildo?"

"Hoo! Hoo! Hoo!"

Johnny Lever was consoling Rita with the tenderness of an executioner. Thirty million people saw the tears streaming down Rita Huelga's face. And then they saw something else. Although Rita Huelga appeared used up and no longer the concern of the camera, she was not passively sitting anymore. In fact, she bore little resemblance to the shy deer caught in the headlights of trash television. Realization played across her face. She grabbed the arms of her chair, her fingers digging into the upholstery; she was rising out of her seat, fighting against her common sense that was telling her not to make drama in front of the television audience. Johnny Lever was oblivious to Huelga's presence, to the change in her demeanor. Chattering into the mike like a parakeet, he never saw her coming. Slowly, purposefully, Rita Huelga had risen from her chair and was coming up behind the talk show host as he laughed into the microphone.

Behind the smiling face of Johnny Lever, just on the horizon of his right ear, an angry Medusa came into the frame. It was a wonderful moment, wonderful for the viewers, wonderful for the audience, wonderful for this lesbian, and probably also wonderful for Johnny Lever's ratings.

"You *bastard!*" Huelga was just behind him, and her roar leaked into his mike. She had put her arm around his neck in a hammerhold. Then her fist curled up into a ball, came around to his midsection, and landed a solid, well-aimed blow just under his rib cage.

"Oof!" The punch had neatly collapsed his diaphragm. As he turned around to fully face his attacker, Rita Huelga pushed her knee into his groin, aiming it right through his belly. Collapsed in the middle, Johnny Lever flew a good three feet. His rump made a hard, final sound on the wooden floor. "Annngghh!" Instinct had taken over. Lever, as an animal, had instinctively rolled onto his stomach to protect himself from further blows. As a television personality, he instinctively held the microphone aloft, never losing his grip. Rita Huelga lost no time. She strode over and started kicking Lever in the buttocks.

Too soon, too soon, the stage managers took control of the situation. Techies pounded the boards, their big belts and gear looking dark and dirty against the pristine silver blue set. Real life was coming onstage and trying to take Rita Huelga off it. Johnny Lever was regaining his composure quickly. Propping himself on one elbow, his lips grazed the silver ball of the mike. Then, sitting cross-legged on the stage, he took a breath, attempted a laugh, and combed his fingers through his hair. There was but a moment of pain as he stood up, one hand clutching his stomach where he had taken the blow. The camera framed a fractured grin in close-up, and I saw that Lever's eyes glittered with the effort of keeping back the pain. He pulled the microphone back up to his lips.

"Lacch—" Breathing, since the Huelga blow, was a somewhat new experience for Johnny Lever. "Harrumph! Ladies and gentlemen." Steady on his feet, a cold sweat had drenched his face. "Let it never be said that journalism is not without its dangers!" The camera pulled away and revealed a stage minus Dr. Rita Huelga.

"Hoo! Hoo! Hoo!"

He was going to make it a pyrrhic victory for television. Johnny smiled like a returned warrior, with the intense pleasures of his kind: applause, instant ratings, and affiliate allegiance.

"Hoo! Hoo! Hoo!"

"Thank you! Thank you, ladies and gentlemen! After the commercial, I have a special surprise guest! From San Francisco's premiere piercing parlor, the Gambit. A florist and former beautician—someone who can tell us more about Audra Léon. Please welcome Thad!"

Thad. Could it be the same person who had pierced my nose last year? Indeed, it was the very same piercer. I had crossed paths with Thad in the land of beauty and pain. He had doled out a little of both.

"Thad will give us some firsthand information on Audra Léon's body enhancements. And tomorrow: how Halloween candy can kill your kids!—"

Rose stopped the tape. "Seen enough? What do you think?"

"I think I'd like to know where Dr. Huelga learned to fight like that."

"Want to take her on as a client?"

"She looks like a loose canon to me," I warned. She also looked beautiful, passionate, and smart, but not smart enough. "Albeit manipulated, exploited, and betrayed."

"She went ballistic on national television," Rose grimaced. "Johnny Lever's people think she might be in danger—"

"That's a laugh. Looks like she's pretty good at defending herself."

"Since the show, it seems Dr. Huelga might need a bodyguard. The Lever people are willing to spring for it. In the name of goodwill."

"That's what they're calling it?"

"They say Tyrone Warren is rough trade. There's talk of his being connected—"

"Aw, the Mafia is all busted up these days."

"Not in Vegas. The press can't find out a lot about him. The people in Vegas keep their mouths way closed. One rumor has it Tyrone's a contract killer and Dr. Huelga's received death threats on a daily basis. Huelga's had to change her number four times. And, as you can see, she went postal on national television. It might be a good idea to keep an eye on her."

"*On* her or *for* her?"

"Same difference."

"Like being a double agent? That simple, Rose?"

"You can be the hired eyes, Emma. Or you can not be the hired eyes."

"I've never worked for bottom feeders before, Rose."

"Johnny Lever may be a prize cad, but *I'll* take his money." Rose sniffed. "If it's to guard Rita Huelga. She *did* tell the truth, Emma. Now, do you want the job or not?"

I looked at the blue square of the television monitor poised above Rose's desk. "Bodyguarding a victim of trash TV? Make sure the money's right, Rose."

"That's why they call it *work,* Emma."

CHAPTER TWO

A PERKY
APPROACH

Rose's secretary popped his head in the door.

"They're here," he said. It was but a few moments before an unlikely duo entered the room.

She was taller than I had remembered from the tube. Five foot eight in low-heeled loafers, maybe a hundred and fifty pounds. Big, and just a bit soft. There were pleasant lines at the corners of her jet eyes that had been wiped away by the television lighting, delicate skin at her throat where the small medal rested in the little depression at the base of her neck. I was already nursing a crush on the scientist trapped in trouble of her own making.

I put Dr. Rita Huelga at a well-kept thirty-two or-three. Her thick, black braid had been plaited very tightly. Rita Huelga looked healthy enough for someone who had just been burned at the stake, and I wondered again what had made her go on television, particularly the *Johnny Lever Show*. Not to mention the revelation of intimate facts about a woman who was supposed to be the love of her life. Something told me this woman wouldn't be bought with a limousine ride or a nice hotel room.

Dr. Huelga had thrown on a few rags for the occasion: a gray T-shirt, cut off at the neck and cuffs, a worn undershirt from Fruit of the Loom that had seen better days. The T-shirt tails traversed ample hips. She moved with grace, in much better command of herself in the space of the office than she had been on the television set. Black loafers were shined and so were the pennies she'd carefully inserted inside. She hardly looked like the type to kiss and tell.

The braid was a problem; it kept landing on the front of her T-shirt and she threw it over her shoulder like so much unlucky salt. The handsome woman was seething with barely controlled anger. And yet, it was in control. She held most of it in her eyes, burning dark and deep like two chunks of coal. I found myself wondering what she was like in bed. My hormones had a wake-up call. Plus, then a lawyer entered the room. I was full of projections that could get me into big trouble.

"George Arbogast." A late-middle-aged man in a three-piece suit and an expensive cowhide briefcase came in. He was the kind of guy who couldn't bear being ignored. He thrust a thick hand into open space. "Attorney for the *Johnny Lever Show*." Mr. Arbogast had the immutable stone expression of the lawyer, the cop, the elementary school teacher. The briefcase was guarded by two six-digit latches, and I doubted if he would even need to open it. He could negotiate a million-dollar ransom for his only daughter, establish a phony corporation to launder cocaine cash, go through a twenty-hour IRS audit, or set his mother on fire, and his expression would probably never change. The attorney for the *Johnny Lever Show* probably never lost a moment of sleep.

"Emma Victor," I said to the legal face and turned to Dr. Huelga. "Emma Victor." I repeated my name.

"And what part are you playing in this charade?" Huelga asked me.

"Excuse me? I'm a private detective."

"This only gets better, doesn't it?" Dr. Huelga turned around suddenly. I watched her check out the room, as if for an exit, like a bird in a cage. Before she had time to do so, I thought I would try again.

"Could we start over? I'm a *freelance* investigator. I'm just sitting in on this conference. My name is Emma Victor."

"Okay." The face that returned was a shade less guarded.

"I *sometimes* take assignments for Baynetta Security Systems. I'm just a freelancer."

"Just?" There was an ironic twist to the lips that held humor. Something in me wanted to make Dr. Huelga smile. Maybe it was because she had been publicly humiliated in front of millions of people; it was a Girl Scout opportunity not to pass up. There were dark circles under her eyes, now a dull black. She looked very tired. She'd probably been exhausted since October 11, National Coming Out Day.

"Rita Huelga," she said with an ironic tone. After the *Johnny Lever Show,* she probably didn't want to be herself anymore. The tennis racket glimmered at the base of the throat. It was slightly damaged, I noticed. There was a small hole in the golden webbing.

I thought I caught a twinkle of life in the *castaña* eyes as she turned her head away from me. What was I doing here, a hired hand of the sleaze trade? Of course I wanted to be a witness to this affair. A big problem solver. Get on your high horse, Emma Victor, and set all right with the world. Except that breathing the same air as Johnny Lever's staff made air pollution smell sweet. And Dr. Huelga rightfully thought I was working for television.

I watched her stride over to a deep chair. She swiveled away from us, from the television monitor. Flopping down, she squared a leg and balanced her ankle on her knee.

"Can we get this over with please. I have work to do." Her words came over the back of the chair. She had a stubborn determination not to acknowledge these people, and yet somehow she was still held prisoner by them, by the *Johnny Lever Show*. Dr. Huelga fixed her gaze on the computer geeks at their work stations. Slowly, she fingered the elastic of her cotton sock. The penny on her shoe twinkled. Rita Huelga was still a furious woman.

The television monitor was a passive blue square. Arbogast cleared his throat. Rose scuttled around the room in her chair, the whir of the motor filling up the uncomfortable space between the big legal gun, the victim of talk TV, and the reluctant bodyguard.

"So, Mr. Arbogast, I understand you are concerned about Dr. Huelga's safety," Rose tried to kindle a conversation. Dr. Huelga's face didn't move. It was stuck. Stuck in front of millions of viewers and drained slowly of expression. "I take it you feel that Dr. Huelga needs a bodyguard after her appearance on the show?"

The big man would never commit to a feeling. "That is the opinion of—" He began to insulate himself as a perky streak of energy in a pleated skirt plunged in the door.

"Hi! Sorry I'm late!" The pale English rose complexion was flushed, the smile was as animated as any histrionic high school student who'd just been elected homecoming queen. Her face was busy; little lips twitching, eyes sparkling with excitement, penciled eyebrows moving up and down like elevators. Her hair had been hennaed, red spikes gathered at the base of her neck.

Moving around the office nervously, her red pleated skirt fanned out at the hips; a fuzzy pink angora sweater was stretched tight across her chest. The sweater was purpose-fully short, her midriff a fleshy exclamation point as she twirled. A tiny black satin purse bounced against her hip, dangling from a velvet rope entwined with gold chain.

"Hi, Rita!" she said to Rita's back. From where we were standing, we could only see Rita's feet. Bevin's perky smile faltered, but only for a nanosecond.

Dr. Huelga was not going to speak to Bevin Crosswell. "George, so glad you could make it!" Bevin chirped.

George nodded ever so slightly; he stood at attention with his briefcase.

"'Scuse me while I check my messages." A very small cellular phone appeared from Crosswell's satin bag. She punched numbers into it furiously and listened to a chattering tape while tapping her foot. Once or twice she turned her head quickly away, as if to shield the room from the messages that were being transmitted. A few nods and grunts; Crosswell shoved the antenna back into the receiver and stuck it back in her purse.

"Do you always use the cell phone?" Rose asked her.

"Only when I'm on the road," she replied.

Rose smiled grimly. "We do like to recommend that communications with us are done on hard-wired phones. It's for your security as well as ours."

"Oh sure, no problem!" Bevin tilted her head, listening to a merry melody that was playing inside. I was glad it wasn't a tune I could hear. And I was glad Rose didn't have to insist on a hard-wired phone. I would have thought that the people who generated trash television would be more careful.

"So!" Bevin was breathing heavily enough for all of us. Crosswell zeroed in on me, a dark shadow against the throbbing blue of the monitor. "We're all here! You must be—" She didn't so much walk, as prance, toward me.

"Bevin Crosswell, segment producer," her grip was strong, but her palm was slick with sweat.

"Emma Victor."

"Yes, yes, that's right. Emma—" Bevin looked me up and

down and sideways. "Okay, Rose," she said after examining the merchandise. "Rose recommended you highly."

"Emma's licensed to carry a concealed weapon," Rose explained. "She can stay awake for twenty hours, and is fully range qualified in handling a variety of firearms. She can work from a fixed post or a roving patrol, that is, in her vehicle or on foot. She's done high-level diplomatic protection and has carried out search, secure, and arrest duties when authorized. She knows getaway driving techniques, the bootlegger's turn, ramming procedures. And she knows what's court-defensible."

"I'm paper trained, too," I said. The monitor behind me was starting to blink. "But I didn't say I would take the job." My voice rang uncomfortably. "Dr. Huelga, what makes you think you're in danger?" I turned the attention toward the scientist.

Rose's office garden seemed to hold Rita's complete attention. Looking at the tips of her finger working the elastic of her sock, I wondered if she was trying to cut off her circulation. Outside the window, workers plugged away, finding people who didn't want to be found. The office cat was stretched out over one of the monitors. Several people conferred over a screen and a large pile of papers. Somebody walked to the water cooler, flipped open a plastic container, gulped a few candy-colored pills.

Rita Huelga had carefully hemmed the neckline of her T-shirt after she had cut it off. Perfect, tiny little black stitches circled around a perfectly straight neck. A small nest of black curls had escaped, gathering underneath the heavy plait. As she swiveled in her chair, I saw a tiny scar on her shoulder, which pointed to a mole. Dr. Huelga looked suddenly very vulnerable to me.

"Dr. Huelga, what makes you think you're in danger?" I repeated.

We waited. The lawyer was good at it; Rose looked anxious: she wanted the gig. Bevin Crosswell was having trouble staying on the starting line; she fingered the chain on her purse nervously.

"Okay, Rita. I guess *I'll* have to explain," Bevin sounded pained, out of patience. As if the talk show guest wasn't even in the room with us, she opened her mouth. I held my hand up, silencing Bevin. I walked to the back of the chair, stopped an impulse to touch the long, black braid that bisected the back of her T-shirt.

"Dr. Huelga, what makes you think you're in danger?" I repeated, more softly, for the third time.

Out of the chair came two words, as final and lifeless as a tombstone.

"I *don't,*" Rita Huelga said.

"There you are." I nodded to Rose, Crosswell, and Arbogast. "Can't exactly bodyguard someone who doesn't think they need it." I fingered my car keys in my pocket. I could last a few more months without this gig. Crime pays, and so does television, but they both extract a high price.

Rose's hand clutched the joystick of her chair. Bevin Crosswell bit her lip, but not for long.

"This has been a difficult time for Rita." Bevin's use of the third person was irritating in the extreme. The understatement was embarrassing.

"You destroyed me," Rita Huelga said simply.

"Now, Rita, I don't think this is the time for a therapy session."

"Oh no, please, let's not *talk* anymore." A bitter laugh from the chair.

"Right," Bevin chirped. "Glad you see it that way. I mean, there's no point in going into all *that* again. You knew just what you were doing when you agreed to come on the show."

"I was *drunk.*" Rita sighed.

"Well, your signature looks pretty clear on the release form you signed."

"My signature is—was—always clear."

"You were willing to share your past with the public, Rita. Come on, admit it."

"I was willing to be your fool, Bevin."

"Now, don't get like that. It's really beyond me. Rita, what did you expect from this experience?"

"Look, I'm not in any danger—at least not since I met you for coffee, Bevin. I just want to be left alone. I want to live my life. What's left of it."

"Are we feeling sorry for ourselves again, Rita?" Bevin's voice held the higher ground. "The fact of the matter is, you've received death threats, and we're very concerned about that."

"Get real, Bevin. All you care about is your ratings."

"That's not true. We do follow up with guests. And Johnny is particularly grateful for your appearance—"

"Yeah, he'd dance on my grave if he could. *Mierda!*" Rita swore softly.

"The fact *is,* Rita—"

"I love your facts, Bevin. You must have a factory for them somewhere." A strong, clear bitterness stained her words.

"The fact, Rose, and Emma," Bevin was including us in her gaze, "Rita signed a release form that includes a clause to protect our guests, should they need it. You remember what happened on the *Jenny Jones Show*? With Scott Amedure?"

Rose shook her head.

"Jenny and her staff are *still* straightening out that legal situation," Bevin whined.

"And counting the money in the bank," I murmured.

Rose kicked me, hard, under the table. "Tell me about the Scott Amedure case."

"The assistant producers kinda screwed up. With the kind of schedule we've got, there's no time to check every guest, every story for every day. At least not as thoroughly as we'd all like to," Bevin said.

"I guess I was just *lucky.*" Rita's disembodied voice came from the chair.

"Hey, on Johnny Lever's show, we hire *therapists* to help us arrange and monitor these reunions. The idea is to resolve problems not create them, Rita. Anyway, Jenny's staff booked a guest who had a crush on this guy Jonathan Schmitz. He was told that his on-air surprise would be the opportunity to meet a secret crush."

"I can finish this story for you," I said. "Jonathan Schmitz walks out in front of a few million viewers and there was a female acquaintance there. Expecting her to be his secret crush, he walked up and kissed her. Then he was told that the secret crush wasn't this woman. Out walks Scott Amedure. Schmitz had no idea that the person who had a crush on him was male. Three days after his appearance, Schmitz went to Amedure's mobile home with a shotgun. The two shotgun shells knocked a hole through his chest about the size of standard television screen."

"Jenny Jones felt terrible about it."

"My heart bleeds." A nasty laugh came from behind Rita's chair. "That is, when my blood isn't running cold."

"I understand how you feel, Rita. But think about the donation to the—"

"I love the way lies trip off your tongue," Rita snarled.

"We did make the donation. What did you expect? Audra Léon to show up onstage?"

"In your dreams, Bevin—"

"No Rita, in *yours*—"

There are people who are naturally violent. They see the fist and the gun as a solution to their problems. Then there are the people who seek violence, they enjoy it, the buildup, the thrill, the payoff of causing someone pain.

But this was not Rita Huelga. Her instinct was pure self-defense, just slightly after the fact. With remarkable speed she'd leaped out of her chair. Her face was flawless in fury as she flew at the perky producer. Her fingernails were short, but they were ready to dig and gouge. Bevin's little bag fell on the floor. For a moment, Rita paused, staring at it. Bevin bent down to pick it up, and Rita attacked her again.

I ducked underneath those furious claws, twisted, and grabbed her wrists, feeling the flesh on her arm twist in my hands. It was not easy to absorb the impact of the large, angry woman. I was grateful that the moment ended soon. At my first touch, Dr. Huelga's fingers uncurled and her arms fell, dangling from her shoulders. I let go. She swallowed and bit her big lip, hard. Huelga's soft arms were remarkably strong. As Rita Huelga raised her head, I saw something besides fury and hopelessness cross her face. Before I could figure it out, the woman had returned to the back of the room. She sank back in her chair; she focused her eyes on the office garden in front of her once again. She flashed a penny at us as she crossed her legs. "Sorry," she said.

"It's good to see you sticking up for yourself, Rita." Bevin Crosswell was undisturbed, picking up her purse. She hadn't reacted at all to Rita's attack. The personnel of talk television were used to it, I thought. Their business is confrontation. "Do you all mind if I smoke?" We all nodded and mumbled. Who wouldn't need a cigarette, something, after an attack like that? We watched as Bevin pulled out a tiny engraved lighter and lit a long Benson and Hedges.

Bevin was talking and talking, a wall of words that I couldn't focus on, so I looked at her, instead. The pleats of her skirt were still knife sharp, and the flesh on her flashing

midriff was pale. "But maybe you're a little too in touch
with that anger. Especially on the *air*, Rita."

I could almost palpably feel the heat rise out of Rita
Huelga's chair, another cork was ready to pop. And then it
didn't. Rita was having another hunk of her lip for lunch.

"Okay, okay," Bevin said to none of us in particular. "As
I was saying, we strive to *resolve* conflicts and not create
them." Bevin had the particular quality of talking as if
everything were a monologue. A kind of war plan you explain, map and push pins in hand. The troops look up, rifles
loaded. "We aren't going to get anywhere like this. The
point is, Johnny simply can't take the risk that you might be
hurt. And he *does* feel responsible, no matter how *you* feel
about it. The fact is, a threat has been made against your life.
Your house has been vandalized. Rita, you are in danger,
and you should be protected. But you are resistant to help,
you've refused to go to the police. "

"The police? You'd love that, wouldn't you Bevin?
Maybe you could sell the story to *The Globe*."

"We are doing the right thing by you. Please don't have
an attitude. Just for the next few weeks. Emma here seems
like a good sort—"

"I don't want a bodyguard," Dr. Huelga intoned.

"The fact is," Bevin addressed her remarks to Rose,
"Audra Léon's husband is heavily connected in Las Vegas.
We hear that there's a contract out on Rita's life. There have
been death threats coming in to the show—"

"Aw, phony phone calls from fans—" Rita protested.

"And someone broke into Rita's house yesterday," Bevin
explained to me patiently.

"Is that true?" I asked Rita.

"There was a lot of cat shit in my closet and my bed when
I came home. I have a lot of cats. That's all there is to it."

"And the death threat?" Bevin prompted.

"The day before, I'd received a death threat. But—"

"How?"

"By phone. Wish I'd never mentioned it."

"It didn't frighten you?"

"No, after last week, there's nothing left to be frightened of."

"Was anything stolen? Destroyed?"

"Nope."

"Any proof of forced entry?"

"Nope."

"Look," I said to Bevin. "I don't like imposing on anyone. And it looks like your guest has been imposed on enough. You'd better find someone else for the job."

"Well, then, we'll just have to hire someone else, *Rose,*" Bevin's breast puffed up in her angora sweater, making her look like a parakeet.

"Sure. I've got a Rolodex full of bodyguards." Rose sighed and avoided my eyes.

"So, you see, Rita, we've got legal authority to protect ourselves." Bevin waved a piece of paper in the air. *Release Form! Release Form! Release Form!* "Even if it means that we have to protect *you.* We'll have a car parked in front of your house night and day, for your own good. We can have you watched around the clock. The streets are public domain, and you heard what Rose said. She's got a Rolodex full of private detectives. And you *will* be watched—"

"I've got a Rolodex full," Rose sighed, "but Emma's the best."

Dr. Huelga addressed us as a group. "Okay, okay, okay. One week. And not while I'm working. I can't have anyone in the house while I'm working."

The lawyer slid his eyes Bevin's way and nodded his head slowly. Bevin was just licking her lips when Rita Huelga suddenly got up out of the chair. I didn't have a second to double-check that smile. I only saw her back as she loped out of Rose's private quarters. We watched the big woman

stride quickly through Rose's office garden. It seemed that
the big, shiny rubber leaves waved in the wake of air she left
behind. A few computer geeks turned around when she
slammed the door, and their eyes flickered back to the
smoked window of the office where I stood, lined up along
the glass, with the lawyer, the segment producer, and my old
friend, Rose.

"Tsk, tsk." Bevin clucked. "That woman is *still* running
away from her life."

But for my money, Rita Huelga had seen the devil and
split.

CHAPTER THREE

BEING MYSELF

"Looks like you've got a job," Rose said to me after Bevin left. "Be at Huelga's residence at nine P.M. Here's the address. Forest Hills, pretty tony."

Rose handed me a piece of paper. I read the address.

"If it's on the block I think it is, your client lives alone in a big castle with a view of the ocean."

"Take a hike around the place every half hour. Write up one of your nice, detailed reports, Emma. It always makes the billing easier."

"I don't think she's in any kind of danger," I advised. "Have you thought that maybe *we're* being set up?"

"We're in the business of providing security. That's what they want, and that's what they'll get. What are you thinking?"

"They'll double their ratings leaking to the tabloids that Rita Huelga is in danger. I don't want to see my picture in *The Globe*."

"They've hired a bodyguard, that's all I know. The rest is their business. Don't worry about it."

"Don't tell me not to worry. Everything I worry about

never happens. But don't you think it's awfully funny the
way they keep mentioning Tyrone? The white bully who
married the black pop queen? The failure of his music
video? How he must be jealous of Gale? Of Rita? Seems
like someone from central casting made him up."

"I don't bill for supposition, Emma."

I looked at my old friend, surrounded by monitors and in-
vestigative worker bees. Rose's investment was big; weekly
salaries alone had put her in the red more than once.

"Oh, Rose." My voice saying her name sounded new.

"Oh Rose, *what?*"

I thought about the situation, the salary, and Dr. Huelga.
A research scientist with a great left hook. It was, if nothing
else, a romantic setup for me. My never-quite-an-ex,
Frances, had been a research scientist. I admired her patience, her detective work, her own feeling for the unending
mitigation of scientific truths. And that was just *one* reason
not to take on this job.

I calculated closely, watching Rose watching me, trying
to get the odds within a few decimal points of principle. The
house was going to take its percentage, it always does. And
it would take it right out of my soul.

Integrity has no price. It is supposed to be its own reward.
That makes it a costly proposition, but I didn't want to look
inside and find myself empty one day. I looked at Rose, her
eyes challenging me. I thought about my friend and her future in the security business. But it wasn't for me to look inside Rose's crystal ball. I could only speak for myself. And
I didn't want this job.

"I can't do it, Rose."

"What?"

"Sorry. No can do."

"Name your price, Emma." Rose's hand worked around
the joystick on her chair.

"You couldn't pay it. It doesn't exist. Not for this job."

"But you *said* you'd do it."

"I never said that. You assumed it."

"Thanks a lot, girlfriend."

"You've got a whole Rolodex full of lady dicks."

"But I trust you the most."

But I don't trust you, I wanted to say. Instead, I edited my remarks. "Trouble is their business, Rose. Every problem a person can have is exploited and trivialized to the point of caricature. They need excitement and conflict. They *ruin* people's lives. I don't want to work for them."

"Ergo, you don't want to work for me."

"You got the picture."

A bad silence hung between us, like dirty wash someone put on the line by mistake. "Well, let me see." Rose drew a Rolodex in front of her with reluctance. On it were all the freelancers and payroll people who did the kind of job I did.

"So, Emma, who would you recommend?" She listlessly flipped through the alphabetical cards. "Surveillance detection, driving, communications . . ."

"Someone good with not using her gun. Doesn't let the glow of celebrities shine them. Stays awake in tight control." I thought about it. "How about Suzanne Benét?"

"She moved to Paris." Rose countered.

"Pity."

"Okay, okay, let's see." The cards flew past her fingers quickly. Rose made a big production of sighing, filling her cheeks up with air, and letting a breath out slowly. "Good with not using her gun. Stays awake, in tight control . . . fame inoculation. And fuck you."

"Just trying to be helpful."

"Shut up and stop being such a Girl Scout. Here! Here's one: Jan Simpson."

"Jan Simpson? I'm not sure how much experience is required for this job," I said carefully.

"Yeah, Jan would do if its just a matter of hand-holding.

But I think this might be more serious. And she would need a fame inoculation."

"That's not all." I sighed.

"We dated a few years back," Rose admitted.

"I *thought* so." My mind flitted back over after-hours conversation. Jan, as I recalled, did not ring her bell. I'd worked with her once on a FedEx job. She cracked at a bad moment, and she pushed my alarm signal.

"I thought I should tread lightly with you on Jan," I ventured.

"I lost interest. Couldn't get a conversation going. No sense of humor. Honest opinion, Emma. Do you think she's butch or femme?"

"I think she's nuts."

"That tears it." Rose pushed her Rolodex away, far away across her desk. She leaned back in her chair and stared at me. "I'm in a hard spot here, Emma,"

I couldn't think of anything to say, so I stared back. The phone rang, and Rose reached behind her to get it, but she never took her eyes off me.

"Yes. Hello? Yes." The expression in Rose's eyes changed. "She's here." Rose handed me the phone. "Expecting a call?" There was a pleased tone in her voice.

"Emma Victor?"

"Yes."

"This is Rita Huelga."

"Yes?"

The line filled with the ambient noise of traffic coming to a halt. I waited for the light to change and wondered if the sounds I heard in the background were made by one or two persons.

"What can I do for you?"

"Well, I just wanted to say I was sorry for—what happened today. I seemed to be—lacking in control."

"I thought you showed marvelous restraint."

"The fact of the matter *is,* Emma—may I call you Emma?"

"Yes," I watched Rose wheel around the room, adjusting monitors to view some faraway Italian Renaissance paintings. A guard strolled in front of a nursing Madonna.

"The fact is, I *do* think I could use a bodyguard." Traffic started up in the background and someone walked by with a boombox.

"Where are you?"

"Eighth and Howard. Why?"

"Why did you call?"

"Emma, some—something else has happened. I just picked up my messages. Mariposa told me—told me that it happened again."

"Mariposa?"

"She works for me."

"What happened again?"

"The cat, uh, excrement."

"I thought you had that figured out."

"No, this was different—"

"In quantity or quality?" I tried to hit a lighthearted note. There was no point in alarming Dr. Huelga until I could get on the scene.

"Well, I guess there was a lot *more.* Mariposa walked in the room and screamed. It's just that they'd put it on the walls. Smeared it all over the wallpaper."

"Too high for cats to shit?"

"Well, yeah, there's that, but also—" I heard the squeal of brakes in the traffic behind her. "Cats don't know how to spell my name." Rita Huelga sighed.

"Ugh. I'm really sorry that happened. And you do need security. This kind of person is often just a prankster, but in this case, with a lot of anger and aggression. I think it would be a good idea to come over and check out your house, go through some basic security systems that will make you safe from this kind of—occurrence."

"Good. I'll see you at my house?"

"Yes," I said. "I'll be there." I repeated her address out loud, reading off the piece of paper Rose had given me. "Seven o'clock okay with you?"

"Fine," and without another word, Dr. Huelga cut the line. It was impossible not to notice the smile snaking across Rose's face.

"Give me that tape, will you?" I asked. "And what's the field Dr. Huelga is in? Some kind of medicine?"

"No, she's a mycologist, Emma. Mushrooms. Maybe she's a gourmet. I hear those chantarelles cook up real nicely."

"Let's not try to make a gourmet meal out of gutter tripe."

Rose shrugged as she pulled out an invoice form with the attached time sheet. "Thanks for taking this gig, Emma."

"I want to be paid from Baynetta Security, okay?"

"You can morally launder the money any way you want, girlfriend." She passed me the required forms used by every lady dick in her Rolodex. "Just remember the basic body-guarding maxim."

"What's that, Rose?" I asked, but I knew anyway what she would have said. And Rose knew that I knew. Instead, Rose wheeled around in front of her monitor, an ever so slightly haughty dismissal from an old friend. Her unsaid words hung in the air like a hangover breath. The basic bodyguarding maxim, as far as Rose was concerned, was simple: Dead clients don't pay.

"Don't forget your earring, girlfriend." The etched hoop, which purported to be pure gold, was lying on her desk. I picked it up and tried to rethread it through my ear. A moment of pain convinced me to put it in my pocket. I would return it to the jewelry store from whence it came. In the meantime, I had a short gig to complete.

And so I came to work for television. It wasn't that pop culture hadn't touched my life before. It had raised me and bottle-fed me through most of my adolescence. It had taught me that my armpits smelled, my body was too fat, too flat, and my laundry whites would always be yellow. The people who made this media were beyond my ken, thus interesting in a perverse sort of way.

The second reason was harder to admit. At first, the twitchy way Dr. Huelga sat staring out that window and her monosyllabic responses merely intrigued me. She wasn't playing the victim, although her cry for help sounded genuine enough on the phone. In the office, her silence and her body language had the ring of truth in a world where truth is a very bendable element.

The speed and strength of her body was still with me, in the resistance of my own arms, in the flash of her dark brown eye.

The third reason was so obviously painful. Television, its producers, guests, audiences might think they were a big group therapy session. But throughout it all, nobody, absolutely nobody, asked what kind of song Audra Léon might be singing these days.

CHAPTER FOUR

COST-EFFECTIVE

San Francisco is best tasted in October when Indian Summer comes for a visit. Whoever was responsible, the current San Franciscans were in their debt. Suddenly, the windy days and nights calmed to a comforting, almost constant warmth. We called it earthquake weather.

On this day, Hurricane Helen held steady to the south and El Niño was residing in the west, creating a low pressure disturbance that combined to keep things hot and interesting. The starched white shirt was cool on my skin; my jacket draped on my arm. Finally, it was summer.

Actual summers in San Francisco were cold. All through July and August, you could watch summer happen on television. People sprayed mosquitos with Raid, wiping sweat off their forehead as they caught summer air-conditioning colds. Images of summer flickered across the tubes in the Castro, the Haight-Ashbury, and Telegraph Hill. Happy families, somewhere else, anywhere else, gathered around the latest in Weber grills, inhaling the smell of roasting animals. The smiles of nubile blond models were mocking as they frolicked in warm waves showing the latest model in bathing attire. These were not the residents of San Francisco.

No, the truth was, our sun finally became warm when our shadows were long, right around Halloween. Only when the valley cooled off and stopped dragging the fog in off the Pacific did the place get a chance to warm up. For a few months in the fall and spring, the fog hesitated, in a moment of forgiveness, off the edge of the Pacific Ocean. The sun became brassy. Surfers reveled off Seal Rock, where the waves could reach fifteen feet and the undertow would suck you into the ocean's belly forever. Downtown San Francisco posted a record 97 degrees. For a few weeks in October, the mercury would rise.

And so, in the fall, the fog finally forgave us, not quite reaching over the peaks, leaving San Francisco with a false sense of summer. The bay and all its surrounding concrete heated up, making for an air inversion. Cars filled up the space in between with carbon monoxide until it hit the ceiling of hot air where it collected in a long, dark stripe. The cars just kept going, two, three, four hundred thousand a day over those bridges to and from the endless bedroom communities that collected outside the peninsula city that was Baghdad by the Bay. The air was tan, and not to breathe.

A small, yellow, slightly dented Alfa Romeo convertible awaited me. My car: She shifted as smooth as a fog bank. She'd followed the hairpin turns of the freeway, hugging the road like a long-lost girlfriend. Romea had a beautiful interior, too. The driver's seat still had the original black leather upholstery. The passenger seat was vinyl, but the dashboard was mirror matched walnut, the grain of the wood extending like some big Rorschach test around various gauges and gadgets.

Walnut gearshift in hand, I backed out of Rose's lot and headed east, toward that big smudge of horizon. The radio told me that the air was so bad the elderly, infirm, and infantile should stay inside. For the rest of us, well, we could take our chances. "Stay clear of the Black Hole, an accident has left toxic fluid on the road. If you've got a headache, Hospital Curve is clear, but Devil's Slide saw a big accident last night. They're still clearing away the debris." As usual, Bay Area traffic was a mess.

Getting over to Guaranteed All Risk wasn't easy; the Central Freeway had been damaged in the last earthquake. What was left over were concrete ribbons that disintegrated in chunks, hopefully within the huge safety nets wrapping the old freeway. Helicopters buzzed overhead, monitoring the traffic. They reported the progress of traffic and pondered the question, "What happened to all the traffic since the Central Freeway was demolished?" But they weren't down on the ground where the traffic was snarled around jack-hammers, cranes, rubberneckers, double-parkers, and fuming Muni buses stalled on their overhead electric leashes.

I turned on the radio.

"Wet kisses only,
Drowning in time,
I always wondered,
When you'd be mine. . . ."

The voice of Audra Léon hit a high note and stayed there, a feat of lung power and vocal chords that was truly remarkable. It nearly drowned out the noise of demolition, but I turned it off. *We always wondered if you'd come out of the closet, Audra.*

Downtown, businessmen and women rushed by paper skeletons and witches exhibited in the windows of greeting card stores and cafés. The Guaranteed All Risk building looked just like the people who built it made sure there was no risk. A concrete slab, reinforced foundation, the thing was a box bolted into the bedrock of San Francisco. San

Francisco, despite its wild reputation, was a banking and insurance town.

Who made money in the Gold Rush? The people who sold the shovels and the pickaxes. And people like the folks at Guaranteed All Risk, who never took a risk unless it paid off.

I made my way through a path in what is referred to as a cube farm. The open floor plan meant merely that more worker bees could be crammed into more spaces. Positioned in front of computer monitors, without benefit of windows or sunlight or air, they typed up claim reports and figured risk calculations. Mr. Fremont was waiting for me on the fourth floor in a dim room.

Mr. Fremont, claims supervisor, had his own office, a room at the end of the corridor. There was a window that showed the sunny side of a brick building, two vertical four-drawer filing cabinets, and a coat rack next to the Formica-topped desk. Mr. Fremont was a lean, bored-looking man who could have been thirty-five, forty-five, or even fifty. He sat in front of a window, blinds tilted downward to subdue the light or to get a better look at me. A light was tilted toward me and away from him. He wore a navy blue suit of a custom cut. His white shirt was starched, and his cuff links were silver ovals, maybe monogrammed, maybe not. A large, masculine ring slipped on one of his long, brown fingers. He instructed me to hang up my coat on the coat rack and asked me my terms.

His face didn't move when I told him that my fee was two hundred dollars a day and two thousand dollars for the video/photo. I explained that I liked to work that way because it gave me an incentive to do everything possible to get the evidence.

"Really, Ms. Victor? We like our employees to go the extra mile."

"I've put a lot of miles behind me."

"Are you busy working on many cases at the moment?"

"Nothing that would interfere with this one."

"I'm hoping we're on the same page, here, Ms. Victor."

"What page is that?"

"Encouragement—a little prodding at the right moment, getting our subject into the right position, so to speak."

"You mean entrapment?"

He sat up a little straighter, his dim silhouette straightened. I thought I saw him nod.

"I know that book. Doesn't hold up well in court."

"Get me the evidence."

"I'll see what I can do, sir."

And the photo I would provide would be certifiable. All my processing was done at one of the finest legal photo labs in San Francisco. Mr. Fremont liked that. It took him the better part of two minutes to give me my forms, take my Social Security number, and tell me all about one Phillipe Pendrinkski who lived out in the avenues. An on-the-job accident. Mr. Fremont passed me the file. He busied himself with a file cabinet while I read the report. It was a common story, almost a cliché.

Petitioner was injured in a work-related accident. On Dec. 3, 1998, while operating a flatbed tractor-trailer unit, a load of large concrete slabs shifted, which resulted in one or more of the slabs pinning the petitioner in the vehicle when it had tipped over as a result of the shift in weight. Emergency workers were called. Petitioner was removed from the vehicle by emergency workers.

An MRI was taken of the low back area following the incident. Dr. Wemple, the petitioner's orthopedic rating expert, noted that the same was interpreted as "Normal." Exhibit B-2.

Petitioner offered the following complaints in his

testimony: he requires crutches at all times, his left knee is unstable, and will not bend past 90 percent. His left shoulder continues to cause pain and suffers movement restriction and a loss of strength in his left hand.

Mr. Pendrinkski, after a minor bump, was suing for two million and was only appearing in public on crutches. Doctors examined him, but Mr. Pendrinkski had war wounds and a host of other medical histories that was making a clear medical diagnosis difficult to pin down. It would make life much easier for the All Risk Company if someone could get a photo of him sans accessories.

"When can you start?"

"Whenever you like."

"This afternoon?"

"Yes."

"Fine." He nodded, and I took my cue. He wasn't going to stand up or see me out. Mr. Fremont gestured at my coat on the rack and I picked it up. I was ready to get my camera in a nanosecond. Insurance gigs, nice and quiet in contrast to whatever histrionics were playing themselves out around Audra Léon. And All Risk was willing to pay a daily rate. That was good. And insurance companies hire operatives again and again. Mr. Fremont was willing to do a lot—to have me do a lot—for All Risk. The man in his finely tailored suit was a pit bull.

I edged into a nice big parking spot in front of the library. A little knowledge is a dangerous thing. Especially if your clients expect you to be an ignoramus about slippery little plants that grow on dead logs. I entered the new technical marvel of San Francisco, the million-dollar public library. I cruised by the computer banks, hoping I could find a nice, portable, democratic *book* to take home with me. I emerged within meter time with a small copy of *All That the Rain*

*Promises and More: A Hip Pocket Guide to Western Mush-
rooms,* by David Arora.

Back to Romea and a quick trip home. We crawled
through the traffic to the lower lump of Bernal Heights, on
the edge of the Mission, where my hacienda awaited me.
The silhouettes of the clapboard houses along the south edge
of Precita Park hadn't changed in a hundred years. The flat-
topped Italianates were tiny, working-class houses, farmer's
cottages that retained their feel of the old West, just in
brighter colors. Egg and dart moldings were gilded now, but
their fronts were still false. They looked as insubstantial as
the cardboard skeletons that hopped in the front windows.
Parents had begun to carve pumpkins. The toothy grins of
orange jack-o'-lanterns were dark in the daylight; their orange heads were placed lovingly on rickety wood stairways
up and down the street. Children abounded in the Mission,
scores of them were anticipating a sugar-induced hyperac-
tivity that already had parents worried. The brown, parched
mound known as Bernal Heights loomed behind the wooden
buildings. The city hadn't gotten around to chopping down
acres of tinder-dry weeds, and kids liked to set off firecrackers on Halloween.

All Risk Guaranteed, I thought, pulling up in front of my
own blue and white clapboard job. The gilt was coming off
the doodads and the sills on the north side had sprouted a
greenish moss. I'd mended the fences and caulked the tiles
around the tub before I'd taken my vacation. It would be
good to sand the sills down and paint them while the wood
was still dry.

I got out of the car and disarmed the security system with
the little round key. The red lights blinked on and off, wel-
coming me to a home covered in jewel-toned Kelim carpets
and lined with books for the days when I didn't have any
gigs. Feeling a deep softness on my calves, I looked down at
Mink. The cat was furiously rubbing against my legs, whin-

ing; she could have knocked me over. I placated her with a saucer of kibbles and put a second bowl of food on the landing for Mink's semiferal companion, Friend. Once the animals were fed, I went into my office. I packed a big green knapsack with a pager, a cell phone, and film. I had a million appliances now. They all came with warranty papers I forgot to fill out and a whole administration I chose to ignore.

The Pentax camera was an old model, its little mechanical gadgetry more reassuring than anything that was operated from a circuit board. A huge telephoto lens was as intrusive as it looked. I never forgot my tiny Minox camera. The original spy camera, it had a silent shutter and double light setting.

It was 2:30 P.M. by the time Romea crested Twin Peaks. The timed lights on Nineteenth Avenue to Taraval Street kept us moving. The avenues run north and south, perpendicular to the Pacific. The rest of the street names are alphabetical: strange-sounding names like Taraval, Ulloa. I turned right on Thirty-seventh Avenue and cruised by a dozen little cookie-cutter houses with Prussian-pruned bushes standing at attention outside. Pink, yellow, green, or blue, crutches will slip and won't scam *you*. Number 1618 was one of the most well-kept on the block. Someone had spent hours with one of those little barbed wheels on the end of a stick, making sure that there was a trough between the sidewalk and the lawn. Not a green blade invaded the concrete. The windows were veiled in sheer curtains; I sped Romea up and around the block. Two blocks east, on the edge of an empty lot, a bank of eucalyptus trees draped their branches nearly clear to the gutter. I pulled Romea under the handy shrubbery, nearly laughing at my good fortune.

Oh, happy day. To any passerby, Romea looked like she had been parked there for weeks, abandoned for her parking tickets. I got out my binoculars and zeroed in on the green square and the nice straight line bisecting it. The veil of curtains hadn't moved. *Come on,* I said to the anonymous face of the house. *Come on, the grass is sprouting. It's going to grow all over that pretty little sidewalk of yours. Come on, you fraud, Mr. Pendrinkski. Weeds are extending their roots, ready to poke up in the air pockets of your driveway. Don't you want to come out and do a little gardening?*

But I'd used up all my luck that day. My anxiety visualization failed to ruffle the facade of the house. The curtains didn't move. No one came in or went out. The car, if it was in the garage, stayed there. Only the grass grew. If it was grass.

The *Bay Area Reporter* had done a number of articles about outing, forcible outing, being out and outness.

Politics of Outing—Out or In?
Once Out, You Can't Go Back In

First there was the Diana Finally case, where the actress's photo appeared on telephone poles all over New York. "Undeniably Queer" ran the text underneath the photo.

Diana Finally's friends said that it was mean and spiteful and unfair. Those who were already out suffered from closet-envy, said others. They had to force everyone else out, especially famous people, to justify themselves. Once you are out, you can't go back in. The sexual orientation issue still so divides people that the distinction is heavier than the Iron Curtain. There is a reason why gays and lesbians have a ghetto. And there is a reason why the Lesbian Revengers have started a coven. I interviewed her yesterday.

"General Gertrude, I understand that you initially approved of the outing of Audra Léon on the *Johnny Lever Show.*"

"That's right."

"It is true that Mr. Lever made out a check to the Women's Cancer Information Center?"

"So?"

"What's your beef, exactly?"

"The producers of the *Johnny Lever Show* sounded like they were interested in lesbian and gay rights. Last week, Lever donated a hundred thousand dollars to the Christian Coalition. We were naive. Johnny Lever has no morals, no point of view at all. Many people go on television talk shows thinking that they're getting their point across when they're merely being used. Rita Huelga was used. Audra Léon was used. It was tragic."

"You mean the way Rita Huelga hit Johnny Lever?"

"No. That was way cool."

"What's the tragedy?"

"Lever's people lied. They said they had a call from Léon. But, of course, Léon would never show up. She's in the closet deep, it's a bank lobby to her. And Lever is still getting publicity! Rita Huelga is being hounded."

"Have you had contact with her?"

"No. She doesn't need our help. We need hers. Meanwhile, as Revengers, we denounce the Hollywood machine in all its forms: cinematic, pornographic, moralistic, hypocritic. It's a rot upon the brains of our community. They're sociopaths, that's all."

"And the Revengers, no doubt, will provide some surprises for the patriarchy this year on Halloween."

"The thirteen generals of the Lesbian Revengers are meeting tonight."

"Care to reveal your plans?"

General Gertrude gave a derisive snort here.

"Anything else, General?"

"Yeah. Kill your television."

Following the article was information about the telephone tree, whispered invitations to the angriest and most activist of dykes to meet at the Club Lexington on Halloween night. According to unnamed sources, the thirteen generals of the Lesbian Revengers were very clear: There was a drag king contest at the Lexington, and they needed an army.

For a little lighter relief, I did a little background reading on the amazing world of mushrooms and fungi in general. I still didn't want it eating away at my house, but the history and uses of the not-plants was pretty interesting.

I stayed at 1618 Thirty-fourth Avenue until 6:30. It was a very quiet place. Quiet like the dead. Or someone on vacation. I filled out my time sheet and billed for a hundred bucks, a half day.

Long tendrils of eucalyptus branches brushed across my windshield, like fingers brushing away a tear, as I pulled away. I was ready for more exciting fare, like Dr. Huelga and Audra Léon. I looked at the address again and found the exact location of Huelga's house. It would be up toward Twin Peaks, where the contractors built individual homes instead of blocks of look-alike tract housing that the Pendrinkskis of the world lived in. Dr. Huelga would have a house with French doors and a gourmet kitchen, I thought. What I wasn't expecting was her strange staff.

CHAPTER FIVE

THE JOY OF
NATIONAL ATTENTION

The property taxes on her driveway alone could have paid my mortgage for a year. Rita Huelga's house was backed up onto a hill, shrouded so deep inside shrubbery, it made surveillance—and security—nearly impossible.

Actually, Dr. Huelga's house was more tasteful than the grandiose faux French villas plunked on the hills with their iron gates and mansard roofs. Hers was an English Tudor job, but so large in size and refined in detail, it might have been a castle, a hunting lodge for a lady in waiting, a duchess, or for Queen Elizabeth herself. Dr. Huelga had not chosen the architecture of French aristocracy; she'd chosen the architecture of British elves.

Unfortunately, it was under siege. How could anyone have broken in and vandalized the place with all the journalists around? I could hear the car doors slamming and the patter of journalists' feet upon the pavement.

Today's *San Francisco Chronicle* was on the front walk. "Disney Wants Cruise Port at S.F. Piers." I picked it up. "The Disney Company has quietly approached the Port of San Francisco . . . a 10-story hotel . . . mall of restaurants and shops . . ." Leave it to L.A.: a faux city inside the city. "Barbie Doll to Get More Real . . . smaller bust, wider waist, flatter feet, see Nation," suggested the top of the paper. The journalists descended upon me.

"Hello! Hello! Are you a friend of Rita Huelga's?"

"Can we ask you a few questions?"

"Tyrone has disappeared. Is it true that Tyrone has taken a contract out on Dr. Huelga's life?"

I didn't say anything. I had an invisible shield that automatically went up in the presence of journalists. Whether stalking surreptitiously or running in plain sight as they were doing now, no one from the press penetrated that shield. Least of all, not the quality of rascals that were hounding me as I walked toward Dr. Huelga's manse.

"Can I ask you just one question?" A woman in a lightweight cardigan, grasping her microphone, hadn't given up the chase. My peripheral vision showed me her cameraperson holding a video-cam like a short-range missile launcher.

"Just one question? Please, miss!" the reporter was whining, her eyes looking up at the mansion like a lost puppy.

Living in the place must have been something else. A circular brick staircase curved around the front of the house and ended at a small tower and the bolt-studded front door. A brass lion's head knocker held a large ring between its fangs. An ornamental iron roof shielded the duchess from any condensed fog as she fit her key into the lock. Above the door and inside, the staircase probably continued up to the second story. Big, leaded windows had been thrown open to the night. They danced with yellow and blue diamonds of bottle glass. A chill wind jostled the pruned trees, causing rustling inside the gallery of opened windows. Stratford-on-Avon with palm trees and traffic along the million-dollar view. Three large brick chimneys graced the roof. Supported with easy-to-grab ironwork, they were a cat burglar's delight. Copper gutters snaked around a cedar shake roof.

"Please, please, just one question?" Cardigan was persistent, but kept her distance. She could feel the invisible shield. I resumed my most professional perusal of the mansion.

Below the first story, a number of smaller windows suggested servants' quarters or a guest room, a den. Although the rooms were dark within, I could see that bright, batik curtains covered the windows like stained glass. A six-inch-high box hedge was a tight cuff of green hugging the base of the building. The grass was mowed to a flattop; a hidden sprinkler system kept it green in the parched October heat. Other trees had been pruned into bonsais—tortured tree sculptures. The two-car garage door featured brass lamps on either side. Neither lamp was burning. A long, brass slash of a mailbox had been recently fitted into the door. To the left of the garage, in a white brick wall, a door led to the garden. Almost invisible in the shrubbery, it was topped by a low piece of matching timber. A kid could crawl over it in a minute. A SWAT team might take two, and no one would even notice, so far back and hidden from the street was the house of Dr. Rita Huelga.

"Just one question? One itty-bitty question?"

The tabloid press gave up; returning to sulking in front seats of their rental cars. I returned to my job.

There were always opportunities, if you could call them that, to do bodyguard work for rich people. Sheiks with money usually wanted off-duty police officers or private detectives to ride around with them and their money. Knuckle-dazzling simian types were available for a nice fee, and lady dicks were useful at Nieman-Marcus. I mounted the stairs. I pulled a wrought-iron bell pull that hung from the bolted door in the tower. A lot of chimes bonged deep within the manse. A sheer curtain was pulled aside, then dropped.

"So, miss, are *you* a lesbian?"

I looked at her face, her person, her microphone. "Get out of my way, or I'll prove it to you, lady."

This was *not* the kind of job I liked. Bodyguarding was the only kind of job that made me really, really nervous.

"Maybe I'll take you up on that," she said, having clicked off her microphone.

I sighed.

I like jobs with products, objects, tangible physical entities. I like it when the goal is a bag with thirty-five thousand dollars in it. Or a videotape, or an old hatbox with letters that could be the conclusive evidence in a criminal trial. Things I can seek and find. Even a signature is a tangible item, once you have it in your hands on the right piece of paper. As Dr. Rita Huelga knew all too well, contracts were very clearly a kind of property.

The product in the bodyguard situation was to have nothing happen. And the way to that goal is the complete and utter focus on an individual, usually a totally unknown quantity. Furthermore, trying to secure a location is always a problem. You do your best to be quick and efficient. But even with the minimum of expense and concrete, you have to break a lot of bad news. For example, boring into someone's mock Tudor finish to mount the required closed-circuit monitors necessary for security. Explaining such things to the client was time-consuming and irritating.

Objects don't talk. A rock star assignment I had once didn't work out too well. She got protected from everything except herself, and I got to witness a lot of things that made me uncomfortable.

Expensive doodads can fit well in your pocket. People aren't like that.

It's a weird gig, bodyguard, somewhere between social and servant. You can't be yourself. You have to be what they want you to be. And you have to put up with all their questions about what it's *really* like to be a private detective, a bodyguard. But Rita Huelga would be different, I thought. I prepared myself for bodyguard duty, which included bodyguard face, talk, and counseling. But Rita Huelga would be different beyond my expectations.

She opened the door. The flashbulbs started going off, and Dr. Huelga didn't even blink. "Thanks for coming over. Let me show you what happened." Huelga was barefoot. She had broad feet, and no one had painted her toenails.

Only a vestige of her earlier plait remained. Damp strands of salt-and-pepper hair escaped from her braid, making a curly dark halo around her head. Long black strands clung to her cheeks and curled at her neck. She wore the same clothes I had seen her in earlier that day, only now they were much dirtier. Her baggy jeans were coated with grime and damp from splashing water. They hung off her hips, revealing a tawny bit of flesh at the waist. The gray T-shirt was peppered with dirt; heavy-duty blue rubber gloves extended to her elbow. A bucket at her feet exhumed a lethal cloud of chlorine steam. Her eyes were veiled. She seemed comfortable barefoot. The big, broad feet looked strong, accustomed to the tiles of the hallway.

"Miss, excuse me—" The plaintive journalistic cry followed me inside. Dr. Huelga may have looked tired, but the hand that grabbed my arm was still strong as she pulled me inside.

"Pretty busy outside."

"Yep."

"Been this way the whole time?" I asked.

"I don't even notice anymore," she muttered. Rita Huelga closed the door on the world, which so wanted to press in.

"Here's your paper."

"Thanks. I hardly go out the front door anymore."

"How long have you been under siege like this?" I asked.

"Oh, a week. It'll let up soon. I hope. I just keep the draperies closed."

"Except for the upstairs windows," I remarked.

"Oh, that. Well—" For no reason, Rita looked behind her. A willowy blond loomed over another bucket of bleach water. About six two, her thin frame was encased in stretch fluorescent fabric. A tiny star winked between her eyebrows. She wore lightweight yellow gloves on her hands. Her eyes were the eyes of a servant; she didn't look at me, she didn't not look at me. I practiced that gaze.

"Sure, Mariposa." Rita turned her back on me, handing Mariposa the bucket of hot water.

Mariposa took the heavy buckets in either hand like they were filled with Ping-Pong balls, and danced off.

"Come in, Emma."

"Thanks." I stepped into the rounded tower hallway that was more Tolkien than Tudor. Walnut woodwork framed Gothic arches with carved ivy winding over the portal. A few decorative battle-axes about eight feet long were crossed underneath a mock flaming torch lending to the room a dungeon effect. Through the timbered doorways, cavernous, dim chambers stretched into velvety darkness on my right and left. I could tell they were big rooms by the way our voices echoed into the distance. Past the cavern on my left, I could see a kitchen door swinging, flapping open and closed as Mariposa floated silently into the kitchen. A white rectangle of light appeared and narrowed to a stripe as the door closed behind the burdened figure.

"Excuse me, do you mind if I go change?"

"Not at all."

"Make yourself at home," she said, leaving me in the hallway. A pedestal chair with a slung leather seat made me feel like Sir Lancelot. The crossed battle-axes were suspended over my left shoulder. The blades looked sharp. As I had expected, a large, timbered stairway lumbered up the tower. The base of a newel post shielded a mischievous carving of a squirrel. It tried to climb up to where an intricate ma-

hogany acorn awaited it, atop that newel post. Frozen in
wood, the squirrel would never lose the gleam in its eye that
the carver had wrought. A thick, red carpet had a romantic
William Morris design in the kind of flowers they call tendrils. It flowed up the stairs, six feet wide, its pile deep
enough to still the footsteps of a small mercenary army.

I sidled under the arched doorway to my left and felt
around the side of the wall. Two buttons protruded from a
switch plate. I pressed one and the dining room, decked out
as a medieval gallery, lit up. Dr. Rita Huelga had the computer technology of a dedicated scientist; no less than four
laptops squared off on her table. She had been a busy elf, indeed. Three perfect columns of chain-linked paper appeared
to be filled with columns of data. Two laser printers, a scan-
ner, and a band of four-drawer file cabinets lined one wall.

Behind the table was a sideboard displaying the requisite
silver and crystal of the realm. The kitchen door to the right
of the sideboard was still swinging. I could hear the water
rushing behind the door. The whole place still stank of chlorine.

I felt rather than saw Dr. Rita Huelga behind me. She was
wearing a high-necked velour T-shirt in a bright parrot
green. The tiny golden tennis racket nestled at the base of
her neck.

The rest of her was a brand-new fashion queen. Baggy
jeans were tightly cinched; silver stars studded across a
black leather belt. The velour T-shirt was tight across her
chest. She'd rinsed her face and pulled her hair tightly to the
back of her neck and plaited it into a newer, tighter, braid.
The penny loafers were back on her feet. I kind of missed
those feet. A long finger sparkled with a small diamond,
which she hadn't bothered to wear at Rose's office.

"Can I help you?"

"Oh." I smiled. "Sorry, I just don't like dark rooms."

"Okay," she nodded slowly. "I guess I'm just a little jumpy."

"It's understandable. If the press doesn't let up, we'll get a restraining order to keep them a certain distance from your house. They are probably in minor violation of something or other."

"They'll go away soon." Rita sighed. "There's a break in that murder of a six-year-old beauty queen in Boulder. There'll be plenty for them to feed on in Colorado. I don't care about the reporters, but someone broke into the house while I was at Baynetta Security this morning. They came into my bedroom—upstairs. I'll show you." The dark walnut stairway waited before us. "Come on." The stairs groaned as we mounted them.

"Nice place you've got here."

"Thanks. It's real half-timber construction. Most of the mock Tudors you see are just decorative beams sunk into stucco. This place was designed by Patricia Pendlebury. She was a student of Frank Lloyd Wright. You can see his influence in the rooms upstairs.

"Of course it has some pretty eclectic torchieres, like the crossed battle-ax lighting fixtures in the hallway, but I kind of left them there as a joke."

"Are they sharp?" We'd reached the landing. My fingers grazed along the lead stripes that held the wavy bottle glass panes in place. Swirls and bubbles played themselves out in the glass.

"I cut a little firewood last Christmas with one of them. My quarters are to the right." She stretched her hand out with the formality of a first lady giving a White House tour. Two large double doors led into a wood paneled hallway. She opened one of them. The stench of bleach enveloped me. I blinked away two quick tears as I stepped inside. I held my breath and squinted in the darkness. Rita found the switch with a practiced hand. With a click and a kindling of light, I saw one of the most beautiful rooms in the world.

A long, deep room swept along the ocean wall where deep red curtains billowed in the gusting wind. A strong, salty breeze caught the heavy velvet. The material made a sound like an audience of big, gloved hands, clapping. But all the luxurious appointments were housed in a horrible aftermath of highly personalized aggression.

If it weren't for the bleach and the damaged walls, it would be a bachelorette's boudoir. But even the salty ocean wind couldn't compete with the chlorine. And worse, the walls of the entire room were scraped unevenly. Wallpaper hung in long, peeling strands like dead skin, a tan that had gone terribly wrong.

Timbers stretched across the ceiling, above the damaged plaster. Across the beams, simple geometric designs had been stenciled, lending a festive, folksy air. A worn, polished wood floor led to a small alcove fireplace. Above the half-burnt logs, a brilliant display of photos and memorabilia, glittering with pungent marigolds and strange statues, caught my attention.

The fireplace mantel was, in fact, an altar dotted with the sugar skulls of *Día de los Muertos*. Candles, now unlit, sprouted from their glittering craniums underneath a large hand-tinted portrait of a man whose eyes might have been Rita Huelga's eyes. Chocolates, shells, a bottle of mescal, and glittering marigolds in crystal vases made their way through all the frames.

"It's an *ofrenda,* an altar."

"Who's that?" I pointed to the big portrait of the man with Rita's eyes.

"My father."

The big frame had an oven wreath of marigolds, and the largest sugar skull was poised beneath the picture: *Carlos* was written on his sugary forehead, over the black-rimmed, shit-eating grin. Behind them, more photos, which were propped up, resting against the wall, against each other. I wondered if Audra Léon's was one of them. I wondered if her face would be friendly now.

"Everyone on this altar dead?"

"No." Rita twisted a grinning skull around; red sequined eyes winked at me. "There's a saying: We have to worry more about those of us who remain on Earth, than those who've died. At least they rest with God now."

"So, who's over the fireplace, the living or the dead?"

"Both. The *calaveras,* the skulls, have been in my family for years. The marigolds are the traditional flower of the dead. There's a community feeling about death in Mexico. We don't feel as alone as the gringos."

"That's a good thing. I guess."

A winged armchair was placed to catch the warmth of the fire, when there was one. A small occasional table stood ready with ashtray and reading glasses poised over an orderly pile of books and magazines and a faux antique telephone.

"So, about the cat—the cat shit—the place was covered?"

"They concentrated, so to speak, on the walls. I didn't really feel like preserving the evidence."

"But they didn't touch the altar."

A pause. "No."

I could see the places where the stucco had been scrubbed white, past the paper right down to the plaster. To the right of the fireplace, an inset panel had been scrubbed especially hard. Did I see the brown stain of her name, Rita, on the wall? It was pretty adolescent stuff.

"What did they write?"

"Just my name."

"Your first name."

"Yes. *Rita.* That's all."

A large, round bed, covered with brocade, was pedestaled

in the middle of the room, raised about a foot off the floor. All the bedding had been stripped off of it and the silver-patterned bare mattress was naked to the air. Marks of the recent scrubbing were visible along all the walls, but it was the horrible smell of bleach that was most repugnant, a chemical sear that took the charm right out of the room. Along with the fact that somebody was acting out a hostility that was hard to comprehend, a hostility that was personally aimed at Dr. Rita Huelga.

Something at the far end of the room caught my attention. I walked over to the fireplace. A long clod of dirt—or shit—about two inches long caught my attention. I picked it up and sniffed it. Dirt.

"Would you mind getting me a small cellophane bag, please?"

"What?"

"A Zip loc. You know. A Baggie."

"Sure," Rita hesitated uncertainly, then turned. I heard her leave the room and descend the creaking stairway. Soon I would hear the flapping of the kitchen door, the plastic bag request buying me a few minutes to take a look around.

The occasional table with its reading material and faux antique phone was tops on the list. One small drawer was just visible under the magazines. Inside, a leather manicure set was carefully zipped closed. A bottle of aspirin was nearly empty. A second set of reading glasses was tucked in the back. Pushed into the back of the drawer was a tiny address book.

The little cardboard covers reminded me of Woolworth's. A dime-store document with first names and initials carefully recorded inside. Rita Huelga had a whole set of friends outside her professional life, I thought, looking at the first names and cities listed within. And there it was, under L: "Audra. 777 Horizon. 90291." A phone number began 310. The codes, zip, and area weren't for Texas; the numbers

spelled out La La Land to me. Santa Monica, perhaps. Or
Venice Beach.

I heard the kitchen door open and close downstairs as I
whipped open my wallet and recorded the numbers. I put the
book back, sliding the drawer quietly closed. I turned my attention to Rita's reading material, which lay ready under the
half-moon reading glasses. I pulled a tabloid out from underneath a few books. The smell of chlorine was nearly
toxic. I wiped a tear away from my eye and focused on what
was Dr. Rita Huelga's late-night topic of interest.

All Talk! The Talk Show Magazine! The faces of Jenny,
Oprah, Rikki, and Regis stared out at me. The tabloid
promised dish and scoop: "Why Regis and Kathie Lee Don't
Speak!" "Talk Show Wars!" "Johnny Lever Did the Dirt on
Audra!" "Oprah Defends Her Friend against Invasion of Privacy!" It was hard to believe the mycologist would find
tabloids of such interest.

More interesting was the gallery of faces perched on the
mantel over the fireplace. They smiled for posterity, wearing
double-breasted suits and ties as wide as steel-belted radials.
They stood proudly next to crank-start cars, little bungalows
in what looked like Los Angeles, with and without grandchildren.

More recent Kodak photos showed Rita at a variety of
public functions, at a podium receiving some award, her arm
slung around a young man, a much younger man, as they
sunned on a foreign beach, perhaps in Mexico. I squinted.
The mountains in the distance suggested Acapulco. The
young man was swilling a Dos Equis. There were two more
photos stationed behind the vacation picture.

I pushed the vacation photo aside. A stern grandfather
looked back through time. I peered behind the two-
dimensional face. There. A tiny, heart-shaped frame was
perched behind the false front of the patriarch, inlaid with
mosaic flowers. I turned the image toward me. Audra Léon,

in far earlier times, was barely recognizable. Audra Léon with an Afro and a tennis racket and a gleam in her eye that was unlike any sparkle she put on for the publicity shoots. We were all teenagers, once. I returned the tiny photo to its place behind grandfather. I heard the kitchen door swing open and closed again.

I picked up *Tuning in Trouble: Talk TV's Destructive Impact on Mental Health* and a smaller trade paperback, *All Talk: The Talk Show in Media Culture,* by Wayne Munson. I opened it up. "One of the talk show's most striking attributes is its depth of intertextuality. No other form owes more of its fundamental substance to other media texts, thus making its closure—to the degree it can be closed—especially dependent on the spectator-participants intertextual cognition."

Soon Rita would be coming up the stairs. I wondered if this kind of stuff was helping the doctor to make sense out of her experience, but I didn't have time to wonder for long. I put the book down. The massive timber staircase was groaning with Dr. Huelga's hurried steps. I put the magazine back carefully and walked over to the central window.

I peered outside. Fresh air finally cut the stench of bleach. Underneath, the shrubbery looked like it had been disturbed. I bent down double, reaching through the leafy vines. Several of the lattice slats had been broken.

"Here's the plastic bag." She handed me a small, sandwich-sized bag. I dropped the clod of dirt inside.

"Just dirt," I said.

"How do you think they got in?" she asked.

"I think they might have climbed up the trellis into the bedroom window. Was it open?"

"Yes, I'm afraid so. I never thought I would have to worry on the second story."

"I'll go downstairs and double-check the ground. It's October, so the ground is pretty dry, but I noticed you had a sprinkler system. We might be able to pick up a footprint."

"What will that tell us?"

"It would be nice to know how they got in here. Based on my assessment of that and the grounds, doors, and windows, we will need to make some modifications to the building for your security."

"I understand. Let's just try not to affect the style—the feeling—of the facade."

"I don't think Queen Elizabeth had video cameras."

"Had they been available, I'm sure she would have been completely wired." Rita sighed. "Shall we go downstairs?"

"I'd like to see where the cat facilities are. And I'd like to discuss the security requirements with you. By the way, I'd also like to talk to Mariposa."

"Oh, you can't. She's gone to bed by now. She had a hard day."

"First thing in the morning then."

"I hope that this—situation isn't going to impact my life—"

"You did want a bodyguard, didn't you?"

"Yes . . ."

"But you're not brimming over with enthusiasm?"

"It's not anything I ever thought I would need." Dr. Huelga sighed and looked around at the room.

"Where do you keep the Kitty Litter?"

"I have a courtyard for the cats out back. There's a facility that Mariposa cleans every three days. Unfortunately, it was due for a cleaning."

"So Mariposa paged you, and you stopped at a pay phone. What did she say, exactly?"

"That someone had come into the house and had put shit on the walls."

"That's all?

"She was very frightened."

"Where was she when this happened?"

"Out shopping. She goes down to West Portal, walks to the little village area to visit the greengrocer, the baker."

"She shops at pretty much the same time every day?"

"Yes."

"We might have to change around her schedule. It looks as if someone were casing your house. How long has Mariposa been working for you?"

"About three years now."

"She is a housekeeper?"

"More like an au pair. She has a variety of duties. She's very good with making decisions about the house, arranging things."

"Does she live here?"

"Yes. There's a small bedroom in what used to be the basement. It has a bathroom and leads out onto a patio. The way the rents are in San Francisco, its worked out really well. She knows a lot about botany, actually. It was her hobby in Brazil. Mariposa does a variety of tasks, whatever needs to be done."

"Such as?"

"Supervising general maintenance around this place. For example, painters. I always let her pick out the colors."

"How did you come to employ her?"

"I met her in Brazil. She knew a lot about plants."

"What did she do before your employ?"

"Why all the questions about Mariposa?"

"It's just routine, believe me. Had she just been doing odd jobs—"

"Yes, in between boyfriends. "

"A straight girl?"

"Yes. She used to be a runway model in Brazil. She's very hardworking, kind, and conscientious. And *quiet.* She's probably in her bedroom, painting, right now."

"Does she have a boyfriend at the moment?"

"No, not for the last three years."

"Three years? That's a long time."

"Look, Emma, I don't pry into Mariposa's personal life. She parties, she travels, she saves her money. Mariposa is the only way I can live the life I need to get on with my work."

Sounded pretty dependent to me. "I see you've been reading up on talk television?"

"What!?" A suspicious note in her voice.

"The books. By the fireplace."

"Yeah, well, they say knowledge is power."

"Do you believe that?"

"Sort of." Dr. Huelga was obviously uncomfortable with my looking around her bedroom. Except for the fireplace mantel and books, the room was rather empty. How long had Rita lived here? Three years? She traveled light, maybe she lived light, too.

"Emma, your assignment as bodyguard—what are your plans? What will be expected—of me?"

"I'd like to see the place first." Walking past the battle-axes I squinted at the edges of their crossed blades. They looked plenty sharp for decorations.

"I'm not ready to show it to you."

"Okay." Decorations don't order you around, either.

"Come into the living room." Huelga's hand stretched out and beckoned me inside the other dark room off the hallway. I could see her biceps flex under the soft, high cuffs of the velour T-shirt. Her fingers curved slowly, and when I came to the arched portal, she pushed three abalone buttons into the wall. Before us, a large, timbered room was both massive and as cozy as a French farmhouse, but with one difference. Except for the furniture, there was a remarkable lack of doodads.

On one side of the room, cherry-veneer shaded lamps spilled light on massive, moss green velvet sofas. A black walnut cabinet took up most of the wall behind the left-hand couch. A decorative key hung nonchalantly from one of the blackened front doors. Resting on huge turnip-ball feet, the cabinet looked like it had been brought through the Reformation to make its way here to America.

The sofas were new. But the padded curves, like bustles, on either side, were stolen from an earlier time. Amber and dark red pillows stood ready to soften the sit for the boniest hip. The two sofas were perpendicular to the rustic flagstone fireplace. A leather-covered brown steamer trunk was studded with nails. A bowl of mixed nuts was held aloft on a brass pedestal. It all looked like it was ordered out of a very expensive catalogue.

I looked around me and wondered one thing: How did Dr. Huelga pay the mortgage?

A large Livingston fireplace dominated the room. It came to Dr. Huelga's shoulders. An iron rotisserie hook hung down on a heavy chain. I could have roasted my car in there. The huge fireplace was unadorned except for the timbered mantel. Kindling and wood had already been laid on the grate, perhaps one of Mariposa's tasks. Huelga drew a long fireplace match from a copper kettle, struck it on the rock. She leaned inside the yawning mouth of the fireplace. I took the opportunity for a surreptitious scan around the room.

The other side of the room was a wall of French doors and transom windows that probably let out onto some kind of patio. Moonlight didn't quite make it past the deep velvet curtains, but a ray or two made it over the beveled transom windows. An eye or two could have made it over there, too. In front of the windows, incongruously, a wrought-iron screen, stretched with bleached muslin, appeared to guard a small, low table covered with more books and papers in front of the window. It didn't do a very good job of it.

Dr. Huelga was looking into the flames, transfixed. Maybe she was thinking about "spectator-participants intertextual cognition," but I wouldn't want to bet on it. I looked away, not meaning to intrude on her moment.

The flames sparkled throughout the room, on the nailhead studs of the steamer trunk, in the deep shine of oil paintings that lined the walls. I could just make out the subject matter of the paintings: luscious bouquets of roses and a few dead swans, their necks broken in a way that the Dutch had once thought was romantic.

Maybe it was the bleach, maybe it was the swans, maybe it was even a guilty conscience. Whatever it was, I fell into an uncomfortable silence. The intensity of Huelga as she watched the fire was unnerving. When she turned around, I could feel her eyes eating me.

"Sit down," Rita commanded. I sank deep into the lap of one of the velvet couches, the overflow of throw pillows threatening to suffocate me. I fought back, leaning forward with effort; I felt like I was trying to escape the upholstered proto-mother. I stretched my hands out toward the dish of mixed nuts displayed on the top of the leather trunk.

"You can help yourself." Dr. Huelga, with eyes in the back of her head. Pecans and cashews, fruits of the Amazon. Every nut in the bowl was unbroken. I picked out a perfect half moon nut, as I watched Dr. Huelga's silhouette. She was balanced on her heels, she looked feline, crouched and ready to spring.

Her long fingers seemed to make circles; they pointed to the ground as she stared at the fire. The flames jumped up quickly behind her. I sank back into the arms of the couch, watching her figure light up with the intensity of the blaze. I could see her in profile. Her face was cast in red, the black hair, like marble, reflecting the light. Her lips seemed to be moving, to be saying something to the fire. It was as if she'd forgotten I was there.

"Dr. Huelga?"

"Oh! Yes!" As she turned around, I saw that a film of moisture—of sweat or tears—had broken out on her face.

"So, its been hell trying to get your work done around here, you say."

"Yes."

"What do you do, exactly?"

"It's sort of difficult to explain."

"Try."

"Uh—not now." The flames drew her attention again.

There are some people who need time to think, rethink, perhaps even do major edits before they speak. They have had good reason in their lives to keep quiet, to keep things secret. In normal social intercourse, there is no point in rushing these people. But my life was sometimes a balancing act between good manners and bad behavior. I looked at the lit-up face of Dr. Rita Huelga, at the intensity of her eyes, fixed on the flames, and I knew that I would have to bust this woman for any answers. I would give her as much time as possible to come up with some exposition. And I certainly hoped it wouldn't be about "spectator-participants' intertextual cognition."

Dr. Huelga stood up, her shadow form moved behind the couch, hesitating by the massive carved oak sideboard. I heard the ornamental key turn. I turned around just in time to see the cabinet light up from within. A fine liquor collection in all shades from port to gin and sherries to vodka stood there in carefully lined rows. An assortment of stemmed and unstemmed glasses were poised on glass shelves over a small, stainless-steel bar sink.

"Would you like a drink?"

"Just water, if you have it. Bubbles are okay. That's quite a cabinet you've got there." I heard a small refrigerator open, a cap turn, the crush of ice and fizzling. The next drink didn't fizzle but needed a lot of stirring.

"It's original Tudor." She closed the door and turned the key with finality.

"Very nice. Must have set you back a piece. By the way, you don't have to hide the key. Except for wine with dinner, I never touch spirits."

Dr. Huelga turned and looked me in the eyes as she put her drink down, way down, on the leather steamer trunk. She may or may not have known that she had given me a clear shot of her cleavage as she bent over.

Dr. Huelga walked over to the other couch, fell into it, keeping her martini nicely balanced in her hand during an attack of the throw cushions. She seemed to be waiting for me to say something, so I did.

"I'd like to outline a plan for you. There are a number of choices you will need to make. There are—or there could be—two parts to this plan. First of all, it seems imperative to defend your privacy and your property. And, if necessary, your person."

Dr. Huelga nodded. The martini seemed to give her some comfort along with the words *privacy* and *property*. She was visibly relaxing into the velvet cushions.

"I'd like to be on the premises at night. At the moment, your home is vulnerable simply because of the amount of vegetation. Eliminating some of your abundant greenery seems like the first and simplest step." Huelga's sigh was audible. She was, after all, a plant lover. "In any case," I continued, "it would be prudent to position video cameras on all four sides of the house, with closed-circuit monitors. We can put the monitors right inside your liquor cabinet, for example."

Dr. Huelga sniffed. She leaned into a pillow, exposing a soft moment of midriff underneath her soft velour T-shirt. The martini was loosening her body but not her lips. She was clasping her drink with both hands.

"Or we can install the monitors down in the cellar or in

the laundry room. Somewhere where I can sit and watch them for a week or two, if that's what you decide is necessary."

Dr. Huelga stretched out across the couch. A hand lazily drew her fingertips back and forth over her belly. "I'd prefer it if you didn't stash yourself away in the basement," she said.

"Dr. Huelga, I will always assume that you want me to be in the background. But I'd be happy to station myself closer to the center of the household."

"Good. Tell me what's the second part of this plan of yours?"

"It might not be a bad idea to pursue an active investigation as to who—if there is any one person—has done this—this act. I don't mean to alarm you, but this attack seems like a very personally aimed aggression. Maybe we need to look at who might be motivated—provoked—to make this kind of attack?"

The fire crackled and sparked suddenly. "How about one of Audra's legions of fans?" she suggested.

"It's a thought."

"But do you think fans, even crazy fans, would go to the trouble? They would have to climb in a two-story window."

"They've been known to do a lot more than that to get to a star."

"Hmm! Well, never mind the horror stories. Ms. Victor, tell me what I'm going to see on these monitors."

"You will be able to see the entire perimeter of your house. There will be motion-detector lamps—"

"Motion-detector—"

"Yes."

"Lamps?"

" We can run the lights continuously after dark, if you prefer."

"Lights? I don't think so. That's not possible."

"Why?"

"That's strictly on a need-to-know basis."

"Ms. Huelga, most people don't feel safe or even comfortable in the dark."

"It's not going to be easy."

"I'm sure we can work something out." I sighed. My earlobe was giving me trouble. I rubbed it, pulling the earring and sending a small shoot of pain up to the top of my head. I wished I was on another assignment, any assignment. I could be getting pierced in exchange for life-saving information, for example, or crawling along a rain forest floor in the misty moonlight toward a dead body and thirty-five thousand dollars in cash. Anywhere but in a six-figure mansion in San Francisco with a fussy homeowner who was going to hate me by the time all the boring and threading and pounding was over.

"Emma, I'm going to take you into my confidence about the work that I'm doing. There's more than one reason why I feel I need a good security system around here. I've got a really important project going on. And I don't want it to be sabotaged. Or stolen. That's what I feel *really* needs protection."

Oh good. Projects, papers, objects, and secrets with a tangible value, things that didn't order you around. Things that you could put in your pocket, deliver, sell, or save for later. I could almost like this assignment, I thought. That is, until Rita Huelga returned from behind the white screen with a pile of papers. Two legal-sized eight-by-fourteen pieces of paper, stapled at the end with a blue card stock cover. A legal document.

"I want to tell you all about my work. But first, Ms. Victor, you'll have to sign *my* release form."

CHAPTER SIX

THE OLDEST ART

I took the documents, knowing that I was soon to find out exactly how Dr. Huelga paid the mortgage of her Tudor manse. Squinting at the form, I saw it was a boilerplate contract swearing me to complete secrecy about a project known only as TKTK1477, which was the sole property of Dr. Huelga and Consortium Bell-Worless. There were a lot of clauses about if I should make any use of the research of Dr. Rita Huelga and Consortium Bell-Worless, I would be liable for civil and criminal prosecution, and my firstborn child. Surveying the document, I scratched my earlobe. Then I scribbled my signature on the bottom as Dr. Rita Huelga strolled over to the big black oak cabinet.

"All signed and released." I put my glass on a coaster next to the nut dish.

"Okay." Rita finished her martini and pondered the olive. Then she ate it. I looked over at the white curtained window with the moonlight stretching through the transom windows. Rita Huelga was all soft in velour and velvet. She sure was a lot more beautiful than the guy on crutches. And, unfortunately, a lot more mysterious.

"Come on, then," Rita Huelga stood up, the copper pennies flashed. Strolling quickly toward the opposite end of the room, she pushed a few buttons. The lights in the living room dimmed. The white curtains parted. A red light lit a tableau that was unique in all the world.

A huge, nocturnal greenhouse, about twenty by thirty feet, had been built into the north face of the house. Covered with glass, moonlight freely entered through a thin veil of condensed moisture on the glass roof. Underneath the huge skylight, a large, curving wall of stone, thirty feet long, formed a series of grottos where gnarled and rotting wood sprouted a kaleidoscope of mushrooms. There were several partitions, glass doors, which led into further misty chambers, allowing different temperature and humidity controls. In front of us, a fairyland scene played itself out.

Delicate white bells shone in the moonlight. Brilliant orange toadstools perched jauntily atop moss-covered logs. Freckled faces, little hats, and black-spotted thumbs emerged from soft beds of moss. A tiny waterfall made a silver crack in the rocks.

And everywhere, the blinking of yellow and green eyes as cats, scores of cats, woke to see what was happening. Their cat houses were built into the grotto. Like the ancient Anasazi in their cave dwellings, these cats seemed equally at home, curled up in their baked clay nests. Many, most of them, were black cats, a few tuxedo models with white breasts and gloves. Amber eyes narrowed and rough pink tongues scoured furry faces, the morning wash.

Dr. Rita Huelga's eyes focused into the darkness, watching the felines as they slowly emerged, stretched.

"Mushrooms and cats. You've still got me guessing, Dr. Huelga."

"Call me Rita."

"Okay. Rita." The name came on a sharp intake of breath.

"You know that the Amazonian rain forest is the source of

thousands of varieties of plants that are on the verge of extinction?"

"So I've read."

"I began my research ten years ago, Emma. When I was a graduate student at Columbia, I spent every summer in the rain forests. While everyone else was working on their tan, I was working in the rain. There's nothing like the feeling when you push aside the carpet of the forest and find the brilliant treasures that wait there. I collected cultures of every species of mushroom I could find. I researched the particular environment of each species and replicated it here, in my own personal laboratory. At first, it was just a challenge. And then I started synthesizing some of the chemical components. The applications are, to say the least, remarkable."

"I take it that's where the cats come in."

"You know about feline leukemia?"

"Yeah. All my cats are inoculated against it. They call it kitty AIDS."

"That's right; there are some real similarities between the two diseases, as they both impair the immune system. What I've found is that not only do some of the mushrooms seem to retard the progress of the disease but actually lower some of the viral presence."

"Didn't you win an award from the Cancer Institute?"

"It was just for a paper."

"Any human applications?"

"No, now this cat—"

"But you work for the Women's Cancer Resource—"

"I'm just on the board, Emma. Look at this cat, here. The amazing thing is that, unlike people, they seem to know absolutely what's good for them."

I looked back at the amazing grotto. The cats were stretching out on the moss, calling to each other, rolling on their bellies provocatively.

"Definitely a Halloween scene," I whispered.

"Mariposa does a misting of all the mushrooms in the morning. The cats are nocturnal beasts; a midnight romp is what often suits them, and that's when I like to watch.

"Sometimes I sit here and watch them for hours. It's been suggested that I get video cameras, but it's too difficult to control the lighting conditions. And I like seeing the cats with my own eyes. I've spent countless days in front of this window, watching. In the meantime, I correlate a lot of data."

"So none of these cats are house pets?"

"No. I don't want to interfere with their behavior and environment any more than is necessary. It's not exactly a controlled scientific environment, but it's the best I can do."

"Where do you spend most of your time in the house?"

"I pretty much use the whole place. Sometimes I stay up late working in the dining room. Then I sleep in."

"Sounds like you're rather nocturnal, too."

"It suits me," she said simply. "There she is." Rita smiled with satisfaction. "Ganymede."

A small kitten in a top penthouse wobbled on young legs. It was too thin to be healthy. I watched as it climbed carefully down a path cut in the steep stone. It made its way with difficulty, bumping into a stone before it reached a cluster of cute little red toadstools, like the kind garden elves lounged under.

"Cats usually see so well in the dark—"

"But this cat is blind, Emma. Almost all my cats are blind."

"Why is that?"

Sniffing carefully, the fungus held the interest of the young feline.

"Watch." The tones of Rita's voice were of awe, not instruction. The kitten had approached and was very cautiously nibbling on the edge of a toadstool.

"Check this out. I call it toklastaki."

The kitten was backing away from the mushroom, now.

"The taste isn't great," Rita said. "Unfortunately, not all poisonous mushrooms have a bad taste. People put them in spaghetti sauce, like the Sebastiani kid."

The papers last week had tolled the death of the son of a local wine maker. He'd collected the death cap mushrooms and put them in spaghetti sauce. It was surprising, since the papers had been full of warnings about poisonous mushrooms and recent immigrants had been made perilously sick. And the Sebastiani boy, a local, must have had some knowledge about California's dangerous fungi. His liver failed in the hospital; the toxins from the mushroom had destroyed it in hours. After that, it was a race to find an appropriate liver donor and try for a transplant. But the mushroom's poison was too fast and too final.

The year before, Wilhelm Winter, an amateur mycologist from Marin "tasted death and found it delicious." He felt ill after eating mushrooms but denied the symptoms could be from poisonous mushrooms. After a coma, a liver transplant saved his life and kept his menu limited for the rest of his life.

The *San Francisco Chronicle* had published more diagrams of the death cap and the panther's cap, both which looked like the common horse mushroom found in every supermarket. And still, people picked the mushrooms, put them in spaghetti sauce, served them over gourmet pasta, and gave them to their friends, who ate them and died. Livers failed, funerals were held.

"Since penicillin is derived from fungi, you'd think Western scientists would be cultivating and investigating mushrooms," Rita said. "But I guess the profit margins are higher elsewhere. Fungophobia."

"Fungophobia?"

"Mold is freaky, Ms. Victor. It ruins the Wonder Bread.

But in other cultures, people hold mushrooms in great regard and put them to all kinds of purposes. In Russia, people play games with mushrooms, wear them, use them to start fires and plug leaky roofs. They can also break down toxic wastes."

"What about poisonous mushrooms?"

"First of all, what is a poison? What I've found is—in the case of this kitten—that small amounts—*very* small amounts—of some supposedly dangerous mushrooms seem to enhance the immune system to the point where the feline leukemia virus goes into remission."

"Like nature's chemotherapy?"

"Actually, no. The magic bullet concept is strictly a Western concept, Emma. Western scientists are obsessed with finding a 'magic bullet,' the specific molecule that works on specific diseases in very specific ways. Check out the language for the latest HIV development: 'Hunter Virus Kills HIV. A biological weapon that can seek out infected cells. Hunter viruses loaded with biological killer molecules.' The language itself could come from the Pentagon!"

I found myself entranced by her speech. There was no doubt about it—I was developing a competence crush. "The Chinese have a different approach," she went on. "Drugs that have specific effects don't interest them. Wide-ranging effects that affect the entire system is what interests the Chinese—and me. I am in awe of nature, learning from it, and not obsessed with control. As a result, there is a whole body of neglected research—conducted over thousands of years—that has yet to be utilized in the Western world, except by hippies and health freaks."

"Psilocybin? Magic mushrooms?"

"Exactly."

"This kitten was brought to the SPCA in an advanced stage of feline leukemia, passed on from her mother. Her blindness has been caused by the cytomegalovirus. She's put on weight, and every day she eats a little piece of the tok-lastaki. Then she backs off. Sometimes she throws up. And tomorrow morning, she'll eat a huge breakfast. She's getting better day by day."

"Have you been a teacher?"

"Yes. Why?"

"Because you sound like a lecturer."

"What is this, the inquisition?"

"Sort of."

Dr. Huelga sighed. "Sloan-Kettering," she said.

"What are the legal parameters for felines used in research?"

"I get all the cats from the SPCA. The ones with leukemia they have to put to sleep immediately. The disease is too contagious to contain. They have a special intake area. If I get there within six hours of pickup, I can take the cats home."

"Ever been bothered by animal rights people?"

"Animal rights?" Rita's hands were up against the glass, the force of her voice seemed to hit the glass with a disconcerting bitterness. Once again, it was that instant moment of emotion that seemed to take her by surprise. Her fingernails pressed up against the hard surface; I heard them tap as they hit the glass. "Let me tell you about cat lovers! In the late nineteenth century, somebody invented the motion picture camera, which revealed how a cat lands on its feet. Only one-eighth of a second is required for an upside down cat to turn over. So the boys got together and started tinkering. They found out if you both blind a cat and destroy its hearing in one ear, it will drop like a rock from sixty feet." Her bitterness was as deep as it was sudden. "I think my cats here have it pretty good. They don't have electrodes in their heads. Nobody is doing split brain research on them. That's been going on since the 1950s. Curiosity has led to unbelievable cruelty."

"Sort of like journalism, wouldn't you say?"

Huelga didn't say anything. It was a rhetorical question. There was time to get specific later.

"There is so much that is endlessly fascinating about the feline. A dog can be taught to do a variety of things that are unnatural to it. Cats cannot seem to be made to *work*. Cats teach us that hunger and killing are separately motivated."

Rita took her hands off the glass, her arms fell to her sides as she said quietly, "The cat's way of knowledge is another way of knowing. I try to see the cats as my teachers, and not objects to manipulate to answer questions *I* am choosing to ask. I don't need scalpels and torture to find out what they know. The cats will teach me the right questions. So, no, I haven't been bothered by animal rights people."

"The SPCA has seen and approved your work?"

"They've not only approved it, they're really excited about the work. Feline leukemia is a pernicious, heartbreaking disease."

"Any problem with the neighbors? Zoning?"

"Funny you should ask that. A neighbor over the north wall lodged a complaint a few years back. The neighborhood board supported me. A lot of AIDS researchers have made use of my findings. I don't think anyone could make a good case for stopping my research."

We watched the little kitten wobble back to its cave and collapse.

"Why the black cats?"

"Actually, it's just chance. I just seem to have a lot of them at the moment. Black is a dominant gene fur color, often seen with white socks, breast, blaze on the forehead."

"Tuxedo cats."

"Yes, I've had particularly good luck with them. Terrible time with tabbies, though. And Buster, my Maine coon cat, died last week after a two-year remission. Just about broke my heart. I take care to only have a few males per group.

Obviously this means that my placement for male cats is limited."

I looked over at Dr. Rita Huelga, scientist with a heart. The garden grotto loomed behind her in its strange, precise, majesty. Her creation was captivating. "So you see, lack of chlorophyll is what *defines* a mushroom. I simply can't have lights blinking off and on at all moments of the night. *Any* light is going to ruin the ecological balance of the environment. You see the problem?"

What I saw was Dr. Rita Huelga's beautiful face. One side was lit white in the moonlight, the other side reflected the red glow from the grotto. Her lips were wet, soft, and large. She was looking at the sleeping kitten. The only problem was not kissing her.

"I don't think the lighting is a problem. We can work around that pretty easily." My own voice sounded tinny. "It's good that you keep a rather irregular schedule. Would you show me the cat sanitation facilities?" Dr. Rita Huelga must have one hell of a litter box.

"I'll save that for the end. Mariposa deals with all the work around the cats. So, you don't think we need to change the lighting outside?"

"No. The fact that your solarium—so to speak—has a glass roof makes it pretty vulnerable. There's no skylights or vents in it?"

"No. The air filtration and humidifying systems are vented to the outside through the wall. The panels are all floating on a thin metal canopy. It would be pretty hard for it to support the weight of a human. You'd crash through it."

"Good. All the preexisting wiring will mean a lot less alteration to the building."

Rita Huelga smiled. "That's a big relief." Her hand landed on my shoulder and squeezed hard. There was more in that squeeze than a homeowner's relief. "I'm really happy to hear that."

So she was happy. Being a bodyguard for Dr. Rita Huelga was going to be a big problem for me, a bigger problem than I had realized. I didn't want to guard her body, I wanted to take it.

"Could you show me the rest of the house?"

"Nature alone is antique. And the oldest art, a mushroom."

"What?"

"Let me show you the mushroom farm."

"You mean this isn't it?"

"No, I just transplant selected species. I need a much more controlled environment to be able to grow the kind and quantity of mushrooms I require."

The pennies in her loafers twinkled as we made our way back through the hallway. Leading me through a white and sterile kitchen, Rita opened a narrow door and made her way down another munchkin set of stairs. A low light streamed in from the basement area.

Clatter, clatter, Rita's feet made a little jump, landing together on the concrete floor. Before us a large, low-lit room hummed with fans; the air was heavy with mist and a deep smell of the forest, strangely at odds with the laboratory environment. "Mostly, I'm growing medicinal mushrooms, polypores and other wood-rotting species."

Large carts were carefully beset with trays upon trays, which were filled with what looked like sawdust and bark. On the surface, thousands of spores were springing to life, strange life forms, from tiny purple buttons to huge shining caps that looked more like abalone shells than fungus. There was one exit to the large, square room, a door with a dead-bolt and a large two by four held in place by two massive angle irons.

"Mushrooms are very big in China, right?"

"Mushrooms occupy a central role in traditional Chinese pharmacopeia. I actually learned quite a bit from a Siberian scientist, Olga Barkishow, a colleague I've been communicating with via E-mail. Check these out!" She pointed at a large birch log that looked overwhelmed by some horrendous growth. *"Inonotus obliquus."*

Deeply cracked black cankers fed on the silver bark of the birch. They were about as big as a shrunken human head, and had about as much appeal.

"Chaga, or *Inonotus obliquus,* makes a tea that enhances the immune system. It's really helped some of the cats that have come in with light cases of leukemia. After a few months of chaga tea, I've been able to put them into complete remission and the SPCA has adopted them out. They're all house pets now, thanks to *Inonotus obliquus."*

"How do you make the tea?"

"I cut up the cankers with an ax, soak it in water for six to eight hours. Then I run it through a meat grinder and add the powder to boiling water. It looks like shit on the log but has a very mild flavor."

I found myself walking through the carts sprouting fungi of all shapes, colors, and sizes. White caps spotted with ruby red spots, like drops of blood, strange snakelike black tongues poking out of deep green moss, and a whole tray of pastel formations that looked like ocean coral and nothing like fungus at all. Three growths had attained the size of soccer balls, split in half like the hemispheres of brains, they could have fed—or poisoned—an army.

On the far wall, a complete laboratory setup featured rows of test tubes, a Bunsen burner, and a whole lot of wooden boxes and fans and other equipment I couldn't place.

"Do you grow any edible mushrooms?"

"Sure, I cultivated a few chantarelles, shiitake, a few strains of oyster mushrooms you can't find in any of the gourmet food stores."

"A few of these trays look disturbed."

"What?" Huelga's concern was immediate.

I bent over, noticing odd spacing between the spores, the occasional splatter of sawdust on the scrubbed tile floor. There was a scattering of dirt and a little white cap on the floor.

"Mariposa uses them for cooking. Maybe she picked a few," but Huelga's face showed concern.

"Mariposa is knowledgeable about mushrooms?"

"Sometimes I let her take a few chantarelles to friends. It's the *Chateaubriand* of the fungi world. Rita plucked a long, fluted mushrooms from among the group on the disturbed tray. The lacy gills looked like a pleated skirt that blew upward in the wind. The stalk broke with a snap. *"Cantharellus cibarius."*

"Looks a little messy for your maid. Looks more like a cat has been scratching in here." I took a closer look at the tray of sawdust and growing medium.

"Well, they have been known to escape." The mushroom was hidden in her hand. I bent closer to the tray.

"I don't see any evidence they mistook this tray for a potty." I took a quick sniff. "Smells like mold and sawdust. But you did say that the cats had escaped. They've gotten in here before?"

"Yes."

"Would you show me the cat facilities now?"

"Sure, why not?" She put the mushroom carefully down on a paper towel.

"And any other part of the house I haven't seen? Then I'd like to discuss a plan of action with you, a situation that will make you feel comfortable and safe."

We left the carefully cultivated mushrooms behind us, emerging slowly from their sawdust beds. I took another quick look through the kitchen. It was as cozy as an intensive care unit. Dr. Rita Huelga was beyond being a neatnik, the whole house felt laboratory clean. And she must have shined the pennies in her loafers every day. Covering

Huelga's bedroom with shit would be one perfect way to freak her out.

"Here it is," Huelga pointed through a round window in a dead-bolted door just off the kitchen. There was a smell of ammonia. Rita flicked on fluorescent lights. A tiled room featured four large cat pans. The floor sloped down toward a drain. Two cat doors, each leading to the outdoor mushroom grotto, were open. A human-sized door had an insufficient sliding bolt lock on it. The lock had not been broken. A mop was hung on the wall. A large industrial bucket stood underneath it. Other than that, there was nothing remarkable about it.

"May I go in?"

"Actually, I'd rather you didn't. The clumping cat litter tracks in everywhere. They can send men to the moon, but they can't invent a self-cleaning litter box."

As if to illustrate her point, a dignified black gentleman poked his white whiskers through the cat door. He loped slowly toward the cat box and, with a look of supreme concentration, went about his business, after which he spent time excavating as much of the litter box as possible. When he went back outside, he'd left half a cup of cat litter on the tiles.

"I always keep this door bolted so the litter isn't tracked through the house."

"Yes, I understand."

"And that's the end of the tour, Emma. Except for the garage, which has been undisturbed. I have an automatic garage door with a top-of-the-line security lock. I don't drive my car a lot; it's in the garage most of the time." We emerged back into the dining room. I looked across the expanse of table, paper, and computers. Rita Huelga was a busy woman. She worked at all hours of the night, and she still found time to polish the pennies on her shoes.

"One more thing, Dr. Huelga—"

"Rita."

"Rita. Do you want me to actively pursue who did this?"

"What would that mean?"

"It would mean my interviewing you as to all the possible persons who think they have a bone to pick with you."

"I can't talk about my work."

"I don't think we have to worry about that right now."

"What do you mean?"

Maybe this isn't an investigation you're ready for. I'd have to ask you a lot of questions."

"Like?"

"Like who knew you were going to meet Audra in Phoenix?"

"It's not like I haven't asked myself that question."

"I'd have to ask you about Audra."

"Forget it."

"I'd have to ask you the parameters of your relationship. How often you saw her. Under what conditions. Who knew. Who didn't know."

"Like I said, you can forget it."

"By the way, what happened to your medal?"

"What?"

"The tennis racket around your neck. There's a little hole in the netting."

"Just a high school prank. I wear it to remember—"

"Remember what?"

"High school. That's all. Any more questions?"

"I'll just camp out and make sure you're safe, Ms. Huelga."

"I will be sleeping up there." She pointed to a can-tilevered balcony that floated above the room. "In the guest bed up in the gallery. Let me show you." Framed in by the big, black timbers, I had hardly noticed the balcony. Old King Cole could have appeared at any moment. At the end of the dining room, a steep, narrow stairway led to the gallery. A knotted rope served as a handrail. I followed the pleasant line of Rita's flanks; her braid bounced appealingly between her shoulder blades, black on the bright green field of back. Ample hips moved like precious pillows. *Stop it, Emma.*

Alighting in the loft, a narrow bed had a deep red throw cover with embroidered mirrors worked into a pattern over it. Tapestry cushions in jewel tones had satin string tassels on the corners. A built-in bookshelf featured an all-Spanish-language selection. *Día de los Muertos, Un Historica.* A selection of tall, skinny bottles with dark-colored liquids had no labels. A glass decanter with something evil and greenish was paired with a tiny shot glass.

"I'll be awake all night, down by the dining room table, if you don't mind. I can get a good view of the hallway, make a round of the house once an hour. And I'll be right underneath you."

"That's right," she said with a calm confidence, the tennis racket glimmering on her chest. "You will be."

And then Rita Huelga jumped me.

CHAPTER SEVEN

COMFORTABLE
IN THE DARK

At the first touch of her lips, professional ethics were put aside. Way, way aside.

After what I had seen on television and in Rose's office, I was not surprised with the suddenness of her hug, the strength of her arms. Her hands, given permission, lost no time.

Later, I remembered the two reasons why I usually didn't do one-night stands anymore. First of all, it took too much alcohol and secondhand smoke to get into the mood with a stranger, even a stranger as handsome and compelling as Dr. Rita Huelga. Secondly, the immutable fact was that you had slept with a stranger and that a stranger was then suddenly in your life. Your hormones compel you to a second time; then you have a situation. A situation with a stranger. I had tired of situations with strangers long ago. But I always had a thing for science nerds.

This was business. My peripheral vision was far too developed to ignore the sideline issues. These were pushed out with the force of Rita Huelga's tongue in my mouth, and any

120

resolve or common sense was demolished as she laced her fingers through mine.

Later, I told myself that it was not an entirely unprofessional act. It is said that there are three kinds of communicators: speech, sight, and touch. And at that moment, the woman who had been so reluctant to speak finally emerged.

Her lips continued, relentless. My fingers surrendered to her demanding grasp. Her mouth was strong, her lips were not just eager, they were hungry and committed. Her hand held my chin and brought my lips farther inside her mouth. I felt her teeth, and for a breathtaking moment, it seemed that our faces fused and her mouth was of the same flesh as mine.

Rita Huelga was not just a person who was at home in the physical mode; Rita Huelga *was* the physical mode.

Watching Rita Huelga's fingers lifting my shirt, finding those mushroom buttons, I knew that I had already decided that a minor breach of professional ethics might not be inappropriate. Huelga was beautiful and had the strength of a lion. I just hadn't expected her to take the lead. It was nice to know that there were still surprises in store. At least, that was what I was thinking. That is, *when* I was thinking. Mostly, I was reveling in the soft velour of her T-shirt against my breasts and all the things my nakedness entitled her to do.

Rita's leg was hard, topped with a sinewy quad I could feel under the rough denim of her jeans. With a quick twining movement, she had curled her leg around mine, bent my leg back at the knee, and pressed me back onto the coverlet of her bed where she lost no time. Her pants were rough against my thighs as she spread my legs.

"Strong legs from *tennis*—"

But Rita Huelga would have none of words. Her lips stilled me as her fingers found their way. When Rita Huelga touched me, it was as if the hands of all former lovers left the memory of my flesh, flying away like so many sandpipers when the waves hit the shore. And so I let the riptide of Dr.

Huelga pull me under. Later, I remembered thinking that there's nothing wrong with desperate sex. And it wasn't just Dr. Huelga who was desperate.

Later, she would tell me that I had screamed. She said I swore when I came, "Oh God" becoming "Oh shit, oh fuck, oh yes." And when she told me that the gushing that came between my legs was normal, I believed her completely. I thought about all the women who crowded into bookstores to watch television. And now I knew where my G spot was, too.

After the shuddering ceased, she let go of my hand.

"I thought I'd never find myself in *this* position," I said.

"What's that?"

"Undressed, in a client's bed. I could be in big trouble right now. So could you," I said.

"Me?" She laughed.

"It's a bit harder for me to save you from impending danger while I'm stark naked."

"I'm not too worried." Rita Huelga reached behind a cupboard and drew out a small lacquered humidor.

"And you're still fully dressed."

"Stay awhile, Emma."

"I think I'd better get back on the job, thank you."

"An afterglow cigarette?"

"Oh, okay, why not?"

A black arched eyebrow flew, a quick kiss of camaraderie, and the pungent explosion of phosphorus. I lay in the dewy pillow of her arm and watched her smoke; I felt the soft velour on my cheek, the burning between my legs.

My fingers were tracing the smile lines on either side of her mouth. Her lips were pursed around the cigarette. I looked at the stain on the sheet. She watched me and a burst of laughter was accompanied by smoke. I sat up and tried to get back into character.

"You look very pretty." The hot place between my legs, the shock of finding my name written in come on Rita

Huelga's sheets was making it hard to keep the job foremost in my mind. I peeled wet curls off of her cheeks. I looked deep into those honey warm eyes. "Flattery will get you nowhere. Even from highly attractive physicians in fascinating lines of work."

Rita stared at me, inhaled, and blew smoke out. "Sorry, but you do look pretty. Mind the adjective, do you? Or do you have something against doctors?"

"I've met a lot of doctors in my line of work." My voice was going to say something stupid, something straight out of my unconscious, and I was powerless to stop it. "My experience with the medical profession hasn't exactly boosted my opinion of the human race. Doctors are some of the most major criminals around. They take drugs and murder people, just like anyone else. Maybe, more—" I stopped, watching the surprised, bemused expression on Rita's face.

"My, my, where did that all come from, Emma?"

That's when I started to blush. "I'm sorry, Rita, I guess I'm still—"

"Still hung up on somebody?"

"Yes, I'm even a bit worried that you know her."

"Let me guess, she's a doctor."

"You got it. Same line of work and all that. It's more than a little embarrassing."

"What, to make love with one person when all your feelings are for another?"

"Something like that."

"Don't worry, Emma. I've been doing it for years."

"Audra Léon?"

"Yeah. We reconnected three years ago when I got back from Brazil. I didn't realize the depth of feeling I still carried for her. High school was a long time ago, and yet it was yesterday."

"Doesn't exactly sound like a winning situation, Rita."

"I didn't think that something so—clandestine—could be so exciting. So, who's your ex? Or not so ex ex?"

"Frances Cohen."

"Oh, yeah, I do know her. I met Frances last year in Philadelphia. She was giving a paper on reproductive technology." Rita searched my face. "Frances Cohen, huh?" Nodding, she smiled. "I can see that. What happened?"

"We were together for seven years. It was a good thing until it was a dysfunctional thing."

"Frances Cohen," Rita mused. "She's been working on the lesboparthenogensis project for years, right?"

"You could say that I am very familiar with the patience, and money, that biological research requires. Not to mention trying to move things out of the lab and onto the streets."

"Ah, a science wife." Rita laughed.

"Not that I don't have my own business. But a major goal is clocking in as much beach time as possible. Somehow our lives never gelled. We agreed to part last year. It was a mutual thing."

"She's a nice person. I liked her." Rita smiled, a graciousness in her voice that I hadn't heard before.

"Aw hell, who am I kidding. It wasn't a mutual thing at all." I coughed. "Frances dumped me. Now, let me have a cigarette." I pulled a smoke out of the box. She reached an arm to the side of the bed for a slim, silver lighter. Her smile was sweet, her arm helped lift me up off the bed toward the flame. I laid on my back. The cloth of her jeans was rough along the side of my flesh and made me feel suddenly lonely. I floated off into my own thoughts, staring at the same ceiling that Rita Huelga was staring at. There was a lot of timber stretching across it, but a sideways glance at Rita Huelga let me know that architecture wasn't exactly what was on her mind.

I drew the nasty, bitter smoke deep inside me. It made my head spin for a moment. I lost myself back in thought, in the narratives that always play themselves out in the ceilings, when you're smoking a cigarette, when you've just been royally fucked by someone you just met. But silence and cigarettes only serve their purpose for so long. Eventually, someone has to say something, and that someone was going to be me. And maybe, just maybe, sex would be a way to begin.

"Hey, Dr. Huelga."

Her eyes came back reluctantly, but landing on mine, she smiled, little happy lines forming at the corners of her eyes when she saw my face. Rita Huelga, in her off moments, knew how to glow. Even if she couldn't talk about the hard stuff.

"Yes?"

"How *did* you come to be on that television program?"

"I thought two hundred and fifty thousand dollars for the center was a great idea."

"You didn't think Audra Léon would be there?"

"Not for a second."

"That's the only reason?"

"I call it two hundred and fifty thousand reasons. And one in seven women getting breast cancer."

"One in seven?"

"Yeah, it depends how you skew the numbers."

"I'll bet."

"It's an environmental issue, Emma. Top secret."

"Like your feelings for Audra Léon? I don't think there exists two hundred and fifty thousand reasons to ruin your love affair with Audra."

"No?"

"You'd rather mortgage your house and give the center the money yourself. I think there was one reason. One big reason, bigger than a quarter of a million dollars."

"You can believe whatever you like." The tone was cold.

"Hey, I didn't mean to open any wounds." I put my hand

on hers. Warmth to cold dampness. I squeezed her palm, fingers stroking her arm.

"I don't have any wounds, Emma. And you ask a lot of questions, you know that?"

"I know the saying 'Butch on the streets and femme between the sheets.' "

"I've heard that."

"Dr. Huelga, I think you're the real item."

"Femme between the sheets?"

"Hardly."

Silence.

"Your long tresses don't fool me a bit. You're as butch as they come."

She snorted and stubbed out her cigarette, turned over, and held me in her arms, exploring my face with her eyes, with her fingers.

"You have all those butch qualities, Rita."

"Such as?"

"The strong, silent type, for starters."

"Think so, do you?"

"And you're probably possessive as hell, jealousy on wheels, and loyal to a fault. Your brain races as fast as your heart, but it's a real project getting in there."

Silence.

"Tell me I'm right. You don't take your clothes off making love to me."

"Like that, do you?"

"Maybe. You're one fabulous top."

Smiles and more silence. Other than that, she didn't move a muscle.

"Well, what do you think?"

"If I'm a real butch, I wouldn't say, would I?"

And so she kissed me again, saying softly, "I think you're still in love with Frances."

Rita Huelga, Dr. Rita Huelga, gives the complete exam,

keeps you in good health, and only once has she given away a vital secret. And that secret destroyed the greatest love she had ever had. And supposedly wounded her beyond repair. But as far as I could tell, Dr. Rita Huelga was in perfect working order. When she was finished with me, she turned over and gave me a kiss good-bye. She closed her eyes, slowly but finally, and fell asleep, sans cigarette.

And that was that.

I pulled on my jeans, grateful not to be the only naked person in the room anymore. I ran my hand over the soft velour collar of Rita Huelga's shirt. She twitched lightly in the beginning of her sleep. Well, that was a good way to leave the client, I told myself, full of bull and bravado. The mistress of the manor would sleep, and I would make sure the fort was safe from attack. I would make sure the journalists had all been tucked into their mobile units and motels for the evening. I would brave the chill evening air and check for footprints at the bottom of the trellis.

Despite my intentions, I felt phony. I may be calling myself a bodyguard, but Rita Huelga had wanted my body and had taken it with supreme confidence. She'd never even allowed me a turn, and in doing so had touched something deeply hidden inside myself. Something that perhaps she'd taken with her into dreamland. And maybe she could curl around that certainty and come up with some words that would explain how she came to tell her heart's secret on the *Johnny Lever Show*. How much money she stood to make with TKTK1477, and how angry her colleagues at Berkeley were about that. How soon I could meet and interview her maid Mariposa. And how often she had seen Audra Léon and who had known about it. And how did she feel about a bodyguard? And maybe even how did she feel about me?

At least, that's the kind of thoughts that I was thinking as I pulled on my leather jacket and walked into the night air. There were a few dog owners carrying their requisite plastic

bags. I checked the deadbolt to the front door. Beautiful hardware, but outdated. Rose had girl grease monkeys who were
pretty good at making security devices look invisible when
they compromise the aesthetic.

I was cheering myself with these happy thoughts as I
looked into the inky blackness that was the Pacific meeting
the sky. I was giving no thought to any real danger that Rita
Huelga might be in. That's how good a bodyguard I was
being, that's how good I had been fucked. More concerned
with the facade of Rita Huelga's house than I was with the
plain fact in front of me, I almost didn't notice it. I bent down
and put my fingers on the fine sod.

Kitty Litter on the lawn. Either some cat had escaped or
someone had dragged a big bag of shit through the landscape
on their way to climb the trellis to Rita Huelga's bedroom.

The earth at the base of the trellis had been carefully
combed. A row of brown leaves had been scraped up against
the concrete. Someone had covered up their footprints. I
looked at the trellis. A few of the lattices were broken, pulled
out as if someone had used it as a ladder. There were also
broken rungs underneath the window, but none in between.

I remembered how tidy Rita Huelga was. The laboratory
conditions of her kitchen. "I always keep this door bolted so
the litter isn't tracked through the house," she had said. And
the criminal, the criminal who knew her so well, had been
considerate of this household requirement. They had broken
into the Kitty Litter closet and graciously had climbed a trellis with a bag of cat shit to avoid tracking the litter through
the house. Such etiquette from a criminal/maniac fan/gangster
husband! It made me think that maybe, just maybe, there
hadn't been anybody at all.

But I didn't have a lot of time to think about that because
my pager bleeped into an explosion of noise at my hip. I
looked at the number and walked slowly back to the house. I

was still hot between my legs, and it was not an altogether uncomfortable feeling. That was, until I answered my page.

"Emma." Rose Baynetta's voice had an undertone of dread, the kind of dread you only hear in the early hours of the morning. "I have some bad news. Gale Petros died an hour ago in the hospital. Her liver failed. After having dinner with her mother and Audra Léon at her mother's apartment."

"Gee, that's too bad." My neutral tone sounded disinterested. I wasn't. I was wondering what kind of plot twists this was going to throw into the mix, into my life. Guilty for this selfishness, I waited to hear what more Rose would say.

"No, girlfriend, it's *really* too bad. It seems that what killed Gail Petros was a penchant for wandering in the woods followed by some gourmet cooking. She picked some of those deadly white mushrooms, just like the Sebastiani kid. Spaghetti ai tartufi, that's what killed Gail Petros. Does our Dr. Huelga grow bad mushrooms at home?"

Rose let the news filter through my brain.

"I'm not a mycologist; how would I know?"

"Well I hope you didn't have a pizza fungi while on duty."

"Very funny, girlfriend."

"The good doctor could be in a lot more trouble than we thought. The TV talk show would be just the appetizer."

"What are you saying?"

"Rita Huelga might want to get hold of a lawyer. Want me to call Willie?"

Willie Rossini was a criminal defense attorney with whom Rose and I worked from time to time. My brain was turning with the necessary steps. "No, don't call Willie. Not yet." For one thing, it was too late to call the criminal defense lawyer who kept threatening retirement. And it looks really bad when suspects get lawyered up too quickly. For what it was worth, *I* was still on the job. But the terms of the gig were changing quickly. Perhaps they had already been changed. No matter how airtight an alibi Rita Huelga might have—and with her lonely lifestyle, she didn't have much of a chance of one—she was definitely going to be under suspicion for murder.

Because Gail Petros and Audra Léon lived in Los Angeles and didn't spend a lot of time wandering the forests in pursuit of mushrooms. And the liver of Gail Petros had surely been destroyed by the powerful toxins of *Amanita phalloides,* the white death cap.

That put a whole different light on things. That and the way someone went to a lot of trouble to make it look like a person had broken into Dr. Huelga's house by way of the trellis. And the spill of dirt underneath the delicate elfin buds, which had been snatched off one of Dr. Huelga's carts in the basement. I thought again about the delicate white bell she had held in her hand. Then I grabbed my *Mushroom Field Guide* and descended into the basement. Pretty though they might be, the mushroom tray that had been disturbed was not growing chantarelles.

Out of the sawdust grew white-headed, innocuous, but deadly *Amanita phalloides.* The white death caps. The ones that Dr. Rita Huelga had said that Mariposa used to make spaghetti sauce; the ones that Dr. Huelga said were chantarelles.

"I hope you didn't have a pizza fungi while on duty," Rose had joked. I wasn't about to write this down in my report: Dr. Huelga hadn't bothered to feed the bodyguard, she was too busy distracting her by bedding her and discovering her G spot.

Rita Huelga had lied to me about the mushrooms in the basement. Why, if she was busy curing cats, was she growing *Amanita phalloides?* Meanwhile, Gale Petros, Rita Huelga's romantic rival for a decade, had died a horrible and painful death.

CHAPTER
EIGHT

POSTSHOW DISAPPOINTMENT

There are two main poisons that work to kill those who have ingested the *Amanita phalloides,* the death cap mushroom: amanitan, which works slowly and causes hypoglycemia in the victim, and the second poison, phalloidin, which acts quickly to destroy the liver, kidneys, and cardiac muscles. There is no known antidote. It's not a pretty way to go.

Gale Petros probably became nauseous six hours after being served the deadly pasta. By that time, the phalloidin had destroyed a great deal of her liver. The bloody diarrhea would have terrified her, warning that she wasn't just coming down with the flu. She would confide to Audra that she wasn't feeling well. Then she would have been felled by extreme, gut-wrenching stomach pains.

By that time, her mother would have been screaming and calling 911. The local poison center. The ambulance.

An unquenchable thirst would then manifest itself. As Gale lay upon the bed, Audra Léon would be calming her, wiping her forehead with a cool cloth. The three of them would have gotten into the ambulance together. Gale would have remained painfully conscious almost to the end.

131

Nurses and doctors would have pumped her stomach. Long, lucid intervals in the ambulance, in the emergency room gave them time to say good-bye. The famous pop star would have looked into eyes suddenly yellowed by jaundice. Severe dehydration would have meant it was only a matter of time before Gale's potassium level would cause cardiac arrest. Audra Léon would push the copper pageboy back behind her ears as she watched the poisons play out, until Gale fell into the final coma from which she would never awake.

"Emma, are you still there?" Rose Baynetta's voice had an undertone of dread for four in the morning. "How are things going?"

"Fine. Just fine. I think there's a lot of security work here that could be done." My voice was dull. "But I don't think that will be on the top of the list of problems."

"No, I don't think so. Good luck, girlfriend."

"Thanks, Rose, for lobbing this one into my court."

"Don't make me feel like I owe you, Emma."

"Nobody owes me anything, Rose. It's a friendship thing." There was a small air of resignation as we hung up.

I went outside. I studied the lawn, the half-broken lattices. Walking purposefully toward the trellis, my feet danced into the dirt with dread. And then I replicated the work of the supposed vandal. Eyes closed, I reached for each lattice. At six feet and one forty-five, the lightweight pieces of lathe peeled off in my hands. It was like climbing a mandarin orange. By the time I reached the window, the trellis looked like a huge cat had gotten its claws in, using it for a scratching post, shredding it to bits. I climbed into Rita's bedroom, trailing a lot of dirt underneath her windowsill that hadn't been there before. Then I took off my shoes.

"Why Regis and Kathie Lee Don't Speak!" "Talk Show Wars!" "Johnny Lever Did the Dirt on Audra!" "Oprah Defends Her Friend against Invasion of Privacy!" flashed at me from the table by the fireplace. I tiptoed in my socks down the deep carpeting, quiet as a cat or a cat burglar.

By the time I'd reached Rita Huelga, she had fallen into the heavy sleep of the deepest dreams. Her clothed figure twisted in the sheets. She had thrown off the mirror coverlet. The room was warm. I opened the small diamond pane window and let in the sea air. I watched as the draft found her green velour T-shirt. A tongue came out and licked her dry lips and, without moving her head, she opened her eyes. Her arms spread in an invitation of green velour, an invitation to an embrace that would have felt a lot nicer twenty minutes ago. The smell of sea air was woven into the room. It was as sweet an invitation as I had ever had, and I was going to turn it down.

"I'm dressed," I said stupidly, and something in that sentence seemed to change everything after that.

"I can see." The arms closed, and the coverlet was drawn quickly up to her shoulders. "Your hands are scratched," she said simply. Her eyes held a question; she knew, in the way that people like Rita Huelga knew, that something had irrevocably changed between us. The deep, brown depths in her eyes would never be the same once I delivered the news. And perhaps, if I was doubly lucky tonight, she wouldn't kill the messenger.

"Gail Petros died of acute liver poisoning at four-thirty A.M. at Los Angeles General Hospital. Her liver failed after eating a spaghetti sauce apparently made with death cap mushrooms."

"Maria, Madre de Dios!" She turned over on the bed, hiding her face. Her hands moved automatically to her stomach.

"She was at her mother's house. With Audra."

We waited. The clock ticked.

"Apparently, Audra doesn't like mushrooms."

Silence.

"Rita?"

"Yes?"

"You would have known that Audra didn't like mushrooms."

"Yes." The answer was slow but sure, mouth muffled by the pillow. "So?"

"And Gale's mother wasn't hungry. Want to turn over and talk about it?"

"No."

"Get over it, Rita."

"Why?"

"Better me than the cops."

"Cops?"

"They'll be here soon enough."

Rita's backside shuddered. "I don't have anything to say."

"Good. Just keep that line for when the inspector calls you." I sighed. "In the meantime, I have a few questions I'd like to ask you."

"Not now, baby."

Baby?

"I can help you more if I have some information. Who has keys to your laboratory? How long do the poisons remain toxic after the mushrooms are picked?"

"Emma, I'm too tired." She turned over and a soft palm came to my cheek. "Hey, you've got a little infection in your earlobe. An allergic reaction to nickel?"

"We need to talk about—"

"Mariposa has something for it. An ointment from Brazil—"

"Gale's dead, Rita. You should think about getting a lawyer."

Sigh from the pillow. "I know. I know." Resignation, not despair. "I have to think. But I can't think without sleeping. Really." She reached for the small decanter with the dark green liquid in it. She poured the liquid into a tiny shot glass, took a deep breath and threw it down her throat. "We'll talk later, gorgeous. Just—just guard me tonight, okay?" She put the shot glass on the shelf with finality. "Stay here until Mariposa wakes up!" A kiss was blown from the pillow. Huelga turned over, pulled the coverlet over her clothes. I wondered if she always slept in her jeans. I wondered how she could sleep after hearing about Gale.

"Mariposa is up at six-thirty. She'll see you out."

And so I was dismissed.

Downstairs, I scrubbed my hands in the powder room, keeping the door open. A ceramic-handled nail brush did a job on my fingernails and I borrowed a toothbrush I found in the drawer. I peeled off my clothes and took a fast French washcloth bath. Turning off the tap, I listened to the silence of the big house. Clocks ticked in the cavernous rooms of the house, marking slow minutes before I could leave. I thought I heard cats mewing in the distance as I pulled on the silk boxer shorts Rita Huelga had made such short work of. It would be a long time before I could leave the service of the Queen of Cats; I was feeling less like the Queen's consort than her lackey. Emma Victor, at your service, a good fuck and gets rid of all the nasty evidence afterward.

I perused the papers on the dining room table. There were a lot of drawings of molecules with arrows and number/letter combinations. The bank of file cabinets were locked. A green blotter with gold embossed leather siding held a calendar. October: Board Meeting, Finance Committee Meeting. Fashion at the Plaza, Lunch with Ina. That would be Ina Cho, the haute couture designer. Rita had no plans for Halloween, but was expecting a delivery the day before.

It wasn't all that much for a month. Rita stayed home a lot, working. She kept her calendar clean. An assortment of business cards and shopping lists were tucked under the leather sides: Baynetta Security Services; UCSF, Helga

Meyers, Oncology; Bevin Crosswell, the *Johnny Lever Show;* Markoff Pest Control.

I pried up one end of the calendar to see if there were any plans for November.

There was a black X, scrawled violently on November 3. The mark was so big, so final, that I found myself holding my breath. There were no notations after November 3. Rita kept a clean calendar, but November was an empty month. I tucked the corner of October back into the leather side. The blotter slid over the slick table and a white triangle appeared at the corner. A piece of paper was hidden there, a very legal, unpleasant piece of paper. Rita Huelga was being summoned to appear in court. The plaintiff was Consortium Bell-Worless.

So Rita was in trouble with her boss. Was that the reason why she was so careful to have me sign the release? My client was looking less and less viable. She was in trouble from all directions, it seemed. And yet, she lay upstairs, sleeping like a baby.

The television and VCR were hidden in more heavy-timbered furniture in the living room. Maybe there were more answers there. I popped the video into the machine and fast forwarded through the interview with Rita Huelga, the attack on Johnny Lever, and five minutes of commercials. I wasn't interested in commercials. I was interested in Johnny Lever's guests, the ones that followed Rita Huelga. I let the tape run until the silver blue curtains parted for the next guest, the premier piercer of the premier piercing parlor of San Francisco. It was a familiar face because it belonged to the man who had put a hole in my nose. It *was* Thad.

Once I had needed some information about one of Thad's clients. Insisting that I avail myself of his services, I had followed Thad into his piercing parlor. In fact, he'd used the piercing as a ruse to give a friend time to get away. He'd been more loyal to his customers then. He had also put a diamond in my nose. It was that or lose an eyeball. I got him back by nearly stapling his balls together, but that was a long time ago. Thad had moved up. The piercer of plebeians as well as movie stars, he no longer wore his body art uniform. He now sported a black linen suit with patent leather shoes, Thad waved at the audience as he told about how Audra Léon had come to the Gambit to have her piercing work done. He sounded like a doctor describing a presidential heart bypass, talking about the elective body enhancement. The camera did close-ups of audience faces, twisting in their seats with squeamish delight. What was it like to have a cold needle inserted through that most sensitive, erogenous organ?

The part of the interview that interested me was that Thad managed to plug his new business. He wasn't in the piercing parlor anymore but had opened up a florist shop in the Castro. Thad even managed to mention the name of his new venture: Wilde Flowers.

Wilde Flowers. I had passed by the window with its strange dried arrangements like abstract paintings. Nothing for the mainstream dinner table, but national coverage was worth a lot. Wilde Flowers. Wasn't it referred to as "the House of Moss and Sticks"? Was that why Thad was appearing on the television program? To plug his new venture? I looked at his tiny eyes glittering in the camera.

More commercials and the generals of the Lesbian Revengers appeared. "It is the obligation of public figures to come out. And if they won't come out, we will *shove* them out!"

I remembered the *Bay Area Reporter* article. General Gertrude wasn't so happy with Johnny Lever anymore.

"Hoo! Hoo! Hoo!"

Johnny Lever laughed and stilled them with a hand. Before cutting to a commercial, he managed to slip in a few promises to his audience: Tomorrow's show would feature a few grisly Halloween tales about razor blades in apples.

I looked at my watch. Five-thirty, the hour of the wolf, the darkest just before the dawn. I perused the scanty collection of videotapes; Rita was not a tube viewer. A few commercial releases, *Beauty and the Beast*, *Night of the Hunter*, and a series of National Geographic specials on—what else?—the plants and animals of the Amazon. There were a number of Pam Grier films, the first black female action figure. I wouldn't have minded passing the hours with the over-the-top action sequences that featured Pam's muscles bent on victory.

But there were a few surprises. One video was labeled, "To Rita—from Tyrone who loves you too!" That was generous. Way too generous. I slipped the video into the machine and saw why the would-be rap star was doomed to failure.

He couldn't remember his rap. The hood of the big sweatshirt covered his face and most of his features, only a craggy nose caught the light. Baggy pants flowed over tennis shoes. The lyrics were full of *cunt* and *whore* and *pussy,* when he could remember the words. He couldn't sing. He couldn't dance. The blurry black and white technique that defined the style of music videos didn't do much for his sex appeal, either. He sang his bottom-of-the-chart song from the top of the building, all alone in Los Angeles. All except for Audra Léon. Tyrone Warren was just one of a long line of Hollywood hopefuls who'd married fame and hoped that it rubbed off. It hadn't. He wouldn't like the thought that Audra's heart belonged to Gale Petros. Or Rita Huelga.

One video was labeled, *Entertainment Today*. I slipped it into the machine, it began with a gurgle and threw a television image on the screen, a segment from tabloid television journalism. Two blow-dried puppets were burbling on about Audra Léon and her feud with Madonna.

"But back to Audra, Rob. We have a videotape of an exclusive interview with Audra Léon and Madonna—"

"That was a historic moment in TV broadcasting for sure! The rich and famous can always air their dirty laundry in public and get the headlines a publicist can only dream of."

"You better believe it! Let's watch!"

The camera showed Madonna in a teal blue silk dress. Her right breast was just visible from the chosen camera angle. The star was furious in a black net bra. "I wouldn't waste a moment's time on Audra Léon. What has she done for charity? We're in the middle of a crisis in this country, and all she does is build bigger houses and garages for all her boyfriend's cars. If he *is* her boyfriend!"

Audra Léon's brown eyes sparkled black as she shot back from her living room on the other side of L.A.

"Madonna is revolting! I am a wife—" Audra protested, her pageboy flipping back and forth, grazing her cheeks.

"Oh Audra, you should stop going on about your domestic bliss. Launching a bad singer's career into the dumps. You didn't do him any favors. And you didn't do anyone a favor with that commercial for Bell-Worless!" I seemed to recall an Audra Léon commercial for a diet drug.

"That's none of your business, Madonna! You're just jealous because you pick up all the scripts I turn down! Well, you can have the truly trashy parts, my dear. They suit your voice!"

Madonna curled a highly colored lip. "Join the world, Audra."

"Whose world, Madonna? I'm not drooling for a sound bite. Just like my private life, Madonna, my philanthropic pursuits are my own business."

"No kidding. The La Leche League selling Audra Léon nursing bras?" Madonna sniped.

At that, Audra Léon strolled toward the lens, her long,

black-clad legs like a praying mantis. She must have pulled the camera cord, because all went black on the screen.

"Well, screw you, too!" Madonna screamed. Then she went black, too.

"That's the stars for you!" one puppet said. "They lead dramatic and volatile lives, don't they, Jim?"

The tape cut to static, the moment was over. I looked at my watch. A half hour, and I could go. I reached over to stop the VCR. But the tape flickered for a moment, and I watched a very bootlegged copy of Audra Léon's marriage to Tyrone Warren.

It was a civil ceremony, in a setting that looked like Las Vegas. There was a big black smear on the edges; perhaps the lens had been hidden under a coat.

The minister was a tall white man who was mumbling, pursing and licking his lips. Only the backs of the married couple were visible; Audra wore a cream lace cat suit. Tyrone Warren was a bad singer and worse dancer. But he had no trouble slipping a ring on the hand of the woman who would try, without success, to launch his career. It was a moment with very little sentiment until Tyrone grabbed Audra by the shoulders and suddenly started chewing on her mouth. Audra laughed and the minister said, "I now pronounce you man and wife," and the tape went blank. Probably some paparazzi had made his mortgage on the bootlegged images. I remembered seeing a segment of the wedding on one of the *Entertainment Today* segments.

I would be able to catch a few hours of sleep before I made it out to the avenues. I said good-bye to Mariposa, who appeared silently at the living room door, a pale smile on her lightly freckled face. She wore a flowing lavender cotton dress, gathered at the midriff, and a big purple bow on a ponytail. Her eyes were stony with sleep, and she rubbed them with strong but bony hands.

"Good night," she murmured. And then, "I mean good

morning!" A small laugh dropped out of her mouth like a pearl. Such an innocent mistake. I looked back. The smile was still there, hanging, a bit silly, stuck on her face.

"Bye."

Emma Victor leaves another night of work. Sleep would be a wonderful thing. And Rita Huelga, I was sure, would keep close-mouthed for another twenty-four hours, giving me more nap time. I wanted to see if any bad luck had befallen any of the other guests who had appeared on the *Johnny Lever Show* on October 11. I would start with Thad. The little rat had sprung himself out of body art and become a flower child. Wilde Flowers. I was so intent on my mission, I almost didn't notice the Ford LeSabre that followed me to the Castro and lost me somewhere around the corner of sixteenth and Noe.

My house looked fresh, with its new coat of white paint and extra gilding on the columns. The masseuses were still asleep. And I would have just enough time to take a short nap before I headed out to the avenues.

CHAPTER NINE

HOUSE OF MOSS
AND STICKS

Noon, and things were hardly hopping west of Twin Peaks.
Senior citizens were sweeping the streets, but none of them
lived at 1618 Thirty-fourth Avenue, and none of them wore
crutches. The curtains had been drawn. And then one of the
residents returned, pulling a wire cart up from the Portola
Valley shopping area.

A woman in her latish sixties, her posture showed early
signs of osteoporosis. The dowager's hump effect was
heightened as she bent down to pull the cart loaded with groceries. Mowing that lawn must have given the Pendrinskis
a big appetite. She was wearing a pink mohair coat, an
Easter leftover from twenty years ago. It was held closed
against the ocean chill with three big saucer buttons. The
wardrobe of the elderly; the Pendrinskis could use a little
extra cash, as could most Social Security recipients. The big
brown bags jostled as she shuffled up the walk. Three concrete steps posed a challenge. She parked the cart on the two
legs opposite the wheels. She grabbed the skinny iron railing and hauled herself up the stairs. A key on a long, frayed,
red ribbon emerged from her pocket and slipped into the

lock. Before she had a chance to turn the key in the lock, the door opened. I got out my binoculars, focused the right, then left eye. I got my Minox camera with the telephoto lens ready at my side.

Mr. Pendrinkski, I presumed. A half-shaven man stood in the doorway with two crutches under his arms. He poked his head out the doorway and looked back and forth, up and down the street. His eyes probably couldn't even see my car or the magnified eyes that watched him. Pendrinkski scowled with the effort of opening up the door. He emerged slowly on his crutches out to the doorstep. The woman, whoever she was, tipped the cart back on its wheels and pulled it up each concrete step. Pendrinkski waited and watched her effort without a change of expression. Eventually, the cart landed on the top stair. The woman hauled the top bag off the cart. I could see long tubes of white, wrapped in cellophane. Pendrinkski stretched an arm out over his crutches. He took a bag that looked fairly lightweight. Hugging the toilet paper or paper towels in his left arm, keeping the crutch carefully under his armpit, he held the door open. The woman in the pink mohair coat hobbled with the heaviness of her load. Pendrinkski held the door open, and Mrs. Pink Mohair Coat shuffled inside, dragging the cart behind her. I could see him lean over on his crutches to give her rouged cheek a kiss. It was hardly the face of evil.

I took a good, hard look at the couple. They weren't going to be splashed across the front page of the paper in some insurance scam. Were they dining on cat food, lowest in price and highest in protein, the only affordable diet for many of our senior citizens in the land of the free? The Pendrinkskis were hardly bottom feeders, the predators of the criminal subculture. A mass murderer probably lived down the street, working on his car on the weekend, taking the wife and kiddies out for a drive. And I was laying in wait for the elderly couple to make a mistake.

I watched those crutches, lodged firmly under the armpits. Pendrinkski stuck his head out the door once she was in. He took a second look up and down the street, and closed the door. I wondered if they were eating day-old bread and overly ripe produce. There was something tender and sad about the couple.

Elderly people, frightened of the coming years, cold and hungry. And willing to commit fraud. This wasn't such a great gig, either. For two hours, I watched the little bungalow in which two lives played themselves out. And maybe tried to play Guaranteed All Risk Insurance. I filled out my report for Mr. Fremont and stashed the camera and binoculars back in their cases. All the venetian blinds were closed. Maybe the mohair coat was off, and they were putting the groceries and paper products in the cupboard.

I pulled away from the curb and drifted up Nineteenth Avenue, thinking thoughts about Rita Huelga. The thoughts weren't comforting, as my legs grew weak with remembering her practiced hands deep inside me, and how my feet had slipped on her wooden trellis. Intertextual spectator-participant relationship, indeed.

I wondered what kind of trouble she was in with Consortium Bell-Worless. I vaguely remembered that Bell-Worless had been accused of jacking up prices of some of the more expensive protease inhibitors.

Afternoon in the Castro, and another nightmare parking day. Ever since the F line, with its historical trolley cars, had been put into use, tourists were roaming the Castro. A fantastic fleet of streetcars could take you back in time, as well as to the Castro. You could ride the Brooklyn Blue-Green & Silver, hanging onto the original leather handholds, which swung down from the ceiling. A Philadelphia Silver and Cream would carry tourists in the silence of perfectly tuned air-electric motors. A prewar Chicago Green Hornet could take a few dozen old-timers back to 1933, as well as to Gaylandia. Times changed and also never changed at all.

Lesbian couples with babies in backpacks were ogled by Midwesterners in windbreakers. Market Street was expanding, gay businesses were booming, right down to Octavia Street where the seven-million-dollar Lesbian and Gay Center was soon to break ground. Pozole's served low-fat Mexican food in a decor of Madonnas. Skeletons were dancing merrily as they did every day at Pozole's, their highly muscled waiters in white T-shirts wove among them, oblivious to the contrast. Day of the Dead was coming up, right after Halloween. I didn't see how the little streets could support the crowds during the Last Halloween in the Castro.

Rainbow flags flew from every pole; tourists turned their heads to watch the flapping banners and bought tickets to the matinee at the Castro Theatre. I found a spot on "Sixteenth, across from Café Flor and hiked up past Earthtones, with its fashionable baubles, and the Market Street Gym, where we developed our muscles.

I put the black fedora on my head. Two gaudy clip-on earrings, the kind I never wore, clamped on my earlobes, one of which was still tender. I checked the mirror and drew fire-engine-red lipstick across my lips. Hopefully, this facial display would distract Thad from the sight of one of his past projects: the small diamond couched in the corner of my nose had been his handiwork. It was a hostage situation I didn't want to repeat.

Just past the vitamin store, two tourists stood in front of the window of Wilde Flowers. It was worth the view. The window sported flora and fauna of dreams and nightmares and strange fantasies that never would have occurred to those in the floral business in Peoria. It was a strange tableau, spotlights flickering on the floral set, almost like a television.

A strange and deadly chandelier hung in the window:

glass shards were cleverly strung in tiers, with tiny stainless steel blades that glinted in the sunlight. Monkey ladder, the strange vine from the Philippines, twisting throughout, like the brown arm of a Balinese dancer. But that was only the beginning. Spanish moss hung off the postmodern lighting fixture, bright orange Japanese lanterns dotted the dark green fungus. Underneath the chandelier, a sparkling array of autumn provided a carpet for a wedding cake that only a mycologist could appreciate. The cake, if you could call it that, was a three-tiered affair, carpeted entirely of living lichen: a chartreuse wedding confection that would never be eaten. Bright red pods replaced sugar roses and draped seaweed ribbons would look edible only to the Addams family. Wilde Flowers: Where the Customer Is Always Queer.

"Landsakes, that's the strangest thing I've ever seen, Marge."

"Can you imagine serving such a thing?"

"I don't think it's meant to eat, dear."

"No. No, it couldn't be edible—" The woman looked nervously up and down Market Street. Fine young specimens of manhood were emerging from the weight room, muscling gym bags over their shoulders. "They wouldn't eat—"

Clang! Clang! A green and white Kansas City trolley floated up the street.

"Let's go get some ice cream."

"I think . . ." The man rubbed the stubble on his chin. "I think they only have frozen yogurt, dear."

"That would be just fine." The woman sniffed at the window. "Let's keep walking, okay?"

I watched the couple lumber up the street.

The shop was dark behind the strange window display. I made ready to enter the store, pulling my fedora over my head, brushing my hair over my forehead into a fringe of bangs.

The visual interior of the shop was as expected. The

bright leaves of autumn covered the floor. A young man squinted through bottle-thick glasses, perched atop a ladder. He was clipping the thorns off a forbidding cactus whose accomplishment was a three-foot-high orange bloom at its top. Stellated spines, each bundle bearing more spines, were accompanied by needle-sharp bristles emerging from a tuft of wool decorating the fleshy spine. A long counter graced the right wall, covered with half-finished floral arrangements, birds of paradise and other tropical flowers emerging out of shallow basins of water filled with flat, black stones. An array of small shears and large garden loppers lay agape, their jaws still clenching leaves and twigs.

On the left, a large florist's refrigerator, seven feet high, twelve feet long, took up most of the wall. The large cooler was half empty. What flowers were there held the normal floral sentiments: long-stemmed red roses, gladiolus from Mexico, and the ever-present, pedestrian mums in foil-wrapped containers. Pots of fall-blooming crocuses in topaz, pink, and coral were clustered on the floor like precious gems.

A crash came from the back, and a strangled, frustrated sound that might have been *"Shit!"* filled the store. A tall window overlooking the retail area had been fitted with one-way glass; the noise came from a small, open doorway. The man on the ladder blinked behind the thick glasses but otherwise didn't break his rhythm of clipping the thorns off the monstrous cactus.

"Can I help you?" Seemingly oblivious to the problems in the back, Ladder Boy climbed down carefully from the ladder. Cactus thorns as big as screwdrivers crunched under his shoes as he landed on the floor. He put the shears down on the counter among a little pile of pruned lichen and leaves.

"Don't you think that's a rather dangerous floor display?" I indicated the cactus, a monster with flailing arms of needles.

"Fuck!" came from the back. Ladder Boy's smile didn't falter as he approached me with a display of perfect dentures. "That's why I'm trying to take the thorns out." He was exasperated. "It's a Viscountess Maynard's Great Flowering Cereus."

"You guys just can't leave mother nature alone, can you?"

"Art is not an imitation of nature. Now, can I help you?" he repeated, coming a little too close for normal salesperson distance. I realized he was peering almost painfully through his glasses to examine my face.

I approximated the tones of grief. "Something for a—a funeral—"

"Yes, of course." Ladder Boy was immediately and cautiously sympathetic. "I think I have just the thing." Gently ushering me past the cooler, I saw a display for the bereaved. An oval gilt frame housed a smoky mirror hung with black crepe. The display was positively ghoulish, as was the reflection served up to me in the scratched and worn silver of the mirror. A tall woman in a black fedora and truly hideous earrings with a slash of red mouth was wondering just what would be appropriate for the murdered mate of a highly closeted rock star. The diamond in my nose was hardly noticeable.

"May I suggest the Desert Willow?"

A tiny tree grew out of a flat black marble pot, dripping narrow, willowlike leaves. Narrow seed pods hung like sad Christmas tree ornaments off the threadlike branches. The tree survived in a layer of white sand. Tiny obsidian rocks, arranged like tombstones at its base, created a miniature desert tableau.

"The tree can be kept like this, bonsai-pruned, or it can be planted in the ground."

"Hmm. I was thinking of something more traditional," I said.

Ladder Boy sighed, and squinting, seemed to peruse my earrings.

"Something like a big wreath, something that could be displayed on an *easel.*"

"Ah." Ladder Boy adjusted his expression to hide a look of horror. "You want to make a floral *statement.*"

"Goddamn it to hell!" came from the back.

"I can't be there for the funeral. It's in L.A."

"Yes, of course, of course."

"I want a lot of color, and—" I looked around me at the autumnal displays, so sparse, so minimal of cheer. "I want something *big.*"

"Do reconsider the desert willow. During the summer, it bears a succession of showy, funnel-shaped pink flowers in profuse terminal clusters. And, when planted, it can grow quite tall. Trees are always a comfort; they imply a kind of . . . eternity."

"Hmmm."

"Get in here, Frederick, would you *please*?" There was nothing polite in the request. The sound was unmistakably that of a bosses' hissy fit.

"Uh, would you excuse me, please?" Frederick disappeared, a smile strained his lips and a strange glitter entered his eyes.

"I'm ruined! Ruined!" I heard over Frederick's shoulder. The young man sighed and straightened up as he entered the back of the shop.

"There, there. It's okay."

"Okay? What do you mean, it's okay?"

"It's only flowers, Thad. We'll get another delivery."

"Not in time for Halloween," he moaned.

I drew closer and peered around the doorway.

"Don't worry, Thad!"

"Don't tell me not to worry, asshole. These tulips were flown in from Sydney!"

It was a strange sight. The former piercer was a despairing figure, draped over hundreds of flowers, all coated with a black goo that looked very much like roofing tar. Brilliant orange and red striped tulips, their fancy frilled edges the result of endless hybridization, sagged with the weight of heavy blobs of shiny black. A pot of lilies with harlequin checkered petals was just visible under the thick coating. Flaming shoots of Aztec lilies, their tongues permanently darkened with poison, were dying already. Thad held the stem of a fringed parrot tulip in his hands. He stroked the petals with paper towel, applying a solvent that I could smell from the doorway. The flower bent under the pressure and the weight of a shining glob of tar. Thad shook his head and looked like he was going to cry. "I've got a Halloween wedding. I have to have checkered lilies! Halloween is only three days away!"

"Maybe we could order from—"

"Nobody has these, you idiot! I've got an exclusive on the harlequin lily!"

"Let me call the customer—"

"No! No, you ass! It's for Carole Mig—"

Thad looked up, noticing, but not recognizing me. "What are you looking at?"

"Looks like thousands of dollars of destroyed flora," I said.

"Yeah, now Frederick will help you, I'm sure—" Thad turned his back.

"Looks like someone was trying to make a bad floral statement."

Something in my voice made him turn around.

"Who are you?"

"A regular customer of yours, Thad."

"I've never seen you in here before."

"I came to order a funeral arrangement."

"I suggested the Desert Willow," Frederick piped up, a perky employee.

"Yes, the Desert Willow is a frequent choice for memorials."

"It has to be shipped. Will it survive the trip?"

"We have a special arrangement with FedEx. Refrigerated transport, miss. Frederick will take care of you."

"Actually, you've already taken care of me. And someone has clearly taken care of *you.*"

"I don't know what you're talking about. Now Frederick—"

"That refrigerated truck will be making a trek up a long driveway. All the way to Audra Léon's front door."

"Who are you?" Thad dropped the tulip on the floor. Frederick shuffled nervously.

"Don't you recognize your handiwork when you see it? You've seen the white of my eyes when you put this diamond in my nose. Especially when you held your piercing gun to my temple, trying to protect a certain friend of yours, Gurl Jesus, escape. To her death, by the way."

Thad's expression faded as fast as the tulips behind him. I might have dropped a glob of tar on his mood.

"Emma Victor," he breathed.

I took off my hat. It was making my head too warm, anyway.

"You were a lot more loyal to Gurl Jesus than you were to Audra Léon," I reminded him.

"You can leave now, Frederick." Thad's tone was measured, careful. Frederick hesitated. "Go back into the shop, Frederick," Thad repeated, none too nicely. Frederick turned on his heel and slammed the door behind him. I watched him from behind the tinted glass as he mounted the ladder in front. Angrily, he attacked the ten-foot cactus again, pulling the big thorns off the stalk with a vengeance. The big red bloom at the top bobbed its head in disapproval.

"Looking at this mess, it seems like somebody isn't too happy with you, Thad."

"Nonsense. Vandals. It has nothing to do with—"

"No? Did they take any cash?"

"No. We always leave the register with the empty drawer, open, visible to the street. They broke in through the back window, off the alley. Besides, outing Audra is probably going to help her career. Look at what happened to Ellen DeGeneris."

"But that was her choice. Remember choice? That's what we're supposed to stand for. I'd say that someone is pretty angry about the fact that Audra Léon was outed on national television. They say her career has taken a dive. *Wet Kisses Only* is a box office bomb. No one believes her when she kisses Tom Clavier."

"No one believes anyone who kisses Tom Clavier."

"The latest is, Tyrone Warren has taken a powder, according to the *Enquirer*. The police have issued a grand jury subpoena, but they can't find him."

"Nonsense. This has nothing to do with Audra Léon. Lots of stores are being vandalized in the Castro, ever since the tourist trade started coming up Market Street on the historic streetcars."

"I wouldn't put this up to the tourists or the old streetcars. You see, strange things are happening to the people who appeared on the *Johnny Lever Show*. Bad things."

The little lips drew together. The forehead frowned, the loops threaded through eyebrows came together like café curtains.

"Like what?"

"Maybe it was bad karma to out Audra Léon, Thad. Maybe it was an old cosmic debt. Gurl Jesus's atonement."

"Don't guilt trip me, you— you—"

"I'd rather be a two-bit lady dick than a whore, Thad."

"It was time for Audra Léon to come out. Everybody

knows, anyway. It's been on the gay grapevine for years.
The tabloids have been charting the relationship with Gale
for years. It's disgusting the way Gale was always sitting at
the next table. In the backseat of the limousine."

"You knew Gale?"

"Of course. I pierced them both. It was time for Audra to
be outed."

"And you decided that you were the chosen messenger.
How much did Lever pay you?"

"Nothing, I tell you. Now, shut up. Shut up, and get out of
my store."

"It doesn't look like you're in a situation to turn away
business." The harlequin lilies were dead. Encapsulated in
tar, they looked like so many Milk Duds. "Like I said, I
came in for a funeral arrangement."

"A funeral arrangement. Fine. Go talk to Fred—" The jaw
slackened. "Who?"

"Just another friend of yours, Thad. Gale Petros died last
night. She died in a coma at 4:30 A.M.. A poison destroyed
her liver. They say it's a nasty way to go."

"What? No! Not Gale!" Thad breathed.

"Doesn't exactly make you glad that you outed Audra
Léon on national TV, does it?"

"How? How did she die? Was she doing drugs again?"

"No. Someone poisoned her. They did a bad job of making it look like an accident."

"What do you mean?"

"As far as I know, mushrooms don't flourish in LA."

"Mushrooms?"

"You're a florist, figure it out. *Amanita phalloides.*"

"Poison mushrooms?"

"Think again."

"Dr. Huelga——she poisoned—"

"A little obvious, wouldn't you say? Now, about that floral arrangement—I think I'll pass. The Desert Willow is just

a little too dreary for my tastes. But I wish you luck in your selection of the proper memento to send to Audra. It's better to send flowers with your regrets, your most grievous regrets, about Gale's death. It wouldn't be appropriate to show up at the funeral. Don't you think?"

I walked past the customers at the counter. There were a surprising number of females in the shop, usually filled with gay men. Two women, one husky, one frail, leaned over the counter. The slight woman had shaved her head and leaned heavily on the counter as if exhausted from the marathon of life's daily challenges. They both wore matching plaid jackets and golfing shoes. Frederick helped them, seemed to know that the customers just needed some white mums to feel better.

"Two bunches of those white chrysanthemums," the bald woman commanded, her pate peeking from under her cap. Other female customers, jocks, sling backs, and motorcycle boots, were on her heels. A minor amount of eye flickering and cruising took place. And then it was time to leave.

Back in the car, I took the earrings off and wiped the lipstick off my mouth. I watched the floral customers shuffle up the street with their wrapped bouquets of puffy white flowers, with the little cellophane bag of plant food stapled to the paper. The bald woman, the frail man. They knew what time it was. I knew exactly what time it was, too.

THE FUTURE OF
JOURNALISM

Back at home, my head was humming with theories, with lack of sleep. I turned on the television to soothe the thinking mechanism. Afternoon television offered its usual fare: *Now your teeth can become whiter than white!*

Had someone tried to set Rita Huelga up for murder? Someone clever, a childish egocentric, a man with masculinity problems, a Tyrone Warren? Someone with a highly distorted sense of personal reality and too much fidelity to the boss? Like Mariposa? Someone who felt omnipotent, due to their unique profession: talk television, which tears apart its victims for the sake of ratings, like Bevin Crosswell? Or Audra Léon? Murder maxim number one: always suspect the spouse first.

Try the new brown and crisp microwave bags!

Or had Rita Huelga herself made it look like a bad setup to make it seem like someone else had tried to frame her?

"You can cash in your life insurance today!"

The story wasn't simple. Utterly out of character, Dr. Huelga had appeared on national television to discuss her personal life, to betray someone she apparently loved very deeply. Dr. Huelga, a woman who didn't reveal the color of her socks without difficulty, let herself be seen by millions on the *Johnny Lever Show*. A woman who played her cards so close to her chest they might have been a vest. A woman who had made love to me and had never taken her clothes off.

"Entertainment Tonight!" blatted the television. "It's MaryAnne and Rob!"

"Good evening, ladies and gentlemen! I'm MaryAnne Taylor!"

"And I'm Rob Heron!"

It was the same blow-dried puppets who had set up the bitch fight between Audra Léon and Madonna.

"Tonight, we're going to take you to a wedding Hollywood style! Unlike the bootlegged video of Audra Léon's wedding, these are two movie stars who tied the knot in public. Loved that dress, Rob!"

"Can't wait to see it, MaryAnne! Wait—MaryAnne—this just in!" The reporter put his hand to his ear, pressing a microphone closer. Listening to the news, his expression changed, became grave. "Oh, no, this is a sad story, MaryAnne. Secretary of Audra Léon, Gale Petros, is dead this morning—"

"What?"

"Apparently, she ingested poisonous mushrooms—"

"Oh no!"

"Here's a picture from our files. . . ." The tube showed a picture of a dinner party, Audra Léon in the forefront raising a glass of champagne at the lens. Four seats away, an arrow pointed to a young woman who seemed to be examining a trout on her plate.

The reporter listened to the words in his ear and repeated to the television audience: "Gale Petros fell critically ill last night after unwittingly eating the *Amanita phalloides,* the poisonous death cap mushroom, in Los Angeles. Poison experts, noting that the deadly mushrooms proliferate every rainy season, warned Californians not to pick wild mushrooms because they can be so deadly."

"Wasn't there a death just last week from mushrooms?"

"Yes, a young boy." Rob listened to the words in his ear. "And last week, a fifty-three-year-old man from the Bay Area received a liver transplant after ingesting the poisonous fungus. He is still listed in critical condition. Gale Petros, unfortunately, was not so lucky. The deadly *Amanita phalloides* look alarmingly similar to the common mushrooms that are bought and cooked in every supermarket around America.

"What a tragedy!"

"Rob, do you remember a Dr. Rita Huelga of San Francisco recently appeared on television to talk about her relationship with Audra Léon? Dr. Huelga is a mycologist, a specialist in mushrooms. That's quite a coincidence, don't you think?"

"It certainly is, MaryAnne. Wait! Our correspondent, Clarissa Mullen, is at Dr. Huelga's San Francisco home right now. Let's see if we can get a picture."

A long shot of Rita Huelga's Tudor mansion showed its position on the hill and a lot of journalists hovering like vultures.

"Hi, MaryAnne and Rob. This is Clarissa Mullen. I'm standing outside the mansion of Rita Huelga. You remember that Dr. Huelga appeared on the *Johnny Lever Show* to talk about her relationship with Audra Léon? Not only did Dr. Huelga assault talk show host Johnny Lever, but she specializes in mushrooms, something that will indeed be of interest to the police. We have learned that Dr. Huelga raises the mushrooms here in her own house, carrying on experiments that may have promising results for cats who suffer from feline leukemia. Unfortunately, mushrooms led to the death of Gale Petros, who might be seen as a romantic rival for Audra Léon's affections."

Suddenly, the telephoto lens zoomed in so tight I could read the lettering above Rita Huelga's doorbell.

"That's right, Rob." Clarissa smiled grimly. "Last month, Dr. Huelga went on television to air her affair with the pop singer. Although Léon denied Dr. Huelga's accusations, rumors have persisted."

"MaryAnne, wait! More news." Rob's fingers flew to his ear again. "Tyrone Warren, Audra Léon's husband, has disappeared mysteriously. Although many say that the so-called rap artist likes to take off unexpectedly, it is unfortunate that he can't be with Audra Léon at this time of tragedy. Meanwhile, the funeral of Gale Petros will be held tomorrow. Audra Léon is sending her personal caterers, the Luncheonettes . . . although she can't be there herself. There's overdubbing to be done on *Wet Kisses Only.*"

"Yes, I hear the preview audiences weren't enthusiastic enough."

"The film, as they say, is ready to bomb. Let's hope that this tragedy won't hurt Léon's career."

"Once again, Gale Petros, secretary to Audra for ten years, dead from mushroom poisoning, ladies and gentlemen. Reminding us that nature can be deadly. Please be careful when you're out there on your nature hikes, folks. Doctors warn against eating any kind of mushroom not found in the grocery store. Even the experts have been fooled."

"We promise to keep you updated on this tragic story . . ."

And so human lives are found, filmed, and consumed; I aimed the remote and killed the tube. I communed with another tube, this one on my computer. Soon I was racing along the information highway. Waiting, waiting, for the computer screen to find the rest stop on the superhighway. Even with a fast computer, the Internet didn't thrill me. It was an informational tool. A data bank with a lot of freaky tellers. But most of all, the Internet reminded me of slow television.

Ah. A hit. The screen rolled in candy colors and a Luncheonette appeared. Pixelated pomegranates and food that looked more like flower sculptures. Whatever would a Luncheonette do for funereal workware? I logged off and put the computer to sleep. Which is what I should have been doing. But instead, I was thinking.

I was remembering the *Johnny Lever Show*. And the reluctant way Rita Huelga spoke in front of the studio audience. Rob and MaryAnne had it all wrong. The mystery started way before. Why did Rita Huelga go on television in the first place? What would have made her do such a thing?

Somebody, somewhere, owned Dr. Rita Huelga. Perhaps last month, perhaps long ago. A summons to appear in court, a moment she described with a big X on her calendar, couldn't be making her life any easier.

Somebody somewhere was closing in, someone who had a life ruined by Thad, by Dr. Huelga, by the *Johnny Lever Show*. Someone who was a very active *spectator-participant*.

I consulted my uniform closet in the basement. All the drag possibilities that Rose would have applauded waited there: the tuxedo, the three-piece suit, the morning coat with long gray tails like swallows. In another mode, the vampire cape lined with crimson silk pressed up against my split-gender costume. The dress was still cut in half and basted onto the suit. I never undid my handiwork, despite the impossibility of wearing the costume again. Beyond costumes were rows of carefully starched and pressed uniforms in filmy dry cleaner bags: prim Nurse Nancy garb, complete with name tag and stethoscope; the working waitress with a variety of available aprons; both with the well-worn but polished white shoes of the hardworking types. I had used all the demeanors to match: from grim-lipped efficiency to social pleasantries and small talk so tiny you'd need a microscope to catch my drift.

I pushed the hangers aside, along with the memories. A very tight black sequined dress that had felt like a boa constrictor at a major gala would probably never be worn again. Drag of all drags was a bridesmaid's gown that I had to wear as part of a bodyguard gig. Puffed sleeves and a humongous pink bow, I vowed it would never hit the road, but yet I couldn't throw it away.

On the hard-hatted side: a pin-striped mover's uniform had come in handy for lifting the odd piece of evidence. A mechanic's overalls and even a Department of Public Works standard-issue shirt with emblem. I didn't have a police officer's uniform. That, as we all know, is *illegal*.

I pulled out an overnight case. Tomorrow, I would go to Visalia. Tonight, I would finally clock forty winks.

CHAPTER ELEVEN

ETIQUETTE

Etiquette is important for the private detective, especially while attending a funeral for the purposes of investigation. Death leaves the family and friends of the deceased baffled and alone. And, given the element of murder, no doubt *angry*. However, etiquette performs the service of smoothing out the rough edges. The last rites of any beloved person should be performed in such a way that only the beauty and gravity of the situation comes through. And the private detective should be invisible, gray, in the background.

The valley is a place of great fertility, great poverty, and a great, big concrete irrigation trench that runs from the north down to L.A. My yellow sports car sped along endless acres of fruit trees, baking in the early fall sun. Tired, having given of their fruit, they hunkered down into the soil. Not like the worker bees who now drove hundreds of miles to San Francisco. Their housing developments dotted the valley like strange colonies from Mars. The apricots and figs would be cut down for concrete foundations and the toll roads were just a political payoff away.

Visalia was a major business center of the still-agricultural area. It was made up of strip malls, fields, old farmhouses, and the new condominium crops. Agribusiness firmly in place, and everyone else in theirs.

I stopped and picked up a paper. The news of Gale Petros was tucked discreetly on the second page. The funeral was to be held at Christ's Baptist on High Street in a pleasant, tree-lined suburb outside of Visalia. Afterward, the reception would be held at the Valley Arms, in the wealthier section of Visalia. And, as I had learned on the Internet, the apartment complex had been designed and owned by Audra Léon.

Graceful columns of wood and concrete, crawling with passion flowers and cultivated with fig trees, the gated development was an impenetrable garden of Eden. Shit.

I rolled my car around the block. It was easy to be invisible. The paparazzi were out with blood lust in their hearts and the swelling erections of telescopic lenses in their hands. Romea and I looked as innocent as a woman who has to cater for a day job to support a nighttime acting career and her cute little sports car. I rolled down the window and listened to the shop talk.

"Funeral's in an hour at the church."

"Well, Audra won't be showing up."

"Hey, did you take the tape of her wedding?"

"No. I thought you did."

"I wish. Somebody made big money on that."

"No one we know even knew where the wedding was. That was some video."

"That was some kinda inside information. I hear Mr. Warren was way pissed."

They shrugged and turned to each other.

"Time to go to church," they agreed. "There ain't nothin' here."

But there must be a service entrance somewhere. I saw a

break in the ivy. Two iron gates, painted green, were nearly invisible.

I pulled Romea over to let her radiator cool off. I checked my watch. The paparazzi crawled by in a car. They looked at me for a second as they drifted by. I was powdering my nose in my surveillance compact. It was the only thing the compact was good for. The guys had slowed by the gate. I saw the lumpy heads converge, nod. Then they sped off, worried about getting to the church on time.

If the funeral was at one, then the reception would be at two-thirty or three. It would be a wait. But the Luncheonettes would be prepared. Soon, very soon, I was rewarded.

A van of the cute caterers pulled up. They wore exactly what I had expected. White starched shirts and black pegged pants. No earrings or jewelry of any kind, not that I wanted anything metal near my ear. I plucked a cat hair off of the knee of my trousers. But then my heart skipped a beat as I watched the Luncheonettes unload a caravan of cheese and dip. They were all wearing black and white herringbone ties.

They didn't wear those ties on the Internet.

But there they were, each with a black enameled tie clasp with some kind of initial or monogram on it.

Grrr.

A few cars pulled up, spewing groups of grumpy, aspiring actors at their day jobs. They wouldn't even make any connections at this affair, I thought. They all wore the same tie held down to the white shirts with a distinctive monogrammed clip. I watched the fig leaves wave desultorily in the wind; sad hands that bade farewell to all my plans. And then I saw *her*.

She had a long, blond ponytail, pulled back with a simple black ribbon. Her claws were clipped and the sprinkling of freckles read *no makeup*. She squinted into the sun. My gaydar had never been better, I thought. Girl next door, cap-

tain of the softball team. You were fourteen. Two beers and
you took off your bras after the game. It would never be the
same after that. Her name was Jan. Her name was *always*
Jan. And she would be nothing like any scientist I had slept
with.

This woman was in her twenties. She was carrying a fifty-
pound marble slab with some effort. She wouldn't be an out-
of-work actress. She'd be putting herself through school. In
something like sports medicine. Her thighs would be tight
and smooth as marble.

Atop the marble tray was a sparkling, prismatic group of
lilies, complete with long, sparkling stamens. The ice sculpture was quickly melting in the sun. There was a winsome
wince of pain as the caterer hurried along to her colleagues
who relieved her of her burden and scuttled inside the door.

The Luncheonettes gathered according to some plan and
filed through the iron gates with their ice chests, bags of ice,
and boxes of appetizers and pastries, leaving the woman
with the van.

She pulled out a cigarette, tilting her head away from
what little breeze there was. She bent a match out of a folder
and carefully put the cover on before she struck it. Then she
tore the match off, looked around, and put it on the street.

Okay, so she wasn't the captain of the softball team.

Suddenly, the smell of acacias and mock orange trees was
joined by the pungent odor of burning rope.

Okay, so she wasn't studying sports medicine.

I peeled off my ironed shirt and laid it like a lucky flag
across the backseat. Underneath, I had a white T-shirt on. It
had its own handy insignia, a small pink triangle. It helped
if the gaydar was malfunctioning. I tucked the T-shirt into
my pants; my nipples were visible, hardening. My hair
looked wicked in the mirror, and I had a smile to match.

As I strolled toward the van, I saw a moment of panic on
the face of my victim as she sidled along the hot sheet metal

of the white van. I smiled and stopped. She coughed, putting her hand to her mouth. A black bug of an object fell to the ground. She turned and started to get into the van, her heel happening to grind out the butt on the ground. She got into the van, but she didn't have the keys.

"Waste of good weed," I said, picking the ugly stub of burnt paper and weed off the ground. I rolled it between my fingers. "There's a good hit left," I said. The face inside the van relaxed. I lit what was left of the joint and took a deep toke. There I was, on the job, smoking prime sensimillia. But I didn't inhale.

The sun had given this woman tiny wrinkles at the corner of her eyes. She had small, even, white teeth with a split in the middle. I put her at late twenties. She looked healthy enough, until she coughed.

"Hack, hack, hack!" Tears came into her eyes, but I was busy smelling the orange blossoms. She grabbed a small bottle of orange juice and poured some into a plastic cup for me. As I was drinking, I was sneaking a look at her tie. Lying in a valley between her breasts, it looked like a wool/nylon mix, new, special for the occasion. I really wanted that tie.

"Okay, I guess we've got to go inside and get to work," I said.

"Oh, we've got time. Besides, I've got points with Nancy; I stayed late at a reception for John Travolta last night. And I'm the only one who makes the Bette Davis eyes. I haven't seen you around."

"I'm an alternate, just filling in."

"By the way, Nancy's gonna shit when she sees you're without your tie." She was staring at my magnificent orbs of womanhood. I lit the joint again and leaned into the car. I put the joint in her mouth, and then put my mouth on hers. I inhaled the smoke back from between her lips. We were wet with orange juice and more.

"You got a phone number?" she asked between breaths.

"You got an extra tie? I asked.

"You drive a hard bargain, girlfriend." She laughed, but I stopped her with another kiss.

"Hey, you've got the extra points with Nancy, I don't," I reminded her.

She put a moist hand up to my face and drew me toward her. The kiss was long, wet, and unexpectedly passionate. Surprisingly, her hands were on my breasts, a little too fast, too insistent. She was pulling me, but I didn't want to nose dive into her lap. I drew myself out of the car. "Is it really going to end this way?"

"The tie, madam. You shall be justly rewarded."

"You're silly but cute," she mused. "I'm guarding the van, and they're all busy setting up." She drew aside a velvet curtain, and I saw that the van was nearly empty. "Nancy is hell on wheels when we don't show up in complete uniform, don't you know?" She was crawling over the seat into the back of the van. Lying on her side, loosening the tie I so wanted. Opening up her shirt, a pink nipple was revealed. And I found myself wanting that, too.

I was in the door, lying on top of her. There was a hungriness in both of us. My shirt was off, my hands on her smooth shoulders, the pink nipples like hard stones in my mouth. Sex with strangers. We both had our fantasies of what was happening. My fingers, finding the wet grooves between her legs, were touching someone else. Diving inside, she tightened around my hand, moaning. I kissed the lips of the woman I didn't know. She was begging for more, and I turned my hand inside of her, biting the small pink nipple that I had never met before. She screamed, and her body rose off the floor of the van. My hand, inside a stranger, was never happier. Afterward, she lay panting in my arms. I thought about who I had made love to: Rita Huelga, who wouldn't take off her clothes.

"You're wonderful," she said. "I'm sorry if I seem a little—desperate."

"Nothing wrong with desperate sex," I consoled her, helping her back on with her clothes. "We're going to have to go to work now, you know."

I had never struck a better bargain nor had a surveillance end so happily. Very wet between the legs, I was a step ahead of the game. Slightly stoned, and glowing, I thought I was ready for anything. My gaydar was in top order, and so was everything else. A little too top order.

"I can't believe you want this stupid tie!" But she put it around my neck and helped me with the slip knot. I reasoned that I wouldn't need to give her my phone number. I could make a quick getaway, bargain marvelously complete.

"There, you look great." She beamed. I divined, somehow, that she wouldn't leave her phone number, either.

"Don't you think it's fitting? Here we are, two lesbians making love during the funeral of a lesbian who couldn't come out? Or died because she was outed."

"Yeah, well, I'm not out, either. This is just my day job."

"You're an actress?"

"Being a lesbian doesn't go with the territory, Ellen De-Generis notwithstanding. Not that the stars haven't been spotted cruising at the bars: Tiffany, Celesta, Joan, and even Diana, without the wig. Too bad there's no way for a lesbian to sleep her way to the top in tinseltown. Those girls would forget your face faster than the speed of light; such is the glow of stardom."

"And you wouldn't mind being one of them."

"You betcha."

"Would it be worth denying someone you love, yourself?"

She cocked her head quizzically. But she was only worried about the lipstick, which had traveled outside the lipline. "We'll see."

"We'll see what it's like for Gale's family."

"By the way, I might need a little help passing around the cheese," I couldn't resist straightening the knot of the tie. The clip glittered in the naked sun of the valley.

"You mean, you're not a Luncheonette?"

"Sorry."

"Ohmigod—"

"Just keep me busy and out of Nancy's way."

"Are you a reporter?" she called after me. "I'm screwed!" She was not referring to our playful tryst.

I returned and put my hand, softly, on the shoulder that drooped. My hand still smelled of her. "Don't worry. I'm only here to get information."

The young caterer flapped her arms in the air and let them fall by her sides, a wonderful gesture of hopelessness. Ah, Los Angeles, and the stardom and closets it rents outs to the endless seekers. While for some it is their prisons, for others it's a tool. And I wondered what Emily Post would think of that.

"By the way, my name's Emma." I walked in through the gate into the Garden of Eden.

"My name," she sighed, shaking her head, "is Jan."

CHAPTER TWELVE

SEX WITHOUT EMOTION

Murderers attend funerals. They want to be around the results of their crime. They want to know if they are under suspicion. And, along with the weeping friends and relatives, the murderer would speak in hushed tones over the groaning board of the Luncheonettes. Someone who knew Rita Huelga from their mutual past.

The Petros family had been a house of secrets, living in their own kind of closet for years. The atmosphere of lies and recriminations would hang heavy over the appetizers, I thought. Rita Huelga was an easy, unifying target, and I'd bet the Luncheonettes would not be serving champignon anything. Cruising the Net, I'd found out more about the Petros family than they'd ever care to divulge. I knew their credit ratings and their penchant for Italian furniture. I knew who gave them title to a condominium in Visalia. I knew everything except how they felt about having a daughter in the closet, a closet that just might have killed her. "Wet kisses only / Drowning in time / I always wondered / When you'd be mine. . . ."

The Petros family. Was their silence perhaps bought off

by the airy top floor flat of the housing development that
Audra built? The title to the condo was paid for by Pacific
Hollywood Enterprises, a corporation owned solely by
Audra Léon. The rock diva was also a businesswoman.

As I walked through the gate, I thought that Pacific Hollywood hadn't done a bad job. Carefully kept asphalt path-
ways wound their way under an umbrella of palm trees and
jacaranda. The air was fragrant with mock orange, and
flocks of birds chattered overhead. Tall columns of pale
green stuccoed buildings boasted redwood balconies draped
with twining bougainvillaea. Dark windows showed dancing skeletons and leering paper pumpkins. I passed by a
drugstore, tucked unobtrusively under a redwood eave. In
the distance, a few benches held senior citizens, rocking out
on caffeine from a café. The minor retail activity contributed
to a certain amount of foot traffic, a surprising touch for a
gated community.

I followed the black and white figures of Luncheonettes,
a line of penguins bearing paté and clean, wrapped platters
of appetizers. An elevator took us to a door with a large
black and white ribbon—indicating the death of a younger
person—attached to the brass knocker.

The source of this tidiness and etiquette was a no-
nonsense, middle-aged woman in a gray wraparound dress
and black pearls. A family friend, someone who had both
sympathy and capability at the same time. Not to mention
her *hat*.

The hat said it all. A pillbox hat was firmly fastened onto
her thick salt and pepper hair. A conceit of black and white
ribbons hid what might have been a tiny sparrow. Family,
friends, and a neighborhood lost one of their own, one from
the nest, someone whom they still thought of as a child.

A modest dining room looked out on the waving fronds of
palm trees. The redwood balcony was crammed with funeral
arrangements and ribbons. A rectangular table filled the

middle of the room. A three-story tier of sterling vases held enormous lilies, pink speckled and fragrant. Gale, Audra, and Gale's mother must have sat at this very table that night. The dining table of death. I wondered if the apartment, the room, the table, would ever be free of that memory.

So young, so dead. A lover's triangle, ostensibly the motive, was part of the love that dare not speak its name, at least, I thought, in this crowd. The family had held the secret of Gale and Audra so long that there was no place for the fond little stories and anecdotes. "Wet kisses only / Drowning in time / I always wondered / When you'd be mine. . . ." Every topic broached would have the homosexual subtext. That, and a lot of anger.

But I was wrong. Way wrong.

Mrs. Florence Jones, as she introduced herself, in tones that were neither too loud nor too soft, was undoubtedly the family friend who took care of everything. Right now, she was working on a list, probably matching flowers with senders. It was a list that I wouldn't mind giving a long look. She took the half-moon glasses off her nose and let them fall on the starched bib, a bright white against the gray silk. Touching her silver ballpoint pen to her lips, she cast about the faces of the natty caterers. It was time for the food, and she was probably trying to figure out who was the head Luncheonette.

"Hi, Mrs. Jones, I'm Nancy." With the authoritative tones of a supervisor, she introduced herself and entered into a hushed consultation with Mrs. Jones.

Nancy ushered us into the kitchen where other Luncheonettes were busy with plate presentation. Looking them over, I wondered which, if any, would land the coveted sitcom role. A white man with deep black hair looked familiar, like a soap opera rewrite tethered to his day job. There were some perky comedienne types, blond, singing now, as they sprinkled pine nut garnish on small tuna patés. My friend was using a battery-operated blender to whip some cream; I caught an angry corner of her eye. In the end, it was just as expected.

"Who are you?" Nancy looked at me quizzically.

"Emma. I came with Jan. Just brought on last week." I smiled, my lips were iron.

"Humph—" Nancy paused.

"Nancy, do we put the smoked gouda next to the—"

"Just a minute—okay, Emma. You assist Jan. She'll tell you what to do. Jan, are all the glasses checked for spots? Peg, where's the ice? Tiffany, the garní!"

Jan sighed and pointed to a phalanx of crystal. "Don't forget to wash your hands, Emma." Her sarcasm was as heavy as a corpse. She watched me carefully, and when she finally was satisfied that I was catching all the water spots and I wasn't going to cause any trouble, she allowed me a wink. I was glad of that.

"Here—the Bette Davis eyes." Hundreds of tiny grapes had been halved and filled with goat cheese. "They just need to be rolled in crushed walnuts," Jan explained. "You're a good actress." Jan smiled, rolling her eyes. "Thank god for *that*. You owe me a lotta grapes, Emma." Finally, all was prepared and, glancing out the window over the sink, I could see the cortege of black limousines that signaled the beginning of the funeral party. The flock of cars, like black crows, pulled slowly, sadly into the slots of the parking lot, one by one, side by side. A lot of doors opened, and a lot of people in black stepped out. With few exceptions, everyone was African American. The integrated show business life that Audra Léon led did not spill over into Gale Petros's life.

In fact, there were few of Gale's peers. It was a sad fact, testifying to the kind of purgatory in which she must have lived. From what I could see, the ages jumped from people Gale Petros's grandmother's age to a lot of immaculately scrubbed grandchildren and tentative teenagers in somber

Sunday best. There was something very sad in that, as if Gale's closeted life had denied her any real peers.

I looked around for anyone who might represent Audra's organization. I looked out the window at the cars from the funeral procession. What I saw were two bodyguard types: one was too big and in too good shape to be an undertaker; the other one, the white one, was skinny and bored. A toothpick traveled back and forth across his lips. I wondered if they were part of Audra's organization. And I wondered if they needed any appetizers.

Other than the bodyguards, the crowd seemed homogeneous in their grief. I didn't see any press, that I could tell. But what I did see was Audra Léon's mother.

Charlene Léon was famous as the power behind Audra's continued success. A dedicated mother who gave television interviews that sounded more like sermons. The close-ups of her face were dazzling as she said, "I told my daughter, you gotta be true to yourself; forget that crazy world. It's your feelings that count. But it's awfully hard to see clear when your field of vision is crammed with press, fans, and the demands of show business."

Now Charlene Léon looked almost angry as she helped a woman crumpled with grief out of the limo. Mrs. Gloria Petros was frail before her time; she looked broken by the sudden death of her daughter. The two women, supporting each other down the sidewalk, refused any offers of help from the young teenage boys who shuffled nervously nearby.

And then I felt no different than the press vultures, opening a window on the personal pain of others. And I might get just about the same amount of truth out of the situation as the tabloids did.

"Okay, everybody. Graham, I want you to take care of the trays." Nancy was issuing orders, and I worried that she'd look too closely at me, giving me an assignment or realizing I didn't know how to turn radishes into roses. "Emma, arrange the Angels on Horseback!" A plastic box, cool and sealed, was thrust into my hands. Inside, baked oysters were wrapped in crispy bacon. A soft basil leaf curled around the flesh, reminding me of my recent adventure with Jan.

The funeral guests were arriving. Nancy popped back into the kitchen after depositing a tray of half-dollar-sized biscuits and crab cakes on the dining room table. I heard the last car door slam outside and the slow shuffle of sad feet.

"Jan, cover for me." I popped an oyster in her mouth, denying any protest she might make. The soft, tiny hairs on her neck were standing on end as the oyster slid down her throat. It was time to find a spot where I could eavesdrop among the mourners and minglers.

A small powderroom offered seclusion and an excellent eavesdropping position. The mourners were gathered around Gloria Petros. Two wiry women, mid-sixties, broke away from the crowd and strode toward the apartment. As they opened the glass entry door, I pulled deeper into the dusk of the powder room, locking the door, just in case. It was a hollow-core door. With my ear to it, the sad small talk came through loud and clear.

"His sermons have always been a source of inspiration."

"Of course Flossie's been wonderful. Capable and compassionate—"

"Yes, she notified me immediately—"

"The family could always count on Flossie."

"There's always so much to do. I helped her look through all the closets to find the black dresses, and procuring the necessary articles. I don't expect that they will stay in permanent black all year."

"She's got a job, sorting out all the flowers—"

"I went to church first thing this morning. I've got to get back to the deli, so I wanted to help out when I could. Audra sent a florist, a big woman from Minn-e-sota. Now, could she handle the easel arrangements! We put the biggest arrangements in the chancel."

"The biggest, no doubt, was from Audra?"

"Beautiful. I've never seen anything like it. Orchids and lilies—can you imagine—orchids!"

"Did it spell out any sentiment?"

"Only one word: *Love*."

"Oh, Carmine, the whole thing is so tragic, so awful."

"Is Audra coming?"

"Yes, but it's top secret. She wouldn't want the jackal press to swoop down on the scene. Gossip pickin' vultures. Nothin' will stop 'em, not a lifelong friendship that those two girls had, not the grief of a mother. Why, they'd sell their own kids to get a photograph."

"Audra's people are here, aren't they?"

"Yeah, I reckon those two fellas in the parking lot. They might be keepin' them away."

"Audra made the needlework pall that covered the coffin. I remember she worked for weeks on it in my home ec class. 'I put my trust in Jesus.' It's a beautiful piece of work, as was *all* of Audra's work. Those blue daisies on the border. Gale was good at tennis, but she was a bad cook. No eye for color. Everything that came out of the oven looked beige. And those girls, best friends. Beauty and the Beast. Gale was hell on the tennis courts."

"Do you think she picked the wrong mushrooms?"

"Could of. She was always in a hurry, prone to making mistakes. She put baking soda instead of powder in a cake once. Looked more like a soufflé."

"And Rita Huelga, you remember her?"

"Oh, yes. I had all three of them in my class. Audra, class valedictorian. Homecoming Queen. Gale, bad grades and always waiting for the bell to ring, wanting to get on the court."

"And Rita Huelga?"

"Oh, I remember Rita Huelga. Lordy, lordy. That girl was nothin' but trouble from the first day I had her in the class. She was always asking questions. Endless questions. I used to think it was her way of pestering me."

"They say she's under suspicion for murder."

"She was one bad seed, that's for sure."

"You saw it even then, in high school?"

"By the time those kids get to high school, I found I could predict the rest of their lives. Reading the newspapers, the business section, the theater reviews, the obituaries—why, my predictions are borne out in print every week. Never mind telephone psychics and psychologists, high school teachers can tell you the future of three-quarters of these kids."

"And Rita Huelga?"

"I wasn't surprised that she became a scientist. I never saw a girl follow a recipe so closely. A dent in a measuring spoon caused her no end of concern. And then there was the chocolate cake incident. Not to mention the *fire.*"

"I remember that. What a tragedy!"

"Tragedy seems to kind of follow in her footsteps. It was no wonder none of the other kids liked her. And then there was the chocolate cake incident—"

"What was that, exactly?"

"Before the tennis match. Gale was making a chocolate cake. It was Friday, everyone was going to take those cakes home to their families. Well, the next day was the big tennis match. Rita—at least I believe it was Rita Huelga—put Ex-Lax in the batter that Gale was preparing—"

"No!"

"Yeah, that was one tournament that Gale didn't make. And Rita won."

"Really!"

"Yeah, and the *only* tournament she ever won."

"Shocking! Are you going to tell the police?"

"No, I'd just as soon stay out of it. They can dig up all the information they need without me. Besides, I have to get back to the deli—"

"Do you think Rita Huelga did it?"

"Well, I wouldn't rule it out. Gale was a bad cook, but Rita was just bad."

"Hush! Here comes Gloria. With Charlene—"

"Gloria will never get over it."

"Those two girls have been the basis of a lifelong friendship. It's so sad, so sad."

"Quiet now, Charlene's—"

A minister's robe was just visible in the crack under the door. It swept along the carpet next to two pairs of sensible, black pumps, one that stumbled, one that held steady.

After the trio came more shiny black shoes. The mourners traipsed slowly up the hallway into Gloria Petros's apartment, feet that were still in shock, feet that didn't quite know where to step anymore.

When all was still, I emerged from the little room, the light hitting my eyes, bleaching out the entire hallway. I went up the stairs and tried on the expression of the invisible servant. A Luncheonette passed by me with a full tray of appetizers. The room was full of people, speaking in hushed and somber tones. Someone put on some music, Vivaldi's *Four Seasons*. I recognized the strains of "Winter" as I saw Nancy just disappearing into the kitchen. Time to search for Flossie's list. Ducking into a bedroom, I closed the door. I was alone.

It was a small, dim room. Light fought its way through heavy, flowered chintz curtains. A sleeper sofa, covered in a dark red velvet spread, would fold out conveniently for a double bed. Would Gale and Audra sleep in this room when they visited Mom for dinner? A large table stretched out with neat piles of envelopes, engraved funeral announcements, an address book. Large etchings of ripe, blooming roses hovered above the paperwork. At one end of the table a bulky, black fax machine showed a white edge of paper. A spindly-legged table held a built-in sewing machine, now tucked carefully in its interior. A woven basket underneath it must hold fabric and the current sewing project.

There on the desk was Flossie Jones's guest list. In carefully fashioned script three columns listed the floral arrangements, the sentiments, and the givers.

Yellow Roses and White Carnations	With Sympathy	The Fred Addams family, 2240 Main Street, Visalia, CA
Camellias with Birds of Paradise	In Loving Memory	The Samuel Antoneli family, 17 Willow Pass Road, Visalia, CA
Red Roses with Baby's Breath	Heartfelt Sympathy	Ruth San Juan, 422403 Hwy. 27, #14, Modesto, CA
Bluebells with White Chrysanthemums	Our Deepest Sympathy	Carmine's Deli, Carmine Wright, 150 Park Avenue, Visalia, CA

I slid the list into the fax machine and pressed Copy. The machine grabbed the paper, and a tissue-thin copy curled out of the lip along the bottom.

I folded it and put it in my pocket. There was a bookshelf. Danielle Steele. Toni Morrison. And a shelf of videotapes. A very carefully sorted and labeled selection. Videotapes of Johnny Lever's programs. I looked at the dates. All were recent programs, and the selection was topically consistent. "My Teenager—She's a Criminal!" "Girls Who Dress Like Sluts!" "My Baby Wants to Get Pregnant!" "I Chained my Daughter to a Radiator."

There was no doubt about it; Johnny Lever had a particular taste. And tone. I remembered catching one of those programs. Lever admonished the latest band of bad girls. He dried their mother's tears. He provoked and humiliated them. He must have loved it. Over and over again. And here those sad, televised stories found a home in an apartment full of a mother's tears.

The voices became quieter as the front doorbell rang. Someone must have closed it. I looked around the room quickly. A small closet held a fold-away bed, probably for the grandchildren, the visiting relative. A dry cleaning bag covered something bulky, black. I put my hand under its plastic shroud. Sable. Rich, black sable. It reminded me of small, dark animals being slaughtered in the dark to make a twenty-, thirty-, forty-thousand-dollar garment that was useless in California. Did Audra Leon give it to Gale's mother?

The door to the apartment opened and closed. The room was hushed. Then the organized greetings of an impromptu reception line, as if the pope had arrived for tea. A female voice, a familiar voice, was coming closer, footsteps aiming at the door in front of me. "I just need to freshen up. Excuse me."

"Take your time, honey," said Charlene Léon.

The knob of the door twisted. I opened up the closet door and pressed myself into the dark fur. But the closet was full. The door wouldn't even fit against my toes.

By the time Audra Léon entered the room, I was emerging out of the arms of a large bear coat. Her eyes were larger than in the photos. She was maybe six foot two in modest flats, the cat suit had given way to a swaying dark gray silk pantsuit, gathered at the waist with a gray sash. Her lips were rimmed in red and her eyes were bloodshot and big. They blinked behind enough mascara to tar my roof. A large lower lip, covered in copper glaze, fell and revealed two perfect front teeth, and then flew again.

"What the—?"

"Excuse me." I tried on the look of caterer and attempted

an end run around the famous star. Her arm shot out, blocking me. I was transfixed by the famous, furious face. I
needed a fame inoculation, but it was too late. Trapped and
transfixed; getting past Audra Léon would be like making an
end run around Mount Rushmore.

"What the hell are you doing here?" Two hands grabbed
the points of my starched collar.

"Luncheonette—"

"Fuck that shit." She backed me against the wall with her
right hand. With her left hand, she locked the bedroom door.

"I'm Nancy's new supervisor—"

Audra's hands tightened around my collar. "I *own* the
Luncheonettes. What the fuck do you think you're doing
here?"

"I'm from the California Department of Health and
Human Services—"

Audra Léon's hand came across my cheek in a hard, practiced slap. Then she stepped back, looking at what must be
a flaming red mark on my white face.

"You're pretty good at that. Had a lot of practice with
Gale?" I thought for sure she'd hit me again. But I called a
lot of things wrong that day.

"Oh Christ." Audra let go of my collar and collapsed on
the bed in a puddle of gray silk. She lay on her back, covering her face with her hands. "Gale, where did you go,
baby?" she cried. I didn't say anything. I was feeling too
shitty.

After awhile, I noticed she was staring at the ceiling
through her remarkably long fingers. "You know, they
hounded me, hounded me. You can't have anything in this
world without someone trying to take it away from you.
From the inside and the outside."

"It must be rough." My hand rubbed the cheek where
Audra had smacked so expertly. She, like Rita Huelga,
packed quite a wallop.

She'd been watching me. The hands slowly drew back down her face. "I'm sorry, whoever you are—"

"For what it's worth, I'm sorry about the *Johnny Lever Show.*"

"Yeah. Eighty million people have seen it by now. Eighty million people. That's the size of a small country. That's my entire audience. I'm dead."

"You could jut come out. Ellen did."

"She's a *comedian.* I sing love songs. *Heterosexual* love songs. And I don't have Ellen's timing or her writers, Emma."

"You don't have Gale, either."

I watched her chest heave with breath, with air that didn't want to go in or out. "That horrible dinner—that horrible— I didn't know—"

"Didn't know what?"

"Look, just leave me alone, Emma."

"You know my name?"

"Huh?"

"How'd you know my name?"

"Nancy told me, in the kitchen. I keep close tabs on my employees. You'd be surprised." She sighed.

"Actually, I'm surprised you don't just come out."

"Yeah, sure. You can keep your opinions to yourself. I don't care who hired you. Some sleazy rag? Tell your audience that Audra Léon had an empire. Hundreds of people relied on me. Gale's mom. My mom. The Luncheonettes. All the people who live in Valley Arms. All the people who maintain it. Gardeners, plumbers."

"You smack them around, too?"

"*You* deserved it. Invading Gale's mother's home—"

"You're right. It's a shitty job in a shitty business. No, not yours, Audra. Johnny Lever. I'm not with the press. I'm not with television, believe me."

"She had such a good forehand." Audra was far away,

murmuring. She didn't care if I was with the press, anyway. Something in her had given up her right to privacy.

"Gale could have had a career in tennis."

The puddle of gray silk moved, like a stone thrown in a pond. "It was no world for a black girl; at least not then. She was better off with me. At least, that's what I thought. Anyway, we were *all* better off after high school. Well, I'll give you a clue, Nancy Drew. Bevin Crosswell. Dickens couldn't have named her better. She's the termite that rotted out my house. A parasite. She certainly found her match in Johnny Lever."

"And now Gale is dead."

"You got it. Dead, dead, dead. Kinda like my career. Bevin Crosswell. Sniff up her tree. Or wherever. You'll notice a forked tongue. I wouldn't listen to it; no, I wouldn't."

"Are you saying *she* killed Gale?"

"Gale's *dead*. What can a trash tabloid take away that hasn't been already taken away from me? I used to wonder every day what they would write about me. And all the while, I know that it doesn't affect them. They sit up on their perch, and they really don't care if they ruin your life before lunch or after lunch. They can delay your pain for a day with a feature on orphaned pandas. They know how much it hurts, and they don't care. It used to be that my daily life was determined by whatever dirt someone cared to print. Hell, these days, it will probably all end up in the *Times*. My catastrophe is Johnny Lever's success. And worse, he knows it. He arranged it.

"I've got a legion of lawyers right now looking into all the corners and angles. They protect themselves as much as they protect me. An empire is ruined, and *somebody has got to pay*. That's the lawyer's song, Emma. *Somebody has got to pay*. But I don't care anymore. I really don't. They can bring down presidents and ruin the lives of the common folk. It's a torturer mentality." Audra Léon turned over on her side, and her body shook with eddies of tiny sobs. "They're a bunch of sadists. Death now, or death later. What does it matter? So, just let them get on with it and *leave me alone.*"

I left the guest room. It was hard to open the door, so hard was Charlene Léon's ear pressing against it. She flew inside and gathered up her long, tall daughter in her arms. Audra's hairdo was pressed against her mother's bosom. She was crying hard now, and her mama was rocking her. It was all very sad, but Audra Léon—for all her grief at the loss of Gale, her anger against the media—never mentioned *truth.*

Jan met me at the door. She held up a fig, cut into a sized star. It came toward me, pearl seeds studding the sweet, dark velvet innards. "Not to mention the candied violets and pansies. I don't really like eating flowers, though.

"I really don't feel like eating anything—"

"Did you see Audra Léon? God, she's even taller than I had thought. And beautiful." Star-struck eyes met mine. I had been replaced. I took the tray anyway and balanced it on my hand. "Bet the bodyguards eat meat," I said, looking out the window.

"You better stay out of trouble, Emma."

"Too late!" I said, making my way out to the parking lot where "Audra's people" were keeping an eye on the place. There were two of them. A long and lanky white man with a dark tan and a cagey look on his face. His eyes flickered across the terrain. The shorter, stockier man looked like cheap muscle. A walkie-talkie was balanced on the car hood, squawking away. The men were laughing. They'd forgotten they were at a funeral reception.

"Hey, babe, c'mon over here. I'm hung—ray." The white one was licking his lips with hunger, with attitude. He looked vaguely familiar under that tan. Something about his nose, I thought.

"Yeah, c'mere honey," commanded the cheap muscle.

I froze my face and walked toward them. Trying hard

to act like an end table, I offered the tray of food. The men didn't look at me as their hands traveled back and forth from tray to mouth. I was the perfect sculpture, a woman offering food. The continuously overlooked—children, servants, and elderly women—will always make the best spies. They are the forgotten, gray people of our culture. The walkie-talkie squawked. Someone offered a report in code: "Farley to Snake. Farley to Snake. Everything clear at Eighteenth and San Carlos. No journies after I chased away the dude with the telescopic lens in the church. Ten-four."

"Right," the tall man drawled. "You remember what Mr. Warren said about any journies that get too close? He's plenty angry." The words were languorous, not anxious.

"That's right," agreed the voice on the walkie-talkie. "Only Mr. Warren gives that kind of order, right Snake?"

"Hey, stupid. We're on an air phone, you jerk. Shut up and drive the car, Farley. Ten-four, asshole." The words were pseudo dispatch, boys playing with toys, seeing who can pee higher on the tree.

"Eww! What's that, flowers?" Snake asked, thin lips curving under his big, hooked nose. "Are we supposed to eat those?" It was a rhetorical question, and I was being a wooden end table. Hadn't I seen him before? That suit fit him well, for a tall man with legs as long as the Bay Bridge.

"Yeah, what's up with that? Whatever happened to potato salad and chicken wings, eh? I'll trade for the troll duty next time, at least I can stop and get me some decent lunch! Put the word in for me, with Mr. Warren, wouldya Snake? I ain't never had the opportunity to make acquaintance with the dude."

"We'll see what Mr. Warren thinks about it, Wiley. I need you here. You need, as they say, *training*. Did you think there might be a journalist among the catering crew?" Their eyes slid toward me.

"No way, man!" Wiley looked over at me nervously. Aw,

Audra has a heavy contract with the Luncheonettes. They're sworn to secrecy, that's what you told me yourself. Hey, what's this gooey shit?"

"It's a fig, you asshole. You ain't never had a fig, Wiley?"

"Guess not."

"That Farley's a fuckin' asshole," Snake complained. "Ain't got no respect. Audra treats us good."

"And Mr. Warren treats us good. So what's the beef?"

"Some people just cain't handle it." In the shadow of his big nose, his lips sneered. The thin lips, the long legs, his general sliminess would have given him the name Snake.

"Wha?"

"Work. Workin' for somebody else. Farley should go back into the auto body business. Hustlin' busted bumpers. The only bondo we got here is family. And he don't understand it."

"That's right, Snake, that's right. Loyalty, man, it's the whole thing. You can tell Mr. Warren I said so."

Wiley was plucking the smoked ham ruffles off the figs, tilting his head back. "Good ham, though. Smoked. Near melts in your mouth. Try some, Snake."

"Wait a second. I think someone's talking up there." Snake changed the channel, bands of static filling the air. The sounds of the funeral reception upstairs came through loud and clear.

Small talk became muted, and a voice rang out loud and clear. It could only have been Charlene Léon, Audra's mother. I watched the white moons of Snake's nails hover over the tray, looking for the biggest fish possible, as I tried desperately to pretend I wasn't listening. I could almost feel my ears stretch.

"I'm speaking on behalf of my friend here, Gloria Petros, mother of Gale." There was a pause, which could have been a squeeze on the shoulder, a hug. I imagined Gloria's face, tight-lipped but trembling, happy that her friend was taking over the chores.

"We are here to provide loving support and sympathy for Gloria and her three fine sons, now that Gale is gone. Her light has left the world a little brighter, but we must keep our faith in Jesus, who makes all things whole, and all burdens lighter.

"We all know that Gale had a—special—a very special relationship to Audra. We must, in our sympathy for her grievous loss, be ever vigilant of any idle gossip or—God forbid—leaks to the press. If there are any of you present who feel the devil's temptation, we ask you to please consider the burden of grief of this family. Because you will answer, and answer to more than your maker, if you are the cause of any further grief."

"Amen," someone said softly.

I wondered at the veiled threat, retribution dished out by someone more tangible than Jesus. Like Tyrone Warren. Like Snake and Wiley. Perhaps the whole speech was designed for this plea.

Charlene continued. "We'd also like to thank Florence Jones."

A pause, then a murmur of appreciation.

"Flossie has been of invaluable help to the family with her sympathy and capability."

"And they say you can't be black and queer," said Wiley, reaching for a tuna paté.

Snake was eyeing me with suspicion. He'd stopped chewing, a warning note in his voice. "You shut your trap, Wiley,"

"Whaddaya mean? I heard Audra say that she's worried Mr. Warren could get—could go ballistic. Postal. He does have that closet full of guns. Right, Snake?"

"Shut up, man! You talk too much, you know that, Wiley. This ain't a talkative kind of job." Snake's eyes slid toward me, but I had already backed away from them, trying to fade in with the shrubbery.

"Gale was one nice lady—"

"Even though she got the short end of a golden stick," Wiley agreed sadly.

"I hope they bust that Mexican bitch." Snake pursed his lips, the gesture almost familiar.

The other man agreed too quickly, hoping to please his superior. "There's one taco belle that's gotta go. I hear the buttons got the phone records. Brought 'em here just this morning. Gave 'em to the Inspector."

"The butch button?"

"She's tough. From Wilshire."

Murderers attend funerals. So do cops, I thought. And the cop must be Susan Blackman, of Homicide, L.A. I wouldn't want to run across her path. And if anyone could spot a fake Luncheonette at a reception, it would be Lt. Susan Blackman.

"Yeah, Blackman. I met her a long time ago, in Juvie. She's in Homicide now. I don't like the way she stared at me. But I'll tell you, Snake, it don't look good for the Belle."

"Yeah? Whadda *you* know, Wiley?"

"Plenty. Audra, she ain't never called the Taco Belle in the last six months. But Gale, she called her a bunch after the television show: 415, 415, 415, the area code that don't lie. Gale musta been givin' the belle some bitchin'. But the Belle didn't stand a chance. So she killed her. The whole thing is a big mess, now."

"Hmm. You might have something there, bro. Maybe I better be lookin' into some other line of work."

"No, not you, Snake!"

"You jus' never know, bro. And there's a lot that nobody knows in this situation. Mr. T. and his closest associates ain't talkin', are they Wiley? And anybody who does, why, he's a dead man. You hear me, Wiley? You hear what I'm sayin?"

"I hear you, man."

I remembered what the journalists had said outside of Rita Huelga's house. "Is it true that Tyrone Warren has taken a contract out on Dr. Huelga's life?"

Snake opened the car door and popped a cassette into the player. He turned up the volume. "Wet kisses only / Drowning in time / I always wondered / When you'd be mi-i-i-i-i-i-ine. . . ."

By this time, I had heard all I needed to know. I had backed myself into the foliage before they could realize I was in earshot. Their voices faded.

"And don't you think, bro—" The long finger punched into a vest. "That Mr. T. don' know all that's goin' on in this organization. So I'd just keep whatever you know—whatever you think you know, Wiley, to yourself."

"I get the picture, Snake." Wiley's lips seemed to seal themselves. They chuckled and clinked the ice in their glasses. They turned around, looking for me.

"Go get us a refill, honey. Lemonade," came the call.

"A tall, cool one." Snake looked me up and down.

But end tables didn't talk, they only returned to the kitchen.

My afternoon lover was sitting in the back stairwell. She didn't look at me. Her mascara was smeared, running down her cheeks like skid marks.

"What's up?" I stroked her long, smooth ponytail.

"The whole thing kind of ambushed me," she said through tears. "I guess—it's all a bit much for me to handle."

"What?"

"What do you think? Sex, you idiot!"

"Like we had in the van?" The figs, deprived of the ham covering, were throbbing their heavy fragrance into the heat.

"Yeah, like we had in the van. Duh!"

"Sorry."

"Emma, I'm in the program. The Sex and Love Addicts program. Only for me, I'm afraid, it's just sex. Now I've compromised my work with a total stranger—journalist—whoever you are!"

"Don't worry. I'm really just on a search for truth and justice. I'll make sure nothing bad happens to you, no one will ever know who I am. I'll disappear into the woodwork and nothing will ever point to my being here. I'm a very confidential person, Jan."

But she wasn't listening. "I was working the fourth step," she was saying. "And here I am, screwing some stranger in the back of the van, putting my job in jeopardy."

"You're a very attractive and, I see now, a very sensitive woman, Jan—" This only prompted more tears. "Look, you didn't do anything wrong."

"You're not a reporter?"

"I'm a private investigator. With the emphasis on *private*. Just trying to find out some background."

"Did you get what you needed?" There was a tinge of resentment.

I put my hand over hers. "Only that my client is in deeper shit than I'd thought. Gale and Audra's closet door was definitely ajar, at least as far as the family was concerned."

"Yeah, the family seems pretty cool about it. That lady who spoke—"

"Audra Léon's mother, Charlene. Gale and Audra were friends—and probably lovers—since high school. Sounds like the whole family knew and supported her in the arrangement in a kind of semiconscious way.

More tears. "Poor Gale, her mother just looks devastated—"

"Wipe your eyes." I pulled a Kleenex out of my pocket. The mascara came off easily.

Jan hugged me. "Thanks," she said.

"Listen, you might pick up some information with all the Hollywood bar trolling that could help my client. Strictly on the QT, if you hear anything about Audra or Gale, give me a call."

"What about all the other lesbians, Diana Finally and Julie—"

"I don't really care about who's queer in Hollywood. Now, go upstairs and don't worry. Be a good Luncheonette and go easy on yourself. After all"—my lips went in between the strands of soft, blonde ponytail—"there's no sex without emotion."

But for whom, I did not say. Jan turned to go upstairs with, I hoped, a slightly lighter step. She was a nice woman, and she could tie a square knot backward and forward, she just tightened it too much around her own neck. I may have put Jan in a better frame of mind, but I was deeply worried at the number of strikes against my client.

On the one hand, Gale Petros was untouchable. Audra Léon was a fucking saint. Two mothers were grieving together. And Rita Huelga apparently had a history of poisoning.

On the other hand, the whole situation was rife with closets and potential lock picks. And I wondered what Emily Post would think about *that*.

CHAPTER THIRTEEN

THE F LINE

I had gone to the reception of Gale Petros's funeral, and all it got me was a little star-struck. And angry.

Angry is not the detective's friend. Angry is a bad mistress; she is blind, and she doesn't watch her back. She leads me to mistaken assumptions, mistaken conclusions, and mistakes generally. All of which can lead to the valley of death. I wondered if Rita Huelga had any idea of the gravity of her position; I didn't think she'd ruminated on the gas chamber when she lied to me. I was far, far, too eager to share this pearl of wisdom with my client. I left the housing complex, angry legs carrying me to Romea. And I didn't watch my back.

Anger was still with me as I pushed the accelerator to the floor and sped back through the valley to Baghdad by the Bay, where the only closet doors left were in houses, mostly Victorians.

Los Angeles, while it may have been in the same state, was on a different planet. As San Francisco had been created by the entrepreneurs of the Gold Rush, Los Angeles was created by union busters. San Francisco was a city born of the kind of gold people dug up with their hands and pickaxes. Los Angeles was a city born of stars, impossible fires that burned way out of range, but had everyone hypnotized anyway. There were a lot of smart people in Los Angeles, and they made a lot of crap. The place was founded on boosterism.

The dykes of the LAPD were so deep in the closet they'd never seen the world without two inches of wood in front of them. The dykes of the SFPD had softball teams, retreats, and a bowling league. You could get laughed out of the closet in San Francisco. After all, why bother?

I soothed myself with such smug sociological thoughts. I was so busy distracting myself that at first I didn't notice the two men in a dark green coupe following me on the ribbon of freeway. I stepped on the gas, and so did they. They replicated my every traffic move with quiet confidence. They weren't local cowboys; they weren't even state troopers. I looked at the smoked-glass windshield. It was Snake and Wiley; they had caught my early exit, and they were following me. *"Wet kisses only / Drowning in time / I always wondered / When you'd be mine. . . ."*

The walnut and cherry orchards were losing their fall leaves. The fall heat had confused a few trees. Pink and premature, blooms were appearing, not expecting the freezing rains that would pummel them in December. The long, flat ribbon of freeway stretched before me, and still Snake and Wiley stayed politely behind me. I stopped testing them by passing cars and stepping on the gas. I settled myself in for the ride to the city and started making plans.

I touched the diamond in my nose for inspiration. The Gambit, former place of Thad's employ, was right down the street from the House of Moss and Sticks. I looked in the rearview mirror without turning my head. Snake and Wiley were moving their mouths now. They'd settled in for the ride to the city, which is just what I wanted. The unwavering steadiness of my speed, the beauty of the valley, and the straightness of the road would lull Snake and Wiley into a false sense of security. Meanwhile, my brain was working overtime. Suddenly, I was no longer angry.

We passed San Francisco International Airport. The traffic thickened. I crossed over to 280. Airplanes flew over hillsides. Retail outlets for computers, refrigerators, and stereo systems gave way at the top of the hill, Daly City and its pastel houses were made of ticky-tacky. "There's a green one, there's a blue one," the old Pete Seeger tune came back to me, but I never forgot that I was being tailed. The city loomed around the next corner, like glittering rock crystal.

Cars became mean. Drivers became anxious, cutting each other off at intended exits. I got in the far right-hand lane, hugging Hospital Curve, when I saw the Golden Gate Bridge exit. I did a quick and scary diagonal at sixty-five miles an hour, across seven lanes of traffic. The wraparounds woke up, turned their wheel, and almost forgot their blind spot. Tires squealed and motorists barked their horns. But Snake and Wiley had just made the Golden Gate exit and were leaning forward, tasting the thrill of pursuit.

I turned left on Mission and headed up Sixteenth. I thought I would lose Snake and Wiley as Romea darted like a little yellow bug around fruit delivery and *Examiner* trucks. Still, Snake and Wiley kept pace, darting expertly around the snarling traffic. I passed the Harvey Milk Library, with its flapping rainbow flag. Taking a left at Market on a yellow, I entered the impossible intersection of Noe, Sanchez, Sixteenth, and Market. Crowds of confused pedestrians roamed the deadly, star-shaped intersection. Cars aimed for their intended street, often daunted at the last minute by No Left Turn and Left Turn Only signs. Vehicles meandered up the steep hill leading to Divisidero, looking for parking and testing the clutches of the cars piling up behind them. Meanwhile, the historical streetcars of the F

Line, all golden with brass and ringing their bells, rolled
proudly up and down Market Street. Two tons of antique vehicle was just what I needed. Snake and Wiley were still
stopped at the light. They could have run it, but the confusion of traffic and people making up their minds in the middle of the intersection gave Snake and Wiley pause.

Racing up Market, I saw her. The Baltimore Yellow and
Gray. The old trolley was proudly, inexorably rolling down
the big hill that was Market Street with enough momentum
to make her way down to the Embarcadero with no power at
all. Her interior would be redolent of old wood and fine furniture polish. The car came closer and closer. Snake and
Wiley had pulled up behind me. I could just see the lettering
on the magazine that the streetcar operator had carelessly
thrown on the dashboard of the old control panel. *Drummer.*
The people inside the cable car were laughing, but they
wouldn't be for long. The little chrome wings on either side
of its cyclops headlight were flashing, just like the whites of
the operator's eyes. Someone screamed. Sending a silent
thank-you to the Market Street Company, a nonprofit that
kept the old cars running and their brakes in working order,
I did the famous bootlegger turn, stepping on the gas to the
creaky squeal of the trolley's brakes. I pulled into a bus zone
and flew out of the car and into the House of Moss and
Sticks. Past the floating display of moss and glass shards.
The place was packed; many of the customers were women.
There must have been a sale on white chrysanthemums. A
lesbian couple in baseball jackets looked familiar; they
avoided the Viscountess Maynard's great flowering cereus,
the eight-foot cactus that still dominated the front of the
store, many of its thorns still intact on the dramatic succulent. I tore through the customers, the dewy, green scent of
flowers enveloping me, as I aimed for the back room that
would lead to the alley.

It was an excellent plan. Already ticked at being shoved

aside by a rude dyke, the customers wouldn't be so accom-
modating with Snake and Wiley, who hardly looked like floral consumers. Of course, by the time they made it in the
store, I would be long gone. Up the alley and into the endless mazes of wooden stairways and low-fenced gardens,
which could be easily vaulted. They would stop and look at
all the possibilities and give up.

Or if they caught sight of me, I could streak through the
Gambit, whose top floor was a rabbit warren of pseudomed-
ical operating rooms. Snake and Wiley would have to bump
into beautiful tatoos or confront pierced labias before they
would gather that I had run out the front door of the Gambit
to where Romea was waiting. And if I was really lucky, I
would be saved the $350 bus zone parking ticket.

And so I sprinted through clouds of white chrysanthemums, an unlikely choice of bloom for the House of Moss
and Sticks. Thad must have really been suffering from the
loss of his harlequin lilies, trying to set a new trend. I wove
through the clouds of white mums that burst out of buckets
in the back of the store. The door was just closing when I
grabbed the handle. Yanking it open, I flew through the door
to the alley.

Searing sunlight blinded my eyes as I stepped outside.
But that wasn't all that hit me. Someone was waiting for me.
The rap came hard and confident on a part of my skull that
suddenly felt very soft. I fought to keep my eyes open. I
wanted desperately to turn and face my attacker. I wanted
even more desperately to avoid the second blow that would
surely come.

My knees went soft, just as I felt a warm ribbon of blood
run swiftly down to the middle of my back. I fought the
darkness that was bleeding into my view of the alley. In the
distance, a tall, thin woman, a long, neon checkered scarf
flowing off her ponytail, an empty basket dangling off her

arm. That scarf beckoned me. It was Mariposa. She was more than familiar.

Someone grabbed my wrists, and I wanted to yell, but the horrid taste of bile was filling my mouth. These people were serious, violent, seriously violent. My attackers had thick-soled shoes, and one of them landed somewhere in the small of my back; a kidney connection that caused an excruciating pain that traveled up and down my body. I felt hands on me: One of my attackers grabbed me, and I knew that they wanted to move me somewhere else. Abduction has been my worst fear.

At Crime Scene Number One, I was trying desperately to hang onto my consciousness, and I was losing. The place I didn't want to go was to Crime Scene Number Two, where I would be under their control with no chance of escape. Trying to spit, I worried about choking once the lights went out. And they did go out. So I sent up a silent prayer for my autonomic reflexes, which would keep me breathing even as I embraced the dark.

CHAPTER FOURTEEN

GREEK CHORUS

I was waltzing down the freeway, and also waltzing with Rita Huelga. She excused herself to go to home economics, busy as she was with the coffin pall. She was worried because the body would be cremated, and her handiwork would go up in flames. She was worried about a lot of things, like what kind of pajamas she would wear to the slumber party that night. She breathed fire at me, but suddenly we were at a wild same-sex party, a matriarchal bash that knew no limits.

Charlene Léon held Gloria Petros close, her pious lips biting suddenly into the other woman's neck. Gail Petros was a dominatrix; Audra Léon sang in pain. Rita Huelga danced with me in her stiletto heels. The Luncheonettes were something else; a Greek chorus whining about doom and gloom, earthquakes, and Halloween parties where you were stuck in the character you'd chosen for the rest of your life.

Television crews did a cha-cha around the entire scene. Barbra Walters was a floor manager, and Jenny Jones laughed atop a cherry picker, high above our heads. The cords of the cameras wound like snakes around our feet.

Sally Jesse Raphael was complaining loudly that the cameras no longer worked. Oprah had a pinhole camera, a cardboard box with one perforation for the tiny shaft of light that carried the image. It hurt.

Ca-thunk, ca-thunk, ca-thunk.

The cameras would not work, Sally whined.

Ca-thunk, ca-thunk, ca-thunk.

There was too much ambient light, Oprah insisted.

Ca-thunk, ca-thunk, ca-thunk.

Pain hit me square between the eyes. The eyes were swollen shut, but open, the light would become knives. What a bad party; it almost made being conscious an improvement. Except for the pain.

Ca-thunk, ca-thunk, ca-thunk, a jackhammer operated between my ears.

What made the sound so familiar?

"She doesn't have it on her," said the voice.

"If she's got it, she'll tell us."

"And if she doesn't?"

"We'll bust the castle. I think we'll have to, anyway. But the word is, we gotta wait a week."

Ca-thunk, ca-thunk, ca-thunk.

The metal cleats that held the concrete slabs that formed the Bay Bridge filled my head with a tormenting rhythm. I was going to Berkeley.

At least I was not dead.

Looking around the backseat at the empty ashtrays, a view of the glove compartment through the seats. I was in a Ford LeSabre. Whoever was in the front seat was silent. But, as captors have an extra sense about the captives, someone realized I was conscious again. A fist on the soft spot on my skull took care of that, and I was back at the party, dancing this time with Charlene Léon. She kept stepping on my feet, which caused me great pain. She was talking about her most talented daughter. She would read me all her letters home, if only I would stop dancing long enough to listen. I struggled to open my eyes. I remembered thinking that I was so glad I hadn't had my earring in my ear: they might have pulled it out, leaving me with a big tear that would be even harder to heal. I put a finger up to the lobe; tender, still a little flaky, and hard. I would have to ask Mariposa about her remedy, her ointment. I closed my eyes and went back to dancing with Charlene Léon. Once in the East Bay, they would let me know what they wanted. A third blow visited me on the dance floor. Then everything broke up in the shaking floor that only meant one thing: earthquake.

CHAPTER FIFTEEN

CRIME SCENE
NUMBER TWO

It was a bad part of Oakland. A part of Oakland where two men in stocking caps pulled over their nylon net faces would cause no comment or a call to the cops. Two men who half-dragged, half-walked a wobbly female investigator down the sidewalk. A woman who managed, out of her extreme peripheral vision, to catch a license plate number, X422L 957. My legs were rubber, my arms were cooked pasta, as they dragged me into an alley. The sight in front of me sent a surge of adrenaline through my body and came out a scream: "Help! Help!" X422L 957.

But it was too late. They had dragged me into Crime Scene Number Two. A basement.

"Emma Victor, Private Investigator." A voice was reading my card.

"What exactly are you investigating, Miss Victor?" X422L 957.

"I work for the Luncheonette's security service. They can't do without a security person, doing all the celebrity work. There was a whole team at Lyle and Julia's wedding.

Journalists took pictures from helicopters. We called in the state police with radar. It was wild."

"Try this for wild," another kick came, this one on the other side of my back. Blinded by pain, I found myself losing my cookies on the floor. The floor was concrete, so the mess wouldn't be hard to clean up, I thought with the ever-functioning tidiness quotient of my brain. The two men with silk stockings pulled tight over their faces probably hadn't cleaned anything except their guns in the last ten years.

"Looks like we got a soft female dick," chuckled the taller one, the driver of X422L 957. A Ford LeSabre.

I looked around at a basement; damp spiderweb curtains covered all the walls. One window was closed only by a latch and a lot of spiderwebs. Tell us about Rita Huelga."

"Rita Huelga? Who's she?"

This landed me another blow that threw me to the floor. "Look, bitch. You think you're smart. But you'd better talk." One of them raised a black-gloved hand high over my head. If he brought it down with the velocity I expected, it would spin my head around. X422L 957.

"Okay, okay. I'm not smart, and I'll tell you."

"Who's your client?"

"I wouldn't be in business long if I divulged the names of my clients to everyone who slapped me around," I lied. I was ready to spill everything as the hand lingered over my head. "You let me go, I won't press charges. I would say you guys are in much deeper shit than I am. Assault, battery, and kidnapping. As far as the judge is concerned, by going across the bridge, you've even crossed the county line.

"We're really worried." The hand hovered.

"Fuck that." The other mouth came closer. "Fuck that," the lips moved under the nylon stocking, strange, pressed-down lips. I could see the tongue behind a net curtain. "We know you work for Rita Huelga. And we want information. You spent the night. What's going on there?"

"She seems to be doing some kind of experiment."

"What did she show you?"

"A few cats. A few fungi, that's it."

"She didn't give you any . . . papers? A formula?"

"No way. " I didn't mention the release form.

"A sample? Some ground powder?"

"I don't know what you're talking about."

"See anyone come and go?"

"Nope."

The hand came down like a clap of thunder. I laid on the floor and counted the bricks in the foundation. "I really don't know what you're talking about. I was just a body-guard, just supposed to make sure no harm came to her. I just *met* the woman, I swear."

"You know what, Joe. I think she doesn't know what we're talking about."

"She'd better not. What are we going to do with a useless piece of female shit?"

There must have been an answer in Joe's foot, because it came close to my head, and a careful aim with attendant ex-plosion put me to rest once again.

CHAPTER SIXTEEN

A GENERAL MESS

The worst part was waking up. I checked my clothes, my
body, the feeling in my fingers, the feeling between my legs.
I wasn't dead. Or raped, or mutilated, or anything else that
men do to captive women in basements. Somebody was
barking hard, but they were barking up the wrong tree. And
now they would bark somewhere else.

Someone was really angry at Rita Huelga. Tough guys,
just pushing a woman around for a little information.

I peeled myself off the floor. The basement door was
open. My broken body, fed by fear, raced through that door
and out of the alley and into the dubious light of late afternoon. I squinted. The skyscrapers of San Francisco, looking
like Oz, beckoned in the distance, due west. The East Bay
hills were far off, and I figured that I was a half mile hike
from the Oakland West BART station. People turned their
heads as I, a bloodied, broken woman, made her way
through their neighborhood. I still had my wallet, and a lot
of change got me into the BART.

I wasn't made of the stern stuff anymore, I thought, as my
head and I entered the BART. From the way people looked

at me, I could have had my head tucked under my arm. I hoped a hot shower and a short night's sleep would do the trick. As long as I didn't have a concussion, I could cover any wounds by spackling on some makeup.

Some things had changed. I wasn't angry at Rita Huelga anymore, for no apparent reason except that I'd gotten hit on the head. I'd told some lies. Despite my insistence that my check came from AAA Security, the reality was, I *did* work for the press, for the *Johnny Lever Show*. But I didn't. I was working for my heart. At least I had thought that when I headed for one of the biggest gay ghettos in San Francisco on the Fillmore bus.

I readied myself for the experience of: San Francisco General Hospital. The hospital's Emergency waiting room. *Emergency/waiting* was an ironic oxymoron. Pediatricians and Emergency nurses spent a lot of time picking bullets out of young spines, hopeless gestures against the tide of weapons that had swept over the city.

I walked down the path that led through the fortresses of brick buildings, copper roofs, and sugar-tart white edging that laced just underneath the gutters. Past a field of grass and into the large circular driveway that led to Emergency. The sight of the bright red letters seemed to turn my stomach. The ribbon of blood that ran down my back was just starting to congeal. The swinging doors emitted an olive green sheriff and an orange-clad inmate in shackles, her handcuffs locked to the chain around her waist. I stumbled down the white linoleum, a field of snow, into the crowded waiting room. A television was blaring about the Rolling Stones' latest concert, and people watched dully, eyes glazed over from hours of waiting. My feet shuffled over to the sign taped over the bulletproof windows. Welcome to Admitting Eligibility, S.F.G.H.

The man standing just in front of me appeared to be holding his arm together. We listened to the official cards being passed back and forth under the bulletproof glass.

"Pedestrian versus Auto." The words came through holes in the bulletproof glass.

I read the Patient's Bill of Rights and Responsibilities that was posted on the wall. The words seemed to swim by my eyes, their higgledy-piggledy shapes hardly holding still. *Respect and Dignity: You have the right to considerate and respectful care. You have the right to know if the hospital plans any human experimentation or research project which might affect your care or treatment. You have the right to refuse to participate in such research. . . .*

The man in front of me let go of his arm. A large black hole spurted blood, and I grabbed a column for support. Just then, a pink shape drifted by, a pink shape with blue jeans underneath. It hesitated. I looked at the face.

"Chris," I breathed and felt the cold, hard white linoleum against my cheek.

I awoke to Chris, wonderful, Chris. A bright pin of light moved back and forth, searching out the uneven size of pupils. Chris was talking to me as if I'd been there all along. Apparently, I was catching the tail end of a conversation I couldn't remember.

"Some kind of company you're keeping." Chris started carefully wiping away the blood on the back of my head. Her careful fingers wiped at my skull, my neck, until all was clean. She was still wincing when her face came front to front with mine again. "What you been up to, girlfriend?"

"Hell if I know."

Chris whistled. "You're always close-mouthed about your latest case. That's how I know that this *couldn't* be about that plant in your backyard."

"I wish I'd just gotten busted for a pot plant. My head would be in better shape."

"Now, that was good bud."

I remembered a crystal-clear evening in the Castro when I'd bumped into Chris Fong and we'd shared the fruits of my harvest. The lights on the Twin Peaks Tower never looked redder. She'd been an emergency nurse for a few decades and was one of my best sources on trauma and injury. She even made house calls, on the hush-hush. I had been a chocolate raisin with her on Halloween, and she'd stitched up a few friends that, for one reason or another, didn't want to be seen at General.

"Hey, how's Barbara?" Barbara was Chris's ex-girlfriend, but they still lived together. "I haven't seen her in ages." My own statement reminded me that the news could be bad.

"Oh, she hasn't seen anyone in ages. You know she found a lump in her breast?"

"No."

"We've just finished with the chemo. She's not going to do radiation."

"I'm so sorry, Chris, I didn't know—"

"I think she's getting better. We're trying something *else* now."

"What, the new cancer invasive cell treatment?"

"No, we want her liver to recover from the latest battery of drugs. We're trying something more holistic."

"That's good."

"Yeah, any ray of light is brilliant in a dark tunnel." She sighed. "So, girlfriend, let me ask you the standard questions." The blood pressure cuff was fitted to my arm, pumped up, squeezing my arm like a friendly handshake.

"I'll save you the time, Chris. I've lost consciousness twice. Once after the original injury—"

"Someone left quite a dent there." Chris held up her finger for silence while she listened to my arm through the stethoscope. "Your blood pressure's a little low, Emma. That could explain your fainting spell."

"I'll take it easy for a while."

"No blood or fluids from eyes, ears, nose, or mouth?"

"No. I threw up, but that was awhile ago."

"You've got a goose egg there, for sure. Better put ice on it."

"How are my eyes?"

"Your pupils are the same size, and you got away without a shiner. Lucky girl. From the size of this dent, I'd say you were very lucky, Emma. Look, you've got to keep an eye on this for the next twenty-four to seventy-two hours. Don't go to sleep for a while. I don't think there's any bleeding inside your often thick skull, but sometimes slow bleeding can form a subdural hematoma, in which case you'd better get your buns of steel in here, pronto. Might be good to have a friend call you every few hours to make sure you're awake."

"No way. I have a lot of work to do. I can stay busy."

"Okay, but here's my pager number. Call me if you get worried. If you *can.*" Chris sighed and handed me a mirror. "We aim to please, Emma, but it's definitely a bad hair day."

My face wasn't too bad. There was some scraping on my cheek where it had hit the gravel that lined the alley behind the House of Moss and Sticks. My eyes were only slightly bluish underneath. "Oh dear. How soon can I make it home for a wash and set?" Although Chris had washed off my ear, my hair was another project altogether. Flattened out on the left side, the result of being taken on a long ride across the bridge while trussed, my gray and brown curls were now frozen hard with clotted blood.

"I've had a few hairdos like this before." My legs were like jelly as I slid off the table. Chris and I did the hug thing. "I hope Barbara's going to be okay," I said. "I'll light a candle."

"Now, if you'll excuse me, I've had one hell of a day, and I'm going to go kiss my bed."

"Just so long as you're not kissing Rita Huelga," I thought I heard Chris say, but it must have been my imagination. I was quickly out the door and into the shimmering asphalt parking lot. "Barbra Streisand received an award last night. . . ." crowds in the waiting room blinked bleary-eyed at the television monitor. "Cindy Crawford signs deal with NBC." Why were we all watching these people?

The woman who I'd seen earlier at the entrance shuffled by. She was still in shackles, smiling, probably happy to be out of the prison routine for an afternoon. Accompanied by a male sheriff, they went into a door labeled Fast Track.

It was time to go home and lie down in the dark—even if I couldn't sleep—for as long as the situation would permit. And I didn't really know what the situation was. Who did?

The person who owned Rita Huelga. And that, I thought, was a far better way to look at the situation. If I could just gain Rita's trust, she'd tell me why she went on television. And why Gale Petros called her so often after the airing of the *Johnny Lever Show.*

CHAPTER SEVENTEEN

A BIG MISTAKE,
A VERY BIG MISTAKE

I picked up Romea, then stopped at home for a quick shower. On Chris's instruction, I didn't wash my hair but tried to comb the blood out of it. I wasn't very successful. And it hurt.

Clean clothes had never felt so fresh, and I felt nearly human as I picked up the phone and called one of my sources, a dispatch operator for the San Francisco Police Department. For a few favors, I could get a name attached to a license plate number. I placed the call, happy to find that Brenda was on duty, sending black and whites out to citizens in distress.

"May I help you?"

"It's Emma. I need an I.D. on a vehicle."

"Give me a quarter hour, Emma. We're heading into Halloween, and the city is just jumping with more mischief than merriment. Two stabbings in the Tenderloin—"

"X422L 957. A Ford LeSabre." I listened to Brenda's pencil dutifully taking down the number. Then I hung up and plugged my computer into a different phone line and logged onto the Internet.

Rose had given me her book of passwords and cryptology.

In minutes, I'd broken into the National Practitioner Data Bank, which tracks adverse licensure actions, medical malpractice payments, suspensions of clinical privileges actions, and negative professional society membership actions. I typed in "Dr. Huelga, Rita." Nothing came up. Rita Huelga was a research geek; she had almost never engaged in actual medical practice on patients, a situation I found unusual. The Hippocratic oath just passed her by as she had busied herself with petri dishes instead of patients.

The next call confirmed my suspicions. Brenda, the ultimate civil servant, had done her underground work for me. "X422L 957. A Ford LeSabre?" She repeated the number. "It's a company car."

"What company?"

"Consortium Bell-Worless International, Incorporated. Their office is out in Dublin—"

"Thanks, Brenda." Things were getting hot for Rita Huelga, and I wondered how long she could stand the heat. I pulled up to Rita's mansion at the end of a long, harrowing day. I hadn't managed to kiss the sheets yet, and I wasn't sure I wanted to kiss Rita Huelga anymore. It was just getting dark as I pulled into the mansion park of Saint Francis Wood.

The row of white mums circled the drive defensively like covered wagons. The journalists had found fresher blood somewhere else; not a camera was clicking as I pulled the emergency brake. The electrical work would start next week. Meanwhile, the front door, weakly lit, featured the brass fangs of the lion who guarded the door—but didn't keep the tall man who raced out of it from slamming it. The heavy wood met the frame, shuddering the whole structure.

Like a date who'd been left at the door, the man flew past me, stroking a mustache that had been so heavily waxed I could see it shine in the moonlight. His top hat was pulled down low, hiding his eyes. He bumped into me in the darkness. His brown eyes were black with anger. He flew past like a black raven, thinking, no doubt, *Nevermore*.

His wing tips clattered on Rita Huelga's flagstone walk. I was just about to make the trip up the cobblestone walk when a strain of music stopped me. *Dunka, thunka, whee, whee, whee!* The sounds came from the servants' quarters.

If you could call it that. Like a computer with a voice, a song of aliens, I could feel a rhythm that reminded me of the Bay Bridge. The sounds pulsated from the small windows nestled next to the garage entrance. Bright green lizards crawled across a field of magenta flowers on the batik curtains. Techno-sound from the servants' quarters: someone was home.

I moved back from the front stairs and made my way along the bushes. I peered through a split in the curtains. Just to the left of the lizard leg, I could make out Mariposa. She was sitting cross-legged on a pillow, wearing rainbow overalls and leaning her long torso over a canvas spread out on the floor. Quan Yin was there, coming to life in fluorescent pointillist technique. A million tiny dots spelled out the serene features of her face. Mariposa bent her long frame over the canvas. *Dot, dot, dot.* She was touching her brush to the open ends of paint tubes: florescent pink, blue, yellow, green. How long would it take to finish the piece? I watched the artisan at her craft. *Dot, dot, dot,* the brush pecked away at the canvas, which came to life in the hyper-happy synthetic colors that had been invented long after Buddha's time. *Dot, dot, dot.* The music thumped through the room. I watched her for awhile, but I never saw her break her rhythm or concentration.

Garbage cans, their lids firmly latched, had just been put outside the garage. I poked around in the refuse of Rita Huelga. The white trays in which she grew her mushrooms were there. Sand and moss covered a plastic bag, which had been firmly tied shut. Inside, the mushrooms crowded together, a curious kind of refuse. Was Rita Huelga stupid enough to put the evidence against her in her personal garbage? The district attorney would have a field day with this, I thought, if it was *Amanita phalloides*. There had to be a better way of disposing of a murder weapon. I unzipped the plastic bag, the kind with the strip that turns color when it's closed. Mushrooms shouldn't be kept like that. They need to breathe and are best kept in a paper bag. Indeed, the little white buttons were slick, even slimy. And underneath their umbrellas, they showed the lacy brown gills that meant that they weren't *Amanita phalloides*. These buttons were the common Safeway variety. So what was Rita Huelga, mushroom specialist, doing with them? And in a plastic bag? My thoughts turned dark as I thumbed through the slick white buttons. Perhaps they were the mushrooms Gale had meant to serve.

The lion offered the ring between its fangs. I knocked, I rang the Windsor chime doorbell. I was ready for Rita Huelga, I thought, but I was wrong. As usual, the scientist was far better briefed, better prepared. I had no idea what was coming.

"Oh, it's you." Rita Huelga, in her bathrobe, had been crying. Her hair straggled over her eyes, and she didn't bother to push away the damp strands that curtained her face. Her breath smelled unpleasantly of hard liquor.

"Disappointed?" But Rita didn't look disappointed. She looked devastated.

"I—I just thought you were someone else." She hiccuped, from drinking, or from crying, I couldn't be sure.

"Is Top Hat coming back for a rerun?"

"I don't think so. I think it's over, Emma. Hey, what happened to you?" Rita pulled back and took a better look at me. She wasn't going to run her fingers through my bloody pillow perm.

"I was interviewed by your employer." I grimaced.

"My employer?" The small gold medal with the tennis racket glittered at the base of her neck. "I don't have an employer."

"Are you sure? What about Consortium Bell-Worless?"

"Huh?" The confusion on her face looked real. *"Ohmigod.* Are you okay?"

"Thank you for caring. Can we go in the living room and sit down for a spell?"

"Oh, why not?" She looked sick. I had the feeling that there was a Top Hat to blame.

We settled ourselves in the living room. Rita switched on the lamp, which spilled an amber light on my face. I settled into the lap of the velvet sofa. Rita sat across from me, draped on the edge of the matching love seat like a broken doll. She was certainly not in the mood for an interview.

"Rita, I've got to ask you some questions."

"Really?" She laughed, but nothing was funny anymore.

"Sarcasm won't help. And I can't help you unless you tell me the truth."

"But Emma, I don't want any help anymore."

"You said you hadn't had any contact with Gale Petros in years—"

"Yes?"

"Your phone number is on her personal phone bill on a weekly basis. Ever since the *Johnny Lever Show.*"

She poked at the fire. "I suppose Gale and I had some issues."

"Quit stalling for time, Rita. I've got the pieces of four different puzzles that don't add up. You, a publicity-shy scientist, goes on national television to declare a secret affair? Gale Petros calls you on a weekly basis and ends up dead. You don't understand: You're a murder suspect, Rita."

"Don't you think you're being a little dramatic, Emma?"

"All arrows point your way."

"Okay, okay. What do you want me to say?"

My heart sank as Rita's latest denial came on board like a familiar rat. I felt the hair on the back of my neck rise. It was covered with dried blood.

"Rita, you're a scientist, but you don't seem to realize the kind of deductive reasoning the police department and everyone else, including me, uses. The police are going to want to talk to you—"

"I'll have a lawyer—"

"They will ask you many questions. They will ask them many times and in many ways, I assure you."

"I'm not worried."

"You should be. The district attorney will be wanting to know why, exactly, you went on the *Johnny Lever Show* to out Audra Léon. The timing of the phone calls looks bad. Gale started calling just after you'd been on the show. She must have been one unhappy girlfriend."

"Look, I'm sorry about Gale, but the mushroom thing is such an obvious setup. How *could* the district attorney believe such a thing?"

"Easy. He needs to close a case. He's got the taxpayers and the tabloids to satisfy. He's got a suspect with a means and a motive. The weekly calls from Gale Petros are enough to suggest where the digging should begin."

Rita's face was paling. I hammered on. "The trellis outside your bedroom is broken at the top and bottom only. It looks a lot like you broke the top and bottom rungs to make it look like a break-in. I covered it up for you, but I'm not going to cover for you anymore.

"I have answers."

"New ones, no doubt. Why don't you revise the one about the tray of spores in your basement, the ones you said Mariposa used to make spaghetti sauce? They were hardly chantarelles. They were *Amanita phalloides*. You're growing death cap mushrooms down there. I found an empty tray in your garbage can. And a bag of these." I pulled out the plastic bag, damp with its little crowd of white buttons.

"You're not a mycologist yet, Emma." Rita laughed. "Those mushrooms are from the Safeway."

"That's exactly what worries me. What kind of fool do you think I am, Rita?"

"I don't know, what kind of fool are you, Emma?"

"A bigger fool than the district attorney. This is *murder,* Rita."

A change came over Rita's eyes. Something as cold and shiny as the pennies in her shoes took over. "It's all circumstantial. There's no proof—"

"If this goes to grand jury, I'll have to testify."

"You don't have a clue, Emma."

"I have too many clues. And they all point to the moment you decided to go on the *Johnny Lever Show.*"

"Fuck off, Emma."

"Getting a little close to home, are we?"

"No, you just want to get close to *me,* Emma."

"It would do me good to get out of this whole business. I never liked this job in the first place. You're a lousy client, even if you're not a lousy lay."

"Yes, Emma." The voice was cool, the tone was moldy. "All I care about is my work, Emma. Maybe the DA *will* pay me a call. But it's just a circumstantial case. I've got money to buy lawyers to defend me with whatever I care to tell them. And they'll get me off. So I can finish my *work.* That's what you've forgotten about in the whole puzzle. My *work,* Emma. I live for my work."

"Yeah, and you live in the United States, the only Western industrialized nation that executes people. Lethal injection has just become legal in California. Despite their gruesome science, no one is ever really sure how much suffering the executee goes through.

"It will probably be the gas chamber, Rita. You check into

the little green octagonal room; no deposit, no return. They strap you into a chair, seal the door, and sixteen one-ounce cyanide pellets are dropped into a bucket of sulfuric acid. You will struggle and jerk against the restraints and choke slowly to death. It's a slow process and can take ten minutes or more. The asphyxiation is not quick; your face will turn purple and your eyes will bulge. It's agonizing and grotesque; witnesses have described it as the most vile and inhumane of all executions. And there will be witnesses, of course. Gale Petros's mother, Gloria. Maybe even Charlene Léon, maybe even Audra herself."

"You don't scare me, Emma." The woman was as cool a customer as I'd ever met. "I'm not afraid of death."

"Then you're not of the human race."

"I have to go and fix dinner, anyway."

"Come off it, Rita, you think you're as tough as a battleship, but you can sink faster than the *Titanic*. It's time to come clean—if you know the meaning of the word. You're holding out on me, and your holding out on Consortium Bell-Worless, an employer who uses silk stockings as part of their rough-em-up dress code. Now, do you care to share with me anything that might shed light on this matter?"

"No." The ultimate finality in our language. "I think you've just about outlived your welcome here." The voice was chilly, almost automatic.

"Yeah, I just came here to flap my jaw at you. Just like the fella in the Top Hat who just left."

The identity of Rita's top hat visitor was written all over her face.

"That was Audra Léon, wasn't it?" I asked.

"Yes, Emma. It was Audra. She *always* comes in drag." A derisive snort came from between the pretty pillows of her lips, a short, ugly sound, like a bullet. "Audra Léon, the loping gait of the six-foot disco diva with the heart of stone." A small, ugly sound came out of Rita's mouth. "She's not real happy with me at the moment."

"Neither am I. You're ignoring the facts of the case, Rita."

"And you've just fallen in love with me like everybody else I've fucked."

The memory of Rita Huelga's fluttering, soft touch left my memories, like vultures scared off from the corpse. I looked at her face, the face of an El Greco angel, and the demeanor of the devil. I only had a little tiny voice left, but my hearing had been perfect: *"You've just fallen in love with me like everybody else I've fucked."*

"No," I managed to say, sure that my heart was plastered across my face for all the world to see. My mouth moved and managed a sentence. "I've just made a mistake."

I went to the door, and I didn't turn around. Behind me, I was sure Rita's eyes were trained on my back, measuring my every step: like a scientist, like a sex addict, like a trained assassin. I closed the door behind me, slamming it shut like thunder from a gray cloud.

Outside, the air was pure, compared with all the mutual contamination inside Rita Huelga's Elizabethan manse. I looked up at the stars trying to shine through the sick yellow lights of the city. My head was spinning with questions, with theories, with grief.

I would go home and kiss the sheets and dream the dreams of the guilt-free, I told myself. I sank into the deep palm of Romea's leather seat. Rolling down the window, I let the fog and the ambient noise enter the interior. I took a few deep breaths and maybe I shed a tear or two.

Then I unlocked the glove compartment, pulled out the cell phone, and called Rose.

"You've reached Baynetta Security. We're not available to answer the phone. Our messages are monitored regularly, so if this is an emergency, please leave your message after the tone. Otherwise, call back during normal business hours. . . ."

I rehearsed the words I would leave, sad words, angry words, words that Rose didn't deserve. She was still my employer.

"Twee!" The beep sounded, and I coughed.

"Hi Rose." My own voice sounded shaky. "I'm sorry to say that I have to quit the security assignment on Rita Huelga. Maybe you can put somebody else on the job. It's only another week, right? I don't think she needs a bodyguard. She needs a lawyer. There's a lot that's unclear; Huelga is misleading and hostile. It's just a situation that isn't going to work. On a related note, someone didn't like the shape of my head and tried to do something about it. Someone who drives cars for Consortium Bell-Worless, the place that sets up Rita Huelga. Maybe it has to do with this story, maybe it doesn't." I disconnected the phone.

The techno-music bass beat seemed to mock me. Your love life, Emma Victor, is Guaranteed All Risk. Your head has been replaced, rather inadequately, by your heart. You have a thing for scientists. You have been led around by your memories and your hormones.

But, like a scientist, I knew that I would still seek the answers to the questions that eluded me, the ones Rita Huelga wouldn't answer. Driven by the need to know, I could quit a case and still keep snooping around, right?

Dunka, thunka, whee, whee, whee! The green lizards danced on the windows of Mariposa's room to the tuneless noise, only a rhythm. Mariposa was, no doubt, still working on the face of the Goddess with her teeny tiny paintbrush. I took a deep breath and wondered what *she* was up to.

No, not Rita Huelga, Mariposa, or even Audra Léon, but Quan Yin, Goddess of Compassion.

CHAPTER EIGHTEEN

COMPASSION

"Psst! Emma!" A voice came out of the darkness; a big white face approached my car. It was Mariposa, barefoot, tiptoeing shyly through the moonlight. She was smoking a beedie cigarette, her hand traveling quickly to her mouth, waving the red coal of light. "Hi, Emma, what's up?"

"I just got the big brush-off from Rita. In case that makes you happy."

"That doesn't make me happy, Emma. You've misread the situation completely. I'm just here to help Rita with her work."

"Her work for Consortium Bell-Worless?"

"Some of it, yes—"

"They aren't too happy with Rita at the moment. They think she's trying to hold out on them. They're just circling now. It'll be awhile before they decide to interview her themselves. And let me tell you, their questions leave bruises when they don't like the answers."

"Oh dear, the rough trade." Mariposa sighed like a bad cousin had arrived in town. "Bell-Worliss?"

219

"Yeah, they think you're missing some profit off their investment, Mariposa."

"Now, that *is* a problem." Mariposa paused. "Thanks, Emma. I'll remember that you warned me." Her head popped in the window, long blond hair grazing the metal. "I'm not worried about Rita. She can take care of herself. She cares for you, Emma."

"Sure, just like everyone else she makes love to."

"I think she's just trying to put some distance between the two of you. It's not good to get too involved with Rita, Emma. I know. She tells me everything. What she doesn't tell me, I know already."

"That's just great. Maybe you can tell me if she killed Gale Petros?"

Mariposa laughed, her head left the car for a moment as she stood up straight in the darkness, taking a few more quick drags off her cigarette. "I can tell you right now, Emma, that Rita is about *life* and not about *death.*"

"So why did she go on that television program?"

"Same reason."

"The money for the Women's Cancer Center?"

"You got it, Emma."

"Well, the police won't be satisfied with those kinds of answers, Mariposa."

"This is bigger than the police, Emma. Way, way more important. Listen, I've got to go in and clear up, do the dishes, so Rita can get on with her work tonight."

"It's going to be pretty hard for Rita do her work if she's under a death sentence."

"She's not afraid of death."

"What exactly do you mean by that?"

"Emma, didn't you notice?"

"I've noticed that you answer questions with questions."

"But you made love with Rita, right?"

"Yes."

"She thought you were very special. She said it was wonderful."

"Okay, so it was wonderful."

"Then you know, don't you?"

"Know what?"

"Oh dear, she kept her clothes on?"

"She kept her clothes on, yes."

"Oh well." Mariposa stood up in the darkness again. The beedie light traveled fast as a firefly in the darkness. "I guess I might as well tell you. Rita's had a radical mastectomy, Emma. Three years ago, they nearly took away half her torso."

CHAPTER NINETEEN

THE CUSTOMER IS
ALWAYS QUEER

"It happened in Brazil. I was working as a nurse in a hospital in Brasilia. Rita was there on a field trip when apparently she noticed a lump in her left breast. I met her in the hospital. She was in overnight for the biopsy. We—we became friends. I'd been in Brazil for some time, and I knew a lot of the locals. And a lot about their medicine.

"When I saw the results of her test, it was clear that she would have to have surgery. There's no remedy for something that bad except to cut it out. I suggested that I return with her to the States. And so I did, as her personal nurse, during her recovery. And later. We have . . . a unique relationship. So you don't have to worry about Rita, Emma. We'll be fine, just fine. Now, if you'll excuse me."

I drove over the hills, back to the other side of Twin Peaks, thinking about how little I knew of Rita Huelga and how much I was feeling for her, an equation that was out of balance. It was time to head home.

The lights of the Castro were still bright. Despite the lateness of the hour, there was still time for a cappuccino. I turned left at Divisadero and cruised down Market, politely trailing behind a Boston Red-Orange and Cream with its picture windows. Over the gothic lettering of the Gambit, a rowdy crowd was leaning over the balcony of The Café, a misnomer for a bar in a city full of cafés. The balcony was festooned with orange crepe paper, some people were already in costume—big wigs and uniforms—the people of the Castro were ready to party. It was Wednesday night, and nobody on the balcony wanted to wait for Halloween.

I slid into the right lane, cruising past Wilde Flowers, the House of Moss and Sticks, the place where Mariposa was two steps ahead of me—and Bell-Worliss. The place where I'd gotten my head rearranged. I felt the bump on the back of my head. It was healing well, faster, in fact, than my earlobe. Thad had done such a good job with the nose piercing; perhaps he had an earlobe hint or two.

The House of Moss and Sticks displayed its wares to the night. The sharp-edged floating floral tribute was dark. The hour was late; there were no tourists marveling at its strangeness. I slowed down and shifted into neutral. The other window was dark, too. In the ambient light, I could see that a huge bouquet of checkered lilies were sprouting out of a skull. I pulled into the bus stop and surveyed the dim display.

The harlequin lilies, Thad's exclusive, had been delivered in time for Halloween. The brilliant petals were indeed patterned with diamonds in a deep purple on a cream ground. I parked in the bus zone, got out of the car, and came closer.

A perfect tableau, Thad's creation was a provocative Halloween retail strategy. But there was something way wrong here, and it wasn't the creation. Astounding lilies seemed to grow out of an actual human skull. The skull, grinning horribly, wore a wig of Spanish moss perfectly groomed into a pageboy. Big cartwheel mushrooms made for moldy earrings. But the worst and most tasteless touch was a bejeweled cigarette holder, dangling from yellow teeth. It was a bite that was still intact, featuring intact individual teeth, the tiny lines at the bottom, the yellow stains of a cigarette smoker, the cavities of someone who would no longer be eating their share of Halloween treats. I could even make out a glimmering filling in a molar. It was something only a dark dentist could love. I wondered where Thad had gotten the skull and if it was illegal to harbor human remains. But that wasn't what drew me to the darkened window.

The bigger question was why, if this was Thad's exclusive flower, the pinnacle of gruesome floral tributes, why was the gruesome creation not lit? I walked closer. Behind the darkened tableau I could see the counter where the pedestrian white mums formed an impenetrable flank. Something was missing.

Somehow, the cactus had disappeared, making its way out the door, front or back, to some holiday destination.

Market Street was emptying, even of the nighttime gadflys. A couple was looking into Rolo's, the expensive menswear store. Ina Cho had a new unisex line of leather jackets. Donning the expensive duds, scarecrows made of straw looked happy and festive. But they hadn't bought their flowers at the House of Moss and Sticks.

The sign on the door read Closed, but a dark red stain creeping under the door said otherwise. I put my fingers in the stain. Cold and sticky, the stain was spreading. I put my hand on the doorknob and turned. The door was open, just like someone's veins. A quick look to the right and left of Market; leather jackets still held the couple's interest, and there were no newcomers waiting in line outside The Café. I turned the knob and went inside. Only the swish of traffic outside the window broke the sound of my footsteps. Shadows crept along the skeleton and her lilies, keeping light from the interior of the store. The mums spun cartwheels of white across the counter. The refrigerator cabinet hummed. And the cactus, all eight feet of Viscountess Maynard's great flowering cereus, was lying on the floor in front of me.

The smell of iron filled my nostrils. I was standing in a puddle of blood. Creeping backward, I closed the velvet curtains on the windows and lowered the Levolor blind on the glass door. I grabbed a piece of newspaper from behind the counter and stuffed it under the door, watching the blood creep slowly into the newsprint.

Only then did I turn on my penlight, trying to trace the pool of blood. It took a moment; the Viscountess Maynard's great-flowering cereus had fallen on the floor, the green columns of its arms extended. The large, showy blossom, the whole purpose of Viscountess Maynard's great-flowering cereus, was ruined. Big as a hubcap, its beautiful bright pink face was face to the floor. The ugly thorns emerged from the wooly tufts that dotted the water-filled flesh. And many of them were sticking into Thad, trapped underneath it.

Viscountess Maynard was a powerful plant; all she had to do was fall on you, and a slow and painful death would be yours. Leaking blood from a thousand wounds, the body underneath her was firmly nailed to the floor. Thad, who had been ambushed by the desert beast, wasn't moving. A white, pathetic hand lay like a fallen petal on the concrete. My own hand wove past two thorns to find a pulse. There wasn't any, but the hand was still warm. I pulled back quickly, a sharp spike drew across the top of my hand in warning.

A trolley clanged outside, the evening's last ride of the F line. I swallowed, a dry, hard lump that reminded me that I had a throat, that I was alive, waiting, breathing in the darkness, me and a warm body all by ourselves, I hoped.

The penlight led me through the shop. The back door was open, and there was no one behind it. I closed and locked it; wiping off the handle. The back room had been cleaned of the earlier evidence of vandals. The stainless steel sink had been scrubbed clean.

I checked the lavatory; a soiled and tiny washbasin had been crammed into an unvented closet. The medicine chest held only aspirin and cleaning materials. I returned to the front of the store. The cash register was open, as was the custom for retailers after closing. The open drawer displayed its emptiness. But cash, of course, was not what this murder was about. The rolls of mylar paper—silver, gold, and green—were all wrapped up for the night. Spindles dangled black, orange, and rainbow curling ribbon. A box of cellophane bags, plant food ready to be twist-tied to the flowers that required it, was undisturbed. Everything was in order. There was no sign of a struggle anywhere.

I crept back around the counter and surveyed the body, held in the deadly embrace of the great cactus. From the number and spacing of six-inch thorns and the flow of blood, I imagined that about fifty or sixty piercings had just taken place on the floor of the House of Moss and Sticks. It was Thad's final body art, administered by a cactus he never knew and by someone else that he probably did.

I took a soft cloth from behind the counter and wiped off the doorknobs, front, back, and the lavatory. I did my own hurried little cleaning up, imagining that from time to time, the body was writhing or moaning from its position on the floor.

It was a moment of fear, of loathing. Thad's skeleton display would cackle at the revenge it had achieved. What is a cactus without its thorns?

Had someone surprised Thad, tipping the large plant down upon him? I touched my foot to a bald spot on the plant. Full of water, the scary succulent would weigh a few hundred pounds at least. Pulling it off of Thad would not be easy. Even the fire department with their jaws of life would have a hard time chewing away at the vegetable/weapon.

"Viscountess Maynard's great-flowering cereus, you've got some mighty long fingernails," I murmured, just to hear my own voice. I knelt down by the base of the big plant where the thorns had been clipped away. I poked the thick green skin with my toe. At the base of the collapsed plant was a deep, mushy spot.

Preparing to make my getaway, I thought carefully about any evidence I might have left behind. Thad's heart had stopped pumping, so the red stain was oozing more sedately, making its way more languidly toward the newspaper under the door, which was collecting the flow of blood. Here was a mystery for the San Francisco Police Department. A lot of people had run through Thad's back door of late. I took a last look at the white extensions of flesh that had tried to crawl out from under the viscountess. Was Thad dead? Really, finally, and totally dead? My trembling hand tried to make its way toward his neck, but a spike pierced me with a vengeance. Viscountess Maynard was still alive. Unlike Thad, whose other hand was stretched out toward the counter, as if he had wanted to grab the telephone. But he'd missed, and something else was clutched in his claws.

I remembered Thad's hands, as he had pierced my nose, the tattoo on the back of his hand seemed to have wiggled like a belly dancer. The yin-yang symbol was silent now, black against the pale gray of the dead flesh. His practiced hands were clutched in a death grip, holding a final message for the living world.

I was no longer interested in his pulse, but I sure wanted to know what was clutched in his hand. Something garnered from the murderer, no doubt. Some obvious clue that would wrap up the case once and for all. I grasped the counter with one hand and, balancing on one foot, I ex-

tended my arm precariously over the big green beast. On tiptoe, I held my jacket against my stomach. Any leather
caught by thorns would leave the telltale traces that can
make a case for Homicide.

I was a frightened, dark arch, praying that I wouldn't get
snagged as I let go of my coat, my fingers coming closer,
reaching down for Thad's other hand. Dipping down at the
end of my balance point, I held more tightly onto the edge
of the counter. "Don't worry, Viscountess, baby, I never
wanted to clip your thorns." The words reassured me, if not
the large vegetable. Closer, closer.

And then my foot slipped on blood.

For a few moments, I could see the wall slide before me,
the thorns coming closer. But some newfound strength in
three of my fingers grabbed the wooden counter. I could
feel my nails dig into the surface. The thorns waited beneath me, dissatisfied. It would be a horrible, horrible way
to die. It had been a horrible way to die.

I let out my breath and tried again, an arabesque that
would net me a clue that I hoped I could live to decipher.
Once again, I began my descent. *En pointe,* stretching over
the thorns once again, I came closer and closer, a strange
moment from my own Sistine chapel of life and death. My
fingers stretched, grasped a cold wrist, and turned it over.
Finally, I held hands with the dead man. My fingers curled
under his. Holding hands with a dead man was no fun.
What if there was nothing inside the hand and I was impaled for no good reason? But I was nothing if not curious.

One finger, two fingers, my fingers crept under his. I
held my breath and concentrated on the exact angle of pressure to get his claws to retract and release his final cargo.

Perseverance paid off big time. There, inside Thad's dead
palm was a treasure that would lead directly to the killer.
Thad was holding a hoop earring, one that was uniquely

engraved in Indonesia, one that was not twenty-four-carat gold, despite what the jewelry store had said. It was mine.

Standing up like a soldier, I still held onto the counter. I counted to twenty and looked at the minor piece of metal in my hand. It had been worth the effort.

The evidence that could have convicted me was there, a taunt, an insult that made me feel small and stupid. The murderer, if there was one, was *so* organized, with *such* a sense of humor! The murderer, if there was one, was communicating with me.

The connection between Thad and Gale was the *Johnny Lever Show*. The triggering event for the murders would be National Coming Out Day. And the spree was organized, planned to look like freakish accidents. Someone with a high intelligence. Following media coverage, waiting for the unusual case to come into the headlines. Someone who requires the victim to be submissive: both Gale and Thad would have died slow, horrible deaths. Someone who left little evidence and liked to play games. Thad's murder was so personalized. The staging of his death a coup de grace: both his floral and piercing careers had been exemplified. I wondered if Homicide would make the connections. What was the obvious connection between the cactus crime and the deadly dinner? Easy, the killer's choice of weapon was *plants*.

I had managed to retrieve the earring without snagging my jacket, and hopefully without shedding any gray hairs that were becoming more numerous by the minute. I sent a silent prayer up to Quan Yin that I wasn't leaving any trace evidence as I made my way quickly out of the back door, wiping the doorknob carefully again, inside and out.

The moonlight mocked me, and I hustled down the alley. *You're so smart, Emma Victor; too bad someone else is way, way smarter than you are.* Hearing the clattering of trash cans, I noticed the back door of The Café was ajar. The escape exit of the murderer would be mine as well.

I threaded the earring back through my ear. Wincing with pain, I thought about cats. And how they liked to play with their food before they ate it.

CHAPTER TWENTY

I QUIT AGAIN

Romea's windshield was empty, unsullied by official notice or advertisement. My prayers had been answered. Quan Yin, the parking goddess, had let me off again. I had never been in my car faster, swerving down Seventeenth and speeding home. A man who had pierced many and outed one big diva on television, impaled on a plant. A man who, by his very nature, would have enemies galore. For one thing, he treated his employees like shit, as well as his plants. What is a cactus without thorns? Thad, with my earring in his hand.

At home, my answering machine was blinking, blinking, blinking.

"Okay, Emma. So you quit." It was Rose. "I have to tell you that I really don't appreciate it. You've had difficult clients before. What's this about 'misleading and hostile'? For Chrissakes, all you have to do is keep an eye on the woman, not hold her hand! Park your butt in her kitchen, not in her bed. Park your car on her lawn and write up your report. Just put in your two weeks, Emma, and we'll both collect. I need this account, Emma. Don't let me down." The heaviness in her tone was almost a threat, but nothing com-

pared to a mature Viscountess Maynard's Great-Flowering
Cereus.

I wanted nothing more than to go and wash my hands, but
the answering machine began the second message from
Guaranteed All Risk.

"I haven't heard from you, Miss Victor." It had been two
whole days and Mr. Fremont's undies were wedged. He
wanted a progress report, he wanted to see Pendrinkski
throw away his crutches, and he wanted it on film. He'd be
checking in tomorrow afternoon at five, and he expected
that I would have some solid evidence for him.

I took a hot bath, replaying the scene from Moss and
Sticks over and over again in my head. I could pin down a
million reasons for the murder of the retail slime-bag, but no
reason as to how my earring had gotten in his hand. There
must be another explanation. Of course, explanations only
opened up bigger holes in the case; holes that a jury could
swim through and still convict on circumstantial evidence.
The soft spot on my skull was hardening nicely; I massaged
shampoo gently around it. I could say it was an accident. A
floral tragedy just waiting to happen.

Then I remembered: running from Audra Léon's bodyguards, I'd been attacked by thugs from Bell-Worliss; I had
lain in the alley just outside Thad's back door. My earring
could have easily fallen from my pocket onto the pavement.
Thad would look at it, wondering if it was gold. He was still
holding it in his hand when he went back into his shop.
There, behind the looming cactus, would be his last customer. His last customer *ever.*

Now that I wasn't going to the gas chamber, I could clear
my head. Or muddle it up again. I wrapped myself in a fluffy
towel and strolled to the answering machine. I listened to
Rose's message. "Okay, Emma. So you quit. I have to tell
you that I really don't appreciate it. You've had difficult
clients before. What's this about 'misleading and hostile'?"

The infection in my ear had perhaps left some minuscule skin cells, which adhered to the yellow metal. And were now on Thad's palm. A DNA fingerprint that would seal my fate forever. I threw on a pair of flannel pajamas and wrapped the towel around my head. I massaged tea-tree oil under my eyes and thought about my next course of action. First of all, I would clear the field of Guaranteed All Risk. As far as Fremont was concerned, I should jerk Pendrinkski's crutches from under his armpits and watch the guy dance or crawl. And I would play my own pivotal part. It was a lovely line of work. I listened to the singsong, shrill tones of Mr. Fremont, a company man if there ever was one.

"I want evidence. I want it after you complete your surveillance tomorrow. And I expect to see a written report by the end of the week." He wanted a lot of things for his money, and he would get as close to the truth as I could get him. Tomorrow would be Pendrinkski day, but Mr. Fremont would have to wait until I took another little trip to Visalia. It would be nice to wrap up the insurance job so I wouldn't be on the top of *everyone's* shit list.

So far, Pendrinkski had a woman doing his shopping, but he had to leave the house sometime. Cabin fever would get him sooner or later. If it didn't, I could find a way to flush him out. If I was lucky, he might leave for an afternoon stroll. Maybe that time would be in this afternoon. Entrapment was just a kind of criminal encouragement. And keeping the watch on Pendrinkski would keep me out of trouble and give me a chance to figure out why bodies kept falling around me.

The next message was from Rose—again. Her voice was also hitting the higher registers. "Emma, are you there? Pick up. Why aren't you carrying your pager? I want you to check in, and I want you to do it now." There was a long pause. Rose somehow guessed that I was home; avoidance was not one of my character faults. Usually. "Okay, Emma."

Her tone was warning. "Have it your way. But I hope you
have some other clients in the wings. Because you're really
screwing me, girlfriend!"

I let out a long breath. That's why they call it work. I reminded myself to reactivate my pager. Who would have
thought these peanut jobs would have required it?

I spent the rest of the night typing up my reports on Pendrinkski. It seemed to calm my mind; the petty scams of
people on Social Security who'd rather not die dining on
kitty food.

The respondent, Guaranteed All Risk, placed the petitioner under surveillance and videotaped the petitioner
for brief periods on October 27th and 28th. The photographs shows the petitioner consistently using his
crutches. He neither assisted a woman who carried groceries, although he managed to hold the door open for
her. He took a bag which looked fairly lightweight (to
this investigator). This may be in contradiction to his
claim that his left arm is useless for ordinary lifting.
While holding a bag under his left arm, he kept the
crutches carefully under his armpits. He held the door
open, but was never without the support of crutches.

Great. The guy was either actually crippled, a fabulous
actor, and/or he knew I was watching. I scanned the other
papers. "Disability permanent in quality and partial in character means a permanent impairment caused by a compensatable accident or compensatable occupational disease
based upon demonstrated objective medical evidence. . . ."

Still, life is short, compared to death, which lasts for a
long, long, time. Why spend it lifting pallets with a forklift?
Why spend it catching small-time criminals? Why, indeed?
Because it paid the mortgage. I pulled out my checkbook
and paid mine. I would post it next Monday, after Hal-

loween. All the pedestrian desk chores calmed me and made me forget the fearful arabesque that I had just performed. Exhaustion sent me to sleep, something that Chris had warned me against. There could be a blood clot floating around in my head, a clot that would ambush my brain and keep me from waking up.

That night, my dreams offered culinary delights in fluorescent colors. But as I sat down to eat, I realized it wasn't food at all, but flowers, shaped and arranged to look like food. Orange rose petals imitated roasted duck. Chocolate cake crumbled into dead, brown leaves. I was hungry, I was lonely, I was horny. Everything seemed so *sham,* a pretend table in a pretend house on a pretend planet called San Francisco. The message from my unconscious was clear: facts, not feelings should dictate my course of action. The biggest riddle appeared to be: What is a cactus without its thorns?

Waking up was a relief; I was alive. The scab on the back of my skull had hardened. My hair had been restored and clean clothes completed the makeover. My earlobe had healed without Mariposa's secret Amazon remedy. I was ready to drive back down the valley.

CHAPTER TWENTY-ONE

CACTUS JELLY

Carmine's Deli was a modest establishment that ran a booming business just across from Our Lady of Assumption Elementary School. The bright green grass from the park across the street was filled with barking dogs and flying Frisbees. Parents watched toddlers climb on brightly painted jungle gyms. I parked my car and went into Carmine's Deli, purported, according to the sign, to make the best sandwiches in Visalia. The window was plastered with children's drawings: witches flying, pumpkins grinning their evil intent, and happy, carefree ghosts underneath the scrawled signatures of the students of Assumption Elementary.

It was 11:30, I had a half hour before school let out for lunch. Carmine's was done up in orange plastic chairs and wallpaper with abstracted orange and yellow daisies that jiggled and jumped against a green background. Hundreds of pictures of children in plaid uniforms, all scrubbed and polished, their little white teeth smiling. Messages were written on the photos or next to them: "To Carmine, who always feeds us good food." "To Carmine, who lets me wait here when my father picks me up." In the center of the room, a large pillar had hundreds of stuffed animals attached to it. The place was overheated, and Carmine was nowhere to be seen; three old-timers sank into chairs and shot the shit that old-timers shoot. "You don't think about it, but a war with China would be five million soldiers at least! He ain't gonna do that, no sir!" chuckled a man in carefully ironed but very worn overalls. He was speaking to a small man who wiped down the Formica countertop with a vengeance. Behind him, stainless steel bins held the usual garnishes: tomatoes, lettuce, pickles, onions and, in California, jalapeño peppers. A large, refrigerated showcase displayed tidy containers of egg, tuna fish, and chicken salads. Fresh lettuce and spinach leaves were dotted with tiny pumpkins and gourds, providing colorful background for bricks of local cheeses. Resting on the stainless steel shelf above the cabinet were straw baskets, bedecked with orange and green checkered ribbons. Hand-lettered signs described the contents: Local Tomatoes (Organic), Figs from Tom's Garden, Apples from Arnel's Tree, and MaryAnne's Fine Muffins. The last basket held garnet-filled jars. Carmine's Cactus Jelly was therein, a sweet reminder of a brutal plant. A hot-light rested over nacho chips, melted cheese being swirled by an automatic mixer. Next to the cash register, a vase of fresh flowers, daisies and orange mums, in keeping with fall colors.

I took a seat at one of the blond-wood Formica counters, settling into the warm, orange plastic of the chair, just behind the candy rack. Lik-Em-Aid in tiny white wax bottles, Pez, Candy Buttons, Smartees, and even the soapy-tasting Snaps were all present. Déjà vu, the sugar rushes of childhood all over again. From outside the window, I could see the kids playing basketball, girls on one side, boys on the other, on the pavement playground of Our Lady of Assumption. *Bounce, bounce, bounce.*

Carmine herself bustled in from the back room. "Are we ready for the kids, Tom?"

"We got another half hour before school's out, Carmine; not to worry."

But Carmine *was* worried, straightening a lettuce leaf here, an errant tomato there, making sure all the cheese for the nachos was creamy, the onion rings and french fries hot, ready for the kid trade. *Bounce, bounce, bounce.*

Perusing the sandwich selection posted above her head, the decision was easy.

"Cactus jelly sandwich, please."

"Made fresh just this morning." Carmine wrote my order down on a slip and pinned it under the nose of the man standing at attention in front of the garnishes. "Everything, baby? Pickles, onions, lettuce, tomatoes, jalapeño peppers?"

"Hold the pickles."

"Whole wheat, rye, white, sourdough, or Dutch crunch?"

"Dutch crunch."

"Sure, honey. Anything to drink? Chips?"

"Just some hot tea."

"I've got some nice peppermint today. From Tom's garden." She gestured at the small man busy with my sandwich.

"Sounds great."

"Cup or pot?"

"Pot of tea, thanks. Actually, I was wondering if I could have a word with you as well, Mrs. Wright."

The smile fell from her face. Something guarded took her place.

"It will just take a minute. Do you mind? I'd really appreciate it."

Bounce, bounce, bounce. Carmine thought about it. *Bounce, bounce, bounce.* She thought about it some more. *Bounce, bounce, bounce.*

"The kids won't be off the court for another half an hour. And I could use your help," I said.

"Maybe." Her eyes said, *Probably not.*

We sat down at the little table; Carmine wiped its surface off with a clean napkin. "Yes?" she said.

"I was hoping you could help me."

"Who are you? A reporter?"

"I'm not a reporter, Mrs. Wright. I'm a private investigator." I handed her Rose's card, Baynetta Security Services.

"You're working for this Baynetta—" her carefully plucked eyebrows rose a half an inch. I nodded. "Who are *they* working for?"

"An anonymous client is interested in establishing a tennis scholarship in Gale Petros's name," I lied. It was a scary experience, lying to a former high school teacher. "This disinterested third party is curious about Gale Petros's high school career."

"Hmm. It would be a wonderful thing, such a scholarship. Does Gale's mother know?"

"Not just yet. We're still looking for more information about Gale's high school experience. I was hoping you could be helpful."

"But I was only her home economics teacher!"

"You're the only source I could find. Not a lot of retired high schoolteachers go on to start their own business."

"Yes." Carmine would be immune to flattery, but she was innately proud of her orderly establishment. "I could give you a copy of the high school yearbook from the year Gale graduated. She was one of the very best tennis players that Visalia High ever produced. There wasn't a tournament that she didn't win. Everybody wanted her as their doubles partner. I know because I overheard the conversations during the cooking semester. That was followed by the sewing semester, when there was less opportunity to chat. But over the stove, you couldn't get those girls to be quiet, not even for a piece of chocolate cake!"

We'll get to the cake later, I thought. "They don't teach home economics anymore, do they?"

"No, no they don't. And it's a pity. A lot of the girls coming out of high school can't even boil an egg! But not Audra. Her mama taught her good. Charlene's berry pie was a prize-winner. She'd send those girls off, when all these housing developments were still fields. Gale and Audra'd come back with buckets of blackberries. Lips smeared purple. They were younger then, twelve. Real outdoor, country girls. Too bad it didn't stay that way. Show business! Charlene was against it from the beginning!"

"About Gale's tennis career—"

"She went on to become Audra Léon's secretary. Their families were—are—very close."

"What was Audra Léon like in high school?"

Carmine's lips pressed closed.

"Just curious." I shrugged my shoulders. "Did she show her incredible talent at that age?"

"Oh yes, oh my goodness, yes. All that girl wanted to do was sing. She was in every school play, every musical. Visalia High actually became famous for its leading lady. There just wasn't enough talent to keep up with Audra. She got all the best roles—even playing boy's parts—and up-staged the whole cast consistently. Yes, we had a lot of talent that year. Audra and Gale were two of the brightest and best that Visalia High ever produced."

"Did you have a sense of what Audra and Gale's future would be, back then?"

"Audra was already on the fast track. Her senior year, she signed a contract with a major label. Only Charlene's intervention kept her from running off and not finishing high school."

"And Gale?"

"Yes." Carmine shook her head and looked at her hands on the table. "I often wondered what would happen to Gale. She and Audra were best friends, I didn't know quite what would happen to Gale, she was so—attached—almost dependent on Audra. They played tennis together, Gale chose her for doubles, even though Audra's talents were not to be seen on the court. But Gale took all her balls and gave Audra all the glory. Not that she needed any more. The boys were already lined up to try and date the school's biggest star. But Audra, she would have none of it. The minute she graduated, she was off to L.A. Under the watchful eye of her mother. Gale went with her of course."

"What about Gale's tennis career?"

"Well, that's a bit of a sad story. There was an offer from a professional agent. Her senior year. I remember he even came to one of her tournaments. The only one she ever lost."

"Do you remember his name?"

"No." She sought her memory anyway. "It was too far back."

"I thought you said Gale had never lost a tournament."

"It wasn't her fault!" Carmine had a flash of anger from way, way back, visit her again.

"What happened?"

"She—Gale became suddenly ill."

"Ill?"

"Diarrhea. A terrible attack. She had to leave the court."

"Any idea as to what happened?"

Carmine looked me up and down and didn't find me wanting. She leaned closer. I was glad I'd cleaned behind my ears that morning. "She was *poisoned!*"

"What?"

"Another student poisoned her. Put Ex-Lax in the chocolate cake. Home ec was the period just before the end of school. By the time Gale got on that court, she didn't have a chance. She ran off crying. Her chances for a professional career were ruined. You don't get tennis agents to come to Visalia every day, you know!"

"Who did it?"

Carmine's face closed shut like a big, fat cookbook when the turkey's been roasted. "It doesn't matter."

"Why?"

"Why? Honey, ain't you ever been in high school? Jealousy! I'm tellin' you, it was pure green-eyed jealousy. That's why I put my deli across from Our Lady Elementary. I like the little ones. High school students—well, it is a very disturbing time of life."

"Who would want to ruin Gale's tennis career?"

"I don't like to talk about students and their pasts, Miss Victor. I like to think that we all outgrow any problems—any tragedies—that might befall us in life."

"I have information that suggests Rita Huelga was responsible."

"You *are* an investigator, aren't you?"

"What made people pin the poisoning on Huelga?"

"The girls on the team rifled her backpack. They found the Ex-Lax inside. The package was open, and half of it was missing."

"What did Huelga say?"

"That's the interesting thing. She didn't say anything! Nothing at all. But the most important thing was that she didn't deny it."

"Do you think she did it?"

"She would have denied it if she hadn't." Carmine didn't believe in the presumption of innocence. "Rita was a problem student. Brilliant. But quiet, far, far too quiet. After all, there would be no reason to deny it if she hadn't done it, would there?"

There could have been a number of reasons. First and foremost, it was in Huelga's character to clam up whenever a nerve was touched. Stone butch, she would have taken the consequences, guilty or innocent.

"There had been some family problems for the Huelgas that year. Her father was a drunk. Her sister, Miranda, was living in Canada. Miranda was another strange one. Quiet. Turned out to be an electrical engineer!"

"Rita Huelga is also in the sciences."

"Yes, well, you know, girls are suspicious of—of girls who are too smart. They were then, and they probably still are now. I remember, after the horrible scene with Gale, they threw Rita off the tennis team. Even the police investigators—" She stopped herself, her eyes drifting over to the elementary school.

"The police?"

"It was a long time ago, Miss Victor. The Huelgas were a family with problems. High school can be a terribly competitive time for young girls. I think Rita just didn't have the emotional resources to make herself happy. Too smart and too much pressure. A brilliant young lady who was never well liked, who was always hoping for friendship and trying to find some way to make herself popular but ended up being intensely disliked. Like I said, she was just a disturbed girl who was in Gale's cooking class. There was just something *wrong* with her."

"What time of year was that?"

"Actually, it was fall. I remember because the tennis team had just started practice. The cooking semester was in session."

"So it was in the fall that Gale lost her big chance?"

"I believe so."

"All because of Rita Huelga?"

"Like I said, Rita had had a hard year in school. I tried to find some sympathy for the girl, but, to be honest, I found it difficult. So Gale missed her big chance. I remember she cried and cried and cried. My heart just broke for her. The girls had a big slumber party after the tournament; the girls all felt very supportive of Gale. But that night—well, it would be good just to forget the tragedies of the past. Professional tennis wasn't going to be Gale's destiny, anyway."

There was a sad sigh. "It's an awfully tough world, especially for a black girl."

"I hear Gale was quite happy being Audra Léon's secretary."

"Yes." The lips drew together with finality. Tom came from behind the counter with a sandwich on a Melamite plate. "Here's your sandwich." A sandwich on a Dutch roll landed in front of me, cut down the middle on a diagonal. "Is that all?"

"This is a great sandwich!" Something in Carmine's sandwich defined the ultimate comfort food. Cactus jelly was just what I needed, sweet and hot. Not like Viscountess Maynard's great-flowering cereus. "Now, about that high school yearbook—"

"Sure, I'll get it for you right now." A whistle sounded outside. Recess, gym class, whatever had been happening at Our Lady, was over. "You sure you're setting up a scholarship in Gale's name?" The ex-teacher looked right through me.

"Of course, I can't reveal the name of the philanthropist. Otherwise, all kinds of people would be asking for money. You understand how it must be?"

"Sure, sure," she said, but she wasn't really sure at all. Carmine strode into the back, with a quick look at the playground. The yearbook came to rest in my hands, good as gold.

"Make sure you don't get any greasy fingerprints on it."

"Don't worry." I scrubbed my hands with a paper napkin and opened the padded, white plastic cover.

Faces with the frizzy hair, perms, and Afros of fifteen years ago smiled from the thumbprint-sized photos. Carmine's edition had the signature of every student that ever took her class. Her own picture under Staff had a collection of laudatory sentiments in a hundred different colors of felt-tipped pen. Rita Huelga's signature was not among them.

I checked under L and found Audra Léon's photograph, the rock diva unrecognizable as a tomboy tennis player. She was voted Most Likely to Succeed. She'd been in drama club, chorus, and three musical theater productions that year. Audra Léon had the curlicue lettering of the kind that teenage girls experiment with: "For Mrs. Wright, Who Taught Me That Every Stitch Counts!"

I flipped past hundreds of earnest high school faces to Gale Petros's photo. She had a balanced smile within a quizzically tilted head and an awkward scrawl underneath. "I learned a lot from Mrs. Wright, but I'm still trying to get it Right! Thanks for hanging in there with me! Gale." It was a nice, conscious sentiment for someone who'd tried and failed at something she didn't particularly care about. Underneath the photo was imprinted: "Most Likely to Make It to Wimbledon." Finally, I turned to Rita Huelga's photo.

There was nothing attractive about Rita Huelga in her past. She hadn't bothered to wash her hair for the photo. Her mouth was grim and bitter, there was nothing of the hopeful ingenue about her former visage. Acne dotted her full cheeks and shiny forehead. She wasn't a member of anything except the science club and the tennis team. She looked lonely, even in an old photo, and I winced at the scrawled message underneath in bright red felt-tipped pen. Someone had taken the time while in possession of Carmine Wright's Yearbook to write "Jerk!" in tiny little letters at the bottom of Rita Huelga's short list of high school credits. I flipped through the pages, looking at all the hope and pain and pimples on those adolescent faces. And then I saw *her.* The little television producer, Bevin Crosswell, before her days of television production, was also an identifiable nerd. The hair that was now styled for television was then held back by plastic barrettes. She had braces, which flashed through an uncertain smile. She'd been on the tennis team, along with Rita, Gale, and Audra. *So that was Rita's connection with the Johnny Lever Show.* In a foreshadowing of her future, I saw that she was stage manager for the high school musicals and did the decor for the senior prom.

At that moment, a wave of plaid uniforms and plaintive cries entered Carmine's. "Hi baby! Hi honey! Do you want nachos today, baby?" Carmine was happily scuttling back and forth, giving instructions to Tom and taking precious sticky nickels from small palms. I put the high school yearbook on the windowsill, away from the sugar-tacky fingers of elementary schoolchildren. *"I like the little kids better,"* Carmine had said. *"The high school kids can be so mean."*

I knew just what she meant. It had been a bad time for me and, apparently, a much worse time for Rita Huelga. Especially the first semester of her senior year. Only the public library in Visalia could give me the information on the tragedy that Carmine alluded to, that is, if it was a big enough tragedy to make the news a decade ago.

CHAPTER TWENTY-TWO

PATRICIDE

The Visalia Public Library had all the issues of the *Gazette* on microfiche. I pulled up October-November of the year Rita, Audra, Bevin, and Gale had graduated. Threading the strip of film through the machine, I whizzed backward, forward, not knowing what I was looking for. Ads for Halloween costumes and candy gave way to turkeys and tins of pumpkin. And then I saw it. November 1, the column that listed all the minor crimes and tragedies that never made it to the front page. But a photo had caught the photojournalist's eye and grabbed a few column inches on page seven.

A young Rita Huelga looked radiant. She wore a white lacy nightgown and flames were licking her home in the background. She held a young baby, a worried fire fighter next to her, and an older woman in the background.

FATHER OF THREE KILLED IN FIRE

Visalia: Mr. Carlos Huelga died last night in a fire, which burned quickly out of control, gutting the entire three-bedroom home. His daughter, Rita Huelga, acted quickly and is credited with saving her baby brother, Juan. According to the fire department, Miss Huelga put a wet cloth around her head and crawled through the flames, up the stairs, to the upstairs bedroom where the baby was sleeping. Unfortunately, Mr. Huelga, unbeknownst to his family, was asleep in an upstairs bedroom. Mr. Huelga had been missing for several days, and family members were not aware that he was in the house.

The fire, whose origin is undetermined, started sometime after midnight. The fire began in the basement, where members of the Visalia High's women's tennis team were having an after-tournament slumber party. None of the teenagers were hurt. Survived by his wife, Estella, their two daughters, Rita and Miranda, and son, Juan, the funeral is planned for this Friday.

I crawled along the pages more slowly this time. Pumpkins became turkeys, and then another headline caught my eye.

ARSON SUSPECTED IN SLUMBER PARTY BLAZE

Arson is suspected in the slumber party blaze that killed Carlos Huelga, 44, while he was sleeping. Police and insurance investigators have placed the origin of the blaze in a basement recreational area. The arson squad has scoured the charred ruins for clues and have found a burnt match, which may have been the source of the blaze.

"There were no combustible materials or timing devices," stated Lt. Louise Ottoman, head of the investigation team. "The point of origin of the fire is a small basement bathroom, where the lowest point of charring has been determined. It appears that a curtain in the basement bathroom was set on fire. The window being open, the flames traveled up the side of the building and created a chimney effect. The flames engulfed the first story in a matter of minutes. The heat of the fire was transmitted laterally through the residence. The garage shows evidence of fuel oil and oil spills from a vehicle. However, it is almost impossible to kindle a fire with fuel spread on concrete. In order to ignite and maintain a fire of this nature, a more volatile solvent must be added to fuel oil. We have found no evidence of this kind.

"This could have simply been a prank that went wrong," Lt. Louise Ottoman stated. "We encourage anyone who has any information to come forward. We have found a used match just outside the window. And nothing is so easy to trace as a burned match. We are looking into the type of paper that was used in its manufacture to try and determine its source. The members of the Visalia women's tennis team, most of whom were present, are being interviewed, but all the girls profess to be nonsmokers."

Or, in other words, the tennis team was keeping the silence of the sisterhood. A silence that came after a poisoning, a failed tennis career, a thwarted teenage romance. What had happened at the slumber party? I spun back to the photo of Rita Huelga holding her baby brother Juan. And then I knew the very scary reason why in her long, illustrious, medical career she had never treated a patient. And why she had appeared on television to out her best friend and lifelong love.

I would have liked to stay longer at the Visalia Public Library to find out more. The arson investigation did not bring conclusive results, a two-paragraph article told me. The insurance company had paid out. Although the Huelgas' insurance covered the loss of their home, it was a hard fact that there was no statute of limitations on homicide, by arson or any other cause. Murder is forever.

CHAPTER TWENTY-THREE

ENTRAPMENT

I was anxious to complete the Pendrinkski case, a little too anxious, it turns out. The operation would rank me as a first-class jerk, in the crummy company of other insurance investigators who worked for Mr. Fremonts all across the country. I put a new cassette in the videocam, reactivated my pager, and strapped it on my belt.

The lawn at 1618 was browning; it would need to be watered soon. The Prussian-pruned bushes were still standing at attention; the windows were still veiled in sheer curtains. Even a man who didn't want to be seen walking would have to come out sometime.

Luck was with me, setting me up for my own kind of entrapment, that day. Mrs. Mohair Coat came outside; she didn't have her cart with her. Mr. Pendrinkski was behind her, hopping along with notable agility on his crutches. They paused just outside the door, surveying the browning lawn, shaking their heads. Walking down the stairs, Pink Mohair said something that made Mr. Pendrinkski laugh. Perhaps they were chuckling about his theatrical use of the crutches; maybe he was promising to water the lawn once he could dispense with the bulky supports that he hoped would win him a secure income for the rest of his life. The video camera lay ready, like a weapon, on the seat next to me.

Mohair drew her coat closer, despite the warmth of the day. Pendrinkski sighed as Mrs. Mohair took a key from him. She slid it into the lock of the garage, bending over slowly. With effort, her arthritic hand on the handle, she hoisted the paneled door. Inside, an old car, something big and finned from the fifties, in mint condition, waited in its stall. Like the cliché, I could attest that the oldsters used the car once a week. It was Thursday, and they would want to avoid the holiday Halloween rush, I thought, watching the old Buick back out of its stall. Would they be purchasing candy for the neighborhood kids? Dancing a tango behind closed doors?

Confident that I wasn't spotted, I followed Pendrinkski and Mrs. Mohair down the hill to the little shopping street in the Portola neighborhood. Eyeglass shops, a neighborhood hardware store, a few excellent and well-kept fruit stands, the requisite coffee houses all displayed witches, goblins, and the like in their windows. A tiny movie theater showed movies that the Mr. Pendrinkskis of the world would appreciate. An old Boris Karloff film, a Fred Astair Matinee festival, *101 Dalmatians*.

Dominating a corner, First American Savings had kindly provided a bench. It was a resting spot for other retirees as they trolled the tiny shopping area. I parked on a hill street, leading into the area. I could have gotten a cappuccino and a haircut in the time it took Mrs. Mohair to back the big Buick into its space. She fed a quarter into the slot, turning the knob with difficulty. Then she helped haul Mr. Pendrinkski out of the car. He put his crutches on the pavement and settled them under his armpits, catapulting himself out of the car. The guy had the whole act down tight; only his furtive glances from left to right gave him away. Could he see me, feel me, the invisible eyes, waiting to capture the moment of truth?

Mohair helped settle him down on the bench in the corner. A short discussion ensued. What did he want from the store? Was there something at the dry cleaners? Would they be eating kitty food tonight? What about when their ship came in? The disability hearing was in two weeks. Only a little bit more playacting and they would dine on steak for life, staying home and watching the talk shows together, until death took them, separately, or apart.

The shadows were growing longer, and I was getting sleepy with the boredom of watching a man on a bench who never moved. I spotted a crowd of adolescents, just released from school-prison. Two teenage boys were hopped up on hormone changes, teasing girls, looking for action. The girls blew them off with lots of hair flinging disdain. The boys were left behind with nothing to prop up their egos but more trouble. They found it in a small electronics store, Mr. Lee's Televisions and VCRs—New and Reconditioned. Fake spiderwebs housing big rubber tarantulas were stretched across Mr. Lee's plate glass.

I counted to fifteen, and the boys were out on the street, track shoes on the pavement. Mr. Lee was behind them, shaking his fist. I looked up the street. Mrs. Mohair had popped into the dry cleaners, waiting patiently in a long line. Pendrinkski was still parked on the bench, talking to an acquaintance, oblivious to the drama.

"Come back here with that," Mr. Lee was yelling. The two boys laughed and turned the corner where I had parked Romea. Up at the top of the hill, they congratulated themselves; in a few years, they would be ready for bigger crimes. At the moment, the stolen Walkman satisfied their basic ego needs. Headed for Juvenile Hall, it was an attitude I could use.

Pendrinkski was alone now. His crutches sat unused, next

to him on the bench, just where I wanted them. Mrs. Mohair was moving forward in line; there were still two customers ahead of her.

I crossed over the lanes of slow-moving traffic, big cars trawling for the small spaces. The boys were heading to the top of the hill, still high on adrenaline. They were congratulating each other. Up to no good, they were just up my alley. *Ah, the dirty work I do for the Mr. Fremonts of this world,* I thought.

"Hey, psst!"

They turned around with bored and careful smiles, not sure if I was an emissary from Mr. Lee.

"Want to earn ten bucks?"

Guarded expressions were exchanged.

"What?" asked the taller of the two, screwing a baseball cap tightly on his skull. Yellow earphones dangled from the Walkman. A plastic shrink-wrap box lay in the gutter. "What do we gotta do?"

"Easy." I sprinted up the pavement and pulled in closer. Four suspicious eyes looked at me like I was an alien from outer space.

"We don't have a lot of time," the smaller one explained.

"Sure you do. You have time to steal a Walkman, and this will be even easier."

"Like what?" Mute hostility poured off them in waves. I pulled closer to the edge of the building so we could all look around the corner where Mr. Pendrinkski was still sitting in front of the bank.

"Twenty bucks to steal the old guy's crutches."

"What?"

"The old guy on the bench. Steal his crutches, bring them back here to me, and this twenty is yours."

"That's mean, man!"

"Yeah, I know it is. But I'll bring his crutches back to him. It's just a practical joke."

The boys looked at each other quizzically. Then one of them snickered. That's when I knew I had them on the pay-roll.

"Okay, we'll do it," the bigger one said.

"That guy, right?"

"That's the guy." I leaned against the side of the building that shielded us from the street.

"Okay, lady. We'll do it. Why not?" said the smaller one. "Where's the twenty?"

I brought out the bill, Andrew Jackson looking startled and stern as usual. The little one reached for the bill, his hand fast as a snake through the grass. Even faster, I had it in my pocket.

"The crutches, boys. It'll be easier than stealing candy from a baby," I encouraged them.

The boys approached the bench, looking around suspiciously. I had the videocam ready. I looked through the viewfinder. I just caught his expression as the boys were approaching. Pendrinkski could feel the no-goodness of their presence. Fear started to roll off him as they made for him. He knew he was prey, the way the old, weak, and infirm feel. I watched through the lens, a sickening sense of fate and conscience overcoming me. Each boy grabbed a crutch and pulled. Too late, Pendrinkski reached out and tried to grab the crutches. His hand secured the tan rubber knob at the end; his palm tightened, the frightened boy, not expect-ing this twist, pulled harder. Mr. Pendrinkski fell on the pavement with a hard thump. Twisting the remaining crutch violently out of his hands, the boys sped across the street, looking as scared as they should have been. A few people looked up, pedestrians yelled out, pointing at the teenagers sprinting up the hill toward me. I backed away from the building. They arrived, panting, sweating, a glimmer of fear that overcame their egos at last.

"Here you are lady, where's the cash?" Wide eyes looked

back to the street, waiting to be followed and punished. But the shoppers would be too busy helping Pendrinkski. I handed over the Andrew Jackson and took the crutches from them. Worn vinyl on the tops betold of a body resting its armpits for many months on the surface. I put the camcorder away. Turning down the street, I saw Pendrinkski slowly trying to get himself back on the bench, using only his arms. A young woman kindly put her hands under his armpits, attempting to lift him. I was sprinting across the street, bearing the crutches, Emma Victor, the treasonous Good Samaritan on the spot. It was a crummy spot, on a crummy job in a life that was feeling pretty crummy at the moment.

Pendrinkski had a tear in his eye, which he brushed away with embarrassment. "Why would they do that to me?" he asked the world, and there was no answer.

"Oh, thank you, miss, thank you!" Pendrinkski looked at me with relief. "Thank you so much." He looked at the wooden appendages with relief. "Bless your heart. Oh, bless your heart."

"Leave my heart out of it, sir, let's just get you on the bench." Pendrinkski was a big man, a heavy man. The shock had made his hands shake. His arm had a long scrape on it where he'd slid along the pavement in a futile effort to keep his crutches. I helped the woman hoist him onto the bench, each of us taking an arm. The other woman was red-faced with her half of the burden. I could feel the sweat underneath his armpit as I pulled hard. I could feel that his legs were doing nothing to support him. That's when I felt like the biggest jerk of all. I could tell that his lower limbs were as useless as rubber, and I knew that it wasn't Pendrinkski who was entrapped. It was me.

CHAPTER TWENTY-FOUR

DISCO NAP

Images floated through my mind as I drifted home. Thad, dead on the floor. A cactus, mushy flesh at its base. The girl golfers who bought chrysanthemums. Snake, a man who licked his lips and looked familiar. Mariposa, floating out the back of the House of Moss and Sticks. Rita, suggesting an ointment for my ear. Bell-Worliss, hot on her trail, on mine. My earring in Thad's hand. The white chrysanthemums keeping watch in an orderly row over the gruesome scene on the floor of the House of Moss and Sticks. Cats, sick little kitty cats, getting well for all the world to see. I reminded myself to check out the Diagnostic and Statistical Manual, the current bible of the feel-good profession. There were more than a few characters in this drama who could make it into those pages; perhaps the strange, anecdotal science of psychology could make some sense of it all. I couldn't.

Precita Park was full of dancing dogs. A gaggle of little goblins were working the streets. Later in the night would be the time for adults. And I would be one of them. I was a San Francisco lesbian, and it was Halloween; while I wouldn't wear the half-drag costume Rose so loved, I was ready for my own particular brand of revelry. But first I would have to take a disco nap.

I pulled into the garage, a sudden attack of claustrophobia hitting me in the concrete coolness of the old Victorian basement. Mink furiously rubbed against my legs, whining; she could have knocked me over. After I fed her, she crawled onto my chest and began to purr. My eyes were heavy; I drifted with the throbbing, soft sounds coming from Mink's throat.

They say that dreams do not come in color and there are no sound tracks. But my pre-Halloween nap had both. I dreamed of rainbow flags. And a disco party where all the folk wore iridescent costumes. A wonderful voice came from a heavenly party, from a time before AIDS, when people still smoked cigarettes in bars and the word *fabulous* hadn't been overused. It was Sylvester James and the Two Tons of Fun, singing from some very different days.

Got a match? Mm-hmm!
That's some fabulous clothes! I'm tellin' you!
Look at all the fabulous people!

Before I knew it, a half hour had passed, a disco party that had renewed my body and my spirit. An insistent digital sound from my pager awakened me. *Dance! Dance!*

I dragged myself to the phone, wondering if Rose would be nagging me, trying to keep me in her employ. *Dance! Dance!* I dialed her number and heard the news.

The disco beat was dead. Rose was no longer trying to keep me in her employ. The awful predictable happened. An outcome of the *Johnny Lever Show,* of the media, which could just eat people up and throw them away. Rita Huelga had tried to commit suicide. She'd been checked into San Francisco General, and they were doing everything they could just to keep her alive.

CHAPTER TWENTY-FIVE

THIN AIR

Rita Huelga didn't seem suicidal to me, but I'd been reading a lot wrong these days. She was a woman committed to her work, that was one thing I was sure of. Work had kept her going through whatever trauma her childhood had served up and kept brewing all those years. She'd survived cancer. But maybe she didn't survive Audra Léon.

"They're calling it attmpted suicide," Rose said.

"I just don't figure it. The woman lives for work. She's survived a lot, and she's got a purpose in mind, and if I'm reading the situation right, she was getting awfully close—"

"She ate the bad mushrooms, Emma."

"Oh no."

"She's no fool when it comes to mushrooms. She is probably in danger of liver failure."

"Maybe it was heart failure." I sighed. "And maybe she's found what she's looking for and the quest is over."

"Whatever, it's time to light a candle, Emma."

"Thanks, Rose."

"For what?"

"For letting me know."

I put in a call to Chris's pager and stashed away the camcorder, locking it in my office. I was thumbing my copy of the Diagnostic and Statistical Manual when the phone rang.

"Hello?"

"Chris, it's Emma. Where are you?"

"Home. We're trying on our mustache costumes for the drag king party at the Lex."

"Something slightly more important has come up. I have a client in General—"

"That's too bad."

"Can you find out her stats for me?"

"I go on duty tomorrow—"

"That could be too late."

"It's still visiting hours. You can try to slip in for the last half hour."

"Okay. Where would I find someone with liver failure?"

"Let's see, your patient is probably located on the second wing of Emergency. Ask Erin Murphy to help you. She's the head nurse on duty now."

"I'm not family; I don't think they'll let me in."

"Who is it?"

"Rita Huelga—"

"No! Ohmigod, that's terrible."

"You said it, friend. Give me some potential room numbers."

"Anything from 107 to 121 East. That's my best guess. Unless, of course, she's gone into cardiac arrest . . ."

Chris's information gave me the confidence I needed to go into the basement and get out my very best Nurse Nancy uniform. I even had a pair of paper slippers and a shower cap. I slipped my sneakers over the slippers and stuffed the cap in my pocket. In my hurry, I almost forgot the Diagnostic and Statistical Manual, the volume that might confirm for me *if* Rita Huelga had attempted suicide, *why* she had done so.

•   •   •

The corridors of San Francisco General felt different with the paper slippers on. *Scuffle, scuffle, swish, step.* I waltzed quickly on the linoleum; I could have slid even faster down the hallway if it wasn't for the intense pedestrian traffic complicated by wheelchairs and gurneys. Swimming through the sea of sickness and its personnel, I came to an unattended examining room. A plethora of medical safety devices awaited me. A paper mask, fitted over my mouth, obliterated my features. Rubber gloves would keep the casual inquirer away. I looked authentic enough to roam the hallways in a big, important, hurry.

Scuffle, scuffle, swish, step. I followed the yellow line on the floor, which would lead me to the east wing. The busy, blue-clad crowd at the nurses' station didn't look up as I passed by them. A cart of flowers and cards was without its driver, making me wish I had chosen the candy striper uniform instead. I glanced at the cards: nothing for Rita Huelga. The ominous beepings of life-saving equipment leaked from doors that were slightly ajar. *Scuffle, scuffle, swish, step.*

There were old people, frail and sunken, without their teeth. There were young people who looked like old people. *Beep, beep, beep*, the regularity of the sound the only indication that relatives and friends might return someday, sit up, talk, laugh, have a life. *Beep, beep, beep.* More bodies, more white linen. *Scuffle, scuffle, beep, beep, swish, step.* More machines and the anxious faces of family who watched them. And then there was Rita Huelga in Room 117.

She lay in an examination room, still on a gurney. Along the wall behind her were the gray apparatuses and tubes that kept death at bay. Oxygen on one side and suction on the other. The crash cart with its drugs, oral airway, tubes, and needles, a bunch of which were already in Rita Huelga.

An overhead surgical lamp hovered over her, darkened now. The golden tennis racket was still on the chain around her neck; it was a bright point of light on the dim shroud. Her face was bright yellow against the pillow. An IV pole stood guard, dripping, dripping, drip-ing. It beeped once for each number: 98, 97, 98, 99, 95. The monitor for her electrocardiogram beeped, too, the long green waves of Rita's heartbeat filling the room with a throbbing green glow. There was a peaceful expression on her yellow face, as if she had intended this tableau. Flowers in her hair would have made her a perfect Ophelia. I took off my mask and leaned over her face. I could feel the warmth of her breath, shallow and uneven. Her breath smelled like acetone.

Her eyelids flickered, but it was only a reflex. Or a final dream.

Please keep her alive, I asked the machines, the stainless steel agents that could forestall death, bring back life. Rita's color was not a good sign. A heart monitor showed a curve at a very low tide of life. Taking off a rubber glove, I touched her lips, her delicate neck, the strong cheekbones. I brushed her hair back over her forehead. Gently, I pulled the edge of her gown away from her chest. Rita Huelga had indeed had a radical; several ribs and a great deal of her underarm had been removed. The original wound must have been huge. The delicate eyelids fluttered. "I would have understood, Rita, I would have understood everything," I said to her in the darkness. But I knew I could never understand murder.

Underneath those eyelids, the news was not good; pupils dilated, rolled up into her head. There was nothing I could do. I took off the paper hat, the paper shoes, the paper gown. I sat in the chair in my own version of a deathwatch.

Nurses were making rounds with carts, but they were making their way on the other end of the hall. Rita Huelga wouldn't be having dinner anyway, at least nothing that wouldn't fit into her IV drip. I took out the Diagnostic and Statistical Manual.

The volume placed 'Pyromania' between 'Kleptomania'

and 'Intermittent Explosive Disorder' and described all the associated age, gender, and prevalence of the disease. Of course, there were those who hallucinated, for whom the diagnosis of pyromania was not appropriate. If you had to burn down the White House because Martians were inside and they could only be extinguished by flames, you were more likely a paranoid schizophrenic. The definition was also not applied to the obvious paid torches (included under 'Conduct Disorder'). It seemed that people with low IQs and chronic personal frustrations and resentment of authority were candidates for the flaming hobby.

Common to all was a buildup of tension before setting the fire, said the book, and an attendant "feeling of intense pleasure, gratification or release at the time of committing the act was also part of the profile," a description that could fit the sense of gratification common in burglars and bank robbers. But the *real* pyromaniacs had no other motivation than to see something burn.

There was also the gray area of conduct disorder, antisocial personality disorder, and adjustment disorder. A gray area that could cover the intense frustration and fury at being unjustly accused of poisoning. A frustration and fury that would find its release in setting a fire, a fire in which the arsonist would become a hero. "Although fire setting is a major problem in children and adolescents . . . pyromania in childhood appears to be rare. The relationship between fire setting in childhood and pyromania in adulthood has not been documented. In individuals with pyromania, fire-setting incidents are episodic and may wax and wane in frequency."

Rita Huelga's heart monitor skipped a beat.

"Longitudinal course is unknown."

And that's when Rita Huelga went into convulsions.

The book fell from my hands as I watched her limbs stiffen, a puppet brought to a sudden, horrid approximation of life. Jerking on the bed, eyes suddenly open, mouth gasping, I ran into the hall.

"Help! Help!" My cries brought the red crash cart and a team of technicians swarmed around the body, fighting death.

The monitor said *Tweeeeeeeeeeee;* someone was thrusting a tracheal tube and breathing into her lungs. Metal circles on her chest made her jump, the defibrillator doing its freaky work.

"Her heart's too good to die—"

"I hear something."

The monitor said *Tweeeeeeeeeeee, beep, tweeeeee, beep!*

No one paid attention, busy as they were filling Rita Huelga with new liquids and applying new machines to her body.

"Would you mind leaving the room, please?" A nurse rolled her eyes at me. But by then I was already way out of the way.

"Code blue, code blue, one-seventeen, code blue."

My tennies trod the linoleum. "Code blue, code blue, one-seventeen, code blue. Code blue, code blue, one-seventeen. Code blue, code blue, one-seventeen, code." The first murder came at dinner. The second murder contained a piece of my jewelry, pointing to me. A control freak who derived pleasure from control and exerting power over life and death. Left little evidence and a big message. Becoming addicted to the psychic energy derived from the danger involved in killing. And there was an escalation. From a domestic setting to a retail shop to the hospital room, the sites of the murders had become increasingly more public. With every risk taken, each murder was becoming more of an accomplishment. More of a nose-thumb at society. At me.

I wandered back to the nursing station.

"Can we help you, miss?"

"Yes, how's Rita Huelga?"

"I'm sorry, miss. Rita Huelga died two minutes ago."
The hospital routine seemed to stop.
"I'm sorry, miss. Rita Huelga died two minutes ago."
I could not wish the moment away.
"I'm sorry, miss. Rita Huelga died two minutes ago."
As if she'd gone to the cleaners, to the farm, to Mars.
"Miss. Rita Huelga died two minutes ago."
Two minutes ago. Two minutes of dead, medically dead,
horribly dead. There is no word more final than *dead*. The
dead tell no tales. There's no bringing back the dead. Even
the past tense, *died,* didn't do it. *Dead* was always in the pre-
sent, would always be in my present, would always be Rita
Huelga. *Dead, dead, dead.*

A vision of her mansion, the cats, the plants, came to me.
It shrank and shrank into a pin-sized point in front of my
eyes.

"Are you okay, miss? Why don't you sit down—"
"No, I—"
"I left my coat—my book. . . ."
"You . . . want to go back into her room?" The tone of
consolation made me, for no reason, angry. I pushed the
helping hand gently away from me. In the distance, I could
hear myself crying. *Rita Huelga died two minutes ago.* "Go
ahead—just—just don't touch anything, okay? The coroner
will want to do an autopsy."

I had been too late, always too late. Why hadn't Rita
trusted me? I would have understood. She didn't have to live
with the fear of her past. Emma Victor, slayer of skeletons
in closets, could have set her free. Such a bodyguard, you
could take a ride right from under her eyes. Your ticket could
get punched before she'd blink an eye.

I wondered if my book would still be there, turned to the
wrong pages, the pages of pyromania. I should have looked
up psychopaths or, as they are often called, sociopaths. People who were in touch with reality, who know right from

wrong but consciously choose to follow a path of evil. They lack any conscience.

The hallway linoleum stretched in front of me. A few miles away, the door to Room 117 was closed. They would take Rita Huelga away soon. My feet would take me there sooner. The head nurse would make a report to the coroner's office. The coroner and the photographer on night shift would show up at Rita's room. They would put paper bags around her hands to preserve the evidence. They would photograph Rita's body from every possible angle.

They would take a thin file and scrape the insides of her fingernails. They would cut her fingernails. They would cut twelve hairs from her head. The sputum from her mouth would be swabbed onto a filter. Ten cubic centimeters of her blood would be drawn into a red-stoppered tube. And all these items would be labeled, initialed, dated, and sealed. That is, if they were doing their job correctly.

The gurney would come; Rita Huelga's lifeless weight would be wheeled down to the basement refrigerators. There would be an autopsy, a coroner's report, an inquest. And I would be a candidate for intermittent explosive disorder.

"We'd better call the coroner," the nurse intoned in the dark distance behind me. She was a brilliant scientist. All the nurses seem to have heard of her. "There's nothing more that can happen to her now."

I opened the door to Rita's room, wondering when the coroner and the police department would come.

I had time to say good-bye. "There's nothing more that can happen to her now," the nurse had said. But the nurse was wrong.

Rita Huelga might have been technically dead, according to all the facts of medical science, but the only fact in front of my eyes was that the monitor that had made so much noise had been turned off. That, and Rita Huelga was *gone*.

CHAPTER TWENTY-SIX

PRESTO CHANGO

I blinked. The bed was empty. There was a depression in the bed where Rita had died. I put my hand on the sheets. Cold. I half-expected a puff of smoke.

The sheet that had covered her, that had probably been pulled up over her face, had been carefully pulled up over the pillow. I grasped the hem, knowing that Rita's body would not be underneath. There, on the pillow, was a sparkling jeweled message. A tiny sugar skeleton with green, glittering eyes and a horrible grin. *"I live for my work, Emma."* I picked up the confectionary gem, stared into its sequined eyes. A strand of long, black hair curled around it. I put the skeleton in my pocket.

The window was open, and a fire escape loomed outside. It was the only way out, and the person who used the exit did so, carrying a hundred and fifty pounds of dead weight. It wasn't the lithe technician, that's for sure. I looked out the window. No sounds. No crashing about through the garbage cans with a dead body. Just silence. I laughed, my admiration for Rita Huelga rekindled. The woman worked more

266

magic than I could ever have imagined. Even dead, she had me guessing.

The curtain billowed into the room on the cool evening air. The Diagnostic and Statistical Manual had been closed by hands known or unknown; a strange, almost tender gesture in the rush of saving a life, in the grim thrill of stealing a body. Next to the window, a blue gown and paper slippers had been discarded. A face mask had been thrown on the floor. And there was more evidence. Something that made me laugh, even though nothing was funny.

A cellophane bag, square, opened, lay on the floor, underneath the IV drip. Nothing important, its commercial application revealed in a big yellow daisy. Exept it was used to carry Mariposa's strange potions. I put the packet in my pocket and retraced my steps down the hallway. Had Rita committed suicide? *Maybe she's found what she's looking for, and the quest is over.*

My coat was still there. The nurses were still clucking over the demise of Rita Huelga in the hallway. Wait until they found the open window and the disappearing body.

There was only one answer to this riddle: Peter Pan.

It was time for another quick exit so I could try to figure out where never-never land could be. I had a sneaking suspicion that wherever it was, there would be a lot of cats. The hospital parking lot was quiet, and Romea's engine purred, a key bringing her back to life.

I headed over the Peaks again, my homing signal taking me to Rita Huelga's mansion. Whoever had snatched her body might have wanted the accessories—or evidence— from her house. Rita Huelga's soul, if nothing else, would have flown home.

Except for the moon, the lights were out, and no journalists circled the big house. The windows were closed up tight, blinded by heavy curtains. The green lizard on the window of Mariposa's room was still. Not a leaf fluttered nor a cat meowed. I went up to the front door and leaned on the bell. *Dead.*

I edged along the shrubs that skirted the walls. I looked into the windows and saw nothing. The place was closed up tight; indeed, the owner was away on a long, long, vacation. Rita had said that the outer grotto, covered as it was in glass, was secure. But civilians had odd ideas about security. My fingers found easy holds in the rough-hewn brick of the high wall behind the garage. I crawled along the edges, looking at the glass panes for the one that might be loose, that might be cracked. Right in the middle was a section that was meant to be removed; perhaps the last pane, it was the keystone of the glass ceiling. All I had to do was walk on glass to get to it.

Balancing on the brick wall, I spread the weight of my body over the glass, hoping the tensile strength of the material would hold my evenly distributed weight. I crawled slowly forward, and the metal spines that held the glass sank a barely perceptible eighth inch. I put my fingers on the glass; there was a space, as big as a dime, around all its sides. My fingernails, what there were of them, dove into that space. The glass roof groaned, the metal spines protesting. My fingers started peeling up the glass, the sharp edge cutting little slices into the tops of my fingers. Only once did the pane slip back into its frame; the second time around, I had success: the pane lifted, the glass square balanced on its side, and then slid off, giving me about a foot and a half square to squeeze into the hole and fall to the grotto underneath.

I would have to do it quickly. The steel frame wouldn't hold my weight for more than a few seconds; its strength was calibrated to hold a certain amount of glass, flowing smoothly over a large area. A heavy body in one spot would test the little spines of metal, a test I didn't want to fail. The rain of glass would be deadly, the sound would wake all the neighbors. I inched toward the open hole in the ceiling, keeping my weight distributed over as large an area as possible. I pulled myself close to the hole and looked down. The tiles of Rita Huelga's kitty grotto, the damp logs and stones and mushrooms, waited in the darkness.

I did it fast; I did it tricky. Twisting my fingers around the steel frame where a forty-five-degree welded corner might just have held me, I pulled myself forward. Tucking my feet underneath me, using the strength of my arms, I got my feet into the hole without compromising the glass roof. There was a slight shudder, a grinding of glass against metal spines as the roof momentarily held my full weight. Then I dropped.

Letting my knees collapse, I fell with my whole body weight on the floor. I lay there for a moment in the darkness. There was no sound, no scratching or mewling of animals. I stood up and took the penlight from my pocket.

The grotto was only a memory: the cats were gone in the same puff of smoke that had spirited Rita Huelga out of the hospital. Except for a sprinkling of dirt on the floor, there was no evidence of the plants, the fungus, which had grown there. It could have been anybody's breakfast nook, not the laboratory of a scientist with the cure for kitty leukemia.

The French doors were unlocked, revealing more surprises. The large expanse of living room was empty. No velvet couches. No black walnut breakfront. Someone had cleaned out the fireplace. There were no ashes, no silver pedestals, no cashews.

The penlight led me around the house. All that was left were the lighting fixtures and the battle-axes in the medieval torture foyer.

"A uniquely charming decor, don't you think?" I could hear the real estate agents now. I sprinted up the stairs to Rita's bedroom. The curtains fell heavily to the floor, silencing the ocean at the bottom of the hill. *"And a partial*

view of the ocean! You can hear the waves!" the agent would say.

No bed. No address book, kept close to the telephone. The mantel fireplace was embarrassingly empty, naked. Shorn of all the photographs and sugar skulls, it was more than cold and dark. *"And there are two functioning fireplaces!"* A smell pricked my nostrils, something acrid, fuming through the house.

I ran back down the stairs, stopping briefly at the little gallery where I had done the wild thing with Rita Huelga. There was no bed. Below the railing, the dining room table had been cleared of all the books and computers and piles of papers. The table was gone, too. I looked at the large blank square where the bed had been. I thought about the mirrored coverlet, the way Rita Huelga had laughed, for a moment, when fear had left her. A laugh that would be no more. No decanters with potions, but a strange smell, nevertheless.

I placed the odor drifting through the room. Drifting up. Rita Huelga's deserted manse was inexplicably warm. Hot, even.

In the living room, the floor had come alive. The whole surface was moving up and down. The carpet was breathing *"You'll want to replace the carpeting . . ."* Underneath my feet, little puffs of black smoke escaped from the edges of the carpet; the rubber padding underneath was melting, creating a black carbonaceous smoke. You breathed that in, your lungs were coated with melted carpet padding; a plastic covering that would snuff your life out faster than the gas chamber. Gray and black, the room was quickly getting dimmer as the flames fought to reach oxygen.

And then I saw it and remembered: It's not the fire that kills you, it's the smoke.

CHAPTER TWENTY-SEVEN

SMOKE AND
MIRRORS

Smoke is a suspension of solid material in air. Since only one molecule of every five in Rita Huelga's house was oxygen, five volumes of air would quickly diminish to create one molecule of carbon dioxide. Right now, carbon and invisible gases were seeping into the living area of Rita Huelga's house. They could kill me before I even felt a flame. The conduction of heat, the convection of gaseous materials, and radiation of heat waves was a death sentence for me, if not for the building.

I thought about the original timber construction of the house; the tons of dry wood and old stucco that would feed the flames, forcing them upward. The vestibule and stairway would create a deadly chimney effect, flames and gases would fly up the stairs; the large rooms would supply a catastrophic amount of oxygen. In a flash I was flying down the stairs, through the dining room, and opening the basement door.

A roar of flame greeted me, a wall of fire that had

emerged from the kerosene that someone had let flow throughout the basement. I slammed the door, but not before the yellow monster had tried to escape. The doorknob was hot, searing. I put my hand on the floor. It was warm. Soon, the flames would eat a hole through the oak and then burst quickly through the floor, eating through the floor joists and dropping me into a fiery pit where deadly mushrooms used to grow.

I ran to the front door. A double-keyed deadbolt was locked, with no way to open it. That's why there's a law against double-keyed bolts: it locked you mercilessly in the house while you burned to death. The kitchen was filling with smoke, probably coming up a laundry chute, now glowing orange. Back in the living room, the double French doors that led into the grotto were still open. I closed them and breathed the fresh air, looking above me. Unless I could fly up to the glass ceiling, there was no way out. *"The arboretum makes a marvelous breakfast nook . . ."*

I could run upstairs and jump out a window. One of the box hedges could have broken my fall, and I might walk away. But the hallway was already drawing smoke, which was thicker at the top of the stairs than at the bottom where I was standing. The front door, thick and bolted, was before me. As were the sharp-edged battle-axes.

The big weapons were clamped to the wall with a decorative bracket that easily gave way. The ax was heavy. I took a last look around me. The living room was black, the oozing rubber of the carpet panting its deadly black breath.

"Just imagine, two functioning fireplaces!"

The smoke had filled the kitchen; the fire had its own breathing rhythm now. Sounding like a train trapped in the basement, the swinging door that led to the kitchen was moving rhythmically; swinging back and forth, serving up dark gray clouds that puffed my way.

I hoisted the battle-ax over my shoulder and swung the thing at the door. The blade bounced off the oak planks, mocking me. No way. I looked into the dining room, being served up with smoke from the kitchen. I wrapped my coat around my head, trying to keep some of those oxygen molecules for myself. The flames were quite literally licking at my heels, hot little tongues finding their way through the floorboards. To the left of me, the living room was a black and deadly chamber. My battle-ax and I made it into the dining room where the big weapon neatly crashed through the plate glass window.

After the crash of glass, I only remembered two things: the coolness of grass next to a house that had become a furnace and finally the sound of sirens.

I crouched and made my way quickly across the street and down the block. From the darkened interior of my car, I watched the neighbors gathering, awakened by the sound of sirens. I wondered if Rita Huelga's mansion had been adequately insured. I wondered if she had made a will. Together, we watched the mansion go up in flames: neighbors, rubberneckers, and maybe the pyromaniac, too. The velvet curtains of Rita's bedroom danced one last time with fire instead of ocean breezes. The copper gutters were melting like long, cherry-red taffy that dripped down the front of the house. The windows were just starting to burst, glass explosions that punctuated the night like a twenty-one-gun salute. I heard the sirens. Soon the fire people would appear.

Fire, flowers, fungus. There was a lot that was over: Rita Huelga, her work, a frame-timbered house in Forest Hills. I was just pulling away when I saw flames poke up through the hole I'd made in the glass ceiling. A long, fiery spike emerged, crackling with sparks, gorging on curtains and carpets and timber. The big shoot of fire finally broke through the roof, thirty, forty, fifty feet high. The house seemed to be giving me the flaming finger.

I found myself, twenty blocks away, crying, sounds coming from so deep inside me, flaming feelings of pain, I thought I would be consumed.

And, finally, it was Halloween.

I went home, but not for the costume that Rose had so appreciated. While my makeup was perfect for Halloween, there was a murderer on the loose. And a dead body, too. Admiring the soot and blood on my face, I didn't think there was a way to improve on the makeup. Although, a soft black eyebrow pencil offered itself up to me. I penciled in a mustache. Together with the blood and soot, I was quite unrecognizable as male or female. I was just a mess.

The phone rang, freezing me to the spot. Would it be more hot air? A three-alarm fire? Or an invitation to the grave, for which I was perfectly made up.

But it wasn't earth or water or fire. It was but a creature of the air, a sprite who still breathed, who breathed the words that you most wanted to hear. It was Mariposa. Unlike everyone else, she was anxious to talk to me.

"Emma, we've got to meet. Rita needs to see you."

"Right. *The Living Dead* is a movie, Mariposa."

"I'm serious. We have to meet." The voice was calmly insistent.

"Why? You want to get my fingerprints on a pack of matches?"

"Just name the spot, Emma."

"Let's make it somewhere nice and public. Where there will be a lot of witnesses, and I won't get hit on the head."

"Like I said, you can name the spot."

"How about the Club Lexington. Lexington and nineteenth."

"I'll see you there." The line went dead.

So Mariposa would be at the Club Lexington. And Rita Huelga, a supposedly very alive Rita Huelga, would be joining us. I reached into my safe and spun the combination. I took out my trusty .38. I put new rounds into the cylinders. I sent up a silent prayer, hoping that I would never pull the trigger. But the last time I did that, the prayer didn't work. It backfired, just like the thrust of the pistol against my palm when I missed a murderer out at Sutro Cliff. But this wasn't the great outdoors. It was a lesbian bar full of friends and acquaintances. While I could have guessed that I might end up at the Club Lexington, packing, I never thought it would be a gun.

Or that I'd have a date with a corpse. My face, covered in black soot, smeared with blood and darkened with mustache, was perfect for the occasion. I was the person who most looked like Lazarus, and I didn't think for a minute that Rita Huelga had risen from the dead.

CHAPTER TWENTY-EIGHT

SOME OF THEM WITCHES

The Lexington Club is located off an alley just wide enough to be called a street. Lesbians took the long stroll down the tiny avenue called Lexington to Nineteenth Street to the cozy corner establishment; I had walked there many a night with Frances, marveling at the quiet, tree-lined lane with old, one-family stick Victorians. The shadows would play over our faces, and our arms would lace around each other's waists. Kisses planted just past the warm glow of the streetlights.

The Lexington Club displayed its bright red enamel painted doors proudly to the street. The decorative, free-form grillwork that crept over its bright blue windows was both fanciful and fortresslike. Garbage fluttered back and forth across the street to where the New Lexington Market would sell you cigarettes that you couldn't smoke in the bars. Women would be standing on the corner, looking cool and hot at the same time. Kitty-corner from the bar, PG&E Utility Substation E, a windowless square of Greco-Roman concrete, stood silently, like a masonic hall, like a jail.

In direct contrast, the Club Lexington was a nineteenth-century saloon in a nineteenth-century building. It looked like a bordello; the clientele was strictly San Francisco lesbians and their friends, women for whom the taste of compromise would always be bitter, for sluts who claimed the word for themselves. Rita Huelga and her peers would not be found among them.

The saloon was just how a saloon should be outfitted. Five milk-glass Victorian lamps, like flying saucers, provided a warm glow overhead, as smaller matching lamps did throughout. The room was so red, it could make the whitest bar rat look tan and healthy. There was space for seven or eight round tables, although on most nights, you couldn't find a chair. You'd have better luck at the long bench that stretched along the wall, or you could pony up at the bar.

There you would watch Jill, Kathleen, Ginger, or Ann-Mary, with expressions of perfect disdain, serve the customers. Behind them, the huge, antique sideboard stretched fourteen feet. Tiny red lights were inserted into the sockets, and candles in red glasses were red stars that reflected off the old chrome cash register. You could watch the snakes dance on Dreanna's back while she pulled the tap. Two quarters in the Heart of Magic pinball machine and you'd get a shot at the Magic Trunk or, with luck, the Levitating Woman. You could watch other players grinding their hips and using their fingers to score millions of points when they ran the Tiger Saw. The jukebox would play Edith Piaf, Sinead O'Conner, Ella Fitzgerald, the Indigo Girls, Dolly Parton, and Sylvester. The Lexington was a show that never ended.

It was almost too good. Because the Club Lexington was cool, cozy, and sexy, gay men had started to notice the place. Despite the lack of upscale restaurants in the Mission, Castro clones were starting to make their way to the Lexington. If the trend continued, the place could change; gay men could overwhelm the place with their vast numbers and thick wallets. The lesbian midriffs would disappear between the biceps of men muscling up to the bar.

But it hadn't happened yet. And it certainly wouldn't be happening on Halloween. Tonight, almost all of the Lexington customers were drag kings and all of them were dancing angry.

Women in black suits, black moustaches, and black bras revved up Harley-Davidsons, which dominated the sidewalk. Getting inside the bar would be a challenge. It was a night when no Castro clone would have a chance. And I didn't think Mariposa would, either. I looked around for the willowy blond. Nowhere.

"That asshole better not put his camera in my face!" A big woman with a real beard put a little pamphlet in my hand.

NO TOURISTS! NO TELEVISION! NO TOURISTS!

"Johnny Lever in the Castro—Never!
Join the Lesbian Revengers' Protest Against the Exploitation of Our Community! We Cannot Be Bought!
Assemble at the Club Lexington, 8 P.M. Halloween Eve.
March to the Castro! Theatre and Surprises at the Castro Theatre! Let's Show Hollywood What Revolution Is About!
        NO TOURISTS! NO TELEVISION! NO TOURISTS!
                NO TELEVISION!

I took the pamphlet and stuffed it in my pocket.

"Ooooo! Good costume!" A remark floated my way—a diminutive blond woman. Barbed wire tattoos crawled down her arm.

"Thank you." I pushed one of the doors; it hit bodies that grumbled, cackled, and moved aside reluctantly. I pressed into the crowded crimson saloon. There were the hotheads and the coolheads, the shaven heads and the raven tressed. The main attraction was the pool table, lit in fluorescent pink. Three ancient crones with the bodies of teenagers wore black bras and danced on the pool table, leaping like lithe flames. Their long noses bobbed on their wizened faces as they sprang on high-arched feet. A group of drag kings thronged underneath them, she-males who made new territory of the tits-and-ass show. A throbbing beat pulsed throughout the long, red room. The twisting and twining bodies made it impossible to do anything but move with them. The war whoops made it impossible to say anything, think of anything but a coming, liberating battle. I knew that my makeup, even without checking in the mirror, was *perfect*.

"No tourists! No television! No tourists!"

"Huelga, para Huelga!"

"Johnny Lever is a prick!"

"Viva Rita Huelga!"

"Down with Hollywood imperialism!"

"Huelga, para Huelga!"

Strike for Huelga? Viva Rita Huelga?

Everyone seemed to know about the death of the scientist. The news of Rita Huelga's death had been hot on the heels of emergency room personnel. Was I that far out of the loop? Was I a grape on a whole different vine these days?

I pushed through a wall of black suede, black leather, and black velvet.

Drag kings turned their heads; witches' faces cackled and snorted. None of them were the blond Mariposa with the pale blue eyes. It was nearly impossible to make it up to the heavy oaken rail of the long oak bar that ran down the middle of the bar. Kathleen was working behind the bar. She broke her beautifully bored expression, calling to me, "Whaddaya want, Emma? A greyhound?"

"I'm looking for somebody," I screamed.

"You got a lot to choose from, girlfriend." Kathleen turned her back to sort out the requests of a thirsty coven, all cackling orders at once. That's when I saw her: Mariposa, backed up at the end of the bar.

She stood out like a clown at a funeral. Bright, tie-dyed velvet overalls in pink and green, and a chartreuse T-shirt made her look like a parrot. She caught my eye and smiled as if this were a chance meeting in a shady garden. I fought my way, with elbows and shoulders, toward her. A lot of black leather gave way, and I finally reached Mariposa.

"Hey, Mariposa." I gave her a quick look up and down. Despite her vacuous smile, she looked tired; three of her long fingernails were broken. She nervously fingered a ring of keys in her lap.

"Hi, Emma." The smile was taut. The big blond was very tense. "I'm so glad you could take the time to come and say good-bye."

"What'll it be?" Kathleen was ignoring the cries of legions and sauntered over to us. She was curious, taking in Mariposa, so out of place in the company of drag kings.

"Good-bye?"

"Yeah, we're relocating."

"Just like that?"

"Yes. Rita wanted me to speak to you before we left. Want something to drink? Try the mulled cider."

Mariposa smiled with an irritating, smug expression, silently holding up a glass full of an amber liquid. A slightly pungent smell of sweat rolled off the tall, retro-hippie.

Kathleen approached. "The mulled cider, Emma?"

"Sure, Kathleen." I felt disgruntled. Kathleen turned her back, and I watched the Medusa inscribed between her shoulder blades grimace as she strode over to a stainless steel cauldron that bubbled on a hot plate.

"You look like you've been through a lot, Emma," Mariposa commented.

"Nothing like Rita," I challenged.

"She'll survive."

"By the way, I was just over at the Forest Hills place. You sure know how to clean out a place fast."

"If you know the right people, it's easy to move, Emma."

"The movers I know usually need an appointment weeks in advance."

"The movers I use can move an entire life in four hours for the right price." She watched Kathleen ladle steaming brew into a tall glass at the other end of the bar.

"Of course, the cats were a bit of a problem." She looked at the keys in her hands. *Keys to the cats,* I thought, a phrase that made no sense.

"Rita's house burned down, Mariposa."

"Oh dear, you didn't get caught in *that,* did you?" She smiled.

"Caught? I was nearly trapped. Fires set in basements travel *fast,* Mariposa. So, your mover friends, they also know how to torch prime real estate?"

"You really don't want to know, Emma."

"You're right. The company you keep you can keep to yourself."

"No tourists! No television!" A pair of hips bumped into Mariposa and her ring of keys fell onto the floor. I bent down, looking at the hefty bunch of metal. Three car keys and a lot of house keys, color coded. A circular security key for an alarm system, like the one that had never been installed at Rita Huelga's house. Did they have a new place already? "Tsk, tsk." She took a sip of the hot cider. "We tried to be so careful."

"So why did Rita eat the bad mushroom dinner?"

"Come on, you can figure that one, Emma."

Kathleen put the glass down on the bar. "Two bucks, please."

Mariposa put a fifty-dollar bill on the bar. Kathleen rolled her eyes, and Mariposa shrugged.

"Oh no, Rita didn't try to kill herself. She's not the only one with death cap mushrooms, you know."

"So, what other Hansel or Gretel's been busy in the forest?" The cider was hot and left a spicy, sticky tingle on my lips.

"Only the ones Rita still falls for, I'm afraid. But she took my advice, and we're going on a long trip. How did you get in the house, by the way?" She jingled the keys in her lap.

"Through one of the glass panes in the arboretum."

"That must have been interesting. I didn't think that glass roof would hold anyone. With the double-locked doors, you must have had a hard time getting out, Emma."

"I broke a window. Now, Mariposa, what's this all about?"

"I have a message for you, Emma. From Rita."

"Rita's dead," I stated.

"That's what you think."

"That's what the entire crash team thought at San Francisco General."

"People are presumed to be dead all the time—who aren't."

"No tourists! No television!" A witch bumped into me, I steadied the glass of cider with both hands. Kathleen came over with a stack of bills: Mariposa's change. The tall woman looked at the money on the bar; she made no move to pick it up.

"So, Rita Huelga came back to life. And you have a message for me."

"It's just that Rita wanted to say that she's really appreciated all you've done. And she's sorry she couldn't tell you more about what she's been doing. It's for your own good—"

"That's right. It's all been for my own good, hasn't it? Having me guard a woman who isn't in any danger. Waiting for a cripple to throw away his crutches. Somebody had better tell me something soon, instead of taking me out of the action."

"I don't know what you're talking about, Emma." The tiniest crease came between her eyebrows.

"No tourists! No television!" A samba line was forming through the bar.

"Hey Emma, a little rum would get you up and dancing!"

Kathleen, with a bottle of rum, hovered over my hot cider. "The Revengers are leaving for the Castro soon."

"No, Kathleen." I sighed. The bartender offered a shot to Mariposa, who shook her head.

"Okay, Mariposa. You don't know anything."

Mariposa didn't blink; I had to hand it to her, she had one of the best poker faces I'd experienced in my long career interviewing liars. Her expression showed a kind of internal amusement that wasn't cute; under the circumstances, it looked a little crazy and more than a little scary. "It doesn't matter. I'm going on the road again. And I have more ways of disappearing than Bell-Worliss could imagine."

"How about bringing someone back to life? I have a hard time imagining that."

"You do? I've spent a lot of time in the Amazon, Emma. Many plants are poisons. Many plants are antidotes. What went into Rita's IV reversed the amatin. We should really find a way to get this plant on the market. If only people would stop picking and eating those nasty mushrooms. But we've been busy with other things. Now, I've got a few instructions. Just listen. And don't react for a minute. Rita doesn't want to be followed. She . . . she needs to disappear."

"She seems to be pretty good at that. For a dead person."

"Well, I don't know how else to convince you. But I thought that this, this . . ." She fished around in her pocket. "I thought that this just might."

A tiny golden tennis racket on the end of a chain appeared. It had a little hole in the racket, just like the one that Rita Huelga always wore. Had worn in the hospital, when I lifted her gown.

My mouth was open. I could feel it, stretching longer and longer, down to my neck. Mariposa had indeed been in the hospital room after Rita's demise and before her disappearance. The golden tennis racket was proof. In those precious two minutes of time, could Mariposa have entered her room and carried the hundred-and-sixty-pound Huelga out on the fire escape? No. She had to have help. Help from Rita Huelga, who was coming out of a coma via whatever antidote that Mariposa had supplied, who would shakily make it to her feet and out the fire escape.

"Who's trying to kill Rita?"

"Why don't you ask her?" Mariposa had leaned closer to me. Our mulled cider mingled. Her breath was warm in my ear as she said the last words that made sense that evening. "She's in the bathroom, Emma. Rita's waiting for you. She wants to say good-bye." There was no room on the bar to put down my mulled cider. I took it with me; it would keep my hands warm in case I met up with some dead flesh. I started the journey to the bathroom.

Never was a wall of witches more impenetrable. I reached the door where anxious crones crossed their legs. "Hurry up!" they pleaded with the closed door. "Aw, hell, let's go sit on a bumper on the street." A small phalanx marched out the back exit.

I tugged at the door. The small hook and eye that held it closed gave way easily. I looked into the darkened room, covered with graffiti as high as the arm could reach, a sink, a mirror, and a paper towel holder. I swallowed and walked inside the dark dampness. The door to the toilet was closed. A shaft of light peered out from its edges. The toilet flushed, gurgled. The shaky old knob on the door rattled in my hand. The ribbon of light became wider, became a ribbon of light with a silhouette. The woman before me was Rita Huelga.

"Well, hi." I laughed, a hollow sound inside the concrete chamber.

"Hi, Emma. Surprised to see me?"

"Well, Rita." I tried believing my eyes. "The last time I saw you, you were dead." Rita held out her hands. I took them. Flesh, blood, a pulse that pounded with life.

"Emma." She came closer, we held each other. My hands

grasped her ample hips; I felt the strength in her arms. And then I stiffened, went cold myself. Rita felt it in my shoulders. "Emma, I just wanted to say that I'm sorry I was so cruel last night. Hey, Emma—by the way, is that makeup?"

"No, it's an unintended Halloween costume."

"Very effective."

"Not to mention the little cruelty you dished out. 'You just fall in love with me like everybody else I fuck'?"

"I'm sorry, Emma."

"Well, I guess it says more about you than it does about me." I was starting to feel giddy.

"I know I've got a lot of explaining to do." Rita sighed. "I also know that you're still in love with Frances. We were both looking for closeness because our love objects are out of range."

"A little kindness goes a long way with me."

"Emma, the timing was—is just wrong. You're intelligent, attractive. The chemistry was right. We'd bonded, but I'm not exactly the most secure person in the world. I really am sorry, Emma."

"And I'm really glad you're alive, Rita."

"Mariposa fixed that. She's incredible, you know."

"She seems rather . . . controlling."

"Oh, Emma, there's a lot going on. There's no time to tell you the story now."

"No kidding. Two thugs from Bell-Worliss are after you—"

"I don't exactly live the life of a free woman."

"Who owns you, Rita?"

"That's one problem that I believe will be easy to solve. Mariposa and I are on our way to solve that right now. Then we'll disappear for awhile. And you, dear Emma, would be better off not knowing any of the details."

"How come everybody else gets to decide what I know?"

"It might not be good for your health."

"I'll take care of my health, thank you."

"Doesn't look like you're doing such a good job of it. Not to change the subject, Emma, I want to talk to you about Frances."

"Frances? My ex? What's she got to do with this?"

"I called her. Frances said wonderful things about you."

"A real personals ad, huh?"

"The gist of it was, you *are* to be trusted."

"That's a relief. Already I'm a little beaten and bruised from not knowing your secrets."

"Yes. I've had a lot of secrets in my life, Emma. I've learned, since high school, not to make friends."

"Except for Mariposa?"

"She saved my life, Emma."

"The thing you call toklastaki?"

"Yes."

"Why did you take the rap for Gale's pretournament poisoning?"

"I didn't take the rap. I just didn't say anything."

"A lot of people would see that as an admission of guilt."

"But it's my way, Emma. Talking has never come easily. The connection between my brain and my mouth isn't very strong. Words are like stones for me, Emma. They always have been. I've gotten really good at building walls. Sometimes, though, they just fall on me."

"Emma." Rita fished in the pocket of her jeans. A small piece of paper, ruled in pale blue, a half-centimeter grid, emerged. Carefully, folded twice, Rita opened it for a second, just to make sure. A drawing of connecting dots and circles, with arrows and letters flying about. Only one word was readable: *toklastaki.* "I want you to take this to Helga Meyers. She's head of oncology at University of San Francisco—"

"What is it?"

"I'll tell you what it is. It's the only copy, Emma, of the synthetic formula for toklastaki. It needs to go to Helga Meyers *tonight.* UCSF Medical Center. Hand deliver it. Don't let anyone see it, touch it, know you have it. I can't stress how important this is, Emma. I wouldn't want anyone harming your beautiful body—anymore."

"I'll bet. And I'll take care of your chemical notation, Rita." The little folded missive was tucked into the inner corner of the front pocket of my jeans. "This is undoubtedly the synthesis of some fungal product. One that has been distributed throughout San Francisco via Mariposa? In cellophane packages of plant food attached to white chrysanthemum bouquets? A pedestrian flower that those in need could order without suspicion."

"So, you're one step behind me, eh?"

"A lot of dykes in the Castro buying white chrysanthemums somehow didn't add up."

"Just get the formula to Helga tonight, Emma. It's detective work that can save lives. As you can imagine, Bell-Worliss isn't too happy with me. Somebody in the link squealed. We wanted to make our last delivery before we split town. I was going to give this to Helga myself, but I was laid up—"

"By a suicide attempt?"

"Emma, you and Frances and I, we are bit players in this drama. This goes beyond us. The forces at work are greedy and violent—and global."

"Greedy, violent, and global? I think you know what time it is."

"It doesn't matter. I have Mariposa with me. We can construct new identities and carry on our work in Latin America."

There was a long silence. Rita looked away, a lot of words that were just stones in her brain. I stared at all the scrawled names on the wall. There was a lot to look at:

"Jeannie, I love you!"

"Mary, March, April, May."

"Stand by your Grrrrrl."

Rita brushed her hands over my cheeks, nuzzled my neck, breathing deeply. I held her, grasping the softness of her hips, feeling the strength of her legs. And also, I started to feel light-headed.

"Emma, it's time for this chapter to end. You've been great. True blue, the way only a heart that's broken can be. We gave each other comfort on a dark night. It's time to say good-bye. And that's what I'm saying now."

Rita pulled me toward her and kissed me. A new kind of wrinkle in time made it last a year, forever. Her body, pressed against mine, warm, soft, enfolding, even as I was resistant. When we broke away, I thought I saw infinity in her eyes. I stumbled backward, with the stunning experience, with a new chapter in my mind that was only beginning. For a second, I could have *sworn* that I was kissing Frances Cohen. This was one scary Halloween.

"Emma, you have to let me go."

I watched her walk out the door, closing it carefully behind her. I stood in the concrete cell with the sink and thought about Rita Huelga. Her newfound life. Her being that had nothing to do with all the circumstances that seemed to engulf her. The serial killer, the drug companies, the bozo body-guards, what were they to all the graffiti on the bathroom wall? The names of women scrawled there, in love and lust, and seven to ten-digit phone numbers. Layers and layers of names and colors that were wiggling up and down the wall.

The door opened, and an anxious customer appeared, push-ing her way past me. "Hey, it's time to go to the Castro!" she said, and I realized I would soon be a part of a seething wave of pedestrians going to make trouble in the Castro. But where was Rita? Was she really gone? Had she really been there?

I pushed back into the bar. I didn't see Rita anywhere, but I caught Mariposa sliding off her bar stool.

"Hey, Mariposa—"

"Yes, Emma?"

"Rita—"

"We're leaving, Emma. As far as you're concerned, we've *left.*"

"Rita says you have a last errand in the Castro—"

"Stay here, Emma," she cautioned, lips tightening, an iron look that I had never seen on her face.

"But the killer is after—"

"I'll take care of Rita, Emma. It's time for you to bow out. By the way, have you had dinner?"

"Only smoke inhalation. Why?"

"If I were you, Emma, I'd go home and smell the roses. Watch the wallpaper. Whatever you do, don't follow us, and *don't drive a car.*"

Watch the wallpaper?

Mariposa turned and made her way like lightning through the crowd out the back exit. I looked into the empty glass of cider with a question in my mind. And a bad answer. When I attempted to follow Mariposa, it was as if all the gates to my body had closed. My legs didn't work. Only my eyes seemed to be functioning, and they were going into overdrive. Putting aside the visuals, I bumped into shoulders, was barricaded by hips and sprites who decided I was their dance partner.

"Oh, gross!" came from the bar. The television flickered its faces, a voice reminded us that Johnny Lever had taken his San Francisco show to the Castro in a new time slot. An evening time slot. Tonight, in fact. Halloween. Halloween was television and television was Halloween.

"Mr. Lever has offered a two-hundred-thousand-dollar donation, tonight, to Community United Against Violence, but the group has not accepted. . . ."

Bought off again. Cursing the system that left all our institutions broke and begging, hungry for money, getting their funding from Hollywood, I almost forgot Rita Huelga. Fighting through the crowd, I made it out the back exit. A shabby van, covered with gunmetal gray primer and an old logo from a flower delivery service, waited there. The engine was idling, a plume of white smoke danced in front of me like a ghost. Candy wrappers collided in the gutters like spirit money.

I ran closer, peering in through the back, then the side windows. But then the engine started, and it pulled away from the curb. I ran alongside it, trying to see through the smoked glass of the side windows, not quite believing what I saw there. I thought I saw the glowing yellow eyes of hundreds of blind cats in the window.

Across the street, the Greco-Roman fortress of PG&E Substation E was having a party. The marble sparkled and danced on its facade. The columns themselves did a little jig on either side of a copper-shuttered window, which winked at me.

I remembered Mariposa's warning. *"If I were you, I'd go home and smell the roses. Watch the wallpaper. Whatever you do, don't go to the Castro and don't drive a car."*

Watch the wallpaper?

Mariposa was right, of course. She'd fixed it that way, just as she fixed everything else. She could foil a serial killer and she didn't want any help from me. *"Go home and watch the wallpaper."* Mariposa *really* didn't want me to follow them to the Castro. When I'd bent over to pick up her keys, she'd spiked my mulled wine with extract of magic mushrooms and left me on Lexington Street to watch the PG&E Substation E melt into a puddle of gray stone underneath a neon sky. I had ingested something from the Amazon on an empty stomach. Whatever it was, I was tripping my brains out and needed to get to the Castro. Trouble in paradise.

First, I *would* go to my car, but I wouldn't drive. I'd just use the cell phone, while I could still remember how it worked. A black plastic device for instant communications with lesbians on another planet, like Los Angeles.

CHAPTER TWENTY-NINE

FRIGHT NIGHT

The van picked up speed and started making its way up Nineteenth, in the direction of the Castro, where the Halloween festivities would be endlessly snarling traffic. I watched it disappear into a clot of cars, lights, and honking. Around me, the drag kings ceaselessly danced and jiggled. Romea was a pleasant little yellow bug that I could crawl inside and shut out the noise and the city. I sat in the driver's seat, only momentarily distracted by the drive-in movie now showing on the windshield. Goblins and ghosts were marching past, on their way to the Castro. The Castro, a killing ground?

Suddenly, everything made terrible sense. Or nonsense.

Inside my glove compartment I found an envelope. I folded the piece of paper with the formula inside of a pink tune-up receipt. I put it in the envelope, licked the back, and sealed it, running my fingers over and over it. I found a stamp which said 'Love.' It seemed funny that the post office was peddling love. Love was a stamp that you didn't need to lick. This one was self-stick and peeled off a waxy piece of paper. Stamps were *Love* messages that could stick all by themselves.

And it was a federal offense to steal mail! Like a curse!

Now all I had to do was write my name and address on the front of the envelope. There was a pen, and my fingers knew how to hold it. Little blue lines, like magic, appeared. Emma Victor . . . San Francisco . . . 94110. It seemed hilarious that this represented some kind of identity. Next to me, Romea's original leather seat showed some horsehair where the leather had split. I slid the envelope into the seam.

Get it together, Emma. There's a serial killer on the loose. A killer with a lot of hubris and not much to lose. A killer who had gone way off the deep end. Someone who could stage a bloodbath that would make spree killers look like window shoppers in the theater of death. And I was tripping and carrying a gun. Gun, a horrible instrument of death. Gun. Something ugly that could take away a life in a second. A weapon in the hands of a woman whose wits were on a twelve-hour hiatus.

I didn't like my gun. Oiled, cleaned, loaded, and ready: I was not going to be an angel of death. Someone else had that role all sewed up. The gun went deep into the fold in the backseat. No matter what happened tonight, I would not be carrying a weapon.

I picked up the cell phone and called Rose. "Baynetta Security Services . . ." her answering machine blatted. I tried Rose's pager, punched in my number, and waited. And waited. Rose's pager was off. I called her answering machine back. "I've got a Code Blue, girlfriend. Meet me in the Castro." The neighborhood was going to be swarming. "Meet me *directly* in front of the stage." That wouldn't be easy, not in a wheelchair. But Rose's wheelchair could be an icebreaker as well as a weapon. "I'm not armed, Rose . . ." and I was starting to sound panicked. "I just hope that you pick up this message, dear. Just get to the stage of the Castro, Rose."

Dropping the cell phone on the seat next to me, I closed my eyes against the visual world. The darkness behind my eyelids was full of long tunnels, rabbit holes that led all the way to China. I tried breathing very slowly. The beating of my heart was fascinating. What was I to do next?

Call the cops.

I picked up the cell phone again. It seemed more magical by the moment. I marveled that numbers and buttons could connect me to anyone on the globe. I rehearsed over and over again what I would say, holding on tight to the logical threads that would keep my story together. But the fabric was unraveling fast. Quickly, I grabbed the plastic device, found information for Los Angeles. Then I called the Homicide Division of the Los Angeles Police Department.

The night sergeant growled that Lt. Blackman was not available, if I cared to leave a message.

My lips formed words according to my command. I left my name and my cell phone number. I said it was extremely urgent. I waited, closing my eyes against the antics of PG&E Substation E. I rehearsed what to do in case Lt. Blackman did not call back. I wondered at my own hubris. Who was Emma Victor to Lt. Susan Blackman, a woman far afield from my universe, a woman with a very tough reputation, who was always on one side of the law? She would never call me back, I thought, watching a piece of newspaper become a white dove, flying up the street in the direction of the Castro. I closed my eyes again. I willed the lieutenant to call me. I couldn't handle this by myself, anymore. And if, after tonight, I wasn't anyone anymore, then at least I would have passed on the torch to a *lesbian* police officer, who would certainly not be tripping and maybe, just maybe, could make some kind of happy ending to the whole affair.

I closed my eyes. Darkness came in a million colors, and

the noise of the street was that of crowds, cackling, crowing. I opened my eyes to see the black rags, the screaming hags, the drummers in black bras and dykes on bikes, motorcycles which would never make their way through the throngs of revelers in the Castro. Rose's wheelchair didn't stand a chance. Or did it? *Brrrmmmm! Brmmmmmm!* the motorcycles growled impatiently.

Ring! Ring! said the cell phone.

Brrrmmmm! Brmmmmmm! Ring! Ring!

It was a strange opera.

Ring! Ring! I collected my thoughts and closed my eyes and put the device to my ear.

"Emma Victor?"

"Yes."

"You called. This is Lieutenant Susan Blackman of LAPD."

There was magic in the universe. Magic lesbians who had much more authority than I did. "Lieutenant, I believe I have some information relating to the murder of Gale Petros—"

"We haven't ruled that death a homicide, yet, Ms. Victor—"

"Lieutenant Blackman, the murder of Gale Petros was related to the *Johnny Lever Show*—"

Blackman mumbled. Did I hear a pencil scribbling in the background? "Is it true that Johnny Lever is broadcasting from the Castro tonight?" she asked.

"Yes, ma'am. I think there could be a situation—"

"Halloween in the Castro is always a situation. By the way, we've put out an all-points bulletin for Tyrone Warren."

"Let me guess the description: white, about five foot ten, between thirty and forty—"

"Yeah, it is a little vague. But we've got the fuzzy video—"

"Don't bother watching that, Lieutenant."

"It's not like I'm not interested in what you have to say, but I don't need you to tell me how to do my job. I've heard of you, Ms. Victor. Your name has come up a few times. You work for Willie Rossini, a criminal defense attorney, one of the few I respect. Word has it you're on the up and up. Even though you hang with the down and outs. Perhaps you would like to explain to me—"

And so I did. I told Lt. Blackman about the combined past of Gale Petros, Rita Huelga, Audra Léon, and Bevin Crosswell. How Thad came to appear on the program. I left out the part about Consortium Bell-Worless and Guaranteed All Risk. I left out a lot of things but the identity of the killer. While I expected the good lieutenant to show concern, she snorted.

"And what do you expect me to do about it?"

"There may be more deaths—"

"I should send a TAC squad into the Castro on Halloween?"

"Welcome to my world, Lieutenant."

"Listen Victor, I'll take the next plane up, but we're going to have to set this up very carefully. We don't need a Waco, Texas. There's no reason why we can't lure—"

"Rita Huelga's in danger—she doesn't realize—"

"Rita Huelga? I think you may be a bit behind. Rita Huelga died tonight at San Francisco General Hospital at seven P.M. I don't think you need to worry on her account."

I let there be silence on the line. The PG&E substation had turned into a mausoleum. Little pansies were growing at its base. Maybe Cleopatra lived there.

"I'm sorry, Ms. Victor—are you there? I thought you must have known—"

"That Rita was dead?" My mind crawled back into the present, into the phone line. The police thought Rita was dead.

"No, I didn't know."

"Well, then I hardly need to come to the Castro to save her, do I?"

"No, no I guess not." Logic was becoming more difficult. The phone poles were all tilting at forty-five-degree angles. I closed my eyes.

"Don't worry, Ms. Victor. I'd like to have you come down to Los Angeles for an informational interview."

"Yes, yes, of course," my lips mumbled. Lt. Blackman wasn't going to save the day. She'd just suggested the biggest bummer of all: a trip to Los Angeles.

"You sound like you need to go home and get a good rest," the lieutenant said.

"Yes, thank you," I murmured, watching the last of the topless, one-breasted witches stroll by on her way to the Castro.

"And enjoy your Halloween, Ms. Victor."

"Yes, I'm sure." I looked up the street at the backs of the drag kings, now hoisting angry witches onto their shoulders. I knew I would join them. "I'm sure I will. . . ."

"We'll clear this up tomorrow. Okay?" Something in her voice might have been concern. I should take care of myself. Later, I could meet the lieutenant. Later, I might end up in Los Angeles. But later, I was sure, would be too late. If I didn't get to the Castro tonight, tomorrow, Rita Huelga really *would* be dead.

"Thank you, Lieutenant."

"Thank *you*, Emma." *Click.*

I got out of the car and pondered how to lock it. What was there before locks? Curses or chests made from hollow tree trunks?

"Thieves respect property. They merely wish the property to become their property so that they may more perfectly respect it." The words of Chesterton entered my brain. A dandy in a ruffled blouse and knee britches walked past.

Chesterton in the Castro. I was laughing then, the sounds emerging on a visible bubble from my mouth. Oh, this was bad. Very bad.

I looked back inside the car. It was close and leathery, a cave I would have loved to crawl into. But somehow, I wasn't allowed. There was a horrible Halloween in front of me. The witches and warlocks were my friends, at least. We were on parade, marching up the hill to the Castro together. It was going to take all my concentration to get there, what with all the buildings melting, the sky exploding, and bodies with television sets for faces. The streetlights were eyes, the asphalt was crawling with human flesh. I was tripping violently and caught up in the coven of witches, dragged by the denizens of drag kings. My feet moved with the black wave of anger that flooded the pavement, all roads leading to the Castro.

More costumed people joined the throng. I watched everyone and no one. A Virgin Mary head, huge, jiggled atop a Buddha belly. A beautiful fairy sported a tiger's head. There were no fake women in sight—although my sight and its decoder, my brain, had been severely compromised. I was peaking.

There was no doubt about it, I thought, spying Dorothy from the Wizard of Oz. Her head made a three-hundred-sixty-degree turn, an anatomical impossibility, as well as an image from the wrong movie. There was no doubt about it. The new frontier was my mind, and if I really concentrated, maybe I could remember just exactly what my life-and-death mission was all about.

CHAPTER THIRTY

SHE CAME
IN COSTUME

Bubble, Bubble, toil and trouble, we'll turn the patri-
archy into rubble!
No fake boobs, no cripple shoes, we mean business,
and yours will lose!
Poison our ground and revenge will be found,
For a million breasts lost, you'll pay the cost!

The Revengers, headed by General Gertrude and her
coven of twelve top witches, had altered their garb signifi-
cantly. The thirteen generals of the Lesbian Revengers
peeled down to the waist, topless now, their war cries
reached a higher pitch. Each woman had one breast revealed
and one breast missing. Pink scars snaked across their
chests, some embellished proudly with tattoos, none with reconstructive surgery. The thirteen generals of the Lesbian
Revengers had all had mastectomies. And they now drew
long, thin, needles out of their pouches.

And so I marched behind the Amazon generals of the Lesbian Revengers, chanting, "Bubble, Bubble, toil and trouble,

we'll turn the patriarchy, into rubble! No fake boobs, no cripple shoes, we mean business, and yours will lose!"

I was one of their army, melding with the crowd in my own ghastly makeup. As we came closer, the traffic locked bumpers, the hags rushed between stalled vehicles, scrambling onto the hoods of cars, dancing in wild abandon, reveling in their scarred chests, in their one breast. They laughed and set off firecrackers, roman candles that split the darkness in circles of spinning flame.

Coming closer to the Castro, tourists were already lined up, ready to take photos of freaks, something to show the friends in Cincinnati. One of the Revenger generals was handing out small plastic devices to all the regular witches. Tourists, aiming cameras at the fracas, became truly terrified as the women, with blood-curdling accuracy, accosted the camera-toting tourists and aimed preinked stamps right between their eyes. "I GAPE!" "I GAWK!" the text appeared on terrified foreheads. Cameras were dropped, and tourists fled like rats. I laughed. The Revengers laughed. The male revelers laughed and applauded. We were at the corner of Castro and Eighteenth now, the geographic center of the fantasy fracas known as Halloween.

The Castro Valley didn't look like boys town tonight. There was nothing to fear but a lot of fake women, and most of them were Audra Léon. My eyes danced over the strange figures as they came closer. Cat suits and copper pageboys, insect glasses and girlish giggles, the men had replicated Audra Léon in a million guises, black, white, Chinese, and Chilean. They knew her dance steps. They had practiced her pouty lips. They flirted and feuded with each other. *"Wet Kisses Only!"* they called to each other.

The twelve generals of the Lesbian Revengers had drawn their swords, the long, thin needles. Their war plan was revealed. With careful precision, dancing through the crowd, the topless generals of the Lesbian Revengers were shock-

ing the throngs with their one-breast chests. And they were
popping the fake breasts of Audra Léon drag queens.

Poof!

BANG! POP!

"Honey, what you doin'?"

"Hey, it took me two hours to put on this bra!"

"And it took me two decades to grow breasts!"

BANG! POP!

Men had gathered around the witches and drag kings now.
Gay men were catching on and in sudden solidarity, many
unloaded their brassieres, emptied their cat suits, chanting
along with General Gertrude: "Bubble, Bubble, toil and
trouble, we'll turn the patriarchy, into rubble! No fake
boobs, no cripple shoes, we mean business, and yours will
lose!"

I jostled through the crowd, heading for the big klieg
lights at the corner of Castro and Market. The television
crews were busy. Cameras and monitors and a big cherry
picker swarmed within the intersection, a deus ex machina
that wasn't going to promise an anonymous ending. The
Castro on Halloween was all one big freaker circus, free for
the taking. They wanted it live, they wanted it on tape for re-
broadcasting. They thought that our images belonged to
them. National television had no place in the Castro.

And neither did I. The trip I was on was ending; the Victorian buildings were dancing less frantically. Nobody's
head spun around on its axis. Maybe, just maybe, I was
coming down. There were fewer Audra Léons lining the east
side of Castro Street; they had all lined up to the left of the
stage.

"I GAPE!" "I GAWK!" The witches continued embell-
ishing terrified foreheads, cackling with more and more hys-
teria as their actions brought results. Terrified tourists were
fleeing the Castro like lemmings. The sounds of fake breasts
popping filled the night.

And then I saw him. We all saw him at the same time. General Gertrude let out a hellish howl. Johnny Lever was pacing up and down the stage. He was egging on a bevy of fake Audra Léons. He was inviting them onto the stage. The audience would decide who could do the best rendition of "Wet Kisses Only." The army of drag kings shoved aside a score of faux divas, a few dozen fake mammary glands. The cameras were pointing Gertrude's way. The regulars had lined up behind her, and I noticed that the other twelve generals had stationed themselves strategically around the stage where Johnny Lever was pacing, pointing at an Audra Léon who was six foot four. She was waiting for her big break, next to a short and dumpy Audra Léon, who I'd remembered from a nightclub. An excellent singer whose voice, if not figure, could approximate Audra Léon. I scanned the hopeful drag queens. There was a big gong onstage and a fuzzy-headed hammer.

Everyone was getting impatient. The Revengers came closer. Johnny Lever was shouting at the camera crew to aim the cameras into the crowd, at the Lesbian Revengers. I moved closer, shoving through the crowd, whose faces melted and congealed with alarming regularity. Yellow caution tape had been strung around the perimeter of the stage. Five security guards were lining the stage area. Johnny Lever was no fool. He had volunteers from CUAV, Community United Against Violence, doing security while he staged his show. I moved along the rough wooden edges of the stage. All the faces of Audra Léon looked like normal drag queens, makeup trowled on, nervously shifting from high-heeled foot to high-heeled foot, waiting for the big break. Johnny Lever, national television, every queen's opportunity to become a star.

The CUAV volunteers were concerned about the Lesbian Revengers, as well they should have been. The violence of the screen would meet the violence of the street, and who

knows who would win. The security volunteers were looking this way and that. General Gertrude was directing her
troops to either side of the stage.

"Wait there! Stop!" cried the security guards, as Johnny
Lever mounted the stage.

"Ladies and gentlemen—"

"We're no ladies! They're no gentlemen!" screamed the
Revengers.

"People of the Castro—" Lever was addressing the
crowd, who looked less longingly at the spotlights, at the
lines of Audra Léons waiting to make it onstage. He hadn't
spotted the Revengers in their war paint; he was just watching himself on the monitor.

Two drag kings pushed past a pair of towering Léons, one
of whom shimmied on her high heels, stumbled, and fell
into the gutter.

"Oh, oh!" she screamed as fake men helped her up. She
rearranged her breasts. "Goddamn lesbians! Always ruining
our fun!" she whined.

"And now, ladies and gentlemen, the main attraction of
our evening. A whole lineup of Audra Léons, singing the
theme song from *Wet Kisses Only!*" The first drag queen
mounted the steps, almost tripping on the legs of her bell-
bottomed cat suit. Stepping confidently up to the mike,
Lever announced, "Please welcome Audra Outrageous!"
The crowd cheered, the army of Revengers paused.

"Wet kisses only drowning in time I always wondered
When you'd be mi-i-i-i-i-i-i-ne. . . ." Audra Outrageous
couldn't hit the high note; the sour, note made everyone
wince. I could actually see the note in the air. It was algae
green.

The crowd booed and Johnny Lever hit the big gong,
which created a golden pinwheel of sound. The reverbera-
tions traveled down the street and made the face of Audra
Outrageous fall. The next Audra was the chubby singer with

a pixie face; she would hold the crowd for awhile; the next few Audras would have to be patient. "Please welcome our next talent, Audra Awesome. . . ."

Audra Awesome took the stage and, true to my expectations, began to sing. Ignoring the phrasing of the pop singer, and with a voice of perfect pitch and slow vibrato, she paced the lyrics in a totally different way. A way that almost could make you feel the pain of the closeted diva queen: "Wet kisses only drowning . . ." The amazingly strong voice even made the Revengers pause. The CUAV volunteers were entranced. It gave me just enough time to slip under the wooden scaffolding of the stage. Hunched over, playing jump rope with a lot of cords, the stomping of Johnny Lever's feet just over my head, I emerged just in front of the giant cherry picker, which was panning over the crowd. I traveled unnoticed along the pavement. "Drowning in ti-i-i-i-i-i-me." Audra Awesome's voice had the technicians entranced. I emerged from under the stage, crawling past the skinny legs of lighting instruments. Techies were busy with walkie-talkies and a bank of monitors showed Audra Awesome's figure, the powerful voice belting the words into the night, with a soul that Audra Léon could only dream of. "I always wondered I *always* wondered, people . . . when you'd . . ."

That's when I saw her. Bevin Crosswell, behind the stage, was glued to five or six monitors. The line of Audras was getting nervous, ready for their big moment, afraid that it would never come. One Audra Léon caught my eye. So effective was her costume that I blinked twice, just to make sure. A superb likeness, one who was very patient, an Audra waiting her turn to get onstage. That's when I remembered the bodyguard Snake and realized why he was so very familiar. My trip was starting to end. The visuals were much less intense, and I wasn't afraid to look at my hands.

The Audra look-alikes were waiting their turn. A tall and

gawky Audra had the stage now, a bad physical rendition, but a beautiful bluesy voice sang a slow, sad, "Drowning in time" that made the crowd sway. Song over, the next Audra came onstage.

"Our next singer, please welcome Audra Blue!"

Audra Blue was putting it over; the crowd swayed back and forth. The next Audra, the perfect replica, was getting anxious, a big shoulder bag slung over her shoulder. The gong didn't sound, and it seemed like ages to me before Audra Blue made her way through the pop lyrics. The crowd was with her and booed in disappointment when she was escorted offstage.

The next Audra had a hard act to follow. Johnny Lever helped the new diva onstage.

"Ladies and gentlemen, please welcome Audra—what's your name, honey?" This Audra stood in front of the mike, simply, as if she'd been born there.

"Audra Finale," she purred and took the mike. The voice that emerged was beautiful, in perfect pitch, and with enough volume to fill the intersection of Castro and Market. But something was different. Watching that big black shoulder bag make its way up to the podium, I knew I'd have to move fast. The singer, unperturbed, was expertly spinning the mike in her hand and beckoning toward Johnny Lever. The talk show host came closer and closer, always ready to share the limelight, as long as it was flattering.

That's when I started flying toward the stage.

Johnny Lever wasn't going to share the limelight, he was imprisoned in it.

The singer had drawn a semiautomatic weapon from her handbag. Just as she got her finger on the trigger, someone screamed. The barrel of the gun was pointed at Johnny Lever's head with one hand as Audra Léon hummed. The crowd was just realizing that they were out of danger. Audra Léon only wanted Johnny Lever.

"Mr. Lever!" she cried into the mike. "We are gathered here today to make mincemeat outta you!"

Uncertainly, the crowd laughed.

"You're a little bug in my collection." She smiled. "Now squirm. 'One night only, one night only,' " she started to sing. "No, let's not sing right now. Let's not give the audience a pleasure that they will be denied forever. Let's give them something else, Mr. Lever. Let's give them *you!*"

The crowd roared, the outed diva with a gun in her hand was suddenly on their side. Audra Blue sidled closer; she didn't want to be a hero; she wanted to help. "My mother got called onto one of those talk shows about a fight she had with my sister. She ended up committing suicide!" Audra Léon looked at Audra Blue with a whole new kind of sisterhood. "Here, honey, hold my bag, would you?" Léon was having trouble handling the ready-triggered Taurus and her handbag. Audra Blue took the handbag and held it to her chest. *"Anything* I can do to help, sister."

Léon smiled and took her free hand and bent Johnny Lever's head back. "You all are right about these cripple shoes," she shot off to the Revengers. "Now, I'd like to bring on my first guest, *Bevin Crosswell!*" she yelled into the mike. Nothing happened.

"Bevin Crosswell, you get your Valley Girl ass up on this stage, or Mr. Lever's head is gonna be an exploding pumpkin!"

The crowd roared. Within seconds, Bevin was onstage and at her side. Audra Blue gave her a little shove to the front of the stage. Johnny Lever's eyes were crawling over to the side of his head, to where the muzzle of Audra's gun was close enough to smell. The sweat was running down his collar. "Now, where are we gonna start with these folks?" she asked Audra Blue.

"I don't know, you got anything on them, sister?"

"Yeah, actually, I do. I think it's time to switch the tables

a little. The irony of Mr. Lever's profession is that he thinks
he's above ethics himself. He stands to one side and watches
what he does to people on national television. He seems to
think he's above it all. He's paid to produce the pain of others." Audra spoke clearly into the microphone, a perfor-
mance she had rehearsed. "He enjoys his ability to inflict
pain. Just like his lackey here, Bevin, the producer of his
shows, he can feel good in his invulnerability, just as he
watches his victims' ruin, their enslavement to the next revelation. You can make your victims look stupid, evil, or ab-
surd, whatever you choose. Am I right, Mr. Lever?"

"Yes, yes!" Lever swallowed. He'd say *anything*.

"Oh, come on, fight back a little!" Audra chided.

"I can't. You've got a gun to my head!" The microphone
carried the tones of his panic over the crowd.

"And your very own cameras are catching every moment
of it! You'll make great ratings, Mr Lever, if you survive."
Audra laughed. "And you do want to survive don't you?"

"Yes, yes!" The talk show host swallowed hard.

"Well, let's carry on with our own little talk show. I'm
going to leave the talking to your producer, Bevin. First of
all, Ms. Blue, if you would look in my bag—"

Blue fished around in the big leather bag and found a file.
He opened it up and started reading, letting the crowd see
his shocked expression.

"That's right honey!"

"Wow!" Audra Blue's eyes were wide. "How come nobody found this shit out, anyway?" he said into the mike.

"Because nobody is looking at the journalists, Blue. Why,
Mr. Lever here is so busy ruining everybody else's life, he's
just had time to get himself off on his own little fantasies."

"What a pervert!"

"That's right, Ms. Blue. Our esteemed talk show host
seems to have a penchant for little girls. That is, under his

former name, Howard Brockman. That is *you,* isn't it, Howard?" The gun came closer to his ear.

Lever's lips moved.

"What's that? Speak into the mike, you piece of scum."

"Yes," Lever whispered.

"Yes, *what?*"

"Yes, I'm Howard Brockman."

"And what do you like to do in your spare time, Mr. Brockman?"

Lever said nothing.

"You see, ladies and gentlemen, Mr. Lever here is so used to being in control, he just can't get *over* that there's only a quarter-inch of movement in my finger between him and the great beyond. Let's give your career a little boost, Lever. Let's let your lackey, Bevin, read the charges. Give her the sheet, Blue."

The other diva handed Bevin Crosswell the list and shoved a mike under her nose. Bevin looked over the text and bit her lip.

"Read, Bevin, read about this scum," Audra commanded.

And so, Bevin Crosswell read: "Howard Brockman. Statutory rape, State of Alabama, 1976. Charges dropped."

"Didn't think your boss was a pervert, did you Bevin?"

Bevin continued: "Howard Brockman. Arrested in 1979 for child prostitution. Got off on a legal technicality. Idaho, contributing to the delinquency of a minor, statutory rape, solicitation—"

The crowd started booing, hissing. Audra Léon smiled. "So, while you are so busy pointing the finger, you had a lot of strikes against you, didn't you, Mr. Lever?"

The man nodded, his neck muscles moving against the steel barrel of the gun. "It's really too bad, isn't it?" Audra connected conversationally with the crowd. "It's just not fair that homosexuals are fingered as child molesters when it's usually white heterosexual men going after little girls, isn't it?" Behind Audra, I saw a line of sharpshooters atop the Twin Peaks Bar. It wouldn't be long.

Lever didn't answer. But behind the stage, and on the roof of the Twin Peaks Bar, I could see a sharpshooter. They would wait for their moment. They would wait until they were sure Johnny Lever was safe before taking Léon out. That was too bad, and I was trying to think of any other way this story could end.

"Keep reading," Audra Léon commanded to Bevin.

"Public lewdness, child endangerment, statutory rape—"

"I think we've heard enough!" Léon stated. "Haven't we, people?"

The crowd roared, under the strange spell of the doomed diva. The mike came up to Audra Léon's lips, and she sang as the sharpshooters readied their weapons from the nearby roofs. I looked up, then back at the singer, at Johnny Lever's threatened head. Audra's pitch was never more perfect, even as she held a weapon to the head of her victim with one hand and a microphone in the other.

"You are a star," she sang. The familiar words of the late, great Sylvester rang into the night. "You are a star, and you only happen once—"

It was the moment. I focused on the gun in her hand. Her finger moved, and then I started flying. Seconds before I landed on the stage, trying to pull Audra's feet out from under her, she had done the deed.

And then it was over. Audra Léon had pressed the trigger. Johnny Lever's head had exploded. The sharpshooters, ready for the moment, took Audra Léon's life from many directions. The life that she had said was over anyway. The rest of that Halloween night was *red*.

CHAPTER THIRTY-ONE

THE NASTY GIRL

General Gertrude had hopped onstage, providing unwanted assistance to the police. Camera two, perched atop the cherry picker, descended to get a tight shot. Scores of faces, animals and human, eighteenth-century and postmillennium, were freaking in the mayhem of the moment.

The cops came crashing through the barricades. They took their wounded to the ambulances on stretchers. There was blood onstage and the disappointment of the Lesbian Revengers who had wanted Johnny Lever for themselves. The street was relinquished to the community now. Paige Hodel, the DJ under direction of General Gertrude, had commandeered the sound system, and the familiar notes of Sylvester brought us home, to our own community, home to the Castro.

Trouble, trouble in Paradise
So much confusion!
What am I gonna do?

So much, so much trouble, trouble in Paradise
Where do we go? Where do we go from here?
Now that we've come so far, baby?

By this time, sirens were wailing down Market Street, the black and whites made ready to drain the Castro of its normal Halloween festivities.

Dancing through the night
'till the morning light!
Time for beat
Music makes me dance! Dance! Dance!

But all I could think of were the disheartening facts. Audra Léon was dead, along with Gale and Thad and all those that she thought had betrayed her. Johnny Lever, if he survived, would probably found a program for child molesters and start a new career for himself. I would never see Rita Huelga again. And I needed a cigarette.

I could just make out the monitors behind the stage. A best boy gave me a cigarette out of a crushed pack in her pocket and went off to follow orders that were screaming so loud through her earphones I could almost make out the words. It was Bevin, Bevin Crosswell, the producer who was behind it all. Unperturbed by her experience onstage, the little producer was busy taping the mayhem for her own aggrandizement.

The whole story wound around a little flame that flickered in Bevin Crosswell's purse. A flame that lit the skeleton candles on Rita Huelga's *offerta*. The flame that had killed Carlos Huelga. The flame that put Rita Huelga on national television.

"Camera two, get her face! C'mon, close in!" Bevin hunched over the monitors. Cameras loomed and lurched, cherry pickers looked down like God upon the chaos and tried to catch it for their own. Audra Léon's bullet-ridden body evaded them; there was only a lot of blue serge and heavy belts full of the instruments of law enforcement. Bevin was screaming into her walkie-talkie.

"Camera three, pull forward. Can't you get her face? Get her face! Not her shoes, you assholes! Tight in on the ambulance, that's right, that's right."

Trouble, trouble in Paradise
So much confusion!

"Camera two, catch those protesters over there. What are they doing? Are their shirts off? Good. We can edit it out later for prime time."

Where do we go? Where do we go from here?

"Camera four, Léon's being taken into the ambulance. Can I get a shot of—yeah, there she is!"

A monitor showed but a fleeting glimpse of the famous features, finally at peace. Audra Léon had gone down. The monitor in front of Bevin showed only the taillights of the black and white.

"There's—there's Johnny—" her voice faltered. It was a touching moment. Or maybe just *part* of a moment. "Fuck! Camera two—get her! She's gone—they're gonna close the door. Keep the lights off the glass, try and get her face! Her face!"

Where do we go from here?
Now that we've come so far, baby?

I crept up behind Crosswell, staring at four monitors at the same time. Halloween in the Castro was there in four different moving-picture postcards for Middle America to get all worked up about. "Did we get her face?" Bevin demanded, listening to a response over her earphones. The police cruiser had started its engine. Bevin sighed. "Yeah, that's it. I guess that will have to do." The monitors went dead.

"Got a light, Bevin?"

"Yeah." An irritated, resigned Bevin didn't turn around. She surveyed the crowd, the dead monitors, as her hand dove into the little velvet purse by her side. Out came an old pack of matches with the name El Trebol running across the front. On the back, a map of Mexico was imprinted with major cities: Monterrey, Durango, Torreón, Veracruz, Guadalajara. The cigarette came closer, Bevin was still watching the crowd. "We need to line up some interviews. Get the girl who got onstage. Get her to put her shirt back on. . . ." Bevin held the matches out to one side, expecting a techie who needed a light. *Monterrey, Durango, Torreón, Veracruz, Guadalajara.* It was my moment. I grabbed the book of matches.

"Huh?" Bevin looked at me. "Who—" She struggled with my hand, with her memory. "Who are you?" The matches were firmly in my hand. *Durango.*

"Emma Victor, the bodyguard you hired for Huelga."

"So, what are you doing here?" She stared at the silver square in my hand.

"I'm just liberating you of this very old book of matches, Crosswell."

"Give that back!" she screamed. "That's mine!" But the book of matches was already in the inside pocket of my coat, far away from Bevin's little fingers.

"It's not yours," I corrected her. "But I'll return this to its rightful owner, Bevin."

Bevin scanned the television monitors anxiously. The cameras were rolling again. The first monitor showed the Lesbian Revengers who had still flanked all sides of the stage, arguing with the CUAV volunteers. *"Where are we gonna go from here?"*

"You won't be blackmailing Rita Huelga anymore."

"Fuck you, too, Emma Victor. I've got a television program to produce." Her head snapped back and forth as she looked across the monitors. "Camera two, close-up on the Revengers. Are they putting their costumes back on?"

"You know that extortion is a crime, don't you, Bevin?"

"Sure. So prosecute me. You don't have any evidence. You can't make chicken soup from the shadow of a chicken." Bevin aimed her voice back into the walkie-talkie, "Camera three, get the long shot of Market Street."

"The shame industry, Bevin. How does it feel to finally create a bloodbath?"

"It feels great, Emma. Call it whatever you want, it's truth. And we tell it on trash television. And people watch it."

"Fly them, screw them, just get the guest?" I asked.

I am not a violent person—or I like to think that my anger will not take a violent form—but this time, I failed. My hands reached out and shook Bevin Crosswell. Her headset sprang off her hairdo. Her head snapped back and forth like a doll.

"You idiot! You monster!" I was out of control, but I didn't care. I just watched that horrible face full of dizziness and pain. "You freak!" Soon, some of the television people got to me, before the blood lust had completely taken over.

"Get out! Get off of my program!" Bevin was screeching at me, adjusting the midriff of her sweater. "You'll never work in show business again!"

I laughed. I laughed so hard I almost slipped on a pool of blood by the stage.

"I'll get you for this!" she spat into the night.

That was fine, just so long as I never had to go on television.

CHAPTER THIRTY-TWO

GREEN AND CREAM

The crowds were dispersing, the festivities had come to a doleful conclusion. Paige Hodel had silenced Sylvester and this last Halloween had come to a horrible end. The Muni buses strained on their leashes, trying to pick up passengers. Volunteers herded the thinning crowds aside for an old Deco streetcar, the Illinois Green and Cream. The rounded windows showed a variety of faces, masked and unmasked, on their way home or to other parties. Or Latin America.

Clang-clang! Rita Huelga was ready to jump out of the streetcar, but I pushed her back into the crowd.

"Emma! Let me out!" she cried as the old car made the hairpin turn off Seventeenth onto Market. *Clang-clang!* The car drifted through the crowds and down the hill. *Clang-clang!* "Next stop, Church Street!" The driver managed to make himself audible through the din.

"Emma, what are you doing here? I need to get back to the Castro—"

"To the *Johnny Lever Show*? Don't bother, Rita. Audra's dead. It's over."

"I know. I heard it on the radio." She shook her head

sadly. "Why did she ever go off with Gale? We were meant to be. I loved her completely. She should have been with me. Didn't she understand that?"

"By the way, I did your errand for you," I said, pulling out the old pack of matches. I put it in her hand. *El Trebol. Monterrey, Durango, Torreón, Veracruz, Guadalajara.* She looked at it, the little map of Mexico, the twinkling names of cities in gold lettering worn away with all the time they had spent in Bevin Crosswell's possession. "I believe this belongs to you."

"Yes, Emma." The old pack of matches went quickly into her pocket.

"Rita, you didn't kill your father, you know."

Shame, regret, washed over her face. "You're wrong, Emma." The big brown eyes filled quickly with tears. "I did, Emma, I did." We huddled in the back of the car. "I set the fire—"

"Why?"

"So many reasons."

"What happened at that slumber party, Rita?"

Clang-clang! "Church Street!"

Rita's hands went up to her face and came down again. "If only it seemed like long ago—"

"It was long ago. What made you do it?"

"High school, Emma. Remember high school? The cruel girls, bestowing the gifts of popularity and friendship under the dictatorship of the latest prom queen—"

"Who was . . ."

"Audra. Audra Léon."

Clang-clang! "Next stop, Civic Center!"

"What happened?"

"I'd invited the tennis team to my house for a slumber party. The invitations had gone out weeks earlier. There was an exhibition match the day before. Scouts were supposed to be there. Gale was our prize player, but she couldn't play that day."

"Someone put Ex-Lax in her chocolate cake."

"How did you know?"

"Your home ec teacher, Carmine, told me. She said you did it."

"Everyone else thought so. But I swear I didn't. When Gale got out on the court, she could barely return the ball and ran off the court crying. Carmine said it was the cake. And then they found Ex-Lax in my backpack. Everyone blamed me. I didn't know what to do. I didn't cancel the slumber party. The biggest mistake of my life. I should have known that they were planning revenge."

Clang-clang! "Powell Street, Union Square!"·

"Who?"

"The girls, of course. The tennis team was furious with me. My denials meant nothing. Once my mom had gone to bed . . ." her voice trailed off.

"What happened?"

"It was a sort of mock trail. Verbal abuse. Physical abuse. Revenge for Gail. For making her lose her big chance. Girls can be so cruel. Christ!" Rita looked out the darkened window onto Market Street. "And Audra was the judge. The *beneficent* judge. She didn't think I'd done it. Bevin was the executioner of the sentence. When the girls on the team were done humiliating me, they called taxis and went home. They left me alone. All except for Bevin. She was the only one who hung around. No one wanted to go home with her, and her folks were out. She went to sleep on the floor."

"What happened then?"

"I was in shock. I'd been kicked off the tennis team. I'd taken a lot of verbal abuse. The house was closing in on me. The house we were going to lose to the bank. There was no money for college. My father, deserting my mother. Juan, crying, crying. I could hear him in his crib. It was like he was crying for me. For all of us. I felt, at that moment, that my life was over."

"So you—"

"I went into the bathroom. I looked in the mirror and saw the scratches on my face. I could still feel the hands of the girls, my own tennis team, on my body. My tennis necklace was on the floor, a hole through it. It happened so fast. It was so unjust. I remember I picked it up. My life was over. I was—hysterical. Devastated. Gutted. I had the matches in my pocket; we'd been smoking outside. It was the last time I would ever feel like I could have friends. Juan was wailing. I wondered how long we could keep the house. And then I took the book of matches out of my pocket. It was from my father's favorite watering hole, El Trebol. I went into the bathroom to wash myself off. Then I pulled out a match and struck it. It made a flame, and the flame was under the organdy curtains. The flames flew up the fabric. Warm, hot. Almost comforting. The window was open. The flames grew. I just sat there and watched. A wind took away the fire, took it outside, where it crawled up the side of the house. Before I knew it, the whole side of the house was on fire. I ran into the living room and woke up Bevin. She was so sound asleep, she hadn't heard anything. Smoke was starting to fill the hallway. I ran up the stairs, got Juan out of his crib. We all ran outside. And then we watched the house burn down. Mom, Juan, Bevin, and myself. The flames went up, and the timbers fell down. In an hour, our home was gone. I had Juan in my arms and photographers were taking pictures. Suddenly, I was a hero.

"What I didn't know"—Rita was shaking with the memory—"was that my father had come home that night. Drunk, he'd crept into the house and, not wanting to disturb my mother, fell asleep in an upstairs bedroom. Maybe he woke up to flames; maybe he was too dead drunk; maybe the smoke killed him before he knew what was happening. They pulled his body out from under charred timbers that broke his rib cage. And I was a murderer.

"The insurance company investigated, of course. They suspected arson but couldn't prove it. They searched the ashes and found the one match. Meanwhile, Bevin had searched the pockets of my bathrobe. I don't know how she knew, but she did. And she took the book of matches. Little did I know, but a match is very traceable. The end of the match would match perfectly the book from which it came. That match is still around somewhere, in some police evidence envelope. And Bevin kept the half-empty book of matches all these years."

"There's a girl who thought ahead," I mused.

"That's how she got me on the Johnny Lever show. Arson resulting in death is manslaughter one. There's no statute of limitations. I didn't know what she would do. Worse than ruining my life, it would ruin my research. So I went on the show."

Clang-clang! "Embarcadero, next stop!"

"That's my stop, Emma—"

"What happened after the fire?"

"We got a settlement for the house. A life insurance policy on my father got Juan through college. I wouldn't touch a penny of it. And I've been making up for it ever since, Emma."

"You loved your father, Rita."

"I was an angry teenager."

"'So that's why you went into research?"

"Yes. A belated contribution."

"But a valuable one."

"We'll see what Helga Meyers says. You still have the formula?"

"It's in a safe place."

"Just like the matches."

Clang-clang!

"You don't have to fear criminal prosecution."

She hesitated. "Except from Bell-Worliss. They've paid for my research, Emma. They don't want me to give it away. And, once you connect with Helga, it will be gone. The formula will be out in the community."

"And you've been treating the community for awhile . . . the House of Moss and Sticks?"

"Once we synthesized the active ingredient in TK and it worked on mice and then cats, the next trials were human. We had help from a lot of the physicians in General. Patients with a limited life expectancy showed up at Wilde Flowers and asked for white chrysanthemums. They each got a packet of TK, a week's supply. The results were remarkable, better than anyone had expected. Tumors shrank and skinny dykes gained weight and went back to the gym. Even the cytomegalovirus that plagues those with HIV went into remission, saving the eyesight of sufferers. But Bell-Worliss didn't care; potential profits were going down the patients' throats. They were hot on my tail—"

"Very hot. Is that why you had to burn down your house?"

"Don't make it sound like arson is my hobby, Emma. It was just the best way to get rid of all the evidence."

"And now you split town forever?"

"Forever is a word I'm used to."

"Well, I guess this is good-bye, Rita."

"Mariposa's meeting me here with the van. She's got tickets to Brazil. There's still a lot to be discovered in the Amazon. I think I'll go discover it."

"And not a lot on television."

"Enough of Johnny Lever. You know, Gale must have gotten really obsessed by it, actually *taping* all his programs—"

Clang-clang! "End of the line! Embarcadero! Everybody off!"

"Audra—dead," she choked. "I guess she went out taking the last person who betrayed her."

"Not exactly."

We exchanged looks. There were volumes in those looks. An entire new encyclopedia on Rita Huelga.

CHAPTER THIRTY-THREE

THE SEVEN-SECOND
SOLUTION TO
EVERYTHING

Hours later, I was sitting at the dock of the bay. The Bay Bridge lights had just gone out, and I had seen the pink flush of dawn over the East Bay hills.

The rest of the evening had been an anticlimax. After I said good-bye to Rita, I took a long walk back to the Mission where Romea stood, unmolested. The buildings had stopped moving on their own, the correct key fit into the ignition, and the traffic was remarkably still. I drove over Twin Peaks for the last time during Halloween week. I parked Romea in the big, concrete parking garage on Parnassus. I fished the envelope out of the upholstery and even remembered my parking stub. Maybe Helga Meyer could stamp it for me, I had thought.

In the solitude of her office, Dr. Meyers took the formula without comment. She disappeared into a back room as I read the Hippocratic oath displayed on her wall. When she returned, she thanked me simply and suggested I leave the hospital as quickly as I had appeared. She didn't stamp my parking ticket. But Dr. Helga Meyers would have put the formula somewhere safe. I assumed she would find a way to

get the synthesized formula into production, for the benefit
of patients, and without reaping profits for drug companies.
When I got back into Romea, I realized that there was
nowhere to go. My home would be too quiet. I wasn't ready
for nesting. I just wanted to see the water and watch the
dawn. And so I did.

The sky was light now, the city had started to rustle and
get out of bed. There was traffic behind me. A brave sailboat
had ventured into the bay. A car was honking, honking,
honking. Rose's van had pulled up along the curb, radio
blaring.

> There is something, I wanna ask you—
> There is something I want to know
> And to the question
> You have the answer
> So tell me, what I want to know.
> Do you wanna funk?
> Won't you tell me now?

She leaned out the window and looked at the East Bay
hills with me.

"I just got your message, Emma."

"Oh. Where were you?"

"One of my better Halloweens, Emma."

"It was one of the places I could have used some backup."

"Sorry about that. You look pretty strange—"

"You mean you can check your makeup in my pupils?"

"Pretty big and shiny, Emma. Hey, I'm really sorry about
not responding to your call. You just got way ahead of me
on this one."

"We need better communication, Rose."

"Okay, okay. So you don't know what's happened?"

"Audra Léon was killed onstage in the Castro."

"I know. Girlfriend, you've still got the remaining pieces of the puzzle."

"The cops will find me sooner or later. I wonder how long I've been sitting here?" The morning looked very strange to me, its colors bleeding like a red sweatshirt in the white wash.

"Let's take you somewhere quiet. A little coffee, a little left-brain thinking, perhaps," Rose mused.

"Somewhere close to home," I suggested.

"Progressive Grounds. They just installed a wheelchair ramp. And they should have the fire going in the back."

"Yes. *Fire,* by all means." I wasn't quite ready for the day. Or the news. I needed to explain the story to Rose. She could hold the story for me, contain it, drain it of the horror. Make it real. And maybe, for a moment, just hold me.

I followed Rose back through the Mission and Bernal Heights, little stick Victorians becoming bigger and more expensive with the views. At the top of Bernal, a few wealthy pioneers had chosen to perch redwood-shingled equity examples at the top of the rock that used to be a gravel pit.

A quick turn, and we passed the rocky cliffs where, a long time ago, a Frenchman had salted the soil with gold in an effort to raise real estate prices. San Francisco was a town built on scamming.

We parked Rose's van next to Bernal Books, where Rachael Pepper, up early, was dragging in her newsstands off the street in an effort to keep today's news dry and clean. *Good luck, Rachael.* I didn't even want to see the headlines. Rose pulled the van off to a side street where there was room for her ramp to descend off the back of the vehicle. I held an umbrella over her head as we walked and wheeled into the old café. Double cappuccinos were ordered.

The back room was nearly deserted. A student studied, two seniors were arguing about zoning variations. The fire was crackling, and a thread of Mozart was weaving its way through the smell of coffee and puff pastries. I pulled a chair up to the fire and put my feet up on the bricks. Rose put on her brakes, and I went to get our completed cappuccinos. I sprinkled the tall cones of foam with chocolate and vanilla. Rose was ready and waiting, before she'd even had her caffeine rush.

"Here you go, Rose."

"Ready Emma? *Hard Copy, Prime Time*, everyone is doing the closet queen story."

"Swell."

"Charlene Léon is scheduled to appear on all the talk shows."

"Great. Maybe she will become a PFlag member."

"Parents and Friends of Lesbians and Gays may be a bit beyond her at the moment," Rose observed.

The chocolate was descending too quickly through a hole in the foam. The fire flickered in front of our toes.

"Okay, I'll stop tugging on your heartstrings. Tell me how you figured this all out. How did you know it was Audra Léon?" Rose asked.

"First of all, she was the person who was most disturbed by the *Johnny Lever Show*. Her career was hemorrhaging badly after *Wet Kisses Only* flopped in preview. It was, as they say, the *inciting incident* in her breakdown. I ran into her at Gale's funeral reception. She kept saying, 'Someone's got to pay.' She was quoting her lawyers, but as she said the words, I thought she took the feeling on for herself. She probably started making plans and taking action after the *Johnny Lever Show*."

"She and her husband Tyrone."

"Yeah, *right*. Remember the day I met you in the office with the *Johnny Lever Show* people? And Bevin was using her cell phone? The one you warned her against using?"

"Yes."

"Audra had an interceptor and eavesdrop on the Lever people; she would have been both angry and fascinated by their plans. She figured out a way to control the situation with your security firm, Rose. We were but puppets."

"But how?"

"When she heard that a bodyguard had been hired for Rita Huelga, she made it her business to keep me busy and out of the way."

"You mean she hired you herself?"

"That's right. First she did a little research on Baynetta Security. Guaranteed All Risk is on your Web site as a client, dear."

"How'd she pull off hiring you for an insurance company?"

"Easy, but cheeky. She could have gone down to the building. A little casing would have given her Mr. Fremont's lunchtime departure. Maybe she posed as a client or even checked out his calendar. She could have made a lunchtime appointment with him just to make sure he was out of the office. Who could refuse lunch with Audra Léon?"

"A busy woman."

"A desperate woman. She'd spent her whole life working up to stardom. The media, one media man in particular, had trapped her. This is a woman who spent her life trying to make a career. When Johnny Lever and Bevin Crosswell started manipulating the people around her, she felt increasingly helpless. She decided to do a little manipulating of people to her ends. Audra was a big hit in high school musicals and even did a little light opera. *Hosenrollen.* The Mr. Fremont who hired me was Audra Léon in drag. He sat in front of a window and kept the light trained on me."

"Wow. You didn't guess?"

"A perfect example of why you can't trust eyewitnesses, Rose. People see what they need to see. Why would I be suspicious? An office in an insurance company? There was just no reason to suspect it was a setup. It worked for a while. Kept me pretty busy, I'll tell you. I spent a lot of time in a car watching some guy on crutches. It was only when I pulled away Pendrinkski's crutches that I realized I'd been set up; it was a phony gig. The only answer was that someone wanted to keep me out of the way. Mr. Fremont was the perfect person to do it."

"Audra was at the funeral, at the Petros apartment?"

"When I met her, she seemed to know who I was, although she said that the head caterer, Nancy, had informed her that a new person was on the scene. I had the sense that she was familiar. Also that she was just about at the end of her rope. I could feel it; she kept saying that she didn't care anymore, but that someone had to pay.

"Audra Léon hardly fits the description of a killer, Rose. Pushed out of the closet on national television, and Gale's murder, I can imagine she felt that she had nothing to lose. She was dead romantic meat for Hollywood. And she didn't have a private life left. You should have seen Gale and Audra's mothers. It was *sad*.

"And she wanted revenge. She was used to planning, controlling, and winning. Audra Léon's business empire includes real estate developments. She started her own record company with her first breakthrough hit. An only child fed big dreams by her mother. I got the high school dirt on—on a bad thing that happened to Rita."

"High school?"

"Yeah, that was another tip-off. I knew that the connection between Rita and Audra had been in high school. The reception register included the name of Carmine Wright, who was Audra's home economics teacher. Everyone was ready to blame Rita Huelga for the murder of Gale Petros. It was too easy a setup. I wondered if there had been a precedent in high school. I overheard the clucking and the blaming;

Rita Huelga had always been a problem child. She was tailor-made for the blame, and Audra made sure she got it."

"How'd you bust that one?"

"Went and visited Carmine at her deli. I heard about how Gale's chances of a tennis career were ruined by a laxative. Apparently, someone spiked Gale's chocolate cake with Ex-Lax. Her tennis career was ruined. Ex-Lax was found in Huelga's backpack. Rita Huelga was blamed then, as she was now. And she never denied the claims."

"Why not?"

"It's not in Rita's character. She just clammed up. According to her."

"Perhaps Léon gave Gale the Ex-Lax. Audra wanted Gale for herself," Rose reasoned. "She didn't want Gale off on the tennis circuit, making a name for herself. Once Gale's chances were blown, she became Audra's permanent live-in girlfriend and secretary."

"Of course, high school teachers are always proud of students who make good. And Audra made great. No one wanted to think that Audra was the murderer. The quiet, unassuming Rita Huelga was much easier to blame. And the evidence pointed that way."

"So you went with Rita through all this old dirt?"

"She wasn't interested in hearing anything I had to say. And she wasn't very interested in me, either. She had just had a visit from Audra Léon. And Audra wasn't very happy with her. And came to tell her so.

"Huelga was pretty tired of me hanging around her life. Once Huelga made it clear I was no longer needed, I quit. Part of me was still soft and mushy for her, to be honest. I drove home, past the House of Moss and Sticks."

"The minimalist flower shop?"

"That's right. I'd seen Mariposa there, and I couldn't figure out the connection. Thad, owner and operator, had pierced Audra Léon and thus appeared on the *Johnny Lever*

Show. He would have been a prime target for Léon. Cruising past the House of Moss and Sticks, I noticed that the lights were out in the shop windows. Thad would never have darkened his windows. I slowed down and saw that there was a stain coming from underneath the door."

"Yech."

"You got it. The door was unlocked; I went inside. Thad was on the floor, crucified by his own cactus."

"I think I heard something about that—"

"I'm sure it will make the news any day. Just imagine how easy it will be to believe that Audra Léon killed him. They'll say she waited until the shop was closing and then knocked on the door. Thad must have been ecstatic—and slightly guilty—seeing the pop diva in person. He would have let her in. They might have hugged. Maybe Audra told him he was forgiven for appearing on the *Johnny Lever Show*. She would have put him at his ease. Perhaps the phone rang, perhaps he turned his back for another reason. All Audra had to do was push the cactus on him. A score of nine-inch needles pierced him. It would not have been a nice way to go; a cactus crucifixion that slowly bled him to death."

"That's pretty gruesome."

"But an accident nevertheless. A messy, painful accident that looked like a brilliantly planned murder. That cactus had a problem, Rose. It was all mushy on one side of its base; I believe that was the cause of the collapse."

"So you didn't think Audra Léon did it?"

"No, I think she was gunning for Johnny Lever, after all. I found a whole collection of his shows taped at Gale Petros's mother's apartment. I think the family would have helped Audra discredit Lever, but she was too devastated; she wanted nothing less than revenge."

"Why didn't she take out Bevin?"

"Maybe she had to make a choice. Maybe she made the wrong one. What threw me off, way off, was that I noticed

that Thad had something in his hand. It seemed likely that
Thad had grabbed something from the killer that might be a
clue. I leaned over the giant cactus and managed to pry his
fingers open."

"A dead man's fingers . . ." Rose mused.

"I had to lean over a lot of sharp needles, balancing on a
slippery floor to reach Thad's hand. I'm glad I've stayed in
shape, Rose. I could feel my calf muscle just starting to
tremble as I balanced on tiptoe. And then I had to pry open
the dead florist's hand."

"Was there any evidence?"

"Sort of. If you want to call it that."

"What was it?"

"Thad was clutching *my earring* in his hand!"

"What? How'd he get hold of your earring, Emma?"

"I've been having trouble with the piercing in my ear, remember? Even at your office, I kept taking the earring off,
as my skin's continued to be irritated. At some point, I'd left
the damn earring somewhere. And Thad's murderer pock-
eted it. I tried to remember all the places I'd been. It could
have been left anywhere. Later, I remembered that it was in
my pocket during my struggle in the alley. After that, it was
missing."

"You said that there was a connection between Thad and
Rita Huelga, that you'd seen Mariposa at the flower shop."

"That's right. It was a pretty hard one to figure. It didn't
seem likely that Rita and Thad had colluded to go on the
show together. Bevin Crosswell had found them indepen-
dent of each other. So there was something more to Thad.
Something that linked him to Huelga, without her actually
realizing it."

"I found out later that Thad was involved in distributing
life-saving drugs to cancer patients, mostly women, in the
community. Mariposa was busy throughout the city, visiting

a variety of friendly flower shops in the East Bay and San Francisco."

"How'd she set that up?"

"You know, there's been an underground for years to distribute drugs to gay men who have AIDS. You remember when Eric died? His lover took all his leftover medication to a semisecret distribution point. I knew this kind of stuff has been happening in the city for a long time. Half of San Francisco General knows, but unless you're sick, the silence is kept. Even from me. Chris Fong gave a jump when I mentioned Huelga's name. That was one clue."

"So what was the drug?"

"A synthetic version of mushrooms that shrinks tumors."

"So Audra Léon didn't know anything about that?"

"No. All she cared about was revenge. Rita Huelga was being blamed for everything. She was being neatly taken care of."

"Do you think she was in love with Huelga?"

"No. They met a few years ago by chance, at LAX. They went home and did the wild thing. But no, I don't think Audra was in love with Rita. I think she was in love with Gale. And they had a nice, tight little family, Gale and Audra and their mothers. It was a very warm, cozy closet, until Rita Huelga opened the door. The night I bumped into Audra Léon, I think she was breaking it off with Rita. And maybe just trying to break her. With good reason, if you ask me. Rita's suicide followed."

"Why on earth did Huelga go on air?"

"Who knows?" I lied. "Maybe she wanted the two hundred thousand dollars for the Women's Cancer Center. Maybe she was pissed at Audra for not returning her calls. But once Audra was outed, the affair was over. Audra would have been furious. Her career was ruined in one television broadcast."

"And rebroadcast, and rebroadcast." Rose poked at the fire.

"Audra was desperate. Actually, she fits the profile of a spree killer. One incident set her off. Later, I met Audra Léon emerging from Rita Huelga's house, wearing a mustache. I think Audra Léon has been a drag king for years. It was the way she could have a separate identity. It's not like cross-dressing is a new idea for women in the patriarchy. When Pendrinkski turned out to be a bogus—a real cripple—that's when I really started putting the pieces together."

"So Emma, you had a thing for Huelga, didn't you?"

"It was just one of those things I seem to get for scientists."

"I heard she—that she died."

"Yeah. Well, she did a lot of great research."

"But her body went missing."

"Funny, that." There was no reason to fill Rose in on the subplots. Rita Huelga was hopefully forever in the Amazon rain forest which would continue to yield amazing cures. *Very amazing. Monterrey, Durango, Torreón, Veracruz, Guadalajara.* Women wouldn't need to buy white chrysanthemums to cure their cancer, once the formula was out. And maybe no one would be followed by Ford LeSabres anymore.

"You know something else, don't you, Emma?"

"Nothing that really solves the case, Rose."

"Okay, Emma. How did you know Audra would be in the Castro on Halloween?"

"Léon must have seen all her personal accessories adopted by gay men in the Castro. She knew the *Johnny Lever Show* would be broadcast from Castro and Market. Her cat suit was in the window of Cliff's Variety. Léon masks and wigs were for sale in the hardware store. Her fans had deserted her. Castro Halloween, with Johnny Lever and crew present, was the perfect setup for her to go out. There wasn't a life left for her.

"Halloween was a great way to go out. Once the jig was up, she wanted to take Johnny Lever with her. And the crowd was with Audra in her deep, dark, pleasure. Along with the requisite cat suit and insect sunglasses, she carried a Taurus semiautomatic in her big handbag. It was just the finale she was hoping for. It was a moment made for a closet crazed diva."

"You know General Gertrude is taking all the credit?"

"Oh *good.*"

"The *Bay Area Reporter* has photos. No one with a camcorder caught you in the action. I guess all the tourists were scared away by the Revengers. There are only a handful of stills, and you aren't in them. General Gertrude was the one onstage; the photos show the whites of Audra's eyes and Gertrude's postoperative rib cage."

"So my cover's not blown. That's the best news yet." I pushed a log deeper into the grate with my toe.

"You've got an angel watching over you, Emma."

"I'll make sure and pack that in with the crystals and horror-scopes. Done with your coffee, Rose?"

"Yeah. I've got to get back to the office."

"I've got to get some rest."

"Case closed, Emma?"

"Yep."

"I've got a local gig for you—"

"Give me a week to recover."

"The Women's Center is having tenant trouble. You know the Irish watering hole, the Rover Club? They still occupy the corner of the building where a child care center is slated—"

"Later, Rose. I've got a lot of reading to catch up on."

"They've had bomb threats, Emma."

"Is that all?"

"Yeah."

When Rose dropped me off at my house, a dark mantle of reality set in.

CHAPTER THIRTY-FOUR

DÍA DE LOS MUERTOS

The Victorian, however, had never looked better. The gew-gaws sparkled with gold, and only I knew that the southern windowsills needed caulking. Rose dropped me off, and I walked up the front stairs. The mail had arrived early. A lot of bills. I smiled, wondering how I was going to bill Rose for my services. And how she was going to bill the dead *Johnny Lever Show*. So far, this case had just netted me a pair of smoked lungs and some nasty cuts on my neck.

Jessie and Creole came out of their flat, accompanied by their cat, Bear, who acted for the most part, like a dog. See-ing me, their mouths dropped open. By this time, I had no idea what I looked like, but strange and dirty would proba-bly have filled the bill. The two masseuses looked at each other with concern. "Emma, are you okay?"

"Nothing a good hot bath won't cure."

"Come down and watch *Ellen* on television tonight?"

"No thanks, I think I'll go on a tube diet for awhile." I continued hauling myself up the stairs.

"Emma," Creole's dark eyes scanned my stuttering body

language. "You need a massage, girlfriend." Even the words warmed my back.

"Got any available time slots?" I asked.

"Right now, we're free, right, Jessie?"

"Yeah. The next appointment isn't for an hour."

"Jessie and I will give you a full hour, Emma. You look like you need it. All that fatigue and pain will just roll right off, once we get our hands on you."

"Go, girls." I went into their spotless apartment, the one that used to be mine. There were crystals, aquariums and plants, and all things healthful and cosmic. They draped a modesty sheet over me, laid me on a soft table, and got to work.

They washed me with lavender cream and put herbal remedies on my cuts. Creole worked on my feet while Jessie found every sore muscle in my neck and back. They turned me over. They punched me with all their Amazon strength and gentleness. When they helped me off their table, my body was but a warm, happy wrapper for my soul.

Afterward, I floated upstairs to my apartment. I put the little sugar skeleton on the mantel, fed the cats, and laid down on my blissful bier. I could almost stop my head. Almost, but not quite. I could still feel Creole's and Jessie's hands up and down my body. They had worked 140 different points with their 25 different hand techniques. The pain, physical and psychic, had rolled off of me. Some kind of order had been restored, I thought, falling into sleep.

I kept hearing Rita Huelga saying, *"Audra is dead. I guess she went out taking the last person who betrayed her."*

Ring! I had forgotten to turn off the phone's ringer, but there it was. I was right when I told Rose that the cops would find me. They did. At least it was a lesbian cop.

"Good job, Victor." It was Lt. Susan Blackman from Los Angeles.

"Thank General Gertrude."

"I saw the pictures; I wasn't impressed. I'm calling about something you said."

I found myself wondering what exactly I had said to the lieutenant on the cell phone.

"What?" The small moment of nervousness was over soon. Lieutenant Blackman wasn't looking for Rita Huelga; she wasn't interested in arson or Bell-Worliss.

"We've still got that all-points bulletin out on Tyrone. Why did you say we shouldn't bother?"

"Remember the wedding that took place between Tyrone and Audra in Reno? The video of the highly private ceremony that was leaked to the press?"

"We can't find a record of the marriage, actually."

"Check out the video. The man next to Audra is her bodyguard, Snake."

"I'm starting to get the picture, Victor."

"The sham music video, the one where Tyrone is tuneless and mostly a nose? It was Audra Léon herself."

"Let me guess why Ms. Léon never appeared with her husband in public."

"You got it, Lieutenant. Audra Léon married *herself*. A very tan white man."

I could almost see the lieutenant smile. "Thanks, Emma. I'll follow up on that." *Click.*

Audra Léon, Audra Léon, a solution that everyone would want to own. The cops, the district attorney, the people of the Castro, and the people of television. But I had seen that look in Rita Huelga's eyes.

"Audra is dead. I guess she went out taking the last person who betrayed her."

Only Audra *didn't* take out the last person who betrayed her. Or the first.

The look we exchanged told me everything I needed to know. About chocolate cake. And maybe even arson. The problem was that Rita had mentioned that Gale Petros had a whole series of Johnny Lever tapes. There was only one way she would have known that.

The apartment complex would have been easy enough to break into. The doors in the hallways were often open. There were so many balconies with connecting doors, I was sure Rita Huelga had found a way in. She'd noticed the tapes of the *Johnny Lever Show* on the bookshelf of the guest room. And she'd mentioned it to me.

Rita Huelga was the only one without a chair when the music stopped.

I hoped she'd taken up permanent residence in the Amazon. Rita Huelga had killed Gale Petros. After years of jealousy. And she had gotten away with it.

It was time to give the house a good cleaning. The spice cupboard. Dust the bookshelves. Recycle the newspapers. Maybe I would make some bread. I broke open a packet of yeast and dissolved it in hot water and sugar.

Mink brushed up against my leg as I walked into the living room. The warmth of kitty cats, baking bread, and book-lined walls didn't do it for me. I had my own unfinished business and, like Audra Léon, it could only end in death.

There it was: the glass and plastic monolith that dominated the living room. Soon all forty pounds of it were in my arms and out on the street.

It's hard to kill your television. The picture tube is a little vacuum. It implodes.

I didn't want to injure anyone. So I made a plan. I could smash the remote control with a screwdriver, putting me in complete control of the device. And then I would pull off the cover to the control panel. Removing the channel indicator chips would cut it off from the world. Then I would take its voice, puncturing the speakers.

A car boomed up the street, the kind of testosterone-mobile that not only used up gas, but a whole lot of the aural space in the neighborhood. Two large speakers mounted in the trunk thudded against the sheet metal. The ground shook. It was probably ruining the foundations.

My hips moved to the music. My body was strong. Through the thudding, I could make out the familiar lyrics. And I was ready, at last, to kill my television. The car pulled closer. As I cut the cord off from the box, I knew it would make me feel mighty real. Sylvester, disco queen in heaven, purveyor of proud camp, was booming from the trunk, reminding me of funk, of Audra Léon, and singing just the words I needed to hear:

You are a star
Everybody is one
You are a star
And you only happen once. . . .